THE CANNIBAL

By John Hawkes

THE CANNIBAL

BY JOHN HAWKES

INTRODUCTION BY ALBERT J. GUERARD

A NEW DIRECTIONS PAPERBOOK

FOR SOPHIE

INTRODUCTION

Many introductions exist to persuade the reluctant reader that the classic text under consideration is deservedly a classic, with hidden meanings and beauties. But in the presence of a highly experimental novel, and of such a considerable new talent as that of John Hawkes, an introduction should perhaps attempt no more than to clear away some of the peripheral difficulties and obstacles of strangeness which might prevent an early understanding and enjoyment. No doubt the reader has a right to discover the hidden beauties for himself, during the first years of a novel's life. But isn't it also the novelist's own task, a few readers will certainly argue— "to clear away some of the peripheral difficulties and obstacles of strangeness?" My own answer is that this question can be too costly. The merely secondary difficulties and obstacles involved in the first appearance of a Franz Kafka or a William Faulkner or a Djuna Barnes are not comparable to those involved in the first appearance of a conventional realist . . . and perhaps it would be well if we could get at the restless and original Kafkas at least, if not at the Djuna Barneses, over a shorter period of ridicule, without having to wait so long. I use the names of Kafka and Faulkner and Djuna Barnes advisedly, these august names and coldly intense writers . . . for I think the talent, intention, present accomplishment and ultimate promise of John Hawkes are suggested by some conjunction of these three disparate names.* I know that this is to say a great deal, and also to predict most rashly as to the future direction an original talent will take. John Hawkes is now, at the outset of his career and at the age of twenty-three, a rather more "difficult" writer than Kafka or Faulkner, and fully as difficult a writer as Djuna Barnes. *The Cannibal,* written in 1948, is less surrealist than *Charivari,* a short novel written in 1947; † and I suspect Hawkes will move still further toward realism. But his talent, whatever may happen to it, is already a major talent.

The peripheral difficulties, then, and obstacles of strangeness . . . The plot is a simple one, but not to be simply apprehended. There is in the first place an interesting interlocked story of Germany during the first world war and of Germany in "1945"—a mythical year of the allied occupation, when a single American soldier on a motorcycle is left to supervise a third of the country. In 1914 Stella, later Madame Snow, night club singer and daughter of a general, meets an English traitor Cromwell, and marries the feeble Ernst. In 1945 Stella Snow's boarding house in a ruined village harbors her sister Jutta, mistress of Zizendorf . . . new political Leader and "narrator" of the story. Zizendorf successfully plots the death of the lone American overseer and the capture of his motorcycle; and the book ends with the rebirth of an independent Germany. For the tiny gutted *Spitzen-on-the-Dein*—with its feverish D.Ps., its dis-

* I understand that Mr. Hawkes had all but finished *The Cannibal* before reading Kafka, Faulkner and Djuna Barnes. His earlier reading of modern experimental literature was largely confined to poetry.

† Published in *New Directions 11* anthology.

eased impotent adults and crippled children, with its foul choked canals, with its hunger, militarism, primitive memories and its unregenerate hatred of the conqueror—is Germany itself in microcosm. (As a picture of the real rather than the actual Germany, and of the American occupant of that Germany, *The Cannibal* is as frankly distorted as Kafka's picture of the United States in *Amerika;* and also perhaps as true, thanks to that very distortion.) This interesting story is left very much in the dark, however; is obscured by brilliant detail, by a submersion in many different minds and their obsessions, by a total vision of horror . . . and by a very distinct reluctance (the reluctance of a Conrad or a Faulkner) to tell a story directly. As in Faulkner and Conrad, we have the effect of a solitary flashlight playing back and forth over a dark and cluttered room; the images may be sharp ones, but a casual reference to some major happening may be clarified only fifty or a hundred pages later. The inattentive reader would be hard put to make even such a bare plot-summary as mine; though he might easily go far beyond it—to see in Stella Snow, for instance, both Germany herself and the Teutonic female and fertility principles, the traditional earth-mother of German beer and metaphysics, survivor and protectress of the sterile—"for she had survived and hunted now with the pack."

The peripheral difficulties are obvious enough . . . for the reader who vaguely recognizes his own adult world in *The Cannibal,* as well as his own childhood fears. The story is radically out of focus, which was of course intended; yet there is no consistently distorting point-of-view. The narrator Zizendorf was perhaps intended to supply an even source of distorting light. But Zizendorf, a relative failure, poses more problems than he solves. Again, no character —except Jutta in the single episode of the nunnery— receives that *consistent sympathy* which most of all holds the average reader's attention. John Hawkes clearly belongs, perhaps this to his credit, with the cold immoralists and pure creators who enter sympathetically into all their characters, the saved and the damned alike. Even the saved are absurd, when regarded with a sympathy so demonic: to understand everything is to ridicule everything. And it is also to recognize that even the most contaminate have their dreams of purity which shockingly resemble our own. . . . A third difficulty and distraction is provided, as in Djuna Barnes, by the energy, tension and brilliance of phrasing often expended on the relatively unimportant: the appalling and prolonged description, for instance, of Madame Snow strangling a chicken, a description interrupted momentarily by the appearance of the Kaiser's thin and depressed face at the window.

The final obstacle of strangeness—suggested by the Kaiser's face—is that John Hawkes' surrealism is an independent and not a derivative surrealism . . . I use "surrealism" for want of a better word. There is some traditional symbolism in *The Cannibal;* even perhaps a little old-fashioned allegory. The dead frozen monkey who screams "Dark is life, dark, dark is death"—tail coiled about his neck, "sitting upright on the bodies of the smaller beasts"—is an authentic surrealist monkey. But the ghosts who return each night to the single charred and abandoned allied tank belong to an older literature . . . The basic convention of the novel is this: Germany and the world have shrunk to *Spitzen-on-the-Dein,* rather than the little village enlarged. The characters are passive somnambulistic victims of the divine or diabolic process (history), yet to a degree are aware of their historic position. Thus Ernie running after the carriage of Stella and Cromwell in a German town, stopping in an agony of impatience to relieve himself behind a bush, not merely parallels or suggests but for the moment *is* Gavrilo Princip, the assassin of Sarajevo; and Cromwell and Stella in the pursued carriage prophesy war and offer themselves as historic symbols: "I will become, as you wish, your Archduchess for the people." One could even suggest the peculiarly German conception of a narrator possessed of divine or diabolic omniscience . . . *which the characters enter into or share in occasional moments of intuition.* History is blind, inconsecutive, absurd . . . yet a Stella Snow may foresee it: foresee "the naked cowardice of the fencer, the future fluttering wings of the solitary British plane leaving its token pellet in the market place, her mother's body rolling around it like a stone strained forever, the stain becoming dry and black as onyx."

Of the true solid ingredients of surrealism—illogic, horror, macabre humor—*The Cannibal* has a full share. Terror, for instance, can create its own geography. Gerta almost stumbles over the dead body of the Merchant, on her return from the open latrine, the "pea-green pit of stench," behind the *sportswelt* in *das Grab*. But this merchant, said to have fallen here some months before (page 101) actually fell near Cambrai (page 94), in a farmhouse demolished by artillery fire:

> There the Merchant, without thoughts of trade, dressed in grey, still fat, had died on his first day at the front and was wedged, standing up-

right, between two beams, his face knocked backwards, angry, disturbed. In his open mouth there rested a large cocoon, protruding and white, which moved sometimes as if it were alive. The trousers, dropped about his ankles, were filled with rust and tufts of hair.

The line between the fantasy of an Edward Lear and that actual creation of another universe which the best surrealism attempts is a hard one to draw . . . the line, shall we say, between two aspects of Coleridge's "fancy." Where else do the "monumental dogs found in the land of the tumbleweed, glorified for their private melancholy and lazy high song" belong—unless in the pages of Lear? And yet the German dogs to which they are compared are fully as remarkable; and become both real dogs running beside the train in which the invalided Ernie lies, and perhaps also recollections of childhood fear; and some pages later, vague symbols of defeat and death:

Those were certainly dogs that howled. His face pressed against the glass, he heard the cantering of their feet, the yelps and panting that came between the howls. For unlike the monumental dogs found in the land of the tumbleweed, glorified for their private melancholy and lazy high song, always seen resting on their haunches, resting and baying, these dogs ran with the train, nipped at the tie rods, snapped at the lantern from the caboose, and carrying on conversation with the running wheels, begged to be let into the common parlor. They would lap a platter of milk or a bone that appeared dry and scraped to the human eye without soiling the well-worn corridors of rug, and under the green light they would not chew the periodicals or claw the conductor's heels. As paying passengers, they would eat and doze and leap finally back from the unguarded open platforms between cars into the night and the pack.

The temptation to quote from *The Cannibal* is enormous. But no doubt this passage, and the dogs' progressive irresistible taking over of the train and the paragraph, is enough to suggest the author's delight in grotesque distortion—and to suggest the dangers and promises implicit in an imagination so uninhibited and so incorrigibly visual, immediate, obsessed.

How far John Hawkes will go as a writer must obviously depend on how far he consents to impose some page-by-page and chapter-by-chapter consecutive understanding on his astonishing creative energy; on how richly he exploits his ability to achieve truth through distortion; on how well he continues to uncover and use childhood images and fears. Of the larger distortion of *The Cannibal*—of its total reading of life and vision of desolation as terrible as that of Melville's *Encantadas*—there is no need to speak at length. The historic fact of our present effort to reconstruct German pride and nationalism is rather more absurd than the negligent withdrawal pictured by Hawkes. And yet his few "scenes of occupation life" may someday tell us more of the underlying historical truth than the newspapers of 1945 will tell us: the trial and execution of the pastor Miller for having changed his views under the Nazis (the present Mayor betraying him in terror of the curled claws and sharp hooked nose and red terrifying eyes of the eagle on the Colonel's shoulder); the snarling lovemaking of the American overseer Leevey and his diseased German mistress; and the "overseeing" Leevey at work . . . hurtling on his motorcycle through the third of the nation he controls, absorbed in an historical process which transcends any human intention and which he has no hope of understanding. John Hawkes, who saw wartime Germany briefly as a driver for the American Field Service, has written an unpolitical book but not an unhistorical one. As Kafka achieved a truth about his society through perhaps unintentional claustrophobic images and impressions, so Hawkes—abnormally aware of physical disabilities and indignities and degradations—has achieved some truth about his. This is a Germany of men with claws for hands, of women with reddened flesh, of children with braces to support their stumps or their heads. It is a world without food, without hope, without energy . . . reduced for its pleasures to impotent mechanical ruttings bereft of all desire. I think it can be understood that this is more than post-war Germany, whatever the author intended; that this is, to some degree, our modern world. At the end of the novel the liberation of Germany has occurred; or, perhaps, our old world is renewed. This, to be sure, may be looked at in several ways. The insane asylum in *Spitzen-on-the-Dein* is reopened on the next to last page. "At the top of the hill he saw the long lines that were already filing back into the institution, revived already with the public spirit."

ALBERT J. GUERARD

Cambridge, Massachusetts
November 29, 1948

ADDENDUM

Almost fourteen years have passed since the above was written, yet I see no need to revise, erase or retract. There is much more that might have been said. Today, too, I might substitute the term "anti-realism" (vague as it is) for "surrealism" and its often misleading connotations. And of course it would now seem absurd to speak of John Hawkes as "promising." In the years since publication *The Cannibal* never died as so many good first novels do. It kept up its quiet underground life, highly praised from the first by a few, the yellow jacket still present in the serious bookstores where these underground lives occur, the book each year winning new adherents among readers impatient with the clichés and sentimentalities of commercial fiction, or impatient with the loose babblings of the publicized *avant-garde*. *The Cannibal* was reprinted and read.

There was always the possibility Hawkes had exhausted his particular dark vision in this single book, and would write no more. But during these years (while working full time for the Harvard University Press, then as a teacher at Harvard and Brown), he published three more books: *The Beetle Leg* (1951), *The Goose on the Grave & The Owl* (1954, two short novels), and *The Lime Twig* (1961). Each had its different myth and setting, its landscape of an inward geography projected onto a dry impotent American west, onto fascist Italy and San Marino, onto a damp decrepit England of gangsters and gamblers.

The predicted movement toward realism has occurred, but chiefly in the sense that the later novels are much more orderly and more even in pace, and distinctly less difficult to read. The spatial form and dizzying simultaneity of *The Cannibal* are modified. The imaginative strengths remain, however, and the vivifying distortions: the power to exploit waking nightmare and childhood trauma, to summon preconscious anxieties and longings, to symbolize oral fantasies and castration fears—to shadow forth, in a word, our underground selves. And in each of the novels a fine black humor and a nervous beauty of language play against the plot's impulse to imprison us unpleasantly in the nightmare, to implicate us in these crimes. We are indeed deeply involved. But we are outside too, watching the work of art.

Four slender volumes. The achievement may not seem a large one in this day of voluminous and improvising writers, scornful of the right word. Yet it is an achievement roughly comparable in bulk and in variety of interest to that of Nathanael West. Hawkes has of course not written such an easy or public book as *The Day of the Locust;* perhaps he never will. But he has surely exhibited a power of language and an integrity of imaginative vision that West showed very rarely. Hawkes's position is an unusual one: that of the *avant-garde* writer who has imitated no one and who has made no personal gestures of defiance. His defiances—the violence and the indignities and the horror, the queer reversals of sympathy—are all in his books. He has been associated, moreover, with none of the publicized groupings.

Yet for all this lack of politics and compromise, his work appears to be about to prevail. It is being published in France, Germany, Sweden, Italy and England; it has been honored with a National Institute of Arts and Letters award; it has been admired by Cela in Spain as well as by curiously diverse American writers and critics: Flannery O'Connor and Andrew Lytle, Saul Bellow and Bernard Malamud; Paul Engle (one of the first to recognize and praise); Leslie Fiedler, Frederick Hoffmann, Ray West.

The Cannibal itself no longer seems as willful or eccentric as it did in 1948, nor as difficult to read. This is partly in accord with the law that the highly original artist must create the taste that will eventually applaud him. Time, time and powerful reiteration, at last triumph over ridicule. *The Cannibal* prepares us to read *The Lime Twig;* but, even more obviously, *The Lime Twig* and the others prepare us to reread *The Cannibal.* Beyond this, *The Cannibal* doubtless profits from the drift of the novel generally, away from flat reporting and delusive clarities. Readers are no longer as distrustful as they were in 1948 of imaginative distortion and poetic invention, of macabre humor and reversed sympathies, of violence transferred from outer to inner world and from inner to outer. The rich playfulness of Nabokov; the verbal pyrotechnics of Lawrence Durrell and his humorous relishing of decay; the wilder energies of Donleavy and Bellow; the great poetic myth-making of Andrew Lytle and the visions of Flannery O'Connor; the structural experiments of the later Faulkner and the broken-record repetitions of Beckett; and, even, the brilliant ingenious *longueurs* of certain French anti-novels—

all these (to mention only a few of many) show the extent to which the personal and the experimental have been vindicated; have even won public acclaim. Whatever the quickening anti-realist impulse in the novel signifies—whether transformation or annihilation of a *genre* or even a symbolic foretaste of literal annihilation of the self or of matter, a Byzantine decadence or a created myth of dissolution for our time; or whether, more hopefully, a public awakening to new types of fictional pleasure and suasion— whatever all this adds up to helps define *The Cannibal* as a central rather than peripheral work of art and vision.

A.J.G.

Stanford, California
April 14, 1962

THE CANNIBAL

There is a town in Germany today, I cannot say just where, that has, by a great effort, risen above the misery that falls the lot of defeated communities on the continent. It has been slowly bettering itself now, under my guidance, for three years, and I am very nearly satisfied with the progress we have made in civic organization. It is a garden spot: all of our memories are there, and people continually seek it out. But until now there has been only silence for the outside world concerning this place, since I thought it more appropriate to have my people keep their happiness and ideas of courage to themselves.

However, I was forced to leave the town for a short time and while away I made a compromise. For I have told our story. The things that remain to be done weigh heavily on my mind, and all the remarkable activity of these foreign cities cannot distract me. At present, even though I enjoy it here, I am waiting, and at the first opportunity I will, of course, return.

PART ONE—1945

ONE

Beyond the edge of town, past tar-covered poor houses and a low hill bare except for fallen electric poles, was the institution, and it sent its delicate and isolated buildings trembling over the gravel and cinder floor of the valley. From there, one day in the early spring, walking with a tree limb as a cane, came Balamir, walking with a shadow and with a step that was not free, to fall under the eye and hand of Madame Snow. All of Balamir's demented brothers, in like manner, had been turned out to wander far from the gravel paths, to seek anyone who would provide a tin plate or coveted drink. Madame Snow made room for him, setting him at work digging in the basement, in the *bunker,* and the black air closed in about the piles of debris and he was homesick. His feeble brothers were gradually absorbed, whole corps at a time, into the yawning walls, mysteriously into the empty streets and outlying dark shuttered farms, were reluctantly taken off the streets. And yet the population had not grown, the same few brown forms prowled in the evening, the same tatters of wash hung for weeks in the same cold air, and the Census-Taker sprawled, thin and drunk, blue cap lopsided, behind his desk. The town had not grown but the institution had become empty, officials and nurses gone for distant lands, their eyes tight and faces drawn, and over the high narrow buildings no sound could be heard. Every day from the hill, thin children looked down on the empty scorpion that was all that was left of the ordered institution.

A single spire of notched steel hung high above the town, devoid of banners, un-encased by building walls, sticking up above them all in the cold blue evening. Steel rungs hung crookedly exposed all the way up the spire, and steel slabs were driven across the narrow open cellar window where Balamir paused, his white skin wet in the still evening light. Piles of fallen bricks and mortar were pushed into the gutters like mounds of snow, smashed walls disappeared into the darkness, and stretching along the empty streets were rows of empty vendors' carts. Balamir was unprotected from the cold. He found that the wind swept around his wide forehead and parched throat, flew bitterly into the open mouth of his rough upturned stiff collar. He found, in the damp frozen hollow of the cellar, that he could not unearth the wooden bench, the monstrous curling vase, the moldy bureau, or any of the frozen pots in uneven jumbled piles, littering the earthen floor and reaching to the rafters. He found that the earthen padded walls muffled his long howls at night and left the sound only in his own ears. While he worked, picking with the coal shovel, or sat staring up at the window, paper-wrapped feet shuffled overhead, and in the inhabited kitchens of the town the candles flickered, cans of thin soup warmed over flickering coals, and the children whined. Bookstores and chemist's shops were smashed and pages from open books beat back and forth in the wind, while from split sides of decorated paper boxes a shoft cheap powder was blown along the streets like fine snow. Papier-mâché candies were trampled underfoot. In outlying districts, in groups of four and five, Balamir's brothers chased over the rutted and frozen ground after the livestock, angry and cold, their thick arms wagging, or clustered around the weak fires, laughing and cold. A small number of these men, after flinging hatchets or raging momentarily in the dark with stained knives, walked back and forth in the cells of the town jail, beating themselves and damning incoherently. The rest, including Balamir, did not realize that they were beyond the institution's high walls. The population of the town remained the same and thieves from the jail went home to keep the balance.

Madame Snow, owner of the building, living on the street floor above the cellar room, would have been a grandmother had not her son's child died, no bigger than a bird, in an explosion not a block away. In the still morning air, the frosted fields about the town had cracked with the infrequent thudding of small explosions, and those that had discharged in the town had left a short useless whistle in her ears. But the children of Madame Snow's sister had survived, to crawl sexless and frightened about bare rooms. Time after time, for months before Balamir had come, Madame Snow had watched the thin men climbing down from boiling trucks, waiting to see her son's return. When he had finally arrived with his stump and steel canes, with special steel loops circling up about his wrists for extra support, he had not added even one bare number to the scratched-out roster of the drunken Census-Taker. He had returned to his wife and rooms in a corner of the moving picture house, and from then on, worked with the black machine in the hot projection room, showing each day the same blurred picture to no audience. Madame Snow did not see him after that.

She busied herself as janitor, arguing with the residents or giving comfort; or sat in the large gilt chair tying rags together and infrequently pulling the heads from small fowl. The halls no longer smelled of roasting swine or boiling cabbages, no longer rang full with heavy laughter, but remained dark and cold, streaked with mud from the roomers' boots.

The building slanted crookedly and silent in a row of black stained fronts and the canal drained past the back fence; on the corner where the side street met the empty thoroughfare was the rising jumble of the steel spire. When a boy with black peaked martial cap, leather braces and short trousers walked past the drawn curtains, Madame Snow would peer hungrily out and then go back to the darkness. On the third floor of the house was the apartment of the Census-Taker, who left his dripping cape flung in the downstairs hall. Herr Stintz, a one-eyed school teacher, lived on the fourth floor, and above him, with her children and bleached plants, lived Jutta, the sister of Madame Snow. Herr Stintz, ex-member of the band, played his tuba late into the night, and the notes fell on the cobblestones recalling the sound of fat marching feet. But the roomer who lived on the second floor was out.

"Come," said Madame Snow to Balamir, "come in. The room gives no heat really, but off with your coat. You're at home." Balamir knew he was not at home. He looked at the small table with the rows of playing cards and single gilt chair, looked at the bright figures where Madame Snow played alone. He carefully looked about the room of court and puzzled about the oaken whorls above the curtained door and the highness of the spidery black ceiling. "Sit down," said Madame Snow, afraid to touch

6

his arm, "sit down, please." But he would not. He would never sit when anyone could see him. So he stood in the middle of the floor and a dwarfed cat rubbed against his leg. The attendant, hat pulled over his face and rubbers thick and too large, gave a sheaf of worn papers to Madame Snow and left like a shadow.

"Will you drink tea?" He looked into his hands, saw steaming water and watched a single star-shaped leaf turning slowly around near the bottom of the cup. He saw a pale color slowly spread, creeping up the china towards his fingers, watched the star turn and the cup dip like the moon. But he would not drink. The little woman watched him from the side of her eye, the light almost gone. His hair was rough and shaggy and he would not drink her tea. Down in the cellar Balamir put the coat on again, standing until she hurried back up the stone steps, for he could feel the cold. "Good night," she said and turned the brass key.

Jutta's child, shoes undone and lips white, ran along a path through the rubble, stumbled over stones, passed overhanging iron ledges and shattered windows, tried to weep, and fled on. A man followed, swinging a cane, craning into the darkness. The child passed a wall spattered with holes and the fingers of a dead defender, and behind him, the man coughed.

A butcher shop was closing and a few cold strands of flesh hung unsold from hooks, the plucked skin and crawling veins uninspected, hanging, but without official sanction. Wire caught the child's knee.

The town, roosting on charred earth, no longer ancient, the legs and head lopped from its only horse statue, gorged itself on straggling beggars and remained gaunt beneath an evil cloaked moon. Rattling trains turned back at the sight of the curling rails blossoming in the raw spring on the edge of town opposite the hill, and fields, plummeted with cannon balls, grew stained with the solitary need of beasts and men. As the old families returned to scrub again on the banks of the canal or walk singly dressed in black, the prisoners filed out over the hills, either as names on a ticket, or if the ticket had been lost, simply as uncounted numbers. When an old man was gripped dying in a terrible cough, Jutta was betraying her lost husband and bearing child again. The town, without its walls and barricades, though still a camp-site of a thousand years, was as shriveled in structure and as decomposed as an ox tongue black with ants.

The Signalman, girded with a blanket in a wicker chair, smoking a pipe like a porridge bowl, commanding the railway station and a view of empty benches, no longer raised the red arm or pulled down the yellow, and no more lights blinked before his fat eyes to disturb his memories of the war of 1914. He had nothing to eat and nothing to say, and black men in large hats and capes were painted all over the walls of his station. Relics of silver daggers were looted from the nunnery and stored in trunks with photographs, or taken off to foreign lands. The bells never rang out. Fires burning along the curbs and dung heaps smoldering on the farms filled the air and alleys, the empty shops and larders with a pungent smell of mold.

The Mayor, with his faded red sash, was too blind to tend the chronicles of history, and went hungry like the rest with memory obliterated from his doorstep. Their powerful horses of bony Belgian stock, dull-eyed monsters of old force, had been commandeered from the acre farms for ammunition trucks, and all were gone but one grey beast who cropped up and down the stone streets, unowned, nuzzling the gutters. He frightened the Mayor on black nights and trampled, unshod, in the bare garden, growing thinner each day, and more wild. Children took rides on the horse's tail and roamed in small bands, wearing pasteboard Teutonic helmets, over the small confines of the town, their faces scratched and nails long. The undertaker had no more fluid for his corpses; the town nurse grew old and fat on no food at all. By mistake, some drank from poisoned wells. Banners were in the mud, no scrolls of figured words flowed from the linotype, and the voice of the town at night sounded weakly only from Herr Stintz's tuba. Bucketfuls of sand kicked up by minor grey duds had splattered against flaking walls and trickled onto worn doorsteps where chickens left frightened tracks. Rotting sandbags killed the weeds, filled the air with the must of burlap, and when they fell to nothing, left white blotches over the ground.

The townspeople had watched the bands of men march off and later come back with venereal diseases or their ears chopped from their skulls. One night startled eyes watched the coat of arms on the castle wall go up in smoke and flame as if an omen that they were expected to rally round for their sons or weep bitter tears. The Mayor lost at cards, had witnessed executions with his eyes closed, and in the marrow of his thick bones, the town shrank. All bartering was done by hand, the flowing script was chipped from the fat walls of the bank and the barred windows of the institution grew dense with cobwebs. An overturned tank on the north road still

9

crawled with ghosts who left it at night and hung over the canal walls for drink.

The Signalman, his mouth clamped shut, sitting behind the postered window of the station, saw the boy dashing over the torn rails and saw the man with the cane coming behind, his shadow lengthening in the station's candle light. Jutta waited with her hungry little girl bouncing up and down, riding her knee. The damp smell of the river rolled over soldiers' leggings and trousers that had been left in doorways, and a cow lying dead in a field looked like marble. In the tenuous light of day, Madame Snow hunched over her cards, and the silver platters, goblets and huge bowls grew black with tarnish and thick with dust. The merciless light showed each house a clear red or flat sand color and long burned beams and ashen barns were black. The green of cabbages had turned to white, and small automobiles, stalled and punctured to the side of the road, were blood red. Everyone wore grey, and over their shoulders were hitched empty cartridge belts. They begged while queuing for food and pounded their foreheads with their fists.

Throughout these winters Madame Snow could not believe that the worst would come. All her faith was in the knuckle bones of a worthless currency, in the right of the victorious, a coinage covered with the heads of high-spirited men. Bits of gauze were pushed into the clay and women wore coats with epaulettes and brass buttons. In the early days when the patients had rioted at the institution, it was the women who beat them down with clubs, while girls with spirited eyes and bare knees lured officers to a night of round-the-world. Arms and armies and silver blades were gone, the black had come out of the realm of kings, and butterflies and grass were left for children. Freight trains were hit and burned and no more came, and the keys of all machines were welded together. *Wohin gehen Sie?* cried the devils, and the clatter of boots died out of the barracks.

Balamir came eventually to think of himself as Madame Snow's Prince. But for a long while he worked by himself, still smelling drugs and fighting with the terrible shapes that leaped from drawers. He longed to be in the mountains, to leap from crag to crag, fly about the snow fields and find gold at the foot of stunted trees. He longed to tend the sheep and be a gangling black dog racing at the herd over green slopes. He longed to live in a cave. Icicles hung between the slats of the cellar window at night, and Balamir began to think of the jewels hanging from the ears of Madame Snow, began to listen for the turning of the key. He listened for the only accordion in the town and the notes traveled down the rain pipe, over the slate, but no voices sang to the crashing of the steins. There was nowhere to eat in *Spitzen-on-the-Dein,* and tables were piled on one another, chipped with bullet-holes. Sometimes Balamir heard sleigh bells that jingled in the valleys of the Alps, and he flung himself on piles of cold rubbish and earth as on a snow heap. He slept on an army cot, longed for the fir trees, and as he grunted and threw his weight every day into the frozen articles of chairs, springs and picture frames, he felt that his strength was falling away. He remembered photographs of the vicious tigers and the days when all men wore spats or silver braid, and from the mountains to the *Brauhaus,* camps and meeting halls sprang up, precision glasses were trained. He thought of a pigtailed donkey and the bones of men ground

11

into food. But now the guardhouse was empty, his father, who had been the Kaiser, was dead, and the nurses had been taken from the institution as corporals. He began to sit at the top of the stairs waiting for the door to open.

Madame Snow, Stella Snow in the days of laced boots, parasols and Grand Balls, had loved white prancing horses, square-shouldered men with spikes rising from their helmets, and sleek sausages that bulged like pig's hind legs, hanging in the kitchen large as a palace. She had breasts for a young girl, and had sat many times in a golden opera box, her legs growing rigid as if she were posing for a picture. The food in her father's house was served encased in layers of fat and from a basket at the side of her bed she had eaten a hybrid kind of giant pear. She went out with young men dressed in black who could ride a horse up to the point of death on a winter's day and leave him to freeze, feeling the hand of hell's angel, or went with moustached students with orange bands about their caps. She craved candies imported from France and Holland, heard lovers sing in raucous voices, and punting, seemed the image of the passing swan. She had a mouth that inverts envied, and when the first thuds of cannonade rocked the country, the mouth closed and she began to read. She loomed like a waxen noncommittal saint when her mother fell before her in the street from marketing, a piece of metal jutting from the bosom, while the airplane crashed. The policeman blew his whistle and people ran from every hole, looming like roaches before her startled eyes. It was then that she imagined marble bannisters and the candelabra of several generations before, and saw strange men embarking in ice-covered ships. Machine guns slowly rattled in the raked forests. Her sister, young and sullen, tore pages from books and leaped in the snow. Stella took to cards, gambling, to singing, and finally back to cards, and in the meantime crossed barbaric swords hung over her head and she swept through ironclad centuries, a respected crone.

Doors clamped shut and single lamps were lit. Jutta fondled the unformed girl while her son, awkward as a doll, ran over the cold earth. Many boys had been crushed under the tread of monsters and there were no martial drums to roll, though women pulled up their skirts to catch the tears. The shadows about the child seemed like beasts of the circus, groaning out of the empty doorways with nothing to mangle in their jaws. About him the wind began to scream as through the slots of airplane wings. The child ran, but only a sharp eye would have told that he was a boy, for his face, hands and hair were as flat as his sister's, and the light from his eyes was as limpid and sullen as the night. Still, the Duke hooked his cane over his arm, adjusted his suede gloves, and followed, his trouser cuffs becoming wet with mud. The child ran all the faster when the light went out of the butcher shop.

The shutters on the Mayor's house were closed as they had been ever since the time of air raids. The collar of his nightshirt was dirty and torn and he pulled the covers over his head. He smelled damp wood, the stone, goose feathers. And when he heard the footsteps running in the street below he shivered; for as a Hun, only *he* knew responsibility and the meaning of a coat of arms, the terror of a people left without tribunal and with privation. The Duke walked past the Mayor's house, unafraid of a hand in the dark, whistling softly to himself, but his eyes were sharp and he was keen on the scent. Then out of the blackness came a man, fresh from an alley, his hands still wet, breath strong with spirits. He reeled and they bumped below the Mayor's bedroom window. It was the drunken Census-Taker. He stepped back, looked up at the tall figure. "Ah, Herr Duke," he said, and his eyes searched the face. "You are mistaken," said the Duke and pushed on.

There was no sound. It was years since the people had stopped talking, except for fragments of a sentence, "Madame Snow told me to die . . ." And these words were only uttered in the strictest of confidence and in the lowest voice, for they had all the same experience, yet expected an alien ear, waited for disbelieving eyes. Even when the butcher shop door slammed shut, it seemed to say, "Quiet. I am not really closed." "Believe only in ten Gods," most people said. "For Evil is a punctual being; our mothers and fathers founded the State; our prisons have since become empty; the Crown must pass from hand to hand; and Stintz is a good devil with our children. Our money will not burn forever; even the sow's hoof is armed; one of our devils is just the time of day. We recall the rites of Wittenberg, and our tempestuous wives beat the fair young girls." When they spoke of the darkness of the weather, or of the lack of clothes, they were referring to one of the ten Gods of Loss whom they could not trust. And when they spoke their lips hardly moved and they were unable to believe their own words, expecting some agent to rise out of the middle of the table and condemn or laugh. Of Nordic stock, they were silent, the tribal cry long dead from their rolling tongues.

14

The Census-Taker moved away, drunken but conscious, fearing to make a sound. His belt sagged round his waist, his eyes rolled as with columns of figures. In the back of his mind he turned over a hatred for the Mayor, who had witnessed executions with his eyes closed. Pulling his cap more over his ears, he knocked softly on the door of the *Crooked Zeitung,* the town newspaper. At the end of every evening he stopped at the Paper, and it was then that his heart grew bright and the old excitement returned. Each letter in the plates of type was butchered into the next, all the plates had been smashed with hammers, and throughout the office was the smell of gum and the half-light from broken eye shades. The roll-top desks were smashed open and mice crawled over the bottles piled in the corners.

Jutta's husband had owned the Paper, but he was lost among thousands in Siberia, and I, Zizendorf, his friend, sat through every hour of the day thinking of the past. I too awaited this hour after midnight when my visitor would come, when I could cease thinking of lines of inverted print, and of the spoils I had found but had never seen again in Paris. I alone was editor, but my fingers were too blunt to punch the keys and I had no paper.

"Good evening, Editor," said the Census-Taker, "and how are you tonight?"

"Sit down for a moment," I said.

We always talked for an hour, then left together. We drank together and our pale eyes took in the cobwebs and then we would think of songs now unsingable. But we knew that there was something to do after our few words. We could talk of nothing and yet there were smiles hidden under our faces. We adjusted our clothes, drank slowly and carefully,

15

both knowing we would leave when the time was right.

"Well, we still have no government," I said. My eyes looked over the steel glasses.

"My friend, I can only think of plenty tonight. I remember festive costumes and bright lights. But you are right, we have nothing."

We both smiled, legs stretched limply before us, smoke rising from saved cigarettes. The kerosene burned low and problems were as flimsy as its slight flames. We heard our own breathing. I sometimes thought of Jutta's husband, who had been a good fellow, of spring and beerhalls, but more often I thought of the Pastor I had shot to death, of perfumes and earrings, and the keys that would not work, words that would not come. We heard the distant sound of the low water in the canal, felt our hunger growing stronger. The shadows grew larger in the printing office. "Shall we go?" asked the Census-Taker. He could feel the warmth creeping upon him. I strapped the pistol under my arm, blew out the lamp, and we left.

Jutta's girl was named Selvaggia and she was like a small white statue when she was undressed. Her widespread eyes were always afraid, even though the only person she feared in all the world was Herr Stintz. That man, one floor below, was playing a dirge on his tuba, his shiny head reflected from its bell, the sounds falling chromatically down and down. The mother held her child at arm's length, and the child seemed to grow like the pit of a fruit from the dotted kimono sleeves, straddled, as if she could never fall, on the woman's knee. The mother was starved for food, a woman who had gorged herself on nuts, cream, shanks of meat and chocolate, but

16

now filled herself at night in a way that her daughter, or son, could not. Her head belonged to a man, but though the face was male, her breast was still a woman's. The flat couch filled almost all the room and became her larder. Jutta was like her father, a Prussian mouth, a Roman nose, strong legs now, years after her illness, but her daughter was unlike any of them, a child on a poster. Stella Snow resented Selvaggia and her brother for bearing no resemblance to the family, and they would not speak to her. Jutta hated Stella from the first day her small man's face looked up from the crib to see her older sister staring down, mouth too filled with tongue to speak. The candle flickered and Jutta and child heard the double pairs of boots on the stairs, heard the sound clumping up like drummers' flams out of the silence. Selvaggia ran off to the second room to wait alone for her brother. She was wide-awake. She heard the opening of the door, the words *"Guten Abend,"* then shut them all out of her mind. In the next room the three of us lay on the couch.

Madame Stella Snow combed her half-white, half-gold hair, hung her black gown from a hook on the wall and crawled into the bed. A resident of the town for twenty years, knowing them all more closely than the Mayor, she felt the pain more acutely than he, even with her heart more like stone. Even though there was no Post, even though no one came or went and they all had lived or died for many centuries, even though there was no wireless, she felt the vastness of community that was like burial, spreading over all borders and from family to family. No drainpipes, chemicals to cleanse, flames to heat, no word, no food for the young or old, she was puzzled. Despite her years she could not find where it had all begun, for she was aristocratic to the end. Stella was capable of anything with a cold heart, but she could not bear the mutilation of any part of her. So she would not see her son. Distorted trees and rattling windows, dirty uniforms and an individuality that meant death flowed in a dangerous stream through *das Grab*. Even she, feeling the hunger, sometimes hesitated bringing the goblet to her lips. She had spent an oddly sexual decade and was now more unlike her sister than ever. Limbs of trees scraped against the window; she remembered that her sister's boy was still out in the night. She lay in the dark. Then she heard the scratching at the cellar door.

All Germany revolved around Balamir. His feet were in the boots of an Emperor's son, he felt the silver sword of time and tide and strength against his hip. Growing weak and cold, he was the result of commands coming down out of the years. From the farm where he was born to the institution and munition works, he felt that people bowed as he passed. How he sought to be that image, how the Kaiser's ghost needed him, how he would be Honor in the land he had become. But how well he knew it was a reign of terror and felt like pulling his beard as his father would have done. Potentate of the north, he scowled on his subjects, the trees, the chips of broken glass, brass casings and beaten fuse ends, but alone he smiled on his castle walls. He was the true and unknown Prince of *Spitzen-on-the-Dein,* followed by the castrated and the disillusioned, guided by an unknown hand around the signs of the skull and cross-bones planted above the mines. He had crept about the door of the Duke's apartment, watched the tall man come and go. He used to walk in the institution's garden, and now, in the last days of the decline of his kingdom, he was befriended in the home of twittering birds.

The vapors of the canal grew stronger, the Duke gained a hundred feet and eased his pace, cracks and holes in the earth filled with night dew.

I unstrapped my pistol and put it on the floor.

More insistently Balamir's fingers scratched at the door, and hunched on the top step he thought of a balcony and an armored knight. Germany lay below in the darkness.

"Come in, you poor creature," she whispered, and the trenches of the countryside were suddenly seen by the light of her candle.

TWO

To countenance the sickle over the wheat, to sweep out of the years the mellow heartbreak or the grand lie, to strike forward barehanded to a very particular and cold future, a diminutive but exact ending, a final satisfactory faith that is cruel and demonic, is to suffer the highest affection and lose it, to meet the loss of life and the advent of a certain reality. Madame Snow, having once reached the full period of life with her husband Ernst, and having fallen, alone, from such a richness, had met and lingered on this exact desolate end. Whereas Jutta, kin in place only, having spent a barren rigid past, was just now reaching the turn in the road where nakedness seemed to hang like a hundred apples, pink, wet, and running with sweet stiff worms, and she would probably never in her own time recognize the life-less segments of Germany threaded on a string before an open window. She indulged herself where her sister Stella had entered with daring.

The Census-Taker, stretched full length on the flat of his back, attuned to every breath over the bed and with his soul dissociated from the actual room, felt a persistent gentle quiver through the sheets, a rippling noise from the most infantile spaces. The curtains that hung over the window, not around it, the covers that hung from the foot of the couch, were not at all princely, but were washed clean and sparse. They were passed over many counters, spun from an ordinary thread. He had no heart for rebellion, still wearing the blue cap of an official crushed under one ear, had no ability to desire or to crush the tingling noise or presumptuous motion. While Jutta and I needed, in a skinned momentary manner, this vague ordeal, he was only able to absorb some faintly gross misunderstanding of already abnormal passions, some slight frightening tendency toward reversion, darkness and pleasure. The single globe overhead, burning at the end of a current without direction, diffused a light through the wings of moths, yellow, soft—a reality clear enough to see. The floor was swept clean for the children. Jutta did not seem to know of the Census-Taker's presence, did not feel his cold shoes against her bare feet, or the rough stubble on the back of his hands, but moving in an artifice, a play she well knew, pursed her lips into an act, an act to rid herself.

No one could dislike Jutta, though she was as nervously strong in her adult years as Stella was in her turning girlhood; she was as kind as a maternal spirit with a patriarchal plain nature, and whatever wisdom she may have felt lay restless, lost beneath the sheets. To me she lay in beauty, and into the Census-Taker she breathed a tense laughter, still trying to complete in her middle year some joyless cycle. And to the others, the cold white ravenous men and trunks of women, without age, without passion, she was the younger sister of Madame Snow, half-warm, half-friendly. She persisted in believing that both her children were her own, could not admit their creation with any man, and believed that they both loved her with the clarity of children who have not yet reached the size of youth. She breathed closer into my ear, traced the smooth canals, followed those old repeating dreams and murmured words. I was a counterfeit, a transformer for several delicate whims and exasperating needs, was an image for the moment made from past respectable devices. I rolled up on my side as if awake, and I saw in her body something that was not there, something that graced, I thought, the nibbling lips of the goat.

The Census-Taker, feeling the unnoticeable height of his own small passion, moving with stealth and awe as a child before the hanging sock, moving as if he held it in his hands and would not fracture it, slid from the bed and walked tiptoe to the corner chair, hung for a second, then turned to see. The most sensitive pulsations trembled at the corners of his eyes, and leaning slightly forward, verdant under the yellow light, he watched. His pleasure broke for a moment remembering a week the Americans had occupied the town and he had been forced to watch, deadly drunk, eyes red, while the Mayor, wretched and awkward, looked the other way and dropped the handkerchief that ended Pastor Miller's life at the stake. He concentrated and the steady movement returned, broken with the intricate strokes of pleasure. His memories were not as frequent or particular as my own. But I, Zizendorf, had now forgotten all under my undramatic and specialized dark guise, and I looked into the white of the sheets.

"What are you doing?"

"Why, I don't remember. Does it matter?"

"No."

A haunch rose above the white, then receded like an iceberg drawn just below the surface, the springs making hardly any noise, interest waiting for the chance to disappear. Night after night we waited for this summoning of flagged energy, hands cold, eyes closed, while in other beds and lofts the sleepers could not awake, could not breathe. My need to recreate, with amazing frequency, some sort of pastime similar to my comrades' habits, a cyclic affection that had finally, in Paris, become fatal to their health, led me to the quite real bargain of Jutta on the top floor. I, the Editor, did not recognize the head in the hay or fathom the posed deep slumber of the houses I passed on my nightly journey. And somehow the Census-Taker was my relic-brother, whose actions and despairs, whose humorous awkward positions and dry attempts were similar to mine. The Census-Taker, who had stature only through responsibilities that had gone, was muddled and lopsided as the badge of his marine cap, was unable to count or to repeat the names. He sought the appearance of love in the lives of his friends, retaining out of his official experience a disgust only of death. He lived the smallest chip of illusion, bearing along his drunk path a recognition of the way, a small dropsy formula that might in the end lead him out, beyond the overt sorrow of his partially thrilled, sitting figure.

My first days in Paris had been difficult. "Dear Sister," I wrote, "I'm having a bad time and cannot seem to get started in enjoying myself. I find the women very hard to get—the release here has broken down all our official routine and rank, and in consequence I do not seem to have anything with which to gain their respect . . ." Now with Jutta it was different, more like the second part of my Paris trip when I'd somehow found my nerve and hence perfume and boudoir parties. I enjoyed the Census-Taker watching us from the chair.

A low repressed rumble from the cold radiator

sounded like the beating of crickets' wings, his increased breathing slowly died down while our activity on the bed at his feet remained at a constant low level, consistent and unvaried without end. Gradually he sank back in the chair, his knees spread, belt pulled in, while he brushed with one hand at the image of Miller.

The Duke, shortening the pace, picked his way carefully by the cliff of fallen walls and poked with his cane into the dark crevices, hoping to stick the crouched body of his prey, to light upon the thin fox. He came legitimately by his title, and when he had commanded three tanks in the second war, was known as a fearless man. A father much older than himself still stalked far away in Berlin where I had never been, and as his father would have done, he recognized with taste and profound respect the clear high and stable character of Madame Snow. The night was so black that the red lights from the hatches of his tanks would have reflected against the clouds and brought death. Free of the debris he again approached in the path of the child, not quite able to visualize the kill.

Jutta did not know the Duke, did not like him, and immediate instinct told her to beware the second floor, for she feared his clean standing, feared his aristocratic caliber which she, through her own fault, had not grasped from her family. She spoke of most intimate life with her daughter, tried to instill in her son ideas of manhood, and spent a certain part of the day sweeping dust into a little bin and rubbing with a damp cloth. She left her apartment very seldom, but even the Duke, in his most precise manner, had noticed her gentle convolvulaceous long legs. Large and perfect in every detail but not a woman, sensible and sometimes calm but not a man, she failed to understand the German life, failed as a mother, at least for her son. She had never been quite able to allow a love for her country to intrude within her four walls, had never been loyal, and though she gave herself like segments of a fruit, she never envisioned the loyalty due her State. Tears sometimes appeared on her cheeks after our long embrace which I was never able to recognize. Thirty years is not enough time to measure the complete crystallization of a nation, though partially lost; to measure the greatest advance of communal men, though partially destroyed, and Jutta, far removed from the rise, fall, and eventual rise, was far from being within the thirty years, far from being successful or adored.

"Again?" She spoke under my arm. "Perhaps you are right. You certainly are, here . . ." There was hardly a break as the wheel turned, sustaining the light ardor. No movement could be carried long enough to last over to the first minute after, beneath the yellow globe.

Tonight she seemed lovely, now propped against the pillows, resting a knee against my side, her eyes passing once over the sleeping Census-Taker, then towards the door of the other room, robe-top arrested and wrinkled below her waist, lovely, but far from the majesty of Madame Snow, who looked very old. She was never able to tell when I would come, but at a moment she would find me. Now she relaxed while I touched her arm with the flat of my cheek.

Yesterday she had gone for a walk, down the steep loose stairs of the boarding house, grey shawl over the bent shoulders, bringing with love and kindness her daughter Selvaggia, who followed behind. She reached back for the long hand to guide the child in the darkness, pushed open the door with her foot, and outside they found that the town was partially destroyed, that a cold spring sun was cut through by a rough steel shoulder, that cold ruts of mud were beginning to thaw. Her face had no color under the sunlight, mother and daughter walked in the same slow stride, feeling their way forward in a place they did not know, and the child spoke now and then in a friendly way. Jutta drew the shawl closer, tried to keep her black shoes free of the mud.

"What were the invaders like?" asked Selvaggia.

"They were bad people, but they didn't stay long." The child had been protected from their sight the week that the Americans had stopped in the town; now they had scurried on to the further cities, and only a man on a motorcycle came occasionally to *Spitzen-on-the-Dein*. His saddlebags were full and his handsome machine roared across untraveled roads with authority. But his face was covered with goggles and Selvaggia had only seen him bouncing quickly, noisily, through the streets.

"You shouldn't even think about them," said Jutta, and she vaguely hoped that her child would not.

In the sunlight Jutta's hair was not so pretty, pin-head eyelets of dirt were on her nose, spots in the loose dress had run, her legs were large and stiff under the re-stitched swinging hem. Her daughter's face narrowed to a thin point at the chin and it seemed likely that the child would never have breasts. Under the narrow fish-bone chest where they might have been, her heart beat autonomously, unaffected by the sight of the hill of sliding moist clay. The tar-paper houses on top of the hill were sunken at the ends, jewels of tin cans littered the indefinable yards without lawns or bushes, and hostile eyes watched mother and daughter from behind the fallen poles. A dense unpleasant smell arose from beneath the ruins about two standing walls and drifted out across the narrow road on the chilly wind. *"Tod,"* said the mother under her breath. Side by side they stared down the uneven grey slopes to where the brick-red remains of the institution sprawled in the glittering light.

"What's that?" asked Selvaggia.

"That's where they used to keep the crazy people." The pointed head nodded.

Many, many years before, a woman doctor had spoken to Balamir in those same buildings:

"What's your name?"

"Will you tell me what day this is?"

"Weiss nicht."

"Do you know what year this is?"

"Do you know where you are?"

"Weiss nicht."

"You're going to have a good time here."

"Weiss nicht, weiss nicht!"

As they went down the hill the bright sun had become more cold, their feet were wet, and they had been very glad to get back to the quiet of the rooms.

The yellow walls flickered as the electric globe dimmed, rose, dimmed but did not go out, as the generator sputtered and continued to drone far beneath us in Balamir's basement. Below her stomach the white flesh puffed into a gentle mound, then dissolved into the sheets, while her fingers against my arm traced over the silken outlines of a previous wound. Her mind could only see as far as immediate worry for her son, never awoke in anticipation for the after-dark, or in fear to rise in light; and as the thought of the child slipped downwards and ceased, every moment hence was plotted by actions circled about in the room. She tapped my arm as if to say, "I get up, but don't bother," and left the couch, the top of the robe swinging behind from the waist. She poured the cold water into the basin, washed carefully and left the water to settle. In the other room to get a light for my cigarette, she said, *"Schlaf',"* to her daughter at the window and returned with the lighted splinter. In his sleep the Census-Taker heard a few low mournful notes of a horn, as if an echo, in a deeper register, of the bugles that used to blast fitfully out among the stunted trees in the low fields on the south edge of town. Once, twice, then Herr Stintz stood his instrument in a corner and sat alone in the dark on the floor below. The apartment on the second floor was dark.

"They're dancing tonight," I said, paper stuck to my lips, "let's go, I still have a few hours."

"Tanzen?"

"Yes. Let's go, just for a while."

She dressed in a pale blue gown that sparkled in the wrinkles, stepped into the shoes of yesterday's walk and washed again. I wore no tie but buttoned the grey shirt up to my throat, rubbed my eyes, and reaching over, shook the Census-Taker by the foot. The hallway was completely black and ran with cold drafts. We went slowly from the fifth to the fourth, to the third, the second, the Census-Taker leaning with both arms on the rail.

"The Duke's," said Jutta, nodding.

"Ah, the Duke's."

The little girl heard the door slam shrilly far below her vigil at the window.

"What's all this about dancing?" asked the Census-Taker, his hands held tightly over his ears from the cold, his raised elbows jerking in peculiar half-arcs with his stride. We walked quickly to the hill that rose much higher in the darkness.

At night the institution towered upward crookedly, and fanned out into a haphazard series of dropped terraces and barren rooms, suddenly twisted walls and sealed entrances, combed of reality, smothered out of all order by its overbearing size. We walked at an average pace, feeling for each other's hands, unafraid of this lost architecture, unimpressed by the sound of our own feet. There was no food in the vaulted kitchens. Offices and conference rooms were stripped of pencils, records, leather cushions. Large patches of white wall were smeared with dilating lost designs of seeping water, and inner doors were smeared with chalk fragments of situation reports of the then anxious and struggling Allied armies. The institution was menacing, piled backwards on itself in chaotic slumber, and in segregated rooms, large tubs—long, fat and thick edges ringed with metal hooks that once held patients on their canvas cradles —had become sooted with grey, filled with fallen segments of plaster from the ceilings. Strange, unpursued animals now made their lairs in the corners of the dormitories where insulin had once flowed and produced cures. And this was where the riot had taken place.

Each of us walking through this liberated and lonely sanctum, past its now quiet rooms, heard fragments of recognition in the bare trees. For once it had been both awesome and yet holy, having caused in each of us, silent marchers, at one time or another, a doubt for his own welfare and also a momentary wonder at the way they could handle all those patients. Once the days had been interrupted by the very hours and the place had passed by our minds new and impressive with every stroke. But now the days were uninterrupted and the shadows from the great felled wings sprawled colorless and without any voice about our ever moving feet. Then, scudding away through the maze, new, unkempt and artificial, the low clapboard storehouse emerged, champing of strange voices. It heeled, squat beneath its own glimmers of weak light, a small boarded place of congregation, hounded by the darkness of the surrounding buildings.

Without slacking pace, we neared the din and fray above the scratching needle, the noise of women dancing with women, and men with men, shadows skipping without expression across the blind of a half-opened door. They ceased to whirl only for a moment and then the feet shuffled again over the floor boards, and we, walking towards the building, smelled the odor of damp cinders and felt for a moment the black leaves settle about our ankles.

Jutta, the Census-Taker and myself, emerging from flat darkness into light that was only a shade brighter, bowed our heads, fending off the tinted glare that filled the spaces between the rigid dancers. Close together, we stood for a moment sunken in the doorway. Figures stepped forwards, backwards, caught in a clockwork of custom, a way of moving that was almost forgotten. Gathered in the storehouse, back to back, face measured to face, recalled into the group and claiming name instead of number, each figure, made responsible, appeared with the

30

same sackcloth idleness as Jutta. They swung out of the mist and appeared with pocketed cheeks and shaven heads. They seemed to dance with one leg always suspended, small white bodies colliding like round seamless pods, and fingers entwined were twice as long as palms. They danced continuously forming patterns, always the same, of grey and pale blue. The beauties were already sick, and the word *krank* passed from group to group over devious tongues, like the grapevine current of fervent criminal words that slide through wasted penal colonies. The smallest women had the roundest legs that bounced against jutting knees, and the seams of their gowns were taken up with coarse thread. High above their shoulders towered their partners' heads, loose, with cold whitening eyes, tongues the faded color of cheeks, curled back to the roots of forgotten words. Several girls were recently orphaned when Allied trucks, bringing German families back from hiding, had smashed, traveling too fast along the highway, and had scattered the old people like punched cows in the fields. Some of these danced together, stopping to see which way the other would turn.

I touched Jutta's hand and we walked into the center of the floor while, leaning against the wall, the Census-Taker watched, trying to recall each passing couple. Jutta leaned and pushed, hung to my hand, stepped now upon my own foot, now upon another's, and the stiff waltz whispered out of the machine. The Czechs, Poles and Belgians danced just as she, their wooden shoes sticking to the floor, wearing the same blue dresses with faded dots, some with bones broken off-center, some with armpits ringed as black as soot. For it was not the Germans who thought of coming together when there was

31

nothing to say, when no one could understand the vast honored ideal swept under; it was the rest of Europe—bedridden with idleness, dumb with tremendous distance, unhealthy in confinement, these gathered in the storehouse—who had begun this dance in the evenings. A few true Germans were scattered among them. Men wandered through, seeking a girl they had lost. These men, startled and old, still wore unironed hospital gowns as shirts, moved ready to push the others aside with delicate arms, walked with their feet in sandals and with smoke-white faces. A young girl, sitting on a bench, gently rubbed her hands over an Italian officer's trousers while he leaned back, his eyes closed, and she, smiling, watched the circle of dancers and smelled the boneless herring on his breath.

There was no drink to be had in the storehouse. The smell of pasteboard and dust hovered over the walls, Russian ex-soldiers grinned at each other like Mongolians in a corner, a half-French girl with tangled colorless hair, pregnant with a paunch beneath her belt, looked ugly and out of place; all were spiritless from the very strangeness of the country and so they crowded themselves, unwanted, into this end of town. All of them slept in the back rooms on hay that should have been fed to the herds.

In the brick building nearest the storehouse, Balamir had lain half-awake, sometimes in the mornings, or in the late afternoons when flowers were closing, in one of the large tubs, all but his head submerged in water the temperature of blood, and behind him had heard the waiting nurse who flipped the pages of a magazine. The evenings sidled through the long green shade, towels hung like mats from the walls. He was surprised to find that his hands floated. And always the pages flipping one on the other, pages beating just behind his head. The water gurgled out of the tub, disturbing the peace and quiet, the shaded air of the small room.

Through the minutes, the dancers were the same long lines of inmates stamping time to the phonograph, dancing in block-like groups with arms that were too long. In the back rooms, a few figures sprawled on the bunks overcome with an inexcusable exhaustion, weak and helpless under the low make-shift roof of the storehouse. Overhead the stars were clear.

"Shall we rest?"

"I only have a while more. Let's dance." She followed me. Jutta did not know that she looked like the others, that here in public no one knew the dress was washed, that her face, ribboned with long hair, was just as unkempt and unpleasant as the other tottering faces. If I had left her for a moment and then returned, she would not have known who her partner was, but looking over shoulders that were all alike, she would have danced on.

"Is it going to be difficult?"

"No."

I, Zizendorf, like all men, was similar to her husband who had been captured, but it was something indefinable that made me particularly similar. The other men's sleeves were too short, their heads too thin and bare, all actually unlike her husband; yet they were similar in a way, because seeing them she had started on the long glorious path, then had forgotten a great deal. But I was different from them all and was better for her than her husband.

She gussed that the hall might become empty soon and she would be alone. The shoulder was hard under the cloth, her back began to feel stiff and it was difficult not to go to sleep. A figure in a tight green suit kept changing the record, wiping it with a piece of rag. And in one of the back rooms smelling of flour that had long since been hauled away, where some sprawled or sat by windows streaked with dirt, a girl crouched on all fours, her head hanging forward, face covered with hair, the back of her neck shining like a small round coin, and clutched the sides of the bunk in motionless indecision. Down the corridor we danced, trooped like men about to change the guard, voices low and serious. White heads in pairs that were the same size, shape, identical bony structures, came together in the damp place and kissed. The girl lost her hold, fell forward and, face buried in a wrinkled grey shirt, tried to sleep.

Under my arm I felt the pistol, in my head faintly heard the shrill music, and dancing with Jutta, I felt as well as I ever felt. Naturally my eyes looked from face to face, beyond the back of her head, followed the girls that were hugged along and passed from dry smile to smile. It stirred a memory of burnished Paris women and silver bars during the second part of my visit, of murky waters stirred with blinking lights and faint odors of flowers on street corners. I bumped a man and no words were spoken, then I was pushed backwards into a girl and tried to recall the sensation—while all about me moved the bundles of rags, grass sticking to their collars.

The Census-Taker had lost us and squeezed on the end of a narrow bench that sagged with girls whose fingers were chewed at the ends. He looked with distaste from one red knee to another. He hooked his fingers in his shirt and tried to rest his

34

back, felt something soft and loose pushing into his side and pushed away. An Italian with long hair down his neck looked from the Census-Taker to the girl, and catching his eye, shook an olive head "no," in a meaningful way; the Census-Taker shut his eyes.

The lilt and strain moved back and forth in an endless way, foreshadowed and stunted in careless glances, in the unexcited hang of a dress, with words partially exposed to hearing, with all their mixed nationality running out in shuffling footsteps. Something inside me motioned to hold her closer, and I did so, the scratching close now to my ear. I lit a cigarette with one arm hooked around her neck, the flame close to her hair, spaces black between my teeth as I exhaled. Two of the white heads hung together in a corner with breaths stifled, while the music rested on the constant low scuffle of wooden shoes.

"I must leave," I said. My hand rested on the middle of her back; I looked at her kindly. Something about my person could still be called *soldat* but not the crawling, unshaven *soldatto* filth of the Italians who wriggled dog-fashion.

"Yes," she answered. In the Census-Taker's disturbed sleep, the white handkerchief, recently blown into, fluttered down like a child's parachute to the ground.

"You must get him back to the rooms. Be careful not to fall. Get some sleep, you look tired. I'll come and see you in the morning after it's done, and remember, there's no danger." She smelled a breath of tobacco as my cheek touched her forehead for a moment, and I stepped off, no longer recognized, among the grey masqueraders. Alone, Jutta followed the length of three walls, past outstretched thick feet, past bodies hanging arm in arm, until she found where the Census-Taker was sitting, the last in a row of tallow girls. Gently, holding beneath one arm, she made him rise until his strong breath fumed about her throat, until his red eyes were narrowed full on her face, and speaking softly, she propelled him along. Feeling the narrow doorway, they found themselves out in the night air, alone. In the receding storehouse, the dancers massed together in the cold tart atmosphere to perform, couple by couple all night, some distasteful ritual, whereby those with uncovered bellies and tousled hair walked in their midst as easily and unnoticed as the most infected and sparkling damsel.

Jutta's son, the fairy, fled for his life, his knees the size of finger-joints whirling in every direction like the un-coordinated thrashings of a young and frightened fox.

The Duke continued to prod and tap with the gleaming cane, drew the coat tighter about his chest.

Jutta's daughter watched in the window, her golden curls tight like a wig about the narrow face.

Jutta herself, with the Census-Taker heavily against her shoulders, started down the cinder path, while over all the town and sty-covered outskirts hung a somber, early, Pentecostal chill. She moved slowly because the man mumbled thickly in her ear and his feet caught against the half-buried bricks that lined the path. Finally she could no longer hear the music and was quickly back in the thick deserted kingdom of crumbling buildings and roosting birds, the asylum all about her. She wanted to get home to sleep.

I followed, far ahead of them, the clay contours of the railroad tracks, crossed the wooden scaffold over the canal, smelled the rivulets of fog, heard the slapping of deflated, flat rubber boats against the rocks, made my way across ruts and pieces of shattered wood. I knew that soon the American on the motorcycle, the only Allied overseer in this part of Germany, would be passing through the town, shivering with cold, mud-covered and trembling, hunched forward over the handle bars, straining with difficulty to see the chopped-up road in the darkness. The main highway, cracked badly from armored convoys, crossed the town at a sharp bend where the low wet fields faced the abrupt end of a few parallel streets of shapeless brick houses. A log lay across the road, heavy and invisible. For a moment, I remembered my true love, and then I was following the rough line of the log, leaving the town behind, and slipping in haste, I dropped down beside the two soft murmuring voices and leaned against the steep embankment.

"He'll be here soon."

"*Ja, der Tod.*"

Backs to the road, we looked out across the endless grey fields and almost expected to see barrels of smoke and the red glare of shooting flares through the twisted stunted trees.

Jutta could not believe that I was in danger, but some dull warning voice seemed to try to speak from the leaning buildings, and the Census-Taker babbled in her ear; some voice, a consideration, tried to force its way through her blunted journey. As she passed the building where Balamir had once been kept, she felt this new twist in things and did not want to lose me. Years before she would have seen the face pressed to the window and would have heard from his lips what was in her heart: "I don't want to see those birds smashed!" Balamir first screamed so long ago to his startled nurse. Jutta hurried, pushing the drunk man in front of her towards the hill, and began to think that Stella was a strange woman to take a man crazy with the stars into the house, while out in the cold, I, her lover, had to wait for the puttering of the motor-bike, for the saddlebags, the prize.

PART TWO—1914

LOVE

"Stella sings like an angel," cried the crowd, and the Bavarian orchestra played all the louder. Some of them were shocked, some annoyed, others opened their big hearts and wanted to join in the chorus, while some looked out into the sultry night. The largest of them were eager waiters whose black jackets showed here and there with darker patches of velvet from stains, whose stout arms bore platters of beer and who paused near the kitchen doors to hear the new singer. The officers in their new grey tunics were slightly smaller and the girls were smaller yet—but still were Nordic women, straight, blonde, strong and unsupple. Even the vines on the trellises were thick and round, swaying only slightly out in the heat. Heads nodded close together at the tables in the garden. In the brightly-lit room the wooden chairs and tables were uncarved, unornamented, and the white walls and pillared ceiling were remote. It did not seem possible that enough blue smoke and shadow could rise to make the hall alluring. The men talked together, the clatter of cups intruded. Their backs were straight, they nodded cordially, and the light gleamed on undecorated chests. But it was only ten, still dusk, still formal. They smiled. Stella twisted the handkerchief in her fingers, squeezed it strongly into her damp palms and continued to sing and to smile. Then she found it simple, found that her throat opened and her head could turn and smile, that she could move about and thrust into her shoulders the charm of the song. They listened, turned away, then listened again, and like a girl with breeding and a girl with grace, she made them look and sang to them. First, sadly, then with her eyes bright and her shoulders thrust backwards:

"Dass du mich liebst, weiss ich."

Some of them laughed and twisted in their seats. She shook her hair loose, she felt like telling them they could come to her, that they could send flowers.

"Must I then, must I then come back to your heart
    And smile again?"

She moved as if she had a sunflower just beneath her bosom, as if she could draw them sailing on a sacred lake, and first a crackling chicken, then a duckling, then a head of cheese fell under her swoop. But always she looked directly over into their eyes startled from eating, or eyes large from some private imagination. Her bosom, larger than her hips, swayed with pleasure. And only a moment before she had stood in the left wing, hidden by dusty curtains and sheets of music, feeling that never in the world could she face the lights and attention of the drinking hall. The *Sportswelt Brauhaus,* austere and licensed, patronized and rushed upon, coldly kept her out for a moment, then with a smart burst from the accordion, drew her down, deeply as possible, into the fold. After the summer broke, she had come, and tonight she stood before them all, her body slowly showing through the gown, more and more admired for her stately head, singing,

"All my body blossoms with a greater . . ."

They clapped, chuckled, and slowly the undecorated chests slid open, the lights swirled about in the fog, while Stella, arm around the accordion player, sang anything at all that came to mind. Her ancestors had run berserk, cloaked themselves in animal skins, carved valorous battles on their shields, and several old men, related thinly in blood from a distant past, had jumped from a rock in Norway to their death in the sea. Stella, with such a history running thickly in her veins, caught her breath and flung herself at the feet of her horned and helmeted kinsmen, while the Bavarians schnitzled back and forth in a drunken trio.

In an alley behind the hall timbered with consecrated ash, the darkness and odor of wet stone rose in spirals of steam as from below a horse on a winter's day. The sound of the violin, jumping dangerously along the length of the alley walls, merged with the basso wheezing of a lascivious merchant and swept overhead into the heat of the garden.

Ernie, the *Brauhaus* owner's son, shuffled his feet to two dry spots, leaned his shoulder against the slippery rock, and steadied his face covered with dueling scars, down into the green darkness. Stella's unknown, unnamed voice, beginning to reach the crown of her triumph, leaped straight from the small bright window behind his back and fell about the heads of those in the garden, dumb with love. Ernie wiped his hands on his trousers, leaned back and looked up into the sweltering night, his pockets stuffed with hundred mark notes, his eyes blind to the flickering sky. He saw only emptiness in the day's returns, felt the scratches from a skillful bout burn on his cheek. His tongue was thick and numb with beer. The Merchant, barely afloat in the humid atmosphere, still cradling jade and ivory blocks in his arms and girded with a Turkish robe, made a perfect soft target in the darkness. Ernie breathed in and out on the same air, the pig's tail lay heavily on his stomach, and he gave no thought to steel blades or the Merchant's fat bulk. Howls of laughter were muffled inside the hall, low voices floated over the garden wall in tones that said there was something to hide, and the heady smell of tulips, roses, German-valor-petals, hydrangeas and cannon flowers sank into the pea-green pit of stench at his feet. The flowers turned their pistils out to catch the rain if it should come, the Merchant's breath drew closer, and the moon shone once in the heavens, loaded like a sac with water.

Ernie squeezed his left hand, the hand with the last two fingers gone from a hatchet stroke, into his pocket tight with bills, and turned back towards the light, towards the free men of the hall. He would sit on a worshipped pile of granite, a small duelist in the hall of kings. The Merchant tried to follow but, like a laboring hind, slipped and fell, his fat body dragging along over the stones. He could not call out and each time he moved he slid deeper. Ernie heard his thudding fall and walked faster, trying to find again a place for light and song. He measured his steps and seemed to tread upon the whole world of Germany as he walked, half-consciously, back near the aurora of tabled clans, disciplined faces, and all the irony and fellowship of his men-at-arms. A man in grey staggered past, ready with malice or with a bow at the waist, and far in the back of the alley Ernie heard him trip against the fallen Merchant, heard a muffled word against the background of summer nightbirds.

Ernie, because of the fingers gone from his hand and the ugly sight of three remaining claws, could never ride a black mare into the din of volleying balls, or crawl hand over hand through the wet fields of Belgium. He touched the middle and forefinger with the thumb and heard the woman's voice crying out to the men young in soul. Inside he sat at his father's table under the shadows and far to the rear, and melting into the crowd became nondescript, feigned to strike out with ignored curt expressions.

Stella, like her father, held them at bay; and, losing one by one those traits that were hers, absorbed more and more the tradition that belonged to all. She did not lisp when she sang, but boomed the words in an unnatural voice. And the gestures she developed came with ease. She walked from the archway of her father's house to the audience of the *Sportswelt* transgressing natural thought as clearly as she passed the stages of the months. She, the sorceress, sent them boiling and held them up for joy, feeling pain only in the last moment before sleep, half-dressed, on the bedroom floor. Gerta, the nurse, thought the Devil had come a long way from the forest to find her. Every dress she owned, every male plate of armor, every bone comb and silken ban, was stamped with the seal of the camp follower, and screaming in nightmares to the dead ears of her sleeping father, she followed the weeks of 1914. Beneath her eyes she had painted indigo stains as if she had been beaten, and her eyes swept from tall black trees to the glaciers of dead warriors, green with the tint of pine trees, sober with a long-

45

ing that came of eighteen years of summer patios and a partition of a princely nursery.

After the last chorus of the song, she bowed straight-legged from her flaring hips, flushed to their applause, and made her way to old Herr Snow's table, storing appreciation up in her heart, storing each face beside the photograph of the white flaking head of Gerta, the nurse. Blue smoke floated above the sawdust and the tide of conversation rolled in the lion cage. She sat where Herr Snow, with his red beard, indicated, felt his wrists slide her smoothly forward until she touched the table. She looked from face to face. "You were excellent," he said. "This is my son, Ernst, who enjoys your singing so much." Ernie, thin and more alive with beer, pushed back his chair and nodded, fixed her as he might have fixed a rosy-cheeked sister, adult and come alive from his free past. "And," said Herr Snow, "this is Mr. Cromwell, a guest of mine." Mr. Cromwell smiled with an easy drunken grace and filled her glass. He did not miss the charm of London or of the English countryside rollicking in summer but slept late and heard no cocks crowing in the early dawn.

"You're English?" asked Stella.

"Yes, but I particularly like Germany. The lakes and cities seem like vistas cut into the ice age. You sing well."

Herr Snow was proud of Ernie because his other son, a boy of nine, forever wore his head strapped in a brace, and the words that came from the immovable mouth came also from a remote frightening world. Old Snow, prosperous and long owner of the *Sportswelt,* looked with hard admiration on Ernie's face, saw his own eyes and nose staring resentfully back. With mute excitement, Stella followed each jagged crevice of the scars, noticed how they dug beneath the cheeks highlighting the bones, how the eyes were pressed between encroaching blocks of web-like tissue. She waited for the three claws of the left hand to close talon-like just above her knee, grew warm to the close-kept face down in its corner. The orchestra filled out the room behind her, roasted apples fell from the bosom of an oracle, burnt and golden, and gradually the three men drew closer, warm with all the taste of a chivalric age. She covered the glass before her with the golden hair and saw for a moment in its swirling depths, the naked cowardice of the fencer, the future fluttering wings of the solitary British plane leaving its token pellet in the market place, her mother's body rolling around it like a stone stained forever, the stain becoming dry and black as onyx.

The rain had begun to fall and the summer thunder drifted over the wet leaves, coursed over the darkened glistening steeples. The carriage rocked to and fro, water splashing from the wheels, dripping from the deep enclosures of passing doors. They traveled slowly down *die Heldenstrasse,* hearing only the soft rain, the chopping of the steel hoofs, the smooth movements of leather. Oiled gunmetal springs swung them easily through the June night while Mephistopheles, crouching in a choir-room, circled this eighteenth day of the month in red. He, in his black cowl, called the sleeping swans to pass by them on the lake in the park and the coachman flicked the whip over the horse's ears.

"Why did you want to take me home?" she asked.

"I'm fond of the color of your hair and eyes."

Stella felt nothing near her, could feel no man or

beast or spirit lurking under the rain, no hand crept towards hers. She could not even feel or hear his breathing, only the steady turning of the axletree. No man in the world, sitting as Cromwell sat, soft felt brim curling with rain, fine straight features and wide nostrils drinking in the lavender, no such man or leader of men could have caused a single ripple in her even tone.

"Why didn't you stay home, in your English home?" Her hair was becoming damp and heavy.

"Home? Why I don't really have a home, and in fact, I don't believe anyone has." Now, with a change of wind, she could smell his scented breath, but he was foreign, unreal, was a humor she could brush away with her white hand. "I feel that I am one of those middle-aged men whom, in a little while, people will call an expatriate." In full light he looked a little old, resembled a smart but tottering wolfhound guarding its own grave. And Cromwell, like a change of mind or a false impression, like an unexpected meeting or a mistake in the dark, filled Ernie's place and caused in Stella a fleeting disbelief; she expected to see the lacerated face aloof in the corner of her carriage. He rode as an Archduke, unconsciously wiping the rain from his waistcoat, smiling slightly with lonely intoxication. Stella looked beyond the figure of the fat coachman to see the angular street unwind.

"I think that everyone has a home." Her voice was musical like the axletree.

When he spoke, it was not quite as if he wanted to talk to her. His throat was hidden by an upturned flowing collar.

"I, for one, don't even remember my mother's face. England is a land of homeless people, but the

Germans, though just as homeless, are a little slow in realizing it. And besides, they have a beautiful capacity for ideals of conquest, a traditional heroism." His mouth was becoming heavy with a very sour taste of sleep, a taste of finding it still dark beyond the raised shade, the sourness accumulated from many unwanted meals, and still he kept his head in a smiling manner, looked into the flowering darkness with a pleasant friendly way of practiced youth.

"The bedclothes, curtains, my mother's gowns, the very way I looked as a child, were always unfamiliar. Unfamiliar."

The slight layer of accent beneath his perfect speech began to disrupt her isolation. The soft ribbon of street started to break up into glaring bricks, into actual corners, into black patches of shadow against the curb, the horse stumbling and nodding. The rain shook in the linden trees.

"You should have stayed home," she said. Stella thought that she was too precious for this journey and counted, one by one, the statues of Heroes that lined the street on the park side and wished she could recognize the stone faces. They seemed like metal behind an angry crowd, as if they might step out to march up the stifling street, rain falling from their foreheads. Almost like man and wife they plodded along in silence, the late night growing smoky, their clothes wet as if they had been playfully wading in the park lake. How wonderful that they had all liked her singing, that they had clapped and looked after her, that she could sing to State heroes. Somehow she thought that Cromwell had not clapped at all. Again she could almost feel the three claws just above her knee, would offer her firm leg to their frightened touch. Cromwell, though he seemed to be easily considering the black early morning, found that he could not settle back, resigned to the rain, easily riding in the Duchess' carriage, but felt a vague general pain as if the Heroes followed him. He wondered what the Krupp gun would do to Europe, saw the Swiss sliding down the mountains on their seats, saw the English bobbing in the Channel, and saw the rest of the nations falling in line like a world-wide pestilence.

She had seen Ernst for the first time a few mornings ago, out in the empty garden behind the *Sportswelt,* watching the blue shadows give place to the bright rising sun, neither English, Swiss nor German, but a fighter without his trappings, dangling his legs from an upturned chair. She knew he was a coward when the old man screamed out of the window, "Ernst, Ernst," in a loud bellowing unhappy voice that did not have to command respect. But he jumped, stared at the quiet blank wall of the building, and then she knew that it might have been she herself who called, and she laughed behind the shadow of the open window when it bellowed again, "Ernst, Ernst, *kommst du hier.*" She could tell by the way his head moved that his eyes must be frightened, that all his frail arms and legs would be trembling. He was magnificent! She watched him throw the foil from him and it rolled into a flower bed, lay beneath the drooping petals. But she knew that his face was tough, she could see that the blood would be rising into his head, that his ugly hand would be twitching. The garden became Valhalla, he could kill somebody with a single quick movement, and she wanted to be with him in Valhalla. She heard the door slam and the old man's voice rolling angrily out. The

50

flowers turned very bright in the sun; she could, at that moment, sing her heart out. When she saw Herr Snow a while later he was perfectly calm.

The musty odor of the wet carriage mixed with the lavender of Cromwell's hair, the Heroes passed out of view.

"I don't think you should have come with me," she said into the coachman's back.

"You must give me a chance," Cromwell answered, thinking of the vast Rhineland, "after all, I'm homeless."

On a few isolated occasions in his life, Ernie had been swept into overwhelming crisis, and, after each moment of paralysis, had emerged more under his father's thumb than ever. He remembered that his mother, with her tight white curls and slow monotonous movement, had never succumbed, but had always yielded, to the deep irritable voice. Her kind but silent bulk had slowly trickled down his father's throat, easing the outbursts of his violent words, until at last, on a hot evening, they had laid her away in the back yard, while his young brother, head already in the brace, had crawled along at their sides, screaming and clutching at his trousers. His father loved him with the passionate control of a small monarch gathering and preening his five-man army, and only used him as a scapegoat to vent an angry desire for perfection. The old man would have wept in his hands if anything had happened to Ernie, and, as ruler of the *Sportswelt* and surrounding Europe, had given him every opportunity for love. Ernie, dwarfed at his side, sat every evening at the back table in the hall, until, when the stately patrons rolled with laughter and the father became more absorbed in them than in his son, he could slip away and match swords with those as desperate as himself. "You'll get yourself killed," his father would say, "they're cutting you apart bit by bit."

His father had forced one of the few small crises himself the only time he saw his son in combat. They were fencing in a grove several miles from the city, the sun raising steam about their feet, fencing with a violent hatred and determination. They were alone, stripped to the waist, scratches and nicks bleeding on their chests, heads whirling with the heat. The Baron, young, agile, confident, drove him in and out of the trees to stick him a thousand times before actually wounding him. Ernie was sick, fought back, but saw blades through the fogged goggles. Herr Snow came upon the scene like a fat indignant judge, his face white with rage. He wrenched the weapon from the Baron's hand and beating him without mercy across the shoulders and buttocks, drove him screaming from the grove, tiring his thick arm with the work. "You're a god damn fool," he told his son.

Ernie walked in a dark trimmer's night for a long while and in the *Sportswelt* heard the bees buzzing with a low vicious hum. Since he was a Shylock, his face grew tight and bitter and Herr Snow took to keeping a lighted candle by his bed. Even asleep, Ernie's feet jiggled up and down as they had danced in the grove, the bulk of the noble crushing swiftly down on him, and in a frenzy Ernie jabbed quicker and quicker at the raging white face of his father, fell back weeping beneath the heavy broadsword.

"Well," and the words pushed themselves over the end of a wet sausage, "why didn't you take her home yourself? You'll not get any women just sitting with me." Ernie made a move to leave.

"Wait. Just let me tell you that once your mother

looked at me, there was no other man." He held the stein like a scepter. "You want to go for these," his hands made awkward expressive movements around his barrel chest. Herman Snow had not only used his hands but had made tender love to the silent woman and asked dearly for her hand on his knees that were more slender in those days. He thought her sad face more radiant than the sun, and worshipped her as only a German could. On the evenings when she had a headache he stroked her heavy hair and said, *"Ja, Liebling, ja, Liebling,"* over and over a hundred times in his softest voice. They had taken a trip on a canal barge owned by his brother. Herman had propped her in the stern on coarse pillows, away from the oil-smeared deck forward and the guttural voices of the crew, and she had looked warmly with interest on the passing flat country as if they were sailing on the Nile. Herman gazed into her face, held one of the strong hands.

"A little aggression is needed," said the old man. Ernie lost his head in the stein and remembered the fat Merchant, like Herman, like papa, sprawled out in the alley with a string of women behind him and children gorging themselves on attention, sprawled like a murdered Archduke, his face in the bile. The hall was finally game, the troops screamed and stamped feet, dolls with skirts drawn above pink garters perched on elephant knees suggesting the roar of mighty Hannibal. Old Herman made fast excursions into the crowd, urging, interested. "Hold her tighter, more beer, more beer," and returned to the stoop-shouldered Ernie with his face alive in enjoyment. Several times Ernie thought he could hear Stella's voice above the howling, and like an assassin under floodlights, he shivered.

"Don't be such a fearful *Kind,*" said Herman, puffing with excitement, "join the chase." He smiled momentarily at his son above the strenuous noise of the orchestra. When he left the table again to encourage a maenadic blonde and an old general, Ernie rushed from the prosperous Valhalla.

Rain filled his eyes with warm blurred vision, filled his outward body with the heat of his mind, and running until his breathing filled his ears, he clattered past opulent swaying wet branches, past windows opening on endless sleep. "Ernst, Ernst," the summer evening cried and he dashed zig-zag up the broad boulevard, raced to outrun the screaming, raced to catch the dog who rode with her away, raced to coincide with Princip in Sarajevo. He ran to spend energy, tried to run his own smallness into something large, while far in the distance he thought he heard the carriage wheels. If he could spread before her the metal of magnificence, if he could strike lightning from the sky, if he could only arrest her for one brief moment in the devotion he felt whirling in the night. But then the past told him the Merchant, or the Baron, or Herman would steal her off to a nest of feathers—before he could speak.

He felt that his belt would burst, and so, just before reaching the line of Heroes, he stopped in the park. He thought that his mother would see, would stand looking at him in the dark, so he pushed behind the foliage, behind a bush that scratched at his fumbling hands. The rain became stronger and stronger and still he was rooted behind the bush, desperation on his face to be off, to be flying. Then he was running through the shadows like a flapping bird. When he passed the line of statues, each Hero gave him a word to harden his heart: *love, Stella,*

Ernst, lust, tonight, leader, land. He felt that if old Herman ran at his side, he would tell him to get her in the britches. Already the guns were being oiled and the Belgians, not he, would use that Merchant as a target.

"Tomorrow you'll wake up and find we're in a war," said Cromwell. The carriage was turning the last corner, he turned his ready benevolence on the cruel castles, thought he'd like to tell his old father, but that was impossible.

"Then you'll go home?" she asked.

"No. I think I'll stay. It is pleasant, in moments such as these, knowing with certainty an approaching catastrophe, to view the whole incident that will probably extend fifty years, not as the death of politics or the fall of kings and wives, but as the loyalty of civilization, to realize that Krupp, perhaps a barbarian, is more the peg where history hangs than a father who once spoke of honor. If I could get into my father's house, past his fattening memory, I would tell him what's coming and leave him something to carry away with him."

"I, on the other hand, star of maidenhood, having found love, want to tell my father nothing, and if your prophecy should fall on our heads, could do nothing but protect my own. If in this hour of crisis, we must ride side by side, I will become, as you wish, your Archduchess for the people, but where your eyes and theirs cannot look, I am arrogant."

They were none the closer when they heard his running footsteps, when they looked in fear, back to the road they had just traveled, looked quickly over the low rear of the carriage. He ran up to them gasping out of the darkness, clutched the side of the carriage as if to hold it in his hand, and at that moment a bevy of disturbed birds chirped vividly in fright. They did not recognize him, did not speak, and for a moment, Cromwell waited to see the short muzzle of the pistol, to feel his ears enveloped in concussion, and on impulse almost took her in his arms for the last time. But the carriage continued, the coachman sleeping, and the assailant was dragged, half-running, half-stumbling, veins exploding around his eyes. Then, in great deliberation, she leaned and touched his fingers.

"Come, get in," she said.

"No, no, I cannot."

Cromwell was a fool. He wouldn't move, but back straight, hat over his eyes, he sat and waited. His gloved hands trembled on his knees. "I'll come back," Ernst said and once more took to his heels as the carriage reached the curb and a crowd seemed to gather. Stella knew, in this dark disrupted haze, that she was somewhere near her greatest love. Francis Ferdinand lay on the seat of the carriage, his light shirt filled with blood, his epaulettes askew and on the floor lay the body of his departed wife, while the assassin, Gavrilo Princip, ran mad through the encircling streets. Obviously the advent of the great war would not throw them all together, make them friends, or even make them enemies; Ernie was ready, even in the throes of love, for a goal of religious fanaticism; Cromwell simply longed, desperately, to fit into the conflict somewhere; and Stella knew only that she was climbing high and would someday lose him. It all started as simply as the appearance of Ernie's dangerous, unpleasant face. When the people found out, the people of Bosnia, Austria, and the Hapsburg monarchy, they caused a silent, spreading, impersonal commotion over the body of Ferdinand.

"Thank you," said Stella.

"Oh, I'll be around." She did not turn to watch Cromwell go back to the carriage.

The University was black, impressive, most of its archives and bare rooms encased in a drawn restless wine-stupor, part of its jagged face grey, menacing, piled backwards on itself in chaotic slumber. The rain came down in broken sheets covering first one roof, then a ledge, then splashing against a swinging door, sluicing down the crumbling channels, smothering dust-filled caves crawling with larvae. The center of revolution, dogma and defeat, it drew the city into its walls with a crushing will; and behind its ancient and topheavy porticos and crags, behind small windows and breathing flues, lodged the uninhibited, the young, the old. Ernie crossed a hollow court, dodged down ecclesiastical alleys past flowing fonts, made his way past stone connecting arches and hybrid walls, hastened beyond a mausoleum of brain to where the stone eruption gave way to a wooden comb of corridors. Resolved to upset his dying fall, he finally lunged at a solid door, smelled the dank unvarying stench of huddled students and counted forward five doors while the summer rain rolled thickly down the stained windows, and his footfalls still called back from the stone. The door was covered with the prints of ancient nervous fingers, was damp with the palms that had slipped in and out for centuries. Heavy furniture and eaten rug, iron candle holders and unused loving chair, were pushed into dust-covered heaps lining three walls, leaving the

57

scarred floor a wide cold arena, colorless beneath the only lamp that burned in the University, peopled by the only waking men. They slouched, sleepless, like a band of raiders in a thick wood, drinking a colorless water that caused the lungs to heave, the skin to burn, that brought violent images before the eyes. The single light threw stiff unyielding shadows on the horse-collared masks, on the molding chest mats, protective of bowels, front and loins, covered with dry rust and rattling buckles, grey wire-like stuffing from rough slashes.

The Baron, older in time, more vicious and less proud with his bastard Spanish-German head thrust back and upwards at the agony-carved rafters, more hot and princely and dog-like under his eyes and stripped arms, waited until precisely the proper moment when the eyes found their two-sided common target, when the arena drifted with unraked ashes, to slip to his knees and draw as in sleep a weapon from the debris. The onlookers let the liquor trickle down their nostrils, coughed, rubbed their collars, stared with their mouths open in hate. These were the agates that could not grow.

In the first moment their bodies lost form, clashing like roosters with spiked heels, aiming at brief exposed patches of white, striking for scarecrow targets. They struck at the *Physik* of limbs. In the second moment, the arena stained with drops of ink, walls resounding with blows, they aimed at the perilous eyes and ears, the delicate tendons of the neck, fingers, stabbing at the *Kultur* of sense, and a blade-tip sang past his lower lip, splitting the skin the length of his under jaw. In the third moment they found the groin, and he felt a pain from the accidental flat of the blade that traveled from the abdomen to his throat in a brief spasm, the original *Unlust*. He stooped, and the bell of the saber rang through the ashes, dropped to the floor in a finished scoop. Then gradually he began to fall from a high, blunted indefinable space where the Hero's words: *love, Stella, Ernst, lust, tonight, leader, land* revolved out of relation, until he finally reached particulars too extreme to comprehend. Brine filled the hollow of his gum, the cuticle of one thumb bled into a purple half-moon, and an internal kink filled him with pain from the stomach to the blind gut. "Go outside, if you must," said the Baron who sank down among his comrades. Someone threw him a towel and wrapping it about his head, Ernie managed to get into the corridor and hold to the wall. Inside they sang, one voice after another, in a very slow meter, the *Horst Wessel Lied*. "Get back to your room," said an old caretaker moving around him in the darkness. Finally, his head white and bulky in the towel, he made his way out into the rain, leaving a sharp odor of sickness outside the room with a light.

Stella, golden tresses gathered about the waist, a calm determination to survive and to succeed grown upright in her mind, waited for his return, sure he would come, sure she would have to give warmth. She was prepared to make him as happy as her instinct would allow, would overrule the rights of anyone in the house for her own demands. But Gerta was a woman quick to injure. Stella listened to every sound, fought with the desire to dream, and thought at some hour of the night that she heard marching feet. When Ernie finally did come, it was in desperation. "Come in, you poor creature," she whispered,

and held the toweled bundle in her lap. He left soon
after because a bright excited day was beginning to
break, and harassed or jubilant cries echoed up and
down the drying streets.

STELLA

The conquered spirit lies not only in rest but in waiting, crushed deep in face-lines of deprivation, in fingers that no longer toil, the one thing that shall lift, and enlarge and set free.

The house where the two sisters lived was like an old trunk covered with cracked sharkskin, heavier on top than on the bottom, sealed with iron cornices and covered with shining fins. It was like the curving dolphin's back: fat, wrinkled, hung dry above small swells and waxed bottles, hanging from a thick spike, all foam and wind gone, over many brass catches and rusty studs out in the sunshine. As a figure that breathed immense quantities of air, that shook itself in the wind flinging water down into the streets, as a figure that cracked open and drank in all a day's sunshine in one breath, it was more selfish than an old General, more secret than a nun, more monstrous than the fattest shark.

Stella combed her hair before the open window, sunlight falling across her knees, sometimes holding her head up to catch the wind, as wide awake as if she had slept soundly through the night without wild dreams. A few scattered cheers and broken shouts were carried up from side streets, windows were flung open, dust-rags flung out into the spring morning like signal flags. Brass bands were already collecting in the streets, small groups of old men surrounded by piles of shiny instruments. A crowd was gathering about the front of the gated house and she could hear them stamping their feet and clapping each other on the backs, thumping and pushing, waiting for the chance to cheer. She felt completely at rest, self-satisfied, pulling at one strand of thick hair and then at another. She knew her father would be dressing, powdering his cheeks so he could speak to the crowd, and she had reached the time of a strange discovery. If it were not for the idea of love, if her father were a man she did not know at all, how distasteful his fingers would be, like pieces of rotting wood; how unpleasant his white hair would be, a grey artificial mat that she could never stand to kiss; how like an old bone would be his hollow shoulders. Stella enjoyed thinking of her father as one she did not know. He was so old he never understood. Voices shouted at her, she eased her chair to follow the moving sunlight. Gerta came in throwing the door wide.

"Damn that woman, damn that old fool!" Gerta stared about the room. "Always I say I'm not at home, I've gone away to the country, I'm sick, but there she sits, down there with the cook in the kitchen waiting to pounce on me." The old woman raged about the room, hovered over the chair a moment to see if Stella listened. She snorted at the golden head, ripped into the closets, threw forth bundles of soiled linen. She gasped.

"You're no better!" The comb slid up and down, the nurse trembled in the pile of linen.

Down in the kitchen sat Gerta's friend, a new maid from several houses away who traveled across back courts and had paid a call, for no reason, carrying a bag of cold buns which she munched while trying to become friends with Gerta. Gerta was afraid and angry and could not understand this woman who, dressed like an imbecile girl, wore her thin hair plastered to the head, who had no name and talked forever. Gerta would not touch the buns.

"You're no better. And don't think," the voice was a whisper, distorted and low, "that I don't know what went on last night. Don't forget that!"

Her father fussed with his collar, a rouge color filling in flat cheeks, her mother directed him from beneath the sheets, the crowd screamed when a manservant hung a faded flag from the very narrow balcony.

Stella turned, face shrouded in gold. "Get out. Take the clothes and leave." The old woman raced from the room hauling the delicate silks and wrinkled trains of cloth, stumbled and ran, and the hairbrush sailed through the door over the mammoth baluster and fell in a gentle curve to crash many floors below on the hard marble. She turned back to the light. The insurrection passed lightly as the brush, she was bounded by the pale bed, the brightening walls, and summer. The cook howled for more butter from a stuttering girl, the visitor chopped a bun. There on the floor, there beside the small proper bed was the spot, now in shade, where she had held him in her lap.

Despite the dark brown symmetry and shadows of the buildings outside, the air was filled with a light green haze. It patiently and warmly lifted itself over the sagging branches, weakened beneath the load of fresh young leaves scattered on trees caught between the walls and sidewalk. The morning with its widening haze, voices wrangling over the fences, brushes and rags fighting with the furniture, tousled girls scraping and whispering on their knees, the house filled itself with boys and tremendous baskets of fruit, hauling in, it seemed, crowds of people out of the city, awoke with cries and attention. That was the moment to sit in the sun with soft hair falling about one's waist, to doze and wake, nodding and smelling the sweet air, collecting thoughts for years to come or gone by, like an old woman hooded in black in a doorway.

A half-dozen birds, caught in the leaves, tried to make themselves heard and far down the hall she could hear Gerta talking to her father who was trying to dress. The air was like honey to wave beneath her nose; she called forth her own pleasure, plucked anywhere from the moving number of summer sensations. She waved her hand, even on the opening day of war, the public's day, and a gentle lusty swell crowded her head, shoved the half-dozen murmuring birds out of reach. In winter, the snow fell where she wished, in great dull even flakes, in smooth slightly purple walls where far in perspective she was held like a candle, warm and bright. In summer, alone, it was she that breathed the idea of naked moonlight swimming—divers together in the phosphorescent breakers, leaves as clothes on the silver beach—she that breathed the idea of brownness, smoothness into every day of June, July, August, who created hair over the shoulder and pollen in the air.

Her mother, a long mound beneath the sheets, had lost all this, terribly aged with a cold pallor, strong and indolent, unhappy in the oppressive heat. The mother lay in bed day after day, the spring, summer, years dragging by, with only her head two hands long above the sheets, her eyes fastened together, motionless until some forgotten whim, surge of strength, drove her from the bed. And in that hour she would shop. When she shopped, she ventured on the streets in gowns from another date, walked in steady steps, and took Stella along. She never liked the world she saw and her old husband never knew she was out of the house.

A hundred strokes, a hundred and five, the hair quivered in the space of gold; she changed hands, her skin as soft as the back of a feather. Her brothers, a pair of twins, fifteen-year-old soldiers dressed in stiff academy blue and trimmed in brass, walked past her open door, eyes ahead, arms in parallel motion, and she heard their miniature spurs clanking down the wide stairs. The boys never saw their parents, since the old man and woman had been the age of deaf grandparents at the time of the brothers' remarkable conception. The brothers ate and lived alone. The jingling sound hung in her ears, one of the birds had become audible, and she thought of a parakeet with long sharp nails bathing in a blue pond where the green grass swayed and the sun was orange. There was no shock in the day, but the same smothered joy crept up with the morning's trade and old flags that were unfurling along the guarded streets.

"Breakfast, breakfast!" Gerta called, wearied and harassed, from the center of the first floor lobby, lips drawn down, clutching a fist of silver, calling to wake the whole house into an even greater activity. The shabby crowd was growing restless, howling with round faces scrubbed cheery and proud, while inside the high walls the elaborate process of serving the isolated meal began. Twenty thousand feet in the sky, a sheet of wind flashed over the city cold and thin, while below, warm air rolled over the lake in the park, and swans opened their necks and damp feathers, bumping softly together in stiff confusion.

The old man, always seated first at the table, held his head high and rigid so that it trembled, pure white eyes staring and blinking from a skull like a bird's, the whole area behind the thin tissue eaten away and lost. Sometimes he ate his melon with the fork, or spoon, or knife, or pushed it with his pointed elbow so that it fell to the floor, pits and meat splashing over his black curled-up shoes. The moustache fell to his high collar in two soft sweeping strands of pale gold, his long legs were a mass of black veins. His face, narrow and long, was covered with bark and was deep scarlet, and clots of blood formed just under the glaze of fine hair; and he would fall, slipping and breaking in every part at least once a week. But each time the clots would dissolve and be churned away, down the grass-smelling passages, and he would recover.

The table was so short, with the twelve leaves piled out of sight in dust, that she could almost smell his breath, with scarcely a bare foot of candelabra, bowls, tongs, green stems and silver trays between them. When she sat down, his head, like a brittle piece of pastry, tried to swim over the breakfast things, searching as every morning, but was blocked by a twisted maze of fern in an azure vase and a pyramid of butter patties topped with dark cherries. "Stool," he said in a high voice because he could no longer pronounce her name. They sat close together in the middle of the long dining room, the man with his ninety years and the young girl with her peaches, while overhead, set in one of the domes, a large clock struck eleven. Gerta hurried in and out pushing a little cart laden with napkins, rolls, knives, sauces of all kinds and pans of under-done, clear boiled eggs. "Poor man," she said, dabbing at a long run of fresh egg water on his tunic, turning now and then a look of wrath on Stella as if the poor girl herself had shaken his freckled hand and made the long translucent string slide off onto his chest. Stella frowned back, scattering crumbs over the little table and knocking the goblet so that a mouthful of water sizzled on the coffee urn.

"Watch what you're doing," snapped Gerta, her slippers padding angrily on the rug.

This morning he was able to get the pink slices between his fingers, but, slipping through their own oily perfume, they constantly fell back to the tablecloth in irregular heaps of quivering jelly. Stella thought of Ernie and smiled across the floral table at her father, looked with delightful interest at his slippery hands.

The boy didn't realize what he said, 1870, it would take many dead men to encircle Paris, and the responsibility, that's what he didn't understand or no one could speak in such a manner, pride on the heights. "War," her father said, and there was a terrible fire in his eye through the ferns. "War," and he leaned slightly forward as if to strike her, but his arm only raised part way, shivered, and dropped back on the plate. She stopped smiling.

"Where is the railroad station?" he asked.

Stella watched his questioning face for a moment then continued to eat. She was sorry.

"He only wants to go to the bathroom," said Gerta, and throwing herself under his thin erect frame she led him out, the white lace duster fluttering on her head. The two boys clanked by in the hall, stepped in a single motion out of the way. The cook worked frantically to heat more rolls in the oven like a boiler, kept a flame under the pot of coffee, ran from cupboard to cupboard collecting more juices and spices, threw a large ham on the spit. Stella pulled the long brocaded sash and heard the bell jingle out amid the clatter of pans, the swirl of water. Gerta's friend came in, still wearing her brown shawl and hat covered with violets, still clutching the paper bag with grease on her fingers.

"More toast," said Stella.

"Ah, toast," said the woman and disappeared.

Stella thought that her father suffered very much. Some parts of the day she would walk with him up and down the beautiful quiet hallways, his hand resting only lightly on her arm, a smile about his shriveled lips. Sometimes she suffered herself, though usually in the evening in the blue shadows of her room, never in the morning, for she knew that at dusk she would see him half-hidden and in full stately dress behind the tall lighted candles. The dining room walls darkened with nightfall, the silverware lighted by the flames, the immense shadows falling over him from white flowers instead of ferns, covered him with an illusory change that frightened her. In these evenings Stella remembered how, when she was a small girl, he had talked to her, before his voice disappeared, and she heard his voice talking of sieges and courtships, and emerald lands, and she wished him to be a father still. At night she could not tell. From a few long talks with her mother she knew that for five generations the men had been tall, handsome, discreet and honorable soldiers, all looking exactly alike as brother eagles, and all these men had died young. Her father had so outlived the features of those other men and his family that he no longer existed and could not even speak. The man hidden behind the candles made her wonder for all his years.

"You don't have to tell me where he needs to go," she murmured, and Gerta's friend returning with the toast was confused by her words.

The hair nearest her neck was hazel, the rest lemon, and when she walked it was fitfully gliding as if she were already there—there in the mausoleum where he lay in plaster, where rose petals were swept under her prayer. For in the hottest part of the noon, the house was withered away and his white face was in a lasting repose, the idiot of breakfast, the marshal of dinner, become an old masked man in the heat of the sun wherever she walked. She would gladly cut the epitaph herself for just one glimpse before they latched the door—the noon heat made her feel the marble dust as if it were fresh. Never in the world could she know him, only scraps from her mother's carefully guarded chest. Sometimes, when Stella looked most beautiful, she felt that she would collapse with the house around her when he finally left.

Her room nearest the slate roof was warm, the seascapes, spaced regularly over the walls filled it with blue, the birds had become silent under the window. Jutta, an ungainly eleven-year-old child, was taking her nap at the end of the corridor in a cubicle small and low that might have belonged to a boarding school or nunnery white and bare. Her mouth was open and she breathed heavily, thin legs apart as if she were riding a horse. Stella fastened the bonnet with pink and yellow ribbons, drew on her white gloves, started down the stairs, and stopped to listen to the low ugly noises of the sleeping child. Outside she found herself caught in front of the house in the silence of the crowd, and all eyes looked upward. There on the narrow balcony, squeezed side by side, was her father still leaning on Gerta who smiled, laces fluttering against his uniform. All at once he spoke, and the single word fell upon them hushed and excited. "Victory." For a moment they waited for more, watched, listened and then broke out in screams of appreciation while the old man was led back inside the house. They did not realize that he thought the war, which had just begun, was over, and they took up the word and sent it flying along the street from one startled citizen to the next. Stella began to walk, her parasol catching the shade of the enormous line of trees.

Men tipped their hats, drays rolled by with heavy rumps nodding majestically between the shafts, chains clattering, whips stinging; small flags hung limply in shops as if it were a holiday. A tremendous stuffed fish grinned out at her, sunlight skipping between its blue fins, small clams grey and moist piled about like its own roe on the chopped ice. An awning covered part of the street with orange, passers-by parted into even chattering lanes, and children going to the park grinned, tugging ahead. In the Krupp manufacturing works, huge steel barrels were swung by chain and arm, covered with pale green grease and pointed through barred skylights towards the summer sky. In the jail, prisoners looked out into the white limestone yard, carriages skimmed by on frail rubber wheels, and lapel after lapel spotted with a white flower passed by her side. In the thrill of this first warm exciting day with posters going up all over the city and mothers proudly patting their sons' heads, Stella's aunts and uncles, less fortunate cousins and acquaintances, fanning themselves in desolate drawing rooms or writing down the date in diaries, wondered how the beginning of hostilities would affect her father's position, and donning bright colors, prepared to call.

A swallow dipped suddenly down into the center of traffic, and up again, successful. It was then that the headache began. It came as a dull burn might come in noon hours on the beach, a soft sensation in her eyes; pleated under the yellow hair, it coursed slowly down the small of her neck, and made mouthfuls of spit shimmer above the policeman's white-lady gloves. She held her hand to her breast because the headache was so tiny and almost caught in her throat. "Oh, yes," she said to herself, "I've seen so many artists," and indeed she had once passed a man slumped over a table scratching the fleas. The seascapes about the walls of her room reminded her of the warm south, of islands where the white sun hurt the eyes, of pebbles like the tips of her fingers that were pearl grey. She could never laugh at anyone, a velvet shoulder brushed quickly by, sharp blues and reds hurried along the street. "Your father was a wonderful brave loving man," her mother would say. Dogs barked and howled, she glanced from yellow walls to white, creating as she walked small impressions which remained precious and a source of continual inspiration, catching a swift dark eye of possible European fortunes, pitying the shoe with the twice normal heel. The buildings, low, gilded, with their spires thrust a ludicrously short way into the sky, all trying to fall upon the street, protected by iron spikes, cast a yellow fog against the clouds. When her face was serious, when she watched the drays or passing blurred numbers cut into stone, watched the street as it moved, when her face was vacuous, it was a little flower, as if the larger girl had walked away to find Father. But when she smiled the mouth was tense, desire lost upon the waving of her arms. Gerta, when the moon was starting to sink, used to carry her away from the mother's bedside; and, awake with the nursemaid guarding the door, she could hear the old man snoring fitfully somewhere in the corridor. The sun hurt her eyes; it was certainly more difficult to hear now that her head hurt her so. "Your father was a tall man and we went to the mountains before they had railroads." When, infrequently, she talked to her mother, she was speaking through her, as through a black unsteady ear-trumpet, to a very old man who sat listening, pallid in a rocking-chair, some thirty or forty years ago. Now in his toothless eye she was to him some rifleboy with a sack of powder at the hip. "Victory," somebody shouted, and a boy came running down the smoke-filled street without his cap.

The tail end of the park was a narrow stretch of scrubby green caught tightly between high walls in the center of the city, an acre where the sun rarely fell, and low office men smoked at all hours. Strangely enough, today it was bright in the sunlight, and there were more clerks than ever, black and limpid. Stella walked up and down between two benches that left slat marks on shiny britches. Twisted black toes of shoes, stuck by the loungers into the narrow path, touched the hem of her gown, her head fluttered beneath the ribbons, pained worse, and a huge dog with black and white spots trotted by. The sky would darken for a moment with a smudge of cream, then would roll back to sheer white, turning the patches of grass to straw. Once she had hidden from Gerta beneath her mother's skirts, had felt the overpowering comfort of her ruffles, and that was a strange experience. The mother had thrust heavy hands under the folds, caught the wriggler, and handed the daughter over to the nurse, who always gave bad advice, to be secured in a strict manageable grasp. "Your father wouldn't like you to behave like that." Stella shut out all the city but this one pasture, shut out all the light but that which ached in her head, and high above the whispering clerks realized she loved Ernst very much. City and keeps and roadways in the heat, he, by a forest of young hair, protected from that which is dying. She waited patiently.

"My God, simpleton, why don't you sleep?" The mother spoke from a throat puffing over the edge of the sheet drawn tightly above her bosom with both hands. The father, back in the shuttered room with his tunic unbuttoned, wandered more bent and drawn around the three sides of the bed, his fine Roman nose twitching with excitement, the top of his scalp a sullen red. The room was sheltered, warm, an auburn fuzz glowed through the shutters and darkness. The old woman was white and still in the bed and about her the black wood was inlaid with bits, broken wings, of silver. The father was in one of his reveries, counting very slowly some outlandish or important number on his yellow fingers that would never total. Though one body was heavy and the other frail, though one voice bullied and the other barely mumbled, though the man wavered in agitation and the woman lay in state, they both were very much the same, because on both the hair had receded and become pale, leaving the foreheads, eyes and mouths expressionless with old age. A palmist looking at their hands would have seen no life for all the mazes of fine-drawn yellow lines, overlapping soft pads and

untaken crowding roads. "If only he would slip off
into the light of Heaven," she thought. "Sit down,"
she said, but he paid no attention, and she could
hear only the long-legged rustling of his uniform, the
unbearable sun pressing above them on the roof.

Jutta awoke and the room was filled with black
shapes.

The heat seemed to grow more determined, even
the clerks panted, whispering closely in each other's
ears, and Stella believed the sun would never fall
flaming through the torpid clear sky. She wondered
how the strange wild cannibals on tropical islands
or on the dark continent, running with white bones
in their hair, dark feet hardened in the shimmering
sand, could bear, in only their feathers, this terrible
sun. For the headache made her drowsy. She saw
those men, carrying victims high over their heads, as
tall, vengeful creatures who sang madly on their secret rock, who even at night slept on glistening pink
stone in fire, who stretched their tall bodies whether
in repose or in chase, and who kept wives bare from
the waist up. Their ears were pierced, insects buzzed
low over the children, the islands kept rising up out
of the sea. Even when she was tired and desperately
warm and even in such a trembling state, she loved
him. Her temple throbbed, the clerks were watching.
Her fired heart and sweltering faith were beginning
to fall away, swept by impatience. She was tired of
this park filled with noise, so close to the passing
horses that wore skull caps with holes for the ears.
She was afraid of being left alone. Then, before she
had a chance to meet the image come too sudden before her, before she had a chance to guard against
this reflection which she had searched for in all the
shop windows, and guard against the terror of herself,

74

she saw him running across the street and up the path, turned half sideways, thin, excited, smiling wildly through the fresh bandages round his head.

"Stella!"

"Ernst!"

They walked for twenty minutes under the yellow and green leaves and passed the cool pond as clear as the sky, smelled the berries cultivated by the park authorities, a few beautiful dripping flowers, and passed babies who screeched, dwarfed in the carriage. Then he took her home, left her, feeling at last the approach of twilight, feeling his heart full and as vague as water.

By the end of the next week the first thousands were far into enemy land, ammunition trains roared all through the night, the city burned late in tumultuous but magnificent organization, and the house was full of callers trying to pay respects to her parents in the bedroom. All seeking on their padded feet to scale these, her walls, to climb over them in a house that was no more hers than theirs, to seek out the mother, flies over the white sheet, for knowledge of the venerable man, they crawled exactly as she crawled. She caught, unwittingly, scraps of words, part of love during the seven days and forgot about the cannibals. "We met in a beautiful copse on a summer's eve, smelling the dew." But through the hours, while Gerta stamped about serving tea to them in the anteroom, where they still wore their monstrous hats, she felt for some reason as if these short-winged creatures, all but strangers, had come to mourn, and that mourning, visiting with the dead, was the last desperate attempt, the last chance for gossip. She felt that they were taking away the joy of sunshine, casting a blot, like an unforgivable hoard, on the very search and domestic twilight peace that she did not understand. The seascapes lost their color, in the midst of this remarkable mobilization she began to feel cheated. Ernst was gone for that week, and the old house was sealed tight though they squeezed through the doors and windows. Jutta was more rude than usual.

The seventh morning was freakishly cool. All the light was gone, the fruit flat, the clatter of servants obtrusive and harsh, bands playing in the park were loud and off key. They settled down. The old man beat about the empty halls quicker than usual, the brothers whispered, the entire ring of dark chambers was gathered, not wistful but strained, unhappily into the tight present. Men were pushed first on one shoulder, then on the other, off into the grey line, and the whole house from rafters of teak to chests of wine began to shiver. That morning the mother stepped out of the bed as if alive, stared for one moment about her in the unpleasant shadows and with exact stoic movements began to dress and became, gradually, monstrously large. She was dressed in a long black gown, heavy grey gloves, a tight ruffled collar, and a hat with an enormous drooping brim that made the dark patches around her eyes and in the cheeks more prominent, more like injuries to hide. At one time, years ago, the mother had left the father and had come back three months later thin as a rail, lovely. Now her age hung upon her in unlovely touches, though she stepped out today as if to make one last effort to slough them off. Her black patches were fierce and when it was known that she was up, the house fell into silence, though the father still moved fitfully, getting in the way, as if something were wrong. The mother had somewhere forgotten about morals, self-conquest and the realm to come. She was too weighted down, it was time to go, for age filled in the lacking spaces.

Stella carried the deep basket, the streets were empty, a few luminous clouds blew hastily across the horizon beneath a smoke-black overcast thousands of feet higher. She took her mother's arm in a gesture, warmly, of confidence.

"I will have those lemons, please." The baldheaded man dropped them in, flapped his apron at a pink-nosed dog. Flies hung over the blue meat.

"Potatoes." They rolled among the lemons in dust. The silly girl spilled the money on the counter, it grew darker.

"Apples." From the trees, the branches, sprinkled with water, green leaves. The basket began to fill, the vendor limped.

Live fowl in a dirty cage were silent, claws gripping the rods caked with lime, eyes blinking at each movement.

"Melons, your father likes melons." They were scarred and green and made the basket heavier. The grocer's boy peeped out from behind a hogshead of cheese, red tongue wagging, bare feet scuffing the sawdust.

The mother and girl began to cross the street.

ERNST

Behind them one of the chickens began to scream, and a speck appeared in the sky.

"I think I must stop and buy some flowers." A few loiterers got out of their way, the old woman considered her list.

"You don't want to make yourself tired, Mother."

The day was peculiarly uninteresting, a deliberately cold day with all the summer bugs taken to cover, a few shrubs turned under and splashed dismally with a final blue, all open windows shaded, sleepers uncomfortable, a few omnibuses swaying to and fro, empty, unhurried.

"I think I'll get . . . ," said the mother, but spoke nothing more, looking with the utmost distaste upon her desolate native avenue, façades smothered with an uneven hand, scant twigs swept into the drains, not a single mortal. That was all.

The policeman's call faded into nonsense, into unutterable confusion as the speck fell quickly from the sky, two small leathered heads trapped in smoking holes, the engine, no larger than the torso of a man, blasting, whistling, coughing stupidly. It swooped over mother and girl, flapped its fins once, and crashed, typically English, on the other side of the *Platz*. Paper and wood burned quickly, consumed the flyers, leaving the isinglass still intact over their eyes. In so falling with its mechanical defect, the plane sent a splinter flying into the mother's breast that knocked her down.

The policeman kept pushing Stella by the shoulder while the half-dressed crowd asked again and again, "What happened to the old trumpet?" What happened was that they stumbled out into the street and came upon an old dead woman, kicked around, bent, black. "What are you pushing me for?" The sweet grass burned back in the passageway of the street, the old medium was so wrapped in smoke that the father's second voice, this mother, was choked, mute, with cinders in the cleft of her chin and above the open lips.

"Gavrilo," Stella murmured, "what have you done?"

The birds twittered in angelic surmise, reeled high and low, fed, nested, called beyond the curtains in gentle mockery, and the days passed by with the temperate clime of summer stones. The marble dust fell in rest; leaded curtains, lately drawn, hung padded and full across the sunlight, keepers of the room. The seascapes were gone, no shadows were on the walls, silver flukes that seemed arisen from the past hushed their soft seashell voices and at every dead night or noon, she missed the chiming of the bells. Her mourning was a cold wave, a dry flickering of fingers in departure, a gesture resting softly in her throat that barely disturbed the gentle shift of light passing on its way. It was always dusk, rising, waking, falling with indolence, resounding carefully in her sleep, reporting the solitude of each day past. Stella thought the bier was close by. That perpetual afternoon clawed about her knees, each day the spirit grew more dim, sheltered behind the heavy lost mask of falling air, the thick south receding.

Those ships that had once rolled in on the breakers were cold and thin and had traveled far beyond her sorrow. The mother's hands were crossed, the wrinkles had strangely deepened until the face was gone, the flowers were turning a cold earthen brown. Her black collar was aslant on the neck, her own mother's ring before her was tucked into a hasty satin crevice by her side, wrapped in paper. They sprinkled water about trying to keep the air fresh, and the trimmings began to tarnish. In the evening the face changed color. Sweetness arose from the little pillows; she wore no stockings or shoes and the hair, brittle and thin, clipped together, was hard to manage. The eyelids swelled and no one visited.

Stella waited, awake on the chair, listening to the hushed footsteps, her face in the constant pose of a circus boy, misshapen, cold, her isolation unmoved with memory, numb with summer. The mourning of the virgin, as if she were swept close, now, for the first time, to the mother's sagging breast for her first dance, was heightened in a smile as the orchestra rose up and they glided over the empty avenue, the old woman in starched collar leading, tripping. Those dry unyielding fingers brushed her on, poised, embarrassed by the face that never moved. She did not stop, seeing many other eyeless dancers, lured through her first impression of this season, clear and rare, but she waited, sitting, hour on hour. Those fingers rustled in the dark. She heard the perpetual scratching feet of insects who walked over the coffin lid with their blue wings, their dotted eyes, and an old bishop mumbled as he ran his fingers over the rectangle of edges closed with wax. They tried to curl the hair, but the iron was too hot and burned. Her nostrils, rather than dilated in grief, were drawn closely, dispassionately together, making two small smudges on the apex of her nose.

Sometimes she thought she had waved. She saw the ship's poop inching its way farther into the distance on the flat water, a few unrecognized faces staring back, and smelled for a moment the odor of fish. The sea rolled noiselessly away, and walking back, all the paths choked with marble dust, the air smelled of linen, of dead trees. And all Stella's forebears had finally made this journey—the ocean was filled with ships that never met. No matter how much powder they sprinkled on the mother's face the iron grey color would lie stiffly under the skin the following morning. At night they placed a lamp beside her chair, and in the first light took it away again, its flame brushing the stiff folds of her dress, shining weakly as the smooth disturbed crests of the waves, almost extinct. Each morning she sat just as straight, as if she did not know they had prowled all about her during the midnight hours, beyond the globe of the lamp. She would never see them sailing back, and this most distant visitor, lying in state nearby, asleep day and night, so changed by the assumption of the black role, seemed waiting to bring her to the land of desire, where her weeping would cover all the hill above the plain. Stella's face became gradually unwashed, her arms grew thin, the fingers stiff, her mouth dry, trying to recall this person's name. The attendants and sudden last visitors perspired. The old woman grew damp as if she fretted.

Finally they took the coffin out of the house.

On that day Ernie sat at her feet, and again it was so hot that the birds buried their heads in the shade under their wings, the fountains were covered with chalk, the room close. They heard the scuffling in the corridor and on the stairs as the coffin made its way out of the house, and the servants milled about in the lower hall, talking, weeping, holding the doors. Ernie wanted to open the curtains but did not dare.

"You don't even have a cross," he said. His beloved was silent. "You don't even have any candles, no face of Christ, no tears. What can I say?"

Then she began to murmur and he was astonished.

"I'm sorry. I will believe in the eternity of souls, I am bereaved. I will see those places where death talks solemnly to the years, where the breakers roll over their sins and their regrets, where the valley of Heaven lies before the crag of immortality, and I will believe my mother has gained peace. I have lost her. Has anyone felt such terrible grief, known that for all earthly time the eyes shall never see, the heart never beat except with her shadow? What an unhappy loss, the candles are gutted, and the face wanes for this immortality. I have lost my mother."

This was her only glimpse of Heaven, and she wept so much that he was afraid. Finally she held his hand. The two brothers fired the cannon at the burial.

That night Stella went to live in her father's room, since he could not be left alone, and he watched her with troubled suspicion as she slept, filling only half the invalid's ponderous space. She walked amid heaps of soiled nightdresses, rows of enameled pots for the old man, the stale smell of bones and flies, emptied the deep drawers of food he had hidden, awoke in the gloom and confusion of yesterday's air. She sang him lullabies well after midnight, fed him with a spoon, scrubbed the pale face and neck,

82

fought with Gerta over his mad words, and still he could not keep alive. The odor of sweet grass again became heavy, and one morning she found him, tongue rolled under, the top of his head a brilliant swollen red, clutching a feathered helmet across his breast. She had not even awakened.

Where is the railway station?

The leaves turned heavy on the branches, birds coursed away, forgotten, and the cold chill of a new season descended on the city with rain and late fever.

The great ring of chopped ice rumbled thousands of feet below them without moving. Jagged and slender like headless flowers, like bright translucent stems, the quivering clear stalks of ice shot rays of sun back and forth over the soundless field. It was as if the hotel's foundations were buried finally so far below in this unreal brilliant bed that the sudden sensation of holiday traveled up and down the polished floors to the center of the clear colorful ice, that the wine flowed first pink and then golden in sheer chasms where little men in feathered hats filled it with song. With pick, rope, spike and red shirts they climbed in the afternoons, hung waist to waist over the most treacherous graves in Europe, and at night it snowed, or the moon rose ringed with a faint illumination in the darkness. The mornings climbed upwards from the valley in violent twists and turns, leaping from one shelf of ice to the next, turning the flat grey blades into brilliant shattering arms of light until they finally rose above the gasping mouth of the hotel in cold transparent wings of color, holding them motionless, suspended in gravity amidst an unanchored spectrum.

83

Stella and Ernst found themselves in the midst of healthy guests, the men giants, the women tanned with snow, even the old venerable and strong because they were not too old. A few children chased each other about the lobby and bowed when approached by adults. Their short rasping voices were small and unawares out of doors, and there was a fear that they would fall into the ice floes. "It's a great mistake," Stella said, "to think that the youngest children are the most lovely—they're not." And yet she thought these children, the sons and daughters of the straight athletes, were beautiful. She watched them romp with hostility, and yet they flowered before her, danced and played. "The younger they are the more they demand, the more helpless they are. They're capable of more than we think, especially when they can't talk." They lit their cigarettes and passed out of earshot of the children. Ernst was bundled to the throat in a jacket of bright fur and smiled and nodded at all she said, the tufts of long hair rubbing against his neck. Now that he was on the heights and all below him was gone, he walked always with spikes on the soles of his feet so he would not slip. Hearts in their hands, he slung the rope on his shoulder but never went down, for they wanted to be alone, high, in this one place. The whiteness flashed up, clearing away the last traces of summer, and Stella, looking over such a profound staged landscape, clung to his arm as if he would fall. But he was nearer God.

Every afternoon the old horse stood wheezing by the porte–cochere, trembling slightly with head lowered from the terrible exertion of the long climb. The sleigh would be empty, a rug dragging on the packed snow. The horse appeared blind, so limply hung the head, so blank the closed lids, and little drops of frost grew in his nostrils and on the bit, clung embedded in the sparse mane. He was cold, black and thin and hung with red trappings that did not fit, that swung against his damp hide with each painful bellow of air. Stella always tried to feed a piece of sugar to the flabby lips and slime-covered steel, but always the dumb groping nose knocked it from her palm. "Ah, the poor beast," Ernst would say, looking over the sucked-in tail and fragile hocks. "You could count his age on all the ribs." Then the driver would come out, sinister eyes rolling over his muffler, followed by the departing families with their skis. The black horse stumbled down the hill, and the couple continued their honeymoon, two golden figures in the setting sun.

Behind those flat drooping lids, the horse's eyes were colorless and strangely out of shape, but they were deep, shy, inhumanly penetrating. The knees shivered both backwards and forwards.

This was the upper world. Some of the guests whisked in the morning down to the lower and with each sharp descent in the process, the pitch of their enjoyment dropped, until it was too low to bear. And quickly as possible, they laboriously began the crawl back upwards to the clear air, waiting to laugh until they had reached the point where they could turn and let their eyes glide down in cool recreation over those falling fields. The upper world was superior. In the lower, tufts of grass poked dangerously through the snow; snarling dogs ran under foot; the snow turned to rain on the lowest fields, and the isolated huts were grey and sodden. The laughter was above, the easiness that was tense with pleasure, the newness poured itself over the winged guests in sudden, unexpected delight, for a few days or weeks. The cooking was excellent. The black horse thrived better in the lower world. He was the same horse the students rode, shivering with the cold, tied alone to suffer the night. And yet he carried them, their switches flicking in the wind.

Here in this beautiful forest of burnt furniture, amidst the pale coolness of the wide-flung windows, in the crackling of parlor fires, in the songs beyond the thick rustic walls and the love inside, it did not matter that Herman said he was sorry to see her go, that the *Sportswelt* would miss her. The remembrance of the old house and the old parents, her sister, Jutta, was a far-off thing.

The hotel, from its highest porch where Ernie hid himself to watch all those who approached, to its gradually widening foundations where the mountain flowers shriveled and curled against the stone, was the center of a small acre of snow-packed land, was the final peak of a mountain. During the long rail trip they had watched the winter arrive, the smoke from squat chimneys more grey and thick. The snow fell, first in warning flurries, settling more coldly on the weaving branches and huddled animals. Winter was near the hotel.

At the far end of the acre was a small house, the roof curling under a foot of snow, its rear window gazing outward twenty miles and downwards to the depth of a thousand feet. Stella and Ernst, holding hands, silent in wondrous amazement, turning and clapping each other in excitement, walked over this very acre every afternoon and passed the house. A few scrubby trees leaned dangerously over the cliffs. And every afternoon they passed the old man on the doorstep, brittle shavings heaped over his shoes and like yellow flakes blown on the snow. He grinned while he carved, looked up at them, seemed to laugh, and hunching his shoulder, pointed backwards, behind the hut, out into the emptiness. The crosses he carved were both small and large, rough and delicate, some of simple majesty, others speaking minutely of martyrdom. They too fell across his feet, mingled with the sticks of uncarved wood—sometimes a bit of green bark was left to make a loincloth for Christ. Those that were not sold hung inside from a knotted wire, and slowly turned black with the grease and smoke; but the hair was always blacker than the bodies, the eyes always shone whereas the flesh was dull. Tourists paid well for these figures that were usually more human than holy, more pained than miraculous. Up went the shoulder, the knife rested, and he was pointing to the nearness of the cliffs. After the first week, Ernie bought one of the crucifixes, a terrible little demon with bitter pain curling about the mouth no larger than a bead, drawing tight the small outward-turning hands. Then he began to collect them, and every afternoon a new Christ would peer from his pocket through the tufts of fur.

By now his prayers at mealtime were quite audible. The setting sun stained the imperfect windows, made whorls crimson and shot the narrow panes with streaks of yellow until an off-color amber, like cheesecloth, finally smeared them over and gave way to a dismal night. Chairs scuffed in unison as the five long tables filled, and in the first silence, before strange conversations were resumed, before they had recaptured their half-intimate words, while they were still only nodding or whispering, one of the tables would become conscious of an impersonal, pious mumbling. Busily rearranging the silver and china before him, his brow wrinkled, he talked as if to an old friend. The table would be hushed and uneasy until he looked up. The hotel manager, who took this time of the evening meal to appear before his gathered guests and walk up and down between the rows to interrupt a conversation or a draught of wine, was struck dumb with the unnatural monotone, and would cast significant glances at Stella. The lines of beautiful cloths, the habits of silk, the evening dress of others turned inwards upon her, incongruous with the thick china and bare walls and floor, modern and glittering and presumptuous. She touched his hand, but it was stiff and cold, smooth and pious. She thought at first that she could feel something of his Bishop's creed and was part of this furtive ritual that exerted itself more and more, even when the evenings were rich with color.

The crucifixes began to fill the hotel.

Ernst had filled their two rooms with flowers and stones, small misshapen petals that were bright and petrified, delicate and warped with the mountain air, clear opal stones polished with ages of ice. At night before they slept he arranged the flowers in her hair, and with a kiss laid her away. In the morning he would climb to the porch and spend an hour noting carefully who arrived. And he did the same in the afternoon, breathing deeply, peering intently. He and his wife were very happy. An old count nodded to them in the corridor just beginning to grow light; they awoke blushing and warm holding the covers tight with a childish guilt, and below their window the children laughed, danced and clapped. He no longer thought of the Baron, or Herman, or the *Sportswelt,* no longer thought of Stella's singing and particularly did not want to hear her sing. The altitude made him faint, he breathed heavily, and could not stand to think of pain. If anyone twisted an ankle, or if one of the children skinned a knee, or an old woman ached in the chest, he rushed to be by their side, he "stood over them," as he called it. Then the old man, the Christ-carver, began to visit the hotel regularly, bringing with him each day a basket of those crucifixes that he could not sell, so that the black ugly Christs hung upon the walls of their rooms along with the bright new ones. Children were soon seen playing with wooden crosses, lining them up in the snow, leaving them all about the playroom. A small crown prince possessed one with beautifully flexed muscles and a rough beard. Stella began to have him lean on her arm as they walked and knew that the most beautiful bird holds tightest before flying straight upwards.

It was almost is if the whole family lived in the next room, asleep in the pile of trunks under the hanging window. The trunks collected dust and beneath the arched lids one of her mother's gowns slept with Herman's waistcoat, a militant comb lay straight and firm by a yellow brush. A pair of medical tweezers that had plucked the fine moustache grew old near one of Herman's mugs. The trunks were sealed with wax. All together they were happy, and a flute player charmed the two rooms.

On a morning in the third week Ernst left her side and climbed to the porch. Above the snow there was light, but the thick flakes, like winter, covered all the mountaintop in darkness, beat against his eyes, swept over his knuckles hooked to the railing. He watched. It was impossible to see where the acre ended and where the deep space began, the fall. He waited, peering quickly, expecting the messenger, sure of the dark journey. "Look over the plains," he thought, "and you will see no light. No figures, no men, no birds, and yet He waits above the vast sea. Thine enemy will come, sweeping old ties together, bright as the moon."

Ernst had given up the sword; though his wounds were healed, the Heavens gaped, and he had lost the thread of the war's virus. Then, at the bottom of the flurry, he heard the arrival. The horse's bells rang as if he had been standing there, just below, all during the night and the snow and had just come to life. He heard the muffled knock of a hoof, a door slammed. A sleepy-eyed boy, his tongue still flat along his lower jaw, weaved back and forth in the wind, nearly fell beneath the bag that weighed of gold. The driver beat his gloves and pocketed the *Pfennig,* the snow raced. Ernie closed his mouth and saw through the white roof of the passenger's descent. Cromwell ran up the steps and rang the sharp bell that awoke the clerk. By the time Ernst was back in the room, bending over her in the darkness, cold and afraid, it had stopped snowing. The black horse shook off his coat of white.

Still one could not see beyond the fortress of the hotel, beyond the drops of mustard gas and mountain vapors, beyond the day that was only half risen. The children became thin and tired and the adults suddenly were unable to find their own among the solemn faces. With that sharp cry of mother to child, the parents searched among the idle play groups as if through obligation. During the three meals the tables were half empty and a great many plates were broken, as the child bites and the young mother is still forced to feed. All of them smelled the fog, it curled about their hair and chilled them in the bath, and the nurse's playing fingers could do nothing to help, while the air became more thin and the water difficult to pump.

Ernst had become more and more used to the lover's mystery, had learned timidly what strange contortions the honeymoon demands, and she, not he, was the soldier, luring him on against the fence, under the thicket, forcing him down the back road through the evening. He watched her sleep. But now it was painful, it was cold, the snow was already too thin to hide him. He walked up and down the room, could see nothing from the window because he was too near the light, and the early morning, without the hands of the clock or the morning paper, his own time, was about to break. He was already one of the cold bodies down on the ice, he felt the terrible rush of air. After pausing a moment he ran quickly down the stairs, seeing all of them dragged into the university, kicking, clawing, hunched up like camels in the dust, caught and beaten. Someone put both hands on his knees.

No one stirred, the clerk and boy were curled up to sleep again until the real morning came. The lobby was filled with cold shadows, uncollected cups, a discarded shirt, a bucket with a thin edge of ice over the top. For the first time Ernst felt that the windows were closed, the wires cut, and felt the strange sensation that the mountain was moving, tearing all the pipes from the frozen ground, sliding over unmapped places. A magazine was several months old, an electric fan turned from side to side though the blades were still.

He forced himself to speak. "How was your trip?" The man stood up, still in evening dress, smiling with the old natural grace, and he felt the fingers take his own. "Well, Heavens, to think we'd meet again. And, congratulations, you've got my admiration, she's a delightful girl." They sat together, vaguely conscious of the damp air. "I thought I was coming to a place quite different, no familiar faces, a place of rest, but it's more as if I were home. Well, you must tell me all about yourself." No one stirred. They drank the thick black coffee which Cromwell had heated himself, careful not to soil his white cuffs, while he watched the briefcase. The windows were folded in white, the hat and gloves and cane lay by the coffee pot, the heavy cane close at hand.

Gradually Ernst's head began to lean forward, closer to the table. He had told their story, they were happy, he thought someone moved overhead, but then he knew he heard nothing. Cromwell was telling him everything he did not want to know, and he waited for the footsteps of the cook or the old man or a nurse come to heat the bottles. Cromwell lectured, smiled, and spoke confidentially, with ease, about the lower world. Behind the column of figures, the sweeping statements, the old friendship there was the clicking needle, the voice coming from inside the briefcase—with facts and sieges memorized, hopes turned to demands, speaking to convince them all, from the general to the dandy. Ernst's head touched the table. Cromwell was not tired from the long ride up the mountain but spoke quickly, as if he had been everywhere and carried near his breast the delicate maps and computations, the very secrets they lived on.

". . . Antwerp fell. The Krupp gun, 42 centimeter, took them through and luckily enough, I was able to see the whole thing. It was like Hohenlohe's progress in Africa, more, you see, than just a concentration of men for their own good, more than anything like a unity of states, like the Zolleverein, rather complete success, a mass move greater than a nation, a more pure success than Prussia's in the Schleswig-Holstein affair. We fought, gained in the area of Soissons and they couldn't drive us from Saint Mihiel—glory be to the German army! The line is now from the English Channel to Switzerland, and we wait only spring. We extend across Europe in four hundred integrated miles."

It was now dark, morning turned backwards in exasperating treachery. Cold porridge was left on the table. He thought he should perhaps shake Cromwell's hand again, go fetch more coffee. He had lost the thread, the long chain of virus that keeps a man anchored to his nation, instrumental in its politics, radiant in its victory, and dead in its defeat; had lost the meaning of sacrifice, siege, espionage, death, social democracy or militant monarchism. He was lost, the newspapers scattered over the vertical cliffs, the wires coiled, cut in the snow. And he prayed at meals, knowing nothing about the collective struggle of the hated Prussian and genius Hun, knowing nothing of the encircling world, the handcuff, the blockade. That air seeping visibly below the window, through orchard and burrowed haystack, crawled by the red and yellow wires, kissed the worried *Oberleutnant,* and the dumb sapper smoking his pipe in the hole. Eyes burned; it left patches in the lungs amid the blowing of whistles, this yellow fog. It came in the window, the mountain slid lower, railway tracks giving way to on-sloughing feet.

"They are well trained," said Cromwell, "in spring, the valleys will fall under—extension—we must have technological extension. No nation has the history of ours." There was a list of seven hundred plants in his briefcase, where locomotives swung on turntables and the smell of cordite hovered over low brick buildings. The world is measured by the rise and fall of this empire.

The hotel manager was shaving and soon would come downstairs. A nurse, ruddy and young, behaved like a mother, smiling at the child in the darkness. In the neighborhood of Cambrai where an Allied flanking movement had failed to turn the German extreme right, a farmhouse at a fork in the clay roads, demolished by artillery fire, lay half-covered in leaves and snow. There the Merchant, without thoughts of trade, dressed only in grey, still fat, had died on his first day at the front and was wedged, standing upright, between two beams, his face knocked backwards, angry, disturbed. In his open mouth there rested a large cocoon, protruding and white, which moved sometimes as if it were alive. The trousers, dropped about his ankles, were filled with rust and tufts of hair.

When Stella awoke, she was still possessed of the dream; it lingered on in the dim light. When she looked into Ernst's bed, she saw only a small black-haired Christ on the pillow, eyes wide and still, who trembled, and with one thin arm, motioned her away.

"Maman," a child's voice cried below the window, "the old horse is dead!"

LUST

All night long, despite the rattle of the train wheels and the wind banging against the loose window-panes, Ernst could hear the howling of the dogs out in the passing fields and by the rails. The robe hung over his shoulders and was clutched about his throat, the heavy folds coarse and dark, stamped with the company's seal as railroad property. Robes were piled in all the empty compartments, the dim light swayed overhead, and the cold grew so severe that the conductor, who continually wished to see their papers, was irritable, officious. The compartment, or salon, a public beige color, unkempt, with its green shades and narrow seats, heaved to and fro, tossing the unshaded bulb in circles, rattling their baggage piled near the thin door. Those were certainly dogs that howled. His face pressed against the glass, Ernst heard the cantering of their feet, the yelps and panting that came between the howls. For unlike the monumental dogs found in the land of the tumble-weed, glorified for their private melancholy and lazy high song, always seen resting on their haunches, resting and baying, these dogs ran with the train, nipped at the tie rods, snapped at the lantern from the caboose, and carrying on conversation with the running wheels, begged to be let into the common parlor. They would lap a platter of milk or a bone that appeared dry and scraped to the human eye without soiling the well-worn corridors of rug, and under the green light they would not chew the periodicals or claw the conductor's heels. As paying passengers, they would eat and doze and leap finally back from the unguarded open platforms between cars into the night and the pack.

A small steam pipe, its gilt long flaked with soot, bent like an elbow, began to rattle and gasp, but after a few more knocks, a few more whistles from the engine straining at the head of the train, it died. The official ticketed odor of dust and stuffing, the chill around the dark ceiling of cobwebs increased, and Stella tried to rest while Ernst watched the night pass by, annoyingly slow and too dark to see. The firebox in the engine was small, wrapped up, steady and dispassionate for the night, the fireman nodded over his shovel, an old soldier moved abjectly about the empty baggage car, and Ernie, holding the shawl, wondered what terrible illness was falling on his shoulders. And all he had to show was the castoff crucifixion of a half-wit, wrapped in brown paper in the bottom of the carpetbag. They stopped at many small stations and crossings during the night, but no passengers boarded or left the train.

The honeymoon was over, the mountain far behind, and as they had begun walking down the road, the old horse long dead, Cromwell called, "Well, we'll meet soon again, sorry you have to rush," and waved awkwardly with his briefcase. "I don't think so," said Ernst, and dug his pike into the snow. There was no one, no one; they traveled alone except for the dogs over the snow whose edge, leagues beyond, was besieged. But when, the following morning, they drew into the city, into *das Grab,* hundreds of people milled about the shed, pushed near the train but paid it no attention. When she helped him down the iron steps, her face red with the frost, he knew things had changed, that the dogs had beaten them to the destination. That train would certainly never run again, he felt sure, and he knew that its journey was over. The engineer's black face was still asleep, a mailed fist caught on the whistle cord, head propped on an arm in the small unglassed window. "Fare well," said Ernst as he stepped off into the crowd that steamed and rattled like stacks and shovels and feet clattering in the bunkers.

Engines that had just arrived stood on sidings unattended, steaming, damp, patches of ice stretched over the cabs, waiting where the crews had left them, unaccounted for, unfueled. The crowd milled around wooden cars, valises were lost; returning soldiers, unmet, ran towards strangers, laughing, then backed away in other directions. The streets beyond the station were filled with unindentified men who had lost brass buttons and insignia to bands of children. Some soldiers that were carried on stretchers by medical men, waved empty cups or dozed in the shade of awnings, while their bearers drank inside. Some were seasick as they slid along under the towering gangs, bruised by trailing wagon chains, swept by the rough skirts of coats, tossed close to the crowded surface of the concourse. The streets were as close as the sliding dark hold of a prison ship, and since the continuous falling-off of arms and spirit, since the retreat, provided little fare for the dogs that beat the train. They couldn't support the town dogs and certainly not these soldiers.

Stella had carried the bags ever since leaving the mountain, and used to them by now, thin leather sides stamped with the black permits, bulging with nightshirts and a few mementos, she walked along by his side, stepped over the stretchers and stayed as close as possible without any trouble. Ernst had grown stronger during the night, he felt the air sailing past the train; all of them grew stronger as they neared the city, *das Grab*. It looked quite different, not at all as he had expected, not dark and safe and tiring in the middle of the earth, but cold and wide, packed with the confused homecomers, knapsacks filled with the last souvenirs. There were no bugs or insects, no still drooping beaks and shapeless wings on the marble walls. But crowds in front of empty shop windows and endless white platoons formed and re-formed behind the courthouse. Names and numbers and greetings were shunted between rows of bright bleak buildings and they kissed, changed dressings, in the middle of the street.

Ernst began to look for Herman. He didn't want to look for the old man, conscripted father, but felt, as a citizen, that the *soldat* should be met. He looked under the blankets, in the wagons, scrutinized the ranks, walked faster and faster but did not find Herr Snow.

"Ernst, my dear husband, wait, aren't we going in the wrong direction?"

"Where would you expect to find him, except in this way? All soldiers come here and go in this direction."

Every half-hour the trains slowed to a stop in the stockyards, tired brakemen swung to the ground while troops hurried from the cars; each half-hour the streets were more filled with tattered capes and swinging arms, and musette bags and boxes left forgotten on corners. All the soldiers appeared to think that someone was meeting them, and smoking their first cigarettes, hand grenades still in their belts, they appeared to enjoy searching, at least for a while. In any other place but *das Grab* they would not be so joyous. The musicians who had played at the *Sportswelt* were gathered about an upper window of an empty room and soldiers nearing from the distance heard the tune, caught it, sang it until they passed, and then forgot it. There was at that one place before the window some music. Ernst looked a long while for his father, leading Stella halfway around the city before they finally reached the house.

Beyond the outskirts of the grave, beyond the locked barns at the edge of town, beyond the open doorways and colored stock—out past those hundred miles of fields and cow sheds where old Herman had met his fill and lost his supper in the ditch—out past those last outposts and signal stations, far out to sea, the American Blockade turned first one way and then another in the fog. A few more crates and a barrel and orange or two sank away in the foam. There was no noise in this well-organized blockade field except the cold sound of the waves and the slapping of an oar, locks outward, against the blue tide.

Evidently Gerta was out and the house was empty. Stella, weary of the cold and the long march, glad to keep their voices, questions, and songs away from the day of homecoming, let the door sag-to past the sleeping sentry and, lantern in hand, helped her returning husband up the wide dark stairs. While the trench mortars out of town approached and stopped, then continued on, she felt his small burning cheek and, stooping, unbuttoned his fluttering shirt.

Gerta trudged with her thin legs cold among the boys, her wig tied on with a yellow ribbon, her skirt caught up at her black and blue hip, an old ungracious trollop, a soldier's girl. She would have nothing to do with the blind ones, they frightened her. But she'd met a boy the day before and dried his dressing, sang to keep up her spirits while pushing another along in his red box. She was hurried along, talking in a loud voice, in the throng, now and then her hand falling on a damp shoulder or into a loose pocket. The red box rattled on its cart wheels, bandages turned grey with coal dust, whistles called from the tangled depot, and soaked oranges sank slowly through the ocean's thick current. The pockets, she found, contained only the photographs of the deceased.

Two days after arrival, each trainload of men, smiles gone, hair long, found themselves foodless and the tin pans banged at their belts, the queues turned away. But as each group became hungry and camped on the doorsteps, a new load arrived, singing, watching, laughing, waiting to be met. The new laughers filtered through the despondent men; shops were empty but hung with new regimental flags, and as the laughers became, in turn, pale and confused, as last loaves were eaten and crusts lost, more laughers filtered in, singing, pushing, looking about *das Grab* for the first time. Gerta bumped from one to another, laughed, was carried up and down among the *krank* and lost, among the able but gaunt, among the young or bald. No one who walked these connected streets was old; the aged had been blown indoors. Suddenly the *Sportswelt* loomed ahead.

"Try this, try this, try this," she cried, and rifle butts were pitted against the sealed door, a window broke like the breast of a glass doll. They entered the place, weak and shouting, while the blonde trollop found her way out back to catch her breath.

The corridor made by the rock walls down to the

100

open latrine, was filled with wind-blown pieces of paper, and across the walls the tables were over-turned, the lawns long and the valor-petals dry. Re-turning from the pea-green pit of stench Gerta almost stumbled where the Merchant fell, cocoon in his mouth, beams on his chest, months before. Her wooden shoes clicked on the green stones, skirts swung from the sides of her sharp hips. Gerta took a cigarette from a tin box hidden in her blouse, the smoke trailed into the garden and over the dead leaves.

The family was all dead. The Father, the victor, with a cocked hat and pot, had long ago wished her well. The Mother lay in the cold bunker of the street, cinders falling over the rough chin. The Sons, no longer to be with Nanny, having no longer spurs to tinkle against their boots since spurs were always removed before the body was interred, had never been parted and both lay under the wet surface of the same western road. So now alone, she wore her skirts above her knees and her bright lopsided lips were red with the glistening static day of *das Grab;* for she had survived and hunted now with the pack.

The blonde, the old nursemaid, pinched her ciga-rette and went back to the hall. The vandals, with tunics itching on bare chests, with packs paining and eyes red, with rifles still riding strapped to packs, searched, pawed over the dust, sat leaning against the rafters and waited. They seemed to think the orchestra would pick up, the lights flare on; they waited for the singer. The chairs were not made to sit on, the tables were against the walls, and the dust, lately stirred and tossed in the cold light, settled on the darkening planks. A cat called from one of the upstairs empty bedrooms and disappeared. Several white shoes, chair legs, hands, scraped against grey puttees. These were not looters who carried swag on their shoulders and trinkets in their arms, they did not scrounge and run. They searched as if for something in particular, walked softly about the bare room. The girls were gone with the *Schnapps*. The soldiers crowded together, tossed a few periodicals and lists of the dead, to the middle of the stage, and walked up and down the green carpet while the wheels rolled against the snow. They were now taught methodically to meet the train with blistering paws, and iodine stained their green cuffs.

Gerta laughed as she leaned close to an old hatless soldier who dozed far back in the chair, head to one side, shoulders caught against the rungs. His red beard was clipped unevenly, his wedding ring, tight about a dirty finger, was green. His nails were chewed like those of a young girl. His discharge papers rose out of his upper pocket blue and torn, and the paper disks hanging near his throat turned from red to black in the changing light. She touched his knee.

"Captain, have you a match?"

The eyes opened, the lips were moistened, they shut.

"No." The answer came in low bar-owner's German. He folded his thick hands together and slept.

"Have you come home to be rude to a lady?"

A shawl was miraculously unearthed from a bare corner, the black beads hung over a soldier's back. Cold air swept about the walls.

Slowly, eyes still shut, the big man's hand moved towards a pocket, the weight shifted slightly, the hand went deeper, the face was unshaven, dark, still passive. With another movement, he emptied his pocket on the table, the hand dropped back to his side and did not swing, but hung straight and unmoving. Among the dull coins, the knife, the tube of ointment, the cerulean clipping, the bits of wire, Gerta found a match and flicking it beneath the table, cursed and broke its head for being damp.

Children were looking in at the windows, watched with glee the Madame, matron and the uniformed Herr Snow.

"Was it a long journey, Captain?"

"Across the road, over there." She leaned closer to see.

When Gerta was kissed, she clung to his shoulders and looking over towards the light, saw the child's face. It pointed, laughed and jumped out of view. And old Herman, fully awake, touched the soft fur with his mouth and felt the wings through the cotton dress, while in the far end of town a brigade of men passed shallow buckets of water to quench a small fire. Herr Snow did not recognize the *Sportswelt* and did not know that he was kissing Stella's nurse. A rough golden forelock brushed his cheek.

Then old Snow stopped kissing, and for a moment his lips worked uneasily with no desire to speak, and he leaned back, his rough chin raised higher than the blunt nose. He smelled the breath of unsweetened soap, the odor of the comb issued by the government, and all about him were the grey backs, the crackling shoes, the children whose dead brothers were from his own regiment. Old Snow, sitting with a friend he'd never met in the *Sportswelt* he no longer knew, with small bright bugs still pestering his legs, had no right to be tired, no more right to look torn and drab than all the rest. For though he could not remember, bare shell of a man, his eyes and face wore the look on one who knows where he is going

103

—size without substance his expression was yet determined. It was the determination on those ugly features, the fact that he took a stand in the consideration of his own fate, that made him contemptible, that marked him as second rate, only a novice at the business of being a civil servant.

When he laughed it was the last laugh, and his whole mouth quivered as if the paper lips had been touched with feathers. Gerta laughed, but quickly, and looked through his belongings on the table once more. His once black shining boots, once steel padded and reinforced, once scorching in the sun, were now down on one side, scraped and shredded with long bare patches between the seams; tufts of mud and grass stuck to and raised the heels so that the squat man rolled as he walked on the city streets but sank and plodded in the valiant fields. A civil employee must not sink and plod.

"It's a good thing we met . . .," her mouth torn between desires, "it certainly is." She pulled back, stole a glance at the darkening windows, looked down at her thin hands. Somehow the woman, a little more sallow, a little more old, felt herself more than lightly touched. All the preceding boys she couldn't count, all the brilliant days with the city filling every hour with friends, friends, their sudden departure from the dark cold working hours, all this gaiety, the train arrivals sprinkled with glittering medals and redcross flags. All of it was brilliant and time consuming. But meeting the red-bearded man was a little different. She thought he was different and he was, with his sunken chest; he was, with his palsied fingers; he was, with his short hair shaved for medical reasons. But most of all because he had a sense that the stiff-marching, girl-getting fight was out of him. Now it was time for the father to have the son take over, time for the new horse, the milk-fed horse, to take the reins and buck, to trot up the mountain that was now too steep, the going too difficult with the snow. But Herman didn't know he had a son named Ernst, and there was no new horse, only time to try once again. Old Snow would try and try, sinking downwards in a landslide of age that would never end, until in the night, near the death of his son, he would try once more and fail.

"Come now," she said, "aren't you going to bring me close?" While the laughter faded from her voice and it wheezed, the old man seized her in the darkness and was neither surprised nor disappointed to find that there was almost nothing there.

There were no lights in the *Sportswelt*. For a long while, the old patriots were silent, the vandals and depressed soldiers about them were silent, telling stories in hushed voices, readying themselves for sleep on the great hall floor. The children were gone. And then a lone policeman on patrol, his spiked helmet dull and gleaming in the pale moonlight, himself short and thin, defenseless but warmed with beer, stood on a box and flashed his torch into the *Sportswelt* depths.

"My Lord," Old Snow realized by the light of the torch, "she has black stockings on her legs," and they were stretched, thin and taut, across his broad useless lap.

The tremendous scroll letters, so thick and difficult to read, blurring and merging and falling off in the darkness, profuse and graceless on the ornate pine walls, advertising inns that were dark, posts no longer to be filled, tours that no longer existed, plays that were done, loomed outmoded and intricate overhead as they passed in the street. Gerta pulled him along, curls slightly askew, pushing, holding back, intent upon guiding the soft cumbersome elbow. The street, partially emptied of his comrades, twisted fluidly and darkly ahead, an inopportune channel, street of thieves. Tenaciously she drew him on between the banks, led him down into the gathering arches, and for a moment old Herman saw his brother's barge, and on the pillows in the stern a gross unrecognizable female who kept him in tow on the warm musky evenings. He smelled the oil on the water and the powder sprinkled lightly on her pink curls.

"Wait, *Liebling,* please, not here on the corner, just wait a moment, only a moment." Nevertheless Gerta was flattered and this momentary flicker of life raised, deep within her, very false hopes.

He forgot the barge, but the smell of the sea lingered on until they stood before the sharkskin house, larger, darker, more out of date, more boarded up, than ever.

Within the whitewashed walls of the *Saint Glauze* nunnery, a figure, held mesmerized by the four uneven corners, gazed ruefully about her cell's inner haven. Jutta sat upon the cot's unbleached single sheet, hearing from below the tinkle of bells and creak of leather where the sisters walked around and around in precise timeless honor of the evening prayer. The veils were heavy over the young girl's face, they smelled of linen and were not scented with the fresh new rose, did not smell of the garden or heavenly pine or oil-softened hands. They had been laid on quickly and protectively, after the face was washed. The birds and squirrels were thin near the nunnery, theirs was only the fare of rain and prey of lower insects; the high walls were old and bare. She heard the women rustling unevenly in line, heard the soft devout invocation of Superior who was the only one to speak. From down below in Superior's room she heard the occasional stamping of the *Oberleutnant's* boots. She knew that he was standing straight and tall by the narrow window, smiling, patient, watching the revolution of the humble ring. Now and again she heard his voice.

"Now, Superior," he would say in his unnatural tones, "it is time again to invoke the Heavenly Father's love for our men in the field. Battery C is in a difficult position, you know." And the Mother's voice would intone once more. The *Oberleutnant* had recently been relieved of active duty and given the political position of director at the nunnery where he improved the routine and spirit a good deal. He walked fretfully himself in the garden when the nuns were asleep, at their frugal meals, or at their indoor prayers. Jutta, the young girl, imagined him directing the almost perfect prayers of Superior, could see the old woman glancing out of the tight crowded ring at the man's face hidden deep in the recess. A supply officer, he was secretly included in the older sisters' prayers, and when he walked, bent with rank and tension, he gave the impression of deep concern and all knew he was worried about the welfare of Battery C.

With the old man dead, her mother dead, her two young brothers lost to the Fatherland and her sister Stella gone to marry in the mountains, Jutta was left alone while the city was gradually corrupted into war. It was Gerta, in the last days before her flaming debauch, who took her in long arms and presented her, with reverence, to the nuns. And after the family was no more, swept into the great abyss by the ancestral tide, and Gerta had no more chores, nothing but red paint and the empty house, her friend with the buns sent a note of sympathy trimmed in black. But by the time it arrived, Gerta was on the street and it remained in the leaking mailbox with all the other dead unopened letters. After that the postman stopped calling and the old house shrank tighter, where once the Grand Duke came to call. The street fell into ruin.

One by one she heard the feet shuffling through the gravel to the sanctum door, and as each stooped woman entered into the darkness of a century of peace, the sounds in the garden stilled. The circle unwound until the sisters of charity were no more and she could hear only the *Oberleutnant* humming as he paced rapidly back and forth, replacing the characteristic tone with heresy and haste. Not a bird sang anywhere, but a small bell jangled the sisters to board and thanksgiving. Their prayers for the evening meal echoed through the damp plaster corridors and up to her unmolested cell.

Jutta remembered the ladies in plumed hats and velvet gowns with distaste, remembered Stella's sailing around the ballroom with malice, and the thought of her dead parents, so many years too old, left her unfeeling. The old memories came but briefly, as brief as the desire to own anything or to own the black trousers, and when they did come, she summoned down her pride to fight the witchery.

She heard the soup spoons in the bowls, the soldier's quick steps.

The black skirts were held down about her ankles by long thin arms, frail from the disease that calmly ate at the calcium in her bones and drank the humbleness out of her system. As yet she did not know that her brothers had died howling in retreat, and for herself, all of them could go that way. The half-hours went by and the sky grew cerulean, the ointment was under the pillow but she couldn't reach it. She leaned forward, head over the knees, and it took all this effort at balance to keep from toppling over in a black heap. With ankles now as thin as wrists, the disease was cutting deeper, and there was no one to sit her up again if she fell. So she sat as still as she could, her thin fingers clamped firmly with effort.

Her father, the old general, in the days when he could talk and she could sit on his knee, wanted her in the civil offices. But from the first, she was determinedly an architect, she built towers with blocks and barns of paper, built them where they could hardly stand on the thick rugs, built them with childlike persistence; and the smile of completion was always one of achievement rather than pleasure. As she grew older she did not smile at all and hid her queer angles and structures in her little whitewashed room, grew more and more serious, objected rationally to the public documents and taxpayer's history fostered on her by the old general. Carefully she designed herself inwards, away from the laughing women, closeshaven men, away from tedious public obligation, until she was finally accepted, one steaming afternoon, into the Academy of Architecture.

It was almost time for Superior to start her rounds, to observe, to praise and to condemn the girls who were bad physically or bad spiritually. Superior would stand in the doorway with her face that was neither a man's nor a woman's, blocking out the last bit of light with her stiff fan-like hood and robes. With her steel spectacles, pink face and sharp black eyes, Jutta thought of her as the doctor who walked so slowly and stayed, while probing, such a long while. Down below she heard the *Oberleutnant* sit heavily on one of the benches and from down the hall came the sound of an old woman putting Superior's desk in order. While no one in the city even knew the date or what was taking place, knew neither of the blockade at sea nor of the battles in the empty forests, Superior did. Every morning, after her consultations, she sat at her desk composing, in tiny script, a long laborious letter of protestation to the President of the United States. She objected to the starvation and spreading illness. It grew dark, and Jutta could not move to light the candle.

In the Academy Jutta often saw the young men lined up with their brown torsos and tight grey gymnasium trousers. At first they often smiled at her in the cold corridors and looked over her shoulder at the drawing board. But all of them now, as far as she knew, had swords and spurs like her brothers. Winning the favor of her professors, she did not have to force herself to look at them. They passed out of reach and a long line of nurseries and fortresses took their place. Besides devising a new triumphal arch and scraping hard pencils on her sanding block, she studied history. Volume after volume passed under her close disciplined study. She knew all of the Hapsburgs, knew that the Austrians and Germans were all one blood, knew that the light and life was in the East. Her fits of temper were gone, the sabers were no longer within range, but were only of use, like her brothers, in the fields far away.

Superior was coming up the worn stairs, the *Ober-leutnant,* back in his room, stepped out of his trousers. Jutta felt weaker, more weak than ever before, and down in the city the policeman put away his torch and left his beat to go to sleep.

Her remaining isolation had been debased. The General couldn't talk, the mother was absurd in his unmade bed, Stella flew off again and again until she finally met the one with the puckered face and flew for good. There was no one to give clear-headed praise, no one to admire or respect her diagrams of mechanical exultation, no one to recognize, even at thirteen, her great skill. But it was not the language of the dumb, the old, that made the declining days a treachery and not a triumph, not the dead in the streets and silence in the house that drove her to the nuns.

The final blot against absolution, depriving her of sacrifice and intelligent suffering, was Gerta's unpleasant love. When the sores first came and she fell with dizzy spells, the old fool of a nurse put her to bed, and far too old for such exertion, climbed the immense bare stairway with trays for the invalid. Gerta told her stories, sat by the bedside, excited with the drama, with something to do, and with Nordic bravery, plunged majestically into the soiled linen. And worst of all, the nurse told hundreds of stories of ladies and their lovers, treating Jutta all the time as if she were a girl, and worse, as if she were a child. On the final rainy day, when the child could hardly walk, Gerta insisted upon dressing her meticulously and heavily, and tied, grunting, one of the mother's huge old bonnets on her head to shield her, unhappily, from the storm. It was Gerta's care, the coughing attachment and unforgiveable

111

pity, that made the nation's born leader forlorn in the nunnery. How the old fool petted and fawned even before the sisters, who, though not so outwardly comforting, were more, finally, difficult and grasping, feeding on their wards.

The stately steps grew closer; confessions mumbled nearer at hand.

Standing together like obedient black birds at the bottom of the stairway, their heads bent in silent unmeditating respect, the sisters waited until Superior disappeared upwards and out of sight, painfully slow and belligerently in communion. Never, never could she whip these girls into shape, she deplored the ragamuffins, the misplaced childish females. She did not like girls. Superior caught her breath, drew herself up, and made headway through the common lot of problems and despairs, passing unscathed from cell to cell.

The world was growing dimmer for Jutta, the crisis was at hand, her hold on her knees was precarious and sharp. Whether or not she was responsible, she had her weakness, physical and perhaps beyond control, and it made her guilty of disease while the calcium continued to dribble away from the cold, well-bred bones. And despite her praiseworthy nature, her determination, she did fear Superior. Behind all her plotted good intentions, behind her adoration of the East and worship of people in the abstract, the fear always remained, fear of mother, fear of being nursed, fear of Superior. The light was flowing out of the *bunker,* there was nothing more to do except wait for the final unadmitted illusion to disappear, nothing to think of, no one to dislike, no one she needed to love. The little stone-like bumps

112

were hard and rough under her fingers, the hair was straight into her eyes.

"I didn't really want to do it, Superior," the voices were drawing closer with short unpleasant sobs, "I never really wanted to, it was all a mistake, I'm sorry, truly sorry, sorry," and Jutta heard them falling in terror into the slovenly captivity of forgiveness, heard the voices folding into submission. Superior would cross each name, that night, off from the human list. What was it? Yes, she scorned the heroes on *die Heldenstrasse,* they were forgiven, blessed and posed. She would not put on her Sunday shoes to walk that street. But she could not see Superior, she could not, and surely the grey waters of hell would drown her for that treachery, that fear.

The shadows were cold, her hands were unfeeling with numbness. The *Oberleutnant,* warm and restless, tossed off the covers, thought of silken hair and fiery eyes.

Suddenly the light vanished, faster than the moon could be covered with clouds, and the dark angel stood in the doorway cutting off the candlelight from the outside world. The waters opened at the feet of the girl, Superior opened her warm heart, ready to receive the remnants of another mortal. The throat tightened, pulled, and at that moment she heard the General calling, calling from the great room of feasting, "Where is the railroad station, the railroad station?" and he was laughing.

"Child," the woman stayed in the doorway, half in the hall, half inside, "are you ready to open your heart to the Heavenly Father? Are you ready to be insured of safe flight from the pit of everlasting day and weariness? Now is the time to atone." Superior's voice was loud, was always the same whether she was talking to the well or ill, was always clear and harsh. "Now is the time to abandon the wicked man of your soul, now you may come to my arms." She remained rigidly blocking the light. "Child, have you prepared your confession?"

Surely if she lived she would end up a civil official after all, entrusted and forced to take down, patiently, Superior's documents of condemnation. She felt a small, cold throbbing under her arm.

"No." She did not think, but answered dumbly, out of the deathbed. "No. I have nothing to confess, absolutely nothing, nothing." She was talking back to Gerta, telling her brothers to leave her alone, for she was cold and tired. "Nothing to say to you, Superior," and relaxing her grasp, she slipped from the cot, a rude, black, invalidated heap.

The *Oberleutnant,* disturbed by the voices, threw on his trousers and trudged angrily upstairs. This sort of thing had to stop.

Ernie was so small now, propped helplessly in bed, fever and chill making his face now comical, now cruel and saintlike. He was a puppet with two masks and it was up to Stella, weary, to change them as he bid. He had become as bothersome and old as all unhealthy people, but he loved, in the agonizing undramatic last moments of his life, to swallow the thick medicine and make bitter faces. Stella heard from the sentry, who was still posted at the door of the General's empty estate, that the illness was spreading all through the city. He told her rumors of deaths, widespread prostitution, and of imminent victory. "At least," she thought to herself, "dear Ernst is not the only one." The valises were still unpacked and lay crookedly, uncertainly, at the foot of his bed. "He looks," thought Stella, "as if he had a toothache," and indeed the patient's cheeks were swollen and inflamed at the sides of his thin white face. His coat collar was turned up about his throat, it was better to put him straight to bed, even fully dressed. Everywhere Stella moved, he still called, and though his face was turned away, the voice in the depths of his chest, she felt him holding on to her with his last breath of grace. She hadn't even time to wash, the windows were still boarded up, the furniture, except the pile he lay upon, was still in the basement. For the first time since her love on the mountain, she began to realize that he was a fencer in the clouds, stuck through, finally, with a microscopic flu. The room was dark and close as sickrooms are, but the evening chill and ageless year-round dampness made it more like an underground aid station. Holding her breath she leaned over the averted face, pulled it to position, pushed the sugar-grimed spoon between the lips, and straightened with a long sigh.

Stella didn't know what she would do with him when he died. All at once the problem was overwhelming, his remains would hang around for weeks. The idea of disposal seemed so remote and impossible. Surely the man who took care of such things would be long out of business, where could she turn? If only the body would fly away with the soul, but, no, it would linger on, linger on here in this very room. "He doesn't look at all," she thought, "like the man I married in the garden." Where is the railroad station? She helped him through each physical minute, becoming more impatient as he coughed and turned. Suddenly it struck her that this was not old Herman's son, and now she was nursing a stranger, not even a ward of the State. "Dear Ernst," she thought, "you look just like Father."

Every time he opened his eyes, he saw her there, warm, beautiful, efficient. The very breath of the flowers on her shoulder brought new life. When she sat on the bed, one soft dark knee upon the other, one thin elbow pushing gently against her bosom, holding the lovely head, all lofty desire was his, he was in the presence of the white lady of the other world. Ah, to die no longer with the fire but with the dove. The first stages of death took energy, the last mere confidence. The closer she bent with the spoon in her hand, the warmer he felt, the farther he flew.

"Stella?"

"Yes, Ernst?"

"Isn't it time for the black pills?"

Immediately she brought the bottle.

"Herman, stay away," he thought. "The old man must not come back, the wonderful peace of being waited on must not be broken. The corrupter's prime agent should not be allowed out of the war, but should stay forever and ever in some black hole away from the gracious light of Heaven. The maiden voyage of the star, all hands accounted for, safely arrived into the sky. At last to be able to do something alone, without old Snow there to beat the other fellow's back." The dreams arose more vividly, he forgot the star. "Those were fearful times with the old man filled with wrath. Oh, no, that demon could not possibly come back to plague my end, to expect to be welcomed home at such a precarious, serious time." Ernst channeled himself once more into the soft light, the medicine smelled as sweet as the valor-

116

petals, without the demon's horned masterful voice intruding.

"He flicked his eyes open and shut once," Stella later told the guard.

"Stella." He called again, "Stella, in the carpetbag, he's there, somewhere near the bottom, get him, please."

She rummaged through the flabby thing, like a peddler's sack, and there, beneath the newspapers and photographs, sure enough, under the soiled shirt, near the bottom on a pair of black shoes, it lay, wrapped in old Christmas tissue.

"Here." He patted the pillow near his cheek, "Here," he said in bliss.

She put the carving of Christ, almost as large as his head, on the pillow. She waited as if for something to happen. How peculiar, the wooden man and fleshless God, they kept good company. Then she remembered: on the mountain she too lay by Christ, and it was a mistake!

Suddenly he coughed and the little statue rolled over, its arms and legs thrown wide in fear.

"Here," she said, "now drink this, drink it." For a moment it looked as if he would recover. Then, no, no, he smiled again and all was lost. Stella crossed her soft dark knees.

The guard did not bother to open the door for Gerta and Herr Snow, but whistled and wondered at the old woman's return, while the soldier and his girl pushed alone into the darkness of the wide downstairs hall. For a moment, Gerta stood uncertainly in the middle of the vacant foyer, listening for the sounds of the dead, with Herman leaning, drugged, on her arm. She could hear the guard, the last guard, behind her shuffling about on the other side of the door. Herman breathed heavily in the darkness, his weight sagged, she could see nothing. Then she heard them, those dead two, master and mistress, and far overhead she saw a line of light and heard the tinkle of glass, ghosts in their cups.

She wanted to shut the soldier, shirt off, shoes off, into her room with all night, every night for no telling how long, before her. But she began to lead him toward the light. Mistake, mistake to bring such a tender man, so close to popping, within the realm of unwanted, unexpected guests—to let the steam off the wrong end, the end of white, flat apprehension. And she too, by walking up the stairs, was holding off. As they neared the top, he tripped once, twice, and Gerta began to cross the line from love to nurse, from grand-sharer to assistant.

It was Fraulein Stella's room. They waited before the door.

The trains were still arriving. Under cover of darkness, small and squat, they emptied themselves of soldiers home on leave. In the dark the girls milling on the platform could not tell whether the trains were full of passengers, perhaps men, or empty. Signals crossed, whistles argued out of the stops of tangled rail, "Train from 31, train from 9, let me pass, I'm carrying wounded." "Wait, you'll have to wait, 31, there are dogs in front."

Gerta could hear the whistles far out in the night. They were long and old-fashioned and far away.

"Do you hear the dogs?" Ernst spoke, hands picking at the covers.

"Of course, dear husband."

He could hear them barking among the boat whistles in the middle of the night.

118

Stella mixed the potions and wondered about the hour, what could she do when the hour stopped? All about her the phials, the wads of cotton, the handbook of medical instruction, were out of reach, too slow. There was nothing she could do against it, she lost her place in the handbook. All the soft embrace of the mountain was gone, all the humor of his saber wounds was healed; he was stitched and shrouded in that impertinent, unthinking smile. He grew thinner, and staring her full in the face with his three fingers twitching helplessly on the cover, he gagged.

They heard the scratching at the door and at first they thought it was the wind, only the comforting night air.

"Now, what's she doing here," thought Gerta as she stepped into the patient's room with her lover behind.

The red-bearded devil leaned across the bed, staring at the man with a toothache. Herman looked from his son to Stella, the lovely girl, from the colored bottles to the boarded window, and back to the majestic bed.

"He's not sick!" and the devil roared with laughter, his desire for Gerta flickering out in spasms of recognition of his foe, the bedded influenza.

He had horns. Terrible, agonizing, deformed short stubs protruding from the wrinkled crown, and the pipes he held in his fiery hands were the pipes of sin. All of the calm of Heaven evaporated and at the last moment, not knowing what it was all about, Ernst recognized Old Snow. And in that moment of defense, of hating the devilish return of boisterous heroic Herman, Ernst died without even realizing the long-awaited event; in that last view of smallness, that last appearance of the intruder, Ernst, with his mouth twisted into dislike, died, and was reprieved from saintliness. The old man still laughed, "Feigning, he's only feigning!" Stella was irritated with his ignorance, at least this father could rise to the dignity of the occasion by admitting the fact of death. But no, he chuckled and looked stupid.

Herman paid for his mirth, for it had stolen his son and his stamina. He slept uncomfortably with Gerta in the room which she felt was much too small for the rest of the night.

The guard, Stella found, managed in the morning to fulfill her final obligation to the dead. The disbelief and anger were still on the fencer's face as he was carried from the house, saved by the grace of his own ill-luck and ill-will.

Jutta awoke with the vision of spectacles and hood still in the abbey room and out of the weak unending dream, she heard the tinkle of the goodnight bell, while the pain in her arms and legs was numbed by her victory; for Superior was gone.

"Jutta, Jutta, go to bed," but she discounted that voice. The last authority was gone. Superior, rebuffed, sat at her desk down the hall, unable to write, so angry, the cowl that covered her fierce shaved head tossed aside on a chair. The waiting woman stared in concern at the nun turned monk.

Jutta tried to move, but could not, and stayed for a moment, her face turned to the floor, rising from the squeamish pit of the too-easy psalm and too-easy dying bone. She opened her eyes. "There are enemies even within our own State," she remembered and wondered why the *Oberleutnant* didn't stop Superior, and she was glad to know, being allowed to wake once more, that life was not miraculous but

120

clear, not right but undeniable. How narrow and small was the suffocating Superior with part of each day spent bartering with the miraculous medal salesman. Jutta felt, being once more back in the cell where Gerta put her, uncomfortably sick and very tired. She would try to reach the cot.

The nunnery, high and safe within the meek heart, far from the blockade at sea, rested confident and chaste in the middle of the night, spreading its asylum walls outwards over a few bare feet of uninhabited dry earth. Safe, within the Allied querulous dragnet, because a taste of faith was all the inmates knew, because over the years, the hearts grew large and the stomachs naturally small, safe, with the cyclical event of mother, girl, and vanity thrown out. The old white barn rocked gently in the cloudy night. The moss had grown thin, turned brown, and died on the mud walls, water no longer trickled and grew thick in the well, the sand could hardly lift itself through the halls at night on the wind's back, but still in the morning and evening, bells faithfully chimed out the remote and tedious day. "Father, save me," thinking of the girls, "from these merciless infidels," said Superior, and leaning forward, she shrouded herself in darkness and sat for a long while with her pains and troubles by the window.

An oyster shell on the beach far away was shrouded in oil, coming in off the treacherous tide. The dogs barked.

"Perhaps I should call a doctor," thought the *Oberleutnant* bending over the sick girl, but at that moment she stirred, and besides, he remembered, the old horse that used to be in the stables and could have made the journey to the surgeon's house, was dead.

Jutta could not reach the cot, but slowly her anger and childish pain brought her back from the fleece-lined pit, and at that moment, she heard the bell in the tower ring three, heard Superior, who had rung it, padding back, feelings still hurt, to sit by the window. With a sudden lucky gesture, Jutta turned her head upwards, and in the dim light stared at the uncovered masculine chest of the *Oberleutnant* as he bent down, watching her on the floor.

Then, that night, she passed the crisis, and breath by breath, though scrutinized and unloved, she assumed more of life, still alone, more silent, colder than ever.

A few months after the death of Ernst, Stella gave birth to her fragile son, and while she was still on the bearing bed, Gerta and Herman took the child from her, carried it and kept it, down in the first-floor dark pleasure room where they had failed together that first night. Food became more scarce, and Stella never forgave the old woman for the stolen son. Hearing the dogs howling around the station at the port of entry to the grave, she thought, once more, of singing. The Christ carving had disappeared.

PART THREE—1945

TONIGHT

All during the day the villagers had been burning
out the pits of excrement, burning the fresh trenches
of latrines where wads of wet newspapers were scattered, burning the dark round holes in the back stone
huts where moisture traveled upwards and stained
the privy seats, where pools of water became foul
with waste that was as ugly as the aged squatter.
These earthen pots were still breathing off their
odor of burned flesh and hair and biddy, and this
strange odor of gas and black cheese was wafted
across the roads, over the fields, and collected on
the damp leaves and in the bare night fog along the
embankment of the *Autobahn*. This smell not only
rested over the mud, but moved, and with every
small breath of air, the gas of mustard, soft goat
pellets and human liquid became more intimate,
more strong and visible in reddening piles. One's
own odor could always be sifted out and recognized,
a disturbingly fresh stream in the turning ash, a personal mark that could be sniffed and known after
midnight, sometimes as if the tongue were poking
in the incinerator and the warm air curling about
the hewn seat.

The three of us waited by the side of the road,
stockingless feet burning and itching in our unlaced
shoes, plucking at nostrils, listening to a wasted
mongrel paw the leaves, hearing an occasional tile
slide from a roof and fall to the mud with the swish-

ing of a tail. The flats turned away before us, un-peopled, dark, an occasional shell-case filling with seepage, the fingers of a lost glove curling with dew. Behind us the ghosts left the stalled tank and filed downward toward the canal.

"He's late," said Fegelein.

"Yes."

"No sleep for us then."

"Wait, have patience," I answered.

We crowded invisibly together with the road high overhead that extended far beyond this edge of town, and there were no precision transits or plumb lines to point the kilometers of travel or show the curve on the map where the blank spot of this town would be. We never ventured away, though we still wore the grey shirts and had signed our way to the out-side world.

"It's a good machine he's riding," said Fegelein.

"Don't worry. I won't shoot at it."

"Good."

"Remember, no talking. Stintz would be sure to say something when the next rider comes through in a month looking for this one." I constantly had to give commands.

"In a month we'll be ready."

"Yes."

"And the motorbike will be useful."

"Yes." I had to humor them.

In every town there are a few who, though they don't remember how it came about, or how they returned, or when they went away, or what the enemy expects, gather together in the night to rise again, despite the obstacle of their own people or the swarming invader. Behind us the town grew smaller; the sleepers were cold and numberless.

126

"No one will see?"

"No," I answered.

"I don't want to go forward tonight; you mustn't make me . . ."

"Stop that. You know there isn't any forward."

"I'm sorry."

The cold night air quickened my hunger, and I put the thought out of mind, concentrated on the hunched man in goggles and helmet. Once the old horse clattered by above our ears and then moved off as if he smelled nothing, neither fresh grass nor humans nearby.

Jutta's child watched in the window, her sharp eyes darting this way and that among the shadows, hands folded in her lap, knees drawn together, small and wide awake as children who follow the night very long after the usual time to sleep, quickened and tense with the unexpected hours, wretched small keepers. But she did not see her brother, the fairy, nor any forms crawling along the street among the ends of broken pipe. She watched for a light, a swinging lantern, or any recognizable animal or man in the bare branches and felt that she must wait and watch, for she knew that all were not asleep. She waited for Jutta as a child would, and saying nothing she called her mother home. What was the hour? No one could know because there were no clocks. She knew the time by intuition, this dark time, as a thing that ended only with sleep. She knew that one could never see the morning come, and only by turning away, by hiding, would the night leave. For a long while it had been quiet below, from the time Herr Stintz stopped playing his horn until now, and by a few unnatural sounds, the rustling of cloth, the dropping of a shoe, she knew he was no longer asleep. He was fetching his stick. Jutta didn't like him either, because he could commit no crime nor act strongly, but could only bring harm. The child heard the splash of water and then waited, hearing him walk the length of his cage and unlock the door.

The fairy, out of sight, was running for his life.

She was afraid to look at him and barely made a gesture as if to touch the window, thinking to strike up a light.

"It's very late for a little girl to be out of bed, away from the covers, the nice warm quilt."

"I'm waiting for my brother."

"But you should sleep, because the moon doesn't like little girls to look into his bed. The moon sleeps in the world, a very strong man, and God has given him no covers."

"He's not sleeping tonight."

Mr. Stintz could only bring harm; she knew he carried the stick, but knew that little girls were safe because they were the ones who waited and never moved. If she moved, the paw would break off her wing and catch her by the leg.

"Oh," she said, "there's my mother."

"Why don't you," he said, "why don't we look for the moon quickly?"

She heard the door shut gently. Death is in the breaking of a lock, a cut in the skin, it comes with a cough and leaves before the plaster is dry on the chest. Stintz drove the boys in the rain and made the girls repeat and repeat their lessons in the old schoolroom, and no one spoke to him in the streets. "Madame Snow told me to die . . ." Then she saw something more wonderful than mother, something unknown but unmistakable. A light flashed in the distance, and as she watched, it drew closer, a thin quavering beam that seemed to be searching its way out of the darkness. This was what she had waited for and now she no longer watched for her brother but crept off under the covers. It was as if she had just visited the empty apartment on the second floor.

"Good night," she heard her mother say.

The three of us leaning against the clay bank were all that remained of the shadows of sentries, were primal, unordered, unposted sentries, lounging against the earth without password, rifles or relief. The sharp foreign voice had disappeared from the dark road and unlighted doorway, the rolls of wire, the angry tones, the organized guards were gone. Though unmistakable signs remained, a trampled package of woodbines, a tossed-off canteen, a piece of white webbing, these scraps still littered the floors of sheds or hung in the room corners where white women lay. The keepers, who had asked for papers, swore only with one word, lighted the night with red, and confiscated bicycles, and had moved on to the hunting ground of rodents. And we, the three shadows who remained, gaunt for the great land, dependent on the enemy's tin cans to squat in, waiting in our black unbuttoned coats and peaked caps, were sentries of the civilians, unemployed during the day, plotting for the greatest good by night.

The American on the motorcycle knew no more of the country that his eagle-colonels scourged, than did his free-eyed sergeants, roving in their green work clothes. He traveled along hypothetical lines of communication that chased miles beyond the end of the war and he had beer at each stopover. Desperation was not for this plains-rider, bouncing over once endless roads with his sack filled with unintelligible military scrawl, columns of figures, personal resentments, not for this oblivious traveler whose only communication was silence to the dark countrymen and "hi-ya, Mac" to his listless fellows. From the littered fields and overhanging branches, from the town library charred and unpurged, from the punctured rubber rafts plugging the canal, to the hanging mouths, to the enemy colors, to the unexploded traps, to the drunk official and black pox, it was an unrecognized, unadmitted, unnamed desperation that persisted beyond the tied prostitute and enemy news, beyond the cadaverous houses and American outposts, to give strength to us, the hovering sentries, to bring words to the lolling historians. Poison their camps, if only in a quip or solitary act.

I thought of it during each day in the newspaper office and thought of it against the mud-bank; life is not the remarkable, the precious, or necessary thing we think it is. The naked dark pawing of that eternal old horse who lingered on through no fault of his own, bereaved and unquiet in the night, told me that. And with the hoarded, secret sailor's black rum running through my mind, heaped about by past years' correspondence, dead letters, by fragments of broken type, I knew that the tenant was the law. For the final judgment the tenant must build the house and keep it from sliding into the pool, keep it from the Jew's claw or the idealist's pillaging.

You can ask no man to give up his civilization, which is his nation. The old must go, stagger over the failing drawbridge, fall down before the last coat of arms. I thought Madame Snow too old to understand, I thought she should wither away and die, with her long, false, flaxen hair, because I thought she would run rattle-tattle through the night for preservation. Here I was wrong, since she was the very hangman, the eater, the greatest leader of us all. Death is as unimportant as life; but the struggle, the piling of bricks, the desperate attempts of the tenant; that is the man of youth, the old woman of calm, the nation of certainty.

I brushed the hair away from my ears, relaxed against the earthen wall, smelled the flowering manure.

"Soon?" Even old Stumpfegel was impatient.

"Certainly. Have patience."

The child was not yet asleep, the drains were running foul to the basement, the Mayor dreamed, heaping one on another all the atrocities his old heart could dig up, so that they rolled in a paroxysm in his throat. The windows were shut, but he could not guard against the tottering dreams—for honoring the dead he must die. An attempt to stir himself with his own hand, since his wife was long gone, was, like the ventures of foraging children, like their touch to the self, a breath of suicide. Long after he was disturbed by the noise under the window, the dream returned and forced its way, lifelike, before his eyes as if he were awake. Dream after dream the voices and horses were the same, though they wore many figures, the Priest mixed up with the Officer, his own dead wife firing the rifle, a peculiar child pronouncing verdict as the Judge, the onlooking crowd all dressed as the condemned man. But the voices were distinct, and waking he would forget that they had calmly passed sentence, enemies and friends—guilty in the eyes of his own State.

131

He had betrayed the country only through his conscience . . .

Madame Snow held Balamir's hand.

The child could not sleep and listened to the mother's breathing.

Dancers wearied and each time the record stopped, the silence made them anxious.

The wind struggled and sighed and could go no farther than the edge of the canal.

A cow with its eyes shut clawed at the empty board walls of a barn with teeth like a hare but found no straw.

The boy had gotten himself lost in underworld tunnels, caught between hanging floors and rolls of wire, and he caught his pants on a bent thick nail.

The Duke followed closely in his step, cane raised sharply in the darkness, feeling his way carefully into the blind hole, and it began to rain. The tall man followed the boy through the gaping plaster wall and found himself in the theater. Madame Snow's one-legged son and noiseless wife were somewhere overhead near the projection room. The boy traveled in circles among the thousands of molding seats while rain trickled down the sloping floor and a field telephone covered with dust looked like an enormous trap on a chain. The theater grew darker. Carefully the Duke followed the shadows, slid like an elder actor to the ticket-seller's booth and doffing his hat stepped through the door and waited, surrounded with black glass, rolls of wet tickets, a red handkerchief. A rotted playbill masked his face. He saw something walk across the stage in false breasts and tights, heard the boy drawing fitfully near.

". . . It is you who will die," said the Priest to the Mayor. That had been the day when the motorcycle rider and the rest of the Allies had first passed through *Spitzen-on-the-Dein*. The convoy crept up the long bright highway through the snow, through the handful of silent watchers, down the main street like a centipede with the motorcycle first, followed by the jeep, ending with proud band of four riflemen. An American colonel and two corporals rode in the jeep, an automatic rifle propped in the back seat, their canteens filled with rum, and the dispatch-rider in the lead wobbled from side to side and waved the children off, flurries of snow shooting up behind him.

"So this is Germany," said the Colonel, and leaning out from behind the cold wheel he blew his whistle and the convoy stopped. Before the eyes of the crowd he got out and fastened a slender wire-cutter to the smoking radiator, then with a final quick word to the motorcycle man they made their way to the center of town, pulling on their mufflers, eyes frozen ahead. On the floor of the jeep beneath the jutting rifle, they carried their black robes and a few sealed envelopes. The foot-soldiers alternately ran and walked to keep warm.

By the middle of the afternoon they had stripped Madame Snow's apartment and established a headquarters, of three maps, a table and chair, temporary seat of American representation in the evil zone. The jeep was under a tarpaulin in the rear garden in the shed, the four troops billeted in the hall, and the dispatch rider was standing guard over his still warm machine. Through the uncurtained window, glancing for a moment from the red envelopes, the Colonel saw the sky darken for snow, and worried, he peered at his highly secret route through the nation, studied the undecipherable diagram and code. Satisfied, he signaled the corporal who quickly brought forth the three robes. The Colonel, short, heavyset, graduate of a technical institute, a brilliant engineer, thought in dotted parabolas, considered in fine red lines, and while lonely, overworked, and short in the knees, directed the spreading occupation. Except for the silver eagle sewn above the pocket of his black robe, he might have been the foreman of a jury pointed out to speak before the supreme law. Once more he carefully read the letter of instruction, tapped his pen on the bare wood, then dropped the paper into the heater in the corner, an open can of flaming petrol. The Mayor, Herr Stintz and myself stood in a corner, as there was no anteroom, watching these preparations, while out in the cold alone, walking up and down, waited Miller, the prisoner, thinking of the sweet children and his fair wife.

The robed men muttered together at the far end of the room behind the table, and we three, the witnesses, waited while a thin soot from the burning can settled over the floor, the walls, collected on the Colonel's two musette bags and on the neat small row of cracking army boots. The maps, freshly tacked to the wall, grew darker and the chill in the air grew worse with the promise of snow, soot speckled the grease on the Colonel's mess tins tied to the bedroll. Once one of the corporals turned, "No talking there," and we did not understand, for only the Colonel spoke German. Then, after a short silence, the Colonel seemed to remember. "My God, Corporal, get my pistol—and you might bring my pipe." The young man, holding the black hem above his boots, scowled once at us, the witnesses, and searched in one of the small dirty bags. Then a pause while they fumbled under his gown to arm him and he lit the pipe, his black cassock skirt and tough hands stiff with cold. The motorcycle rider's white helmet moved back and forth across the window, scattered flakes of snow dropped on his jacket.

"Mayor," the corporal called, and the frightened old man stepped into the dock, tensed for a dangerous question.

The Colonel took his place and spoke:

"How old are you?"

"Eh, what's that?"

"Your age, age."

"I'm sixty-one." His paper collar wilted, the official sash sagged on his waist, and he was afraid.

"Where were you born?"

"Right here, here in this very place."

"I understand you keep some sort of civil records?"

"I did, quite true, very fine writing. But they're gone, burned up, shells hit my house, zip, zip, and in the fallen glass the flames spread, so my papers are all gone."

"Well, I want to know something about," the Colonel looked at his notes, "a man named Miller."

"I've known him for years, his wife, children."

"Now, is it true he was a pastor?"

"Pastor? Ah, yes, pastor."

"But now he no longer is?"

"No longer? Well, not actively, the war, I don't think there were many people to listen . . ."

"Did he *want* to stop being a pastor?"

"Well, there was a good deal of trouble in this town, we suffered . . ."

I called from the corner, "He *is* a pastor."

"Silence, keep quiet, there."

Then Herr Stintz came forward, a primer under his arm, smiling, and he edged himself in front of the Mayor.

"If you'll permit me," he said.

"Well, what is it?"

Stintz stepped closer, glasses pinching over his nose. "Herr Colonel, I think perhaps you should take into account that there was, you know, a new gospel, the war made a change in what a man might want to preach to the dumb people—other ears heard, the new gospel was a very strong thing, even his wife could do nothing with Miller."

The Colonel looked for a long moment at the Mayor.

"Is this true? Was there a change in Miller?"

"Well, everyone, the war was a hard thing but," the old man found himself staring at the eagle on the Colonel's chest, and it seemed to glow with a phosphorescent sheen, "but I'm alone, I don't know him that well, he was away . . ." The eagle grew bright and the old man wiped his chin, tried to fasten the sash tighter, "but I think, maybe, he did change . . ."

"He did not," I said.

"He's a tough one," whispered the officer to the corporal, pointing at me, and the judges retired. The snow fell harder, the rider covered his bike with a gunnysack. "I think," said the Colonel, "that the case is closed, but we better be just, it will be excellent to impress them with our thoroughness." So for the rest of the afternoon, while the snow became thick and we waited in the corner, while one of the corporals took notes and the can ran out of fuel, a long line of civilians was formed and one by one

136

each citizen of the town passed into the dark room, was questioned, and was returned to the raw cold evening. At last the entire population had come and gone, steel slats had been driven across the cellar window where Miller waited, and the Colonel undid his bedroll and lay down in the deep rich fur to sleep out the night. Long afterwards the Mayor blamed everything on the shining eagle, "It had frightful curled claws and a sharp hooked nose with red terrifying eyes. That's what it did to me."

The Colonel shook himself awake before dawn, five o'clock by his wrist watch accurate as a micrometer, and in only his grey underwear donned a long sheepskin field coat and stumbled into the day's work. Moving about in the dark hallway where his riflemen lay, he left a bright blank cartridge by each man and emptied each weapon of its live ammunition, inspecting each oiled chamber and silver whirling bore. Back in the long bare living room he filled the petrol tin and, hunched in the great curling coat, made himself a pot of black coffee, warming, the while, his hands over the small flame. The Mayor, Stintz and I slept together in the corner, the corporals were buried deep in their cots, and in the basement, trapped amid the piles of debris, Miller waited to see the morning through the narrow slats. The Colonel busied himself with a worn grammar, put his mess kit aside to be cleaned, and let his men sleep for another hour. Finally, ten minutes before six, he dug into his gear and pulled forth his best garrison cap, polished the badge with a rag, left it ready for the important hour and then padded out of doors. His were the first prints through the snow in the back yard; he was the first to break the air still heavy as with waiting flakes. The canal smelled strongly of vermin and slapping rubber, a broken rake handle and emery wheel jutted up through the damp snow, no smoke came from the chimneys on the other bank. Plough handles, shafts of wood, caked earthenware, the jaws of a wooden vice, old scraps of leather filled the slanting shed where the jeep was garaged under the tarpaulin, and a spot of thick green oil spread over the dirt floor. Two planks, nailed along one thin wall that was once a work bench, were bare—for all pieces of metal, tools, iron wheels had been melted down for shells— bare except for a pair of faded pink pants left on one end, shriveled to the size of a fist. The door swung shut behind the Colonel, he rummaged about the shed, thought of the Fraulein who owned the pants, caught with long braids and bright smile, then he reached into the jeep and pulled out another rifle, bright and clean. The odor of chickens, old herbs, mold, mixed with the oil, and he heard the slapping of low water in the canal, trickling over layers and shreds of thin ice. He checked the tires, looked once more about the shed, then walked back to his headquarters across the unkempt white garden.

By six o'clock he had waked the men, decided that the roads were passable and had loaded the new rifle with a live cartridge.

"Here now, Leevey," he called out the window to the still-walking dispatch rider, "you handle the prisoner this morning." Then, while the three of us sat up and blinked, the Colonel shaved, peering into a mechanical mirror that had crooked collapsible legs. After he was dressed, one of the corporals brushed his uniform, helped him bundle back into the heavy coat, and handed him the cap with the bright badge.

By six-thirty the whole town had been raised and stood crammed together in the garden and the motorcycle rider fastened the red cloth about Miller's eyes while, he, the prisoner, stood rigidly on the edge of the canal. The Colonel hurried out, followed by the Mayor, Stintz, and me, and his troop, hurried to see that Miller was placed correctly, checked the time. Though the sky was heavy, he was sure it would not snow, and if they got an early start should be able to cover two hundred miles at least. "Come," he said turning to me, "I need another rifleman. You just take this gun and fall in line with my men." He handed me the new weapon, the fifth, well greased, light, loaded, then arranged our squad in good order. "Mayor," he called, "Mayor, come here." The old man trembled and came forward, his nose grey with the cold, his chest hollow. The Colonel reached into a woollen pocket and brought forth a large white handkerchief, thrust it upon the shivering leader. "Now you hold this over your head, and when you see me nod, drop it." All right, Leevey," called the Colonel, "come away from the prisoner." The water slid by in the canal. Stintz watched carefully, eager for justice, the Census-Taker, drunk, leaned on Madame Snow's arm and held Jutta's hand, watched the white cloth drooping in the dull morning.

"Leevey," said the Colonel when they were abreast, speaking in a lowered voice, "you might see about loading the jeep, we have a long way to go today."

The crowd grew restless, a thin sickly pink began to stain the clouds, the four men and myself raised our short barrels while the two bow ends of the Pastor's red bandanna flapped in a light breeze.

139

His upraised arm began to pain, and the Mayor felt his legs knocking together, backwards and forwards, and he thought he would perish with the cold. Then he caught the glance from the man with the big eagle on his cap and his fingers opened. "It is you who will die," called the Pastor, and the Mayor shut his eyes.

The noise of the rifles sounded small and muffled, padded in the heavy air, and his fingers still felt as if they held the cloth. Miller fell back, dropped through the film of ice and floated jerkily down over the shoals, catching against rocks, dragging over pieces of wood, bumping the flabby rafts, the red cloth flashing for a moment.

"You're a good shot," the Colonel said to me, "that's the gun that did it." The Census-Taker had to be carried back to the house.

A half-hour later the convoy rolled out onto the highway, jeep coughing, the Colonel carefully driving, leaving behind the several posters and proclamations that the motorcycle-rider had pasted up to the peeling walls: "The Government of the United States . . ." For the most part, they were unreadable.

The Mayor thought they were watching him. The sheets were soiled, the Pastor, holding the book, tapped at the shutters, the bird picked at his toes and he took sick because they talked under his window and his conscience was soft, soft as the pink pants . . .

"My God, he's not coming at all!" said Fegelein.

"Don't be a fool, it's almost time." Sometimes I had to be harsh.

"You don't think he'll see the log and stop?"

"Of course not."

I myself began to wich that the *Schmutz* on the little motorcycle would hurry up, morning would soon come and the newspaper office would be waiting, the old women with their bright eyes would be out watching in the streets, the dumb children would be snooping. The land is important, not the *Geist;* the bronx-mongolians, the fat men, the orators, must be struck down. The three of us, the sentries, drew closer together in the low fog.

Herr Stintz, alone in the dark, stood by the open window and listened, looked up at the starless sky, pointed his snout towards the apartment above, straining his muzzle. He, feeling the small girl so close, hearing her breath, felt some of her apprehension, and wide awake did not think of the cold bare walls behind him, or of the pieces of cracked furniture, but concentrated on the heavens, and spied, waiting to see what would happen. And thinking how small and white she was, he tried to divine her secret, thrust his head farther out of the casement, a head that was white, high and narrow, that leaned around corners to hear, and crinkled about the pale eyes with spying. Stintz was hostile to the cold April night air, peered back and forth across the lowering sky, held the birch stick under his arm. He heard Jutta's footsteps overhead as she readied for sleep and pretended to himself that the mother would take the child into her own bed. The nighty was soft and covered with tender prints and only came to the thin knees, the little neckline was flat against the chest.

Madame Snow, erect, frail, wrapped a quilt about Balamir's shoulders where he kneeled on the floor, and by the light of the candle studied the poor creature's face. She found herself listening for footsteps of the second floor roomer, for she knew that the apartment was empty and dark.

The Mayor awoke, wept momentarily, and reached under the bed for a round receptacle. He wanted to know if morning was close but was afraid to open the shutter.

The theater was vast, the audience dead ratters, forgotten bits of paper left on the seats, wet, loose, covered with growth. The drizzle had ceased and a slight wind swept down the aisles, stirring fragments of celluloid, springs, and old playbills. The Duke waited.

"Would you like to buy a ticket?" And his voice still echoing and booming from the cage to the proscenium in unfamiliar strained tones as he stepped from behind the glass and faced the crouched boy.

With winter almost gone, the coagulated underground pipes began to loosen and a thin dark stream of drained seepage flowed, connected every low basement, and trickled about, encircled all the dog-used walls.

Then Herr Stintz heard a voice, small and calm, soft under the covers, "Mother, I saw a light!" And quickly the thin snapping man glanced down over the village, watched the trees, strained his ears upwards, but could hear nothing except a peculiar puttering. Then he saw it, feeble as a flashlight, weak as an old woman's lantern used behind the house, swaying blindly as a bat's eye, gone out behind a sagging barn, free again over the bushes, lost behind a high gate, and then at last it was clear and unbroken, and Stintz, greedy, pop-mouthed, watched it circle slowly along the great curve of, he realized, the *Autobahn*.

At the same time we three heard the sound of the isolated engine as the bastard on the motor approached.

"I'll get him in the behind—*behind,*" I whispered.

The light flared once and went out.

LEADER

A hundred miles from *Spitzen-on-the-Dein* in the
early morning of the day when the killing occurred,
the intended victim, Leevey, lay wearied and in-
jured beside a laughing slut who was covered with
invisible red clap. All through the darkness they had
struggled, baring each other with the point of a
knee, angry and calling each other *schmuck,* and
she had struck his face so that the eyes bled. She
raised her white legs above the sheets, then grimaced
and threw him off, jabbing with her fists as he fell
against the wall. Over and over she said, "My house,
you come to *my* house," but Leevey was afraid that
if he left the safety of his room she would shellac
him, cut with the scissors, and finally leave him
dead with a pin through his neck. For he had heard
the stories, stories of murder in the empty lot, the
special deaths, the vaginae packed with deadly
poison. He clung to her, "You stay here," and her
sharp wooden sandals sliced at his shins and her
unwashed hair fell over his aching shoulder. His
white helmet, goggles, and gauntlets lay beside the
bunk, his tunic and trousers the girl used as a pillow.
"Candy," she said, pinching and poking with her
strong fingers. "Go to hell," he whined and the
forearm crushed down on his nose and mouth,
bruising and dull. Finally, unsuccessful, Leevey tried
to sleep, but she scratched and pushed, whistled in

his ear, squeezed, cried, jammed with her feet, and just as he dozed would slap with all her strength.

The sun gradually brightened the grey walls, the girl's white laughing eyes never left his face, a quick pinch. The heavy tiredness and pain swept over him and he wished he was back in the delicatessen, his long nose pushed among the cheeses.

When she reached the door she turned, leaned her shoulder against the jamb, thrust out her hip and smiled at the feeble one, also filmed now with red invisible clap, tousled and unprotesting, sick in the bunk:

"Auf Wiedersehen, Amerikaner," she said, *"Amerikaner!"*

Leevey doused his face in the basin, slicked down his black hair. "That's life," he said, "that's life," and as the sun rose clear and cold he slung the Sten-gun on his back, polished his boots, fastened the gauntlets, climbed on his rusty motorcycle, and began the tour of his district.

He traveled ninety miles with his palms shivering on the steerhorn handlebars, the white cold air glazed endlessly ahead, his insides smacking against the broad cowhide saddle. He stopped a few times beside an abandoned farm or mis-turned sign or unburied Allied corpse to take a few notes, laying the machine on its side in the mud, and he sweated over the smeared pad and stubby pencil. He was overseer for a sector of land that was one-third of the nation and he frowned with the responsibility, sped along thinking of the letters he would write home, traveled like a gnome behind a searchlight when the sun finally set and the foreign shadows settled. He saw the bare spire rising less than a mile beyond, and crouching down, spattered with grease,

145

he speeded up, to go past *Spitzen-on-the-Dein* with a roar. The late night and crowded broken road twisted around him, flames shot up from the exhaust.

"Wait a minute, I'll be right up, *Kinder*," called Herr Stintz to the upper window. He caught one last glimpse of the slim light with its tail of angry short tongues of fire like a comet, and flinging on a thin coat he bolted for the stairs. He made noise, hurried, was neither meek nor ineffectual, for he felt at last he had the right, the obligation, and his tattling could be open, commanding; for he had seen the light, the unexpected journeyman, the foreign arrival, a fire in the night that no one knew about but he, and now he moved without caution, tripping and whispering, to take possession. Again he opened the door to the top floor apartment, hurried through the first room past the unwaking Jutta where her high breast gleamed from under the sheet, past the full basin and into the smaller, cold lair. "Quickly," he said, "we must hurry. It's up to you and me." She made no protest but watched him with sharp appraising eyes, holding her breath. Stintz picked the little girl from the bundle of clothes, wrapped her in a shortened quilt, tied it with string around her waist, fastened the thick stockings on her feet. He knew exactly what he was about as he dressed the child, considered no question, gave no thought to the sleeping mother. Never before had he been so close; he tied the quilt high about her throat, smoothed the hair once quickly with his hand.

"The moon will see," she murmured, as his good eye swept over her.

"No, no, there isn't any moon at all. Come along."

146

They walked past the woman, hand in hand, into the bitter hallway and he carried her down the stairs, slipped, caught himself, in the hurry. They left the front door ajar and began their walk over the streets smelling of smoke.

The ghosts raised their heads in unison by the canal and sniffed the night air.

I, Zizendorf, my gun drawn, crouching on my knees with my comrades who were tensed like sprinters or swimmers, heard above gusts of wind the approaching light machine. The uprising must be successful, inspired, ruthless.

The Duke carefully reached out his hand and the boy fairy did not move, while the marquee banged to and fro, the projector steamed, and the invisible lost audience stamped booted feet and rummaged in box lunches.

Unconscious, drowned cold in acid, the Census-Taker lay on the third floor, dressed, uncovered, where Jutta had dropped him.

The Mayor, at this hour, groaned, awoke, and found himself pained by a small black-pebble cluster of hemorrhoids, felt it blister upwards over his spine.

The ghosts returned to their cupped hands and sipped the green water, while soft faecal corbans rolled below their faces through the cluttered waves in tribute to Leevey.

Madame Snow thought for a moment that she heard Herr Stintz's voice yelling somewhere up above through the darkest part of the night and drew the robe closer about the kneeling man. Balamir trembled with being awake, frowned and grinned at the old woman, shook as if he was starving on these sleepless hours, tried to speak of the

147

mob of risers, the strength, fear, out in the night, but could not. Stella wondered what they were doing, this anonymous nation, and felt, such an old woman, that she would never sleep again. The candle swayed, her powdered hands fluttered and moved, and then she heard Stintz's sharp footfall and the padding of the girl, and when they left, a breath of air from the front door ajar swept across the floor and stirred the draped figure of her kneeling charge.

Neither could sleep, and somehow the hard yellow eyes of their brethren had told them men were moving, the night was not still. Madame Snow did not find the rooms changed by this darkness or added cold, simply the cups eluded her fingers, slipped more easily, the tea was like black powder and too much escaped, the pot assumed enormous proportions. But waking, she found the same day and night except that in the darkness it was more clear, the air smelled more heavily of the sewer in the canal, the carpets smelled more of dust.

On the fifth floor Jutta awoke and feeling less tired, began to wash a blouse in the hand-basin.

The tea was so near the chipped brim that it spilled over his robe when he peered closely at the cup and twisted it about. Stella drew the curtains but could see nothing, from the front windows neither street nor light, from the rear windows neither the line of the canal nor the shed. At first when the main pipes were destroyed she boiled the water that had to be taken from the canal, but for months the fire did not last long enough, the effort to prod the dull coals was too great, and tonight the tea tasted more sour than usual. In unlocking the basement door she had noticed that the smell of

the canal was becoming stronger, the water seeping
from its imperfect bed, and she decided that she
must find a new place to keep the harmless unmoving man. The old woman, hair thin about her scalp
but falling thickly to her waist, ankles frail without
stockings in the high unbuttoned shoes, sipping tea
through her thin once bowed lips, hated nothing,
did not actually despise the gross invader or the
struggling mistaken English, but would have been
pleased to see them whipped. She knew the strength
of women, and sometimes vaguely hoped that a
time would come again when they could attack flesh
with their husband's sickles, and the few husbands
themselves could take the belts from their trousers
to flay the enemy. It was the women who really
fought. The uprising must be sure, and the place to
strike with the tip of the whip's tail was between the
legs. The candle went out and the brilliant old
woman and crazed man sat in the darkness for a
long while.

They had waited weeks for the riot to come at the
institution and when it finally did descend like a
mule to its haunches it lasted barely an hour. During those weeks disorder accumulated, both inside
and outside the high walls. The German army was
suffering unreasonable blows, the town was bereft
of all men, the food trucks were overtaken by hordes
of frenzied children, the staff itself worked in the
gardens and nurses spent part of their duty in the
bakery. Switchboard connections were crossed; Supply sent barrels of molasses but no meat; the cold
came in dreadful waves. All reading material went
to the furnaces; several cases of insulin went bad;
and the board of directors learned of the deaths of

149

their next of kin. Bedpans were left unemptied in the hallways; and for days on end the high bright gates of iron were never opened. Finally they burned linen for fuel and a thick smudge poured from the smokestack, the snow rose higher against the walls, and they served only one meal a day. One of the oldest night nurses died and her body was smuggled from the institution under cover of darkness. Reports crept out on the tongues of frightened help, of unshaven men, quarreling women, of patients who slept night after night fully dressed, of men who had hair so long that it hung on their shoulders. And those inside the walls heard that greater numbers of the more fit women were being taken to war, that there wasn't a single man left in the town, that Allied parachute rapists were to be sent on the village, that pregnant women went out of doors at night to freeze themselves to death.

The patients would no longer go to their rooms but crowded together in the long once immaculate corridors and baited each other or lay in sullen heaps, white with the cold. They had to be prodded into going out to the garden, white, filled with frozen thistle, and threatened, pushed, forced to retreat back to the buildings. Fearing more than ever erratic outbursts or startled, snarling attacks, the nurses quickly used up the last row of bottled sedatives, and old ferocious men lay only half-subdued, angrily awake through the long nights. One of these nurses, short, man-like, tense, lost the only set of keys that locked the windows shut, so for the last few days and nights, the horrible cold swept in and out of the long guarded wings. Underneath the ordered town-like group of brick buildings, there were magnificent tile and steel tunnels connecting them to underground laboratories, laundries, kitchens, and ventilated rooms that housed monkeys and rats for experimentation. Through these tunnels ran thin lines of gleaming rails where hand-carts of refuse, linen, chemicals, and food were pushed and the carts were guided by a meticulous system of red and yellow lights. During these bad days the carts were pushed too fast, knocked each other from the tracks, the system of lights smashed, the upturned carts blocked the corridors, and broken bottles and soiled linen filled the passages. The lighting system short-circuited and orderlies, now trying to carry the supplies in their arms, stumbled through the narrow darkness, through the odor of ferment, and shouted warning signals.

At last the rats and monkeys died. Their bodies were strewn over the main grounds, and since they froze, they looked life-like, tangled together on the snow.

All attempts at cure ceased. The bearded, heartening groups of doctors on rounds no longer appeared, nothing was written on charts. The tubs were left cold and dry, and patients no longer came back to the wards red, unconscious, shocked. Not only was treatment stopped, but all activity impossible. They no longer wove the useless rugs, no longer ran uncertainly about the gymnasium, no longer argued over cards or shot the billiard balls back and forth across the table. There were no showers, no baths, no interviews, no belts to make and take apart and make; and the news from the outside was dangerous. They could only be driven out to the garden and driven in.

Some insisted that the monkeys on the blanket of snow moved about during the night, and in the day it was difficult to keep the curious patients from the heaps of small black corpses.

The village, as the days grew worse, became a dump for abandoned supplies, long lines of petrol tins along the streets, heaps of soiled torn stretchers and cases of defective prophylactics piled about doorways, thrown into cellars. Piles of worthless cow-pod Teller mines blocked the roads in places and a few looted armored cars still smelled of burned cloth and hair. Women nursed children as large as six years old, and infrequently some hurrying official, fat, drunk with fear, would come into the village of women and bring unreliable news of the dead. Wives did not know whether their husbands were dead, or simply taken prisoner, did not know whether they had been whipped on capture or stood against a wall and shot. Hatless children ran through the deepening snow and chased the few small birds still clinging to the stricken trees. On the day before the riot an American deserter was discovered in a barn and, untried, was burned to death. Several pockets of sewer gas exploded in the afternoon.

It snowed for nights on end, but every morning the monkeys appeared uncovered, exactly the same as the day they were tossed into the yard, wiry, misshapen, clutching in their hands and feet the dead rats. When vigilance became more and more impractical, all poisons, orange crystals of cyanide and colorless acids, were thrown into the incinerator, and with despondent precaution all sharp instruments were destroyed. They were disturbed; several unrecognized, unwashed doctors wandered without memory in the pack of patients and one young dietician thought she was the common-law wife of a fifty-nine-year-old hebephrenic. On the night before the uprising, thieves tore down the wooden sign inscribed with the haven word "asylum," burned it during the coldest dawn recorded, and the institution was no longer a retreat.

Before dawn on the morning of the riot, Madame Snow stood alone by candlelight in a back room where cordwood had been piled, holding a stolen chicken struggling lightly beneath her fingers. She did not see the four stone walls or the narrow open window, and standing in a faded gown with the uneven hem that was once for balls, the untied soiled kimono flapping against her legs, she looked into the frightful eyes of the chicken and did not feel the cold. Her bare feet were white, the toes covered with grains of sawdust. The door behind her was locked, tallow dripped from the gilt holder and the bird fluttered, tried to shake its wings from the firm grasp. The old woman's pulse beat slowly, more slowly, but steadily, and the narrow unseen window began to turn grey. The feathers, bitten with mange, trembled and breathed fearfully. The soft broken claws kicked at her wrist. For a moment the Kaiser's face, thin, depressed, stared in at the cell window, and then was gone, feeling his way over a land that was now strange to his touch. The old woman watched the fowl twisting its head, blinking the pink-lidded eyes, and carefully she straddled the convulsing neck with two fingers, tightened them across the mud-caked chest, and with the other hand seized the head that felt as if it were all bone and moving bits of scale. The pale yellow feet paddled silently backwards and forwards, slits breathed against her palm. Madame Snow clenched her fists and quickly flung them apart so that the fowl's head spurted across the room, hit the wall and fell into a heap of shavings, its beak clicking open and shut, eyes staring upwards at the growing light. She dropped the body with its torn neck and squeezed with fingermarks into a bucket of water, and stooping in the grey light, squinted, and plucked the feathers from the front of her kimono.

A few moments later the messenger, angry, half-asleep, pounded on the window of the front room and shouted, "Riot, riot up at the madhouse," and clattered off, banging on more doors, calling to startled women, distracted, wheezing.

By the time Stella reached the Mayor's, still in the kimono, hair flying, she found a great quarreling crowd of women already gathered. The Mayor, before taking control of the villagers asked to send aid, had girdled the red sash around his nightgowned stomach, and distrait but strong, he stood on the ice-covered steps passing out equipment and words of encouragement to the already violent hags.

"Ah, Madame Snow, Madame Snow," he called, "you will take command on the march and in the attack. I leave it all up to you." Outstretched hands clamored in his face.

"Did you hear?" he shouted.

"Yes, I heard."

When all of the women had shouldered the barrel-staves which he had distributed, and fastened the black puttees about their bare legs, they started off, Stella in the lead and running as fast as she could. Jutta was tickling the Census-Taker at the time and only heard of the trouble afterwards. Madame Snow's hands were still covered with the blood of the chicken, and back in the small room its beak was clamped open. When they reached the iron fence and the gates were thrown open, the women stopped short, silent, moved closer together, brandished the staves, and looked at the band of inmates huddled together on the other side of the heap of monkeys. One of the monkeys seemed to have grown, and frozen, was sitting upright on the bodies of the smaller beasts, tail coiled about his neck, dead eyes staring out through the gates, through the light of early morning as dim and calm as the moon. "Dark is life, dark, dark is death," he suddenly screamed as the women charged across the snow.

All was hushed that morning, and in a dark wing of building 41, Balamir lay waiting among his unsleeping brothers and wished that someone would let in the cat. The male nurse who had been on duty three days and nights sat dozing in the stiff-backed chair and Balamir could see the white lifeless watch with its hanging arms. Along the length of the corridor were the rows of small empty rooms, and the signal lights over the swinging doors were burned out. An old cleaning woman, stooped and bent with the hem of her grey skirt hiding her feet, shuffled from the upper end to the lower of the monastic hall, dragging a mop over the outstretched legs, mumbling to herself, "Now it's quite all right, you'll all be well soon, yes, you'd be surprised at all I've seen come and go." The feathers of the mop were dry and frozen.

From the windows of building 41 one could see the irregular white fields stretching off to patched acres of sparse forest land, the game field with its bars and benches heaped with snow. Sometimes dimly through the grillwork of adjacent buildings, an unrecognizable single figure passed back into the shadows. The cleaning woman fumbled with the key

155

ring fastened by a thin brass chain around her waist and went through the smooth metal door and down the deserted stairs. Suddenly a little wiry man with small fragile hands and feet and a clay pipe clutched in his teeth, ran to the door and facing it, trembled with anger.

"Don't you ever say such a thing to me again, don't you dare say that, if I hear it again, if you dare speak to me I'll break your back, I'll break it and cripple you, so help me," he screamed.

The nurse awoke with a start, reached for his smoldering cigarette. "Here, Dotz," he called, "stop that yelling . . ." but quickly, before he could move, the whole hallway of men, stamping and crying, followed Dotz through the door and out into the fresh air. Once out, no one knew the way in, and already a few white coats were excited and gave chase.

From a fourth floor window the Director, wrapped in a camel's hair coat, watched the struggle until he saw the women, led by Stella, rush the ridiculous inmates; he drew the blinds and returned to his enormous files.

During that hour the monkeys were so underfoot that the patients were saved from worse injury by the clumsiness of the women who shouted and tore and pelted everything in sight. As these women in the midst of changing years ran to and fro beating, slashing, the stiff tails and hard outstretched arms and furry brittle paws smacked against black puttees and were trampled and broken in the onslaught. Several wooden shoes were left jammed in rows of teeth smashed open in distortion by the stamping feet. The barrel-staves broke on unfeeling shoulders, the rats' bodies were driven deeper into the snow.

"Here, you," suddenly cried the cleaning woman from the main doorway, "come back in here," and the troop of men disappeared, kicking the stained snow in violent flurries. Suddenly the deputized women found themselves alone and standing on the mutilated carcasses of little men, and with a pained outcry, they fled from the grounds. "You won't say it again?" said Dotz, but no one answered and they settled back to rest in silence. The sun came out high and bright at nine o'clock and lasted the whole day, striking from the tiles and bricks, melting the snow, and the Director finally issued an order for the burial of the animals.

Leevey was killed outright when his motorcycle crashed into the log. He was pitched forward and down into an empty stretch of concrete. The Stengun, helmet, and boots clattered a moment, canvas and cloth and leather tore and rubbed; then he lay quiet, goggles still over his eyes, pencil, pad, whistle and knife strewn ahead. The three of us quickly leaped upward over the embankment, crouched in the darkness a moment, and then eagerly went to work. I was the first to reach the motorcycle and I cut the ignition, guided it over the bank. We picked up Leevey and carried him down to his machine, lost none of his trinkets, then together rolled the log until it slid down the muddy slope and settled in silence in a shallow stream of silt.

"It's not smashed badly," said Fegelein and ran his fingers over the bent front rim, felt broken spokes brushing against his sleeve, felt that the tank was slightly caved-in and petrol covered his hand. "You'll be riding it in a month."

I put my ear to the thin chest but could hear

157

nothing, for Leevey had gone on to his native sons who sat by the thousands amid fields of gold, nodding their black curly heads, and there, under a sunshine just for them, he would never have to bear arms again. The night had reached its darkest and most silent hour, just before dawn comes. Still there were no stars, the mist grew more dense overhead and even the dogs no longer howled. My fingers brushed the stiffening wrist.

"Are you ready?" asked my comrade by the machine.

I felt closer, more quickly, pulled away the cuff of the jacket, tore as quietly as possible at the cloth over the wrist.

"What's the matter with you? What are you doing anyway?" The voice was close; Stumpfegle also drew closer to my side.

"Eh, what's up?" The hoarse whispers were sharp.

I pulled at the strap, carefully, faster, and finally spoke, "He's got a watch." I leaned closer to the corpse.

"Well, give it here, you can't keep it just like that . . ."

I brought the pistol dimly into sight again, shoved the watch into my pocket, "I'm the leader and don't forget it. It's only right that I have the watch. Take the sacks off the machine and leave them here. We'll share what we can find, but not the watch."

Fegelein was already back tinkering with the engine. I listened to the watch and heard its methodical beat and could see the intricate clean dials rotating in precise fractions. The tongue was now sucked firmly and definitely into the back of Leevey's throat and his knees had cracked upwards and grown rigid. "We had better get him out of here." We picked him up and with the motorman between us stepped into the shallow ooze of the stream and headed out beyond the wall of fog towards the center of the lowlands.

On the opposite side of the highway, hidden in the shadows of unoccupied low buildings and the high bare spire wet with dew, stood Herr Stintz fixing everything closely in his mind, holding the little girl tightly by the hand. The child crossed and uncrossed the cold white legs, watched the black shadows leaping about in the middle of the road. Then they were gone.

Jutta yawned, carried the damp blouse into the next room, and opening the rear window, hung it from a short piece of wire dangling from a rusty hook. For a moment she smelled the sour night air, heard the lapping of water, and then returned to the still warm bed to wait the morning.

The limping English ghosts made their way back to the tank and stood silently waiting for the light when they would have to climb again through the hatch and sit out the day in the inferno of the blackened Churchill.

The Duke, breathing heavily, slowly extended his arm, and as the boy moved, clamped the diamond ringed fingers over the light shoulder and breathed easier. Footsteps sounded in the upper part of the clay-smelling theater and the projector began to grind and hum, then stilled again.

Very cold, the Mayor crawled out of bed, went to his closet and taking an armful of coats and formal trousers, heaped them on the bed. But it was still cold.

Madame Snow lit the candle again and saw that the quilted man was sleeping, and hearing no sound, no one returning to the second floor apartment, she decided to get dressed and simply await the day. She began to tie up the long strands of white and gold hair, and reaching into a bulky wardrobe found herself a formless white chemise.

"My God, the fog is thick."

"We're almost there," I replied.

"Which way?"

"A little to the right, I think."

The formless white puddles of fog moved, shifted among the stunted trees, rose, fell, trailed away in the areas of sunken swampwood where once tense and cowed scouting parties had dared to walk into the bayonet on guard, or to walk on a trigger of a grenade that had blown up waist high. An axle of a gun carriage stuck up from the mud like a log, a British helmet, rusted, old, hung by a threadbare strap from a broken branch.

"He's heavy."

"They feed the Americans well, you know," I answered.

"Well, he's going where they all belong."

Several times we stopped to rest, sitting the body upright in the silt that rose over his waist. A shred of cloth was caught about a dead trunk, the fog dampened our skin. Each time we stopped, the white air moved more than ever in and out of the low trees, bearing with it an overpowering odor, the odor of the ones who had eaten well. More of the trees were shattered and we, the pallbearers, stumbled with each step over half-buried pieces of steel.

"Let's leave him here."

"You know we cannot. Follow the plan."

Past the next tree, past the next stone of a gun

breech blasted open like a mushroom, we saw a boot, half a wall, and just beyond, the swamp was filled with bodies that slowly appeared one by one from the black foliage, from the mud, from behind a broken wheel. A slight skirmish had developed here and when the flare had risen over this precise spot, glowed red and died in the sky, some twenty or thirty dead men were left, and they never disappeared. The fog passed over them most thickly here, in relentless circles, and since it was easier to breathe closer to the mud, we stooped and dragged the body forward.

"You see, no one could ever find him among these. No one would ever look for him here." My idea for disposing of the body was excellent.

After searching the body once more, we left it and found our way again to the roadside. We took the machine and its valuable saddlebags silently through the town to the newspaper office.

"It's time we had our meeting," I said, "I'll be back." Fegelein began to work on the engine; Stumpfegle broke the head from a bottle.

The slut slept alone in her own house.

LAND

Madame Stella Snow's son, awakened by the barking of a dog, lay quiet, holding his breath like a child in the darkness. But it was not the dog that woke him, it was a theatrical sound, some slight effect, some trick of the playhouse itself, and he listened. Perhaps he had left the projector switch on, perhaps the lights were burning, or the spools of film unrolling. Whatever had happened, he did hear, in the intervals of distant howling, a woman's voice, an argument in the floors below between the empty seats. The dampness of the auditorium swept through the building, warehouse of old scenes, and his own bedroom, once a storeroom and place where the usherettes changed from frocks to uniforms, was cold and dark. It still smelled faintly of powder, stacks of mildewed tickets, cans of film and tins of oil. The voice, high and aristocratic, sounded like his mother's, changed, then seemed once more familiar. The girls had actually changed their clothes, changed into pants, in this room. The concrete walls, like a *bunker,* were damp and cold; light sockets, wire, and a few tools still littered the floor. The voices were still below, he thought he could hear someone weeping, the woman scolded, laughed, and talked on. His wife slept, her body shapeless and turned away under the quilt.

It took all of his effort to get out of the bed.

First, with one hand, he reached to the side and clutched the pipe that ran, cold to his fingers, under the mattress. With the other hand, he threw off the covers, and with a quick odd motion tossed his stump over the other leg, twisted his torso, flung his arm out to add weight to the stump's momentum, and precariously threw himself upright. It was even harder to get into the trousers; he succeeded by rocking forwards and backwards, pulling quickly with his hands, always with the good leg in the air, keeping the balance. He smelled the perfume and old celluloid. Fixing his hands into the two aluminum canes, like shafts into a socket, ball bearings in oil, he made his way out into the hall, and since he couldn't as yet manage the stairs, hooked the canes to his belt, sat down, and holding the stump out of the way, made his trip bouncing down the three flights.

He could no longer hear the voices or the dog, only his own thumping on the cold stairs and the rattle of the thin metal legs dragging behind him. He moved like a duck, propelled himself forward with his two arms in unison and landed on the next step on the end of his spine. Something compelled him to move faster and faster until he was numb and perspiring, dropped with only the edge of the wall against his shoulder to guide him, fell with his palms becoming red and sore. Using the canes as props and the wall against his back he rose, laboriously, at the bottom of his flight, and listened for the woman's voice. But the voices had heard him coming, thumping, and were still. He waited, sensing them on the other side of the metal, fireproof door. He hesitated, then with an effort swung open the door and stepped into the rear of the audi-

163

torium, feeling in the dark many eyes turned upon his entrance. Slowly he hobbled forward, and seeing the large hat and magnificent cane, he laughed at himself and recognized the tall man.

"Ah, Herr Duke," he said, "I thought I heard voices in my theater. But did not expect this pleasure."

"You are right," said the Duke. "I've come after my neighbor's child, this boy here."

Then he saw the boy crouching down in an aisle, no longer weeping, but watching the two men. What a peculiar voice the Duke had, certainly a strange one considering his size and bearing.

"Boy, you should be home in bed."

"Yes," said the Duke in now more normal tones, "I'm taking him home. Forgive us the disturbance."

The child made no sound but allowed himself to be caught, in one quick swoop, about the wrist and pulled to his feet.

"Good night," said the tall man and left with his prize.

"Ja, ja, Herr Duke." The lame man watched the two go out into the still-wet streets, and turning himself, went back to the heavy door.

At the foot of the door his shoe was caught in a large poster, and looking down he saw an actress in a shining gown, wrinkled and scuffed about the breasts and hips.

"Good night, Herr Duke," he said, and freeing his single shoe from the woman's hold, he set out to climb back up the stairs. It was painful to his good leg going up, but even so he felt an uncommon pleasure in the visit of the Duke and the night's events.

I had been gone from the newspaper office only a moment, when Stumpfegle, who was drinking from the broken bottle, and Fegelein, who was rummaging through the motorcycle saddlebags, heard my footsteps returning to the door, and became alert. Both men looked up as I, their leader, stepped back into the office. I was hurried, disturbed, absorbed in the underworld of the new movement, bearing alone the responsibilities of the last attempt. I looked at my confederates and was annoyed with the liquor trickling from one chin, the contents of the bags strewn over the floor from the other's hands.

"Somebody saw us take care of the fellow on the motorbike."

"But, my God, Leader, what can we do?" Fegelein dropped a packet of Leevey's letters from him and looked up in fear.

"We'll have to change things. Bring the machinery, the arms, and everything else, to Command Two."

"Command Two?"

"Snow, idiot, behind Snow's boarding house."

Fegelein had the memory of a frog, a despicable blind green wart to whom all pads, all words, were the same.

"Bring the small press, the motor, bring all the materials for the pamphlets. Oh, yes, bring the whitewash."

"Leader, the machine will be ready to ride tomorrow . . ."

"Stumpfegle, you might ride yourself into the canal with ten American bullets, fired by well-armed Jewish slugs, in your fat belly, you childish fat fool. Don't *think*, do you understand, don't

165

think of the machine, think of nothing except what we must do now. The night's not over, fat Stumpfegle, I don't want you shot. There are many *Anglo-Schmutzigs* we've got to poison with our print tonight. So please, just do the work." I nodded, forgot my temper, and slipped back into the darkness. Fegelein began to read the letters.

The oil flickered in the lamp, consumed and consuming, and as it burned, a few hoarded drops in the bottom of the tin, it shrouded the glass and beneath the film the flame was dimmed. After a considerable swig, the bottle, its neck jagged, filled and refilled, was put down on the floor, the dead man's letters were cast aside, unfit for reading, and the scraps, bundles, clips and type were collected. The patriots, fool and tinker, got themselves to work for power. It was no drunken lark. A difficult hour they had of it at that time of night, the worst time of night for odds and ends and order, especially after killing a man and with sleep so near. The light bright, the shutters drawn, the secret hard for dull minds to keep, the arms scattered, the work small and heavy, the very hardest time of night; this was the hour to try the henchmen.

In an alley by the press was a heavy cart, and Fegelein, the quicker of the two, made hurried trips with spools of thread, staples, needles, small loads of paper, and old bottles of ink. He thought of the witness and the accusing finger, saw the jurystand and unpredictable black-robed judge. Each time he dropped his load, so light but necessary, into the bottom of the cart, he looked up at the sky and feared the exposing dawn. There was no one to trust. Inside the shop the cobwebs were thick between the presses, the bottles piled higher near the rolltop desk, and old broken headlines were scattered, mere metal words, about the floor.

Stumpfegle, fat and cold, carried the small press out to the cart and rested. He carried the stitching machine out to the cart and waited, back by the lamp, for his friend to finish. Stumpfegle, ex-orderly and seeking power, torturer and next in command, harbored, beneath his ruthless slowness, the memory and the valor of his near suicide. Months before, he had lost his chance, though a better man than Fegelein. Stumpfegle, forty-two, aggressive, a private, was captured by a soldier from New York cited for bravery, when he wandered, dazed, into an American Intelligence Headquarters set up for propaganda work. Recognizing the *Reichsoldat*, the American immediately took Stumpfegle into the doctor's office, a room with a filing cabinet and fluoroscope. Quickly they put the big man under its watchful, scientific-research eye, and sure enough, imbedded far below his waist, between the sigmoid flexure and the end, they could see the silver object, the *Reichgeist* capsule, container of blissful death. An hour later, and while the soldier and the doctor watched, the purgative which they had given the bewildered prisoner worked, and Stumpfegle's last hope was dashed, in a moment of agony, down the privy-drain. He survived, with a soft pain where it had been, and gained his freedom to return to the new life.

"I'm finished except for the paint. We should hurry."

Stumpfegle slowly carried the can of whitewash to the cart, strapped himself between the heavy shafts, and with Fegelein wheeling the motorbike, they started down the dark street.

The Mayor fell asleep while vague white animals pranced and chattered through his dreams. Miller wished pain upon him, and kicked up his sharp heels and flew away, only to return with the Colonel on his back and a rifle under his belly to plague the poor mare, hot and sore with age. The white handkerchief was over his eyes, his legs were tied, and all those animals of youth and death, the historical beasts, danced about to watch. It was cold and the kitchen was empty.

The Duke and the boy were halfway down the hill towards the institution where a sack was hidden behind the town girls' bush. The dance music ceased in the storehouse below, the only lights were out. The cane once more was raised and the child, spattered with mud, tried without success to break away. A sleeper cocked his legs behind the storehouse.

"We're almost there. But let's try to hurry, will you?" The faster Fegelein tried to go, the more trouble he had with the machine. Yet he urged and he slipped. The shadow of the spy crossed their path.

The ghosts by the canal all watched, their heads together in the turret of the tank, the spirit of Leevey crawling to meet them from the dark water. A gaunt bird settled on the throat of the headless horse statue in the center of the town and mist fell on the grey sideless spire near the *Autobahn*.

The new watch on my wrist showed three o'clock. It was almost over. Tomorrow the loyal would know and be thankful, the disloyal would be taken care of. By tomorrow this first murder of the invaders would be public news; it would be, rather than a resistance, a show of strength. My footsteps echoed behind me in the darkness, somewhere the traitor was about, and then with a new energy swept upon me, I reached the boarding house. This town had no particular significance, as I entered the hall, because all towns were towns of the land, villages where idleness breeds faith, and the invaders hatred. Yet I knew this town, and in the days of power would always return, for I knew each disappointment, each girl, each silent doorway. I began to climb the stairs and on the next landing, knew the second floor boarder was still out.

My order, the new campaign, was planned and begun. It was spreading, conception and detail, to the borders of the land, aimed at success. The initial blow was struck, the enemy unseated, and there remained only the message to be dealt with and the traitor in our midsts to be undone. I opened the door and saw her warm and girlish arms.

It seemed she had been sleeping for only a moment and the bed was still warm where I had been.

The Census-Taker mumbled in his sleep two floors below, his shirt out of his trousers, wringing wet. They danced on his toes, it was so warm.

Gently pushing the covers back, she rolled slowly over, thinking of my warm brown chest.

Softly she spoke, "Come back to bed, Zizendorf." She wanted to fall asleep again.

She seemed to have forgotten, this flush Jutta, where I had been, love without sense. I sat in the chair facing the bed.

Then, curling her hair in her fingertips, stretching her knees, she remembered.

"It's done?"

"Of course. He fell as easy as a duck, that area-commander. He's out in the swamp with his comrades now."

"But how did you stop him?"

"The log." I bent over and loosened my shoes. "The log stopped him. You'd think that when he hit it he'd fly, perhaps swoop over it in a pleasant arc or at least in a graceful curve. But that's not true. He and the whole machine simply toppled over it, spokes and light and helmet flying every which way. Nothing grand about the commander's end at all!"

"You're safe? And now you can come and get warm."

Jutta feared cold as once she had feared the Superior's sun.

"The rest of the plan is still to be done."

Stintz pushed the child ahead with loving hands and silently she crept up the stairs. "You mustn't tell anyone what you saw, the moon will be angry," and she was gone into the darkness.

"I'd like to stroke your lovely heart and your hair. But there's still work."

"And I suppose there'll be even more when you reach success?" She yawned.

"Night should be mine, always."

The child stole into the room, back with Mother, shivering in her thin gown for all the long tiring adventure. I, the Leader, smiled, and Jutta held out her hand across the hard pillows and cold topcover.

"My darling child, where have you been?" Absently she touched the thin arm and it felt hard, frail.

"What a strange little girl," I thought. Something stirred below, more like the sound of night than human, perhaps the mechanical movement of the trees against the house.

"I saw a man with a light, racing along where no one ever goes any more."

Surely this was not the spy, the lean shadow I had seen for a moment. But she must know the traitor, perhaps was taken in his bob-cat steps and walked by his side.

"What was he doing?" I spoke quietly with a special voice for children, carried over from the days before the Allied crimes and war.

"He didn't do anything. Somebody put something in the road and he was killed. His light was smashed."

"How did you go to see the man? Did someone take you for a walk?"

Suddenly she was afraid. She recognized my voice perhaps.

"The moon did it. The moon's a terrible thing in the sky and will be angry if I tell you anything. He'd kill me too."

"You go to bed, go to sleep," said Jutta, and the child ran into the next room. But she didn't sleep, she waited, awake in the dark, to see what would happen.

The honest man is the traitor to the State. The man with the voice only for those above him, not for citizens, tells all and spreads evil. His honesty is a hopeless misgiving. He makes the way intangible and petty, he hampers determination.

Stintz, barely back in his room, stood by the window and raised the sash. Peering with excited eyes, he looked at the turning in the darkness where he had first seen the light of the victim and tense with anticipation he slowly looked across the dark town-site, to the spot, what a joy, where the victim fell.

What a pleasure it had been, he knew I was up to something, and the child, this was the perfect touch, to make her follow the father and murderer through the darkness! Oh, he knew it was I all right, animal-devil, who took the blood tonight, but his thrill was in the justice, not the crime, no one would accuse except himself. Soon he would hear the footsteps, soon he would be the judge and all the knowledge would come to bear, in the rope, on the father of the child. The sky, for Stintz, was clearing; he hoped, in the morning, to inform.

Her face was so flushed, overjoyed with night, that I disliked leaving.

"I'll be back soon," I said, and she turned the other way to go to sleep. I heard the rustling again in the room below.

Stintz expected the knock on the door and said, "Come," almost before he heard it.

"Zizendorf," he said without turning, "come here."

The tuba lay on the floor between the visitor and host, instrument of the doleful anthem, puckered to the school-teacher's thin lips, battered and dull with long, tremulous, midnight sobs. Stintz still looked out of the window, as if to look all night and talk in the morning, alive and gaping over the streets he could never help to smooth and make prosperous, laughing and useless, watching the scenes of other people's accidents and deeds.

"What do you see?" I picked up the tuba and stood by the black-frocked teacher's side. I hated the braying sounds of the horn.

"Look. It's out again. The moon's out from behind the cloud. Look at him, he sees everything,

Zizendorf. He watches the lonely travelers, he hangs heavy over demons, terrible and powerful. The just man."

The edges showed white and distant for a moment and then the moon was gone. So faint, just a patch of grey in an unpleasant sky, that most people would not have looked at it a second time. Only the pious, with an inward craving for communion, would bother to crane their necks and strain their souls. I noticed that Stintz's neck jutted far out of the window, the bony face held rigidly upwards. The musty smell of textbooks lingered on the black coat, his arms were paralyzed on the sill.

The moon, the moon who knows everything, seemed to me like the bell of the tuba, thick and dull, awkward in my hands.

"You like the moon, don't you, Stintz? It seems frail to me, weak and uncolorful, tonight. I wouldn't put my faith in it."

His room should have been filled with clammy little desks, with silent unpleasant children to make faces.

"See here, I don't think I like your tone, you yourself may not be out of its reach, you know. There's retribution for everyone in this country now, justice, and it doesn't roll along a road where it can be trapped. Someone always *knows,* you really can't get away with anything . . ."

I swung the tuba short. I should have preferred to have some distance and be able to swing it like a golf club. But even as it was, Stintz fell, and half-sitting against the wall, he still moved for a moment.

Two things were wrong; there was the lack of room and I had misjudged the instrument itself.

173

Somehow thinking of the tuba as squat, fat, thinking of it as a mallet I had expected it to behave like a mallet; to strike thoroughly and dull, to hit hard and flat. Instead it was the rim of the bell that caught the back of Stintz's head, and the power in my arms was misdirected, peculiarly unspent. I struck again and the mouthpiece flew from the neck and sang across the room. I was unnerved only for a moment and when finally out in the hall, thought I would have preferred a stout club. Stintz no longer moved.

Stumpfegle and Fegelein were already encamped in the chicken coop, in the shed where the Colonel's jeep had been. I could hear them working as I walked across the yard behind the boarding house, their slight scuffle barely audible above the trickling of the canal. The pink pants and the plank that served as workbench had been tossed out into the darkness, and the shed was almost ready for the composition and the printing of the word. However, the cart was still loaded. I was disturbed to think that the press was not yet set up.

It was a heavy job to clear away the coating of chicken debris. The walls were thickly covered with the white plaster-like formations, hard and brittle, the effort of so many hens, less and less as the grain became scarce, finally water, with nothing left but the envied heaps of better days. Here and there a pale feather was half sealed in the encrustation. It would wave slightly, without hope of flight, embedded in the fowl-coral reefs of the wooden walls. The odor of the birds was in the wood, not in their mess; secretly in the earthen floor, not in the feathers. It was strong and un-removable. Fegelein hacked with a rusty spike, Stumpfegle slowly with the dull edge of a hoe, their dark suits becoming slowly speckled with calcium white.

I stood in the open door, trying not to breathe, allergic to the must-filled air, brushing the feathers and white powder from my jacket. I remembered the white women and darkness of Paris.

"I got rid of the traitor."

"But, Leader, that's magnificent." The foreign arm of justice, with its conundrums, lynchings and impeccable homes, lifted from Fegelein's brow, and the hard chicken foam gave with greater ease.

"It's one less fool to worry about, at least. And by tomorrow, we will have our public, proclaimed and pledged, every single one of them incorporated by a mere word, a true effort, into a movement to save them. Put into the open, the fools are helpless."

"Ah, yes," said Fegelein.

Stumpfegle hated the shed so much that he had no time for our talk. The odor of the flown birds, the stench, seemed like the country to him, and he was meant for the city, the shop with machines. "Birds piddle so," he thought, "it's unhealthly and unreal except for the smell."

"Success is almost ours."

Finally the shed was almost clean, with only a few globs left, and after quickly whitewashing the walls, they brought in the press, the stapler, the rollers and the reams of cheap paper. The three of us were spattered with the wash, became luminous and tired. Stumpfegle stood by the delivery table, Fegelein by the feed table, while I, the Leader, the compositor, put the characters, the words of the new voice, into the stick. I wrote my message as I went, putting the letters into place with the tweezers, preparing my first message, creating on a stick the new word. The print fell into place, the engine sputtered, filling the shed with the fumes of stolen gasoline. I wrote, while my men waited by the press, and my message flared from the begrimed black type:

INDICTMENT OF THE ALLIED ANTAGONISTS, AND PROCLAMATION OF THE GERMAN LIBERATION:

English-speaking Peoples: Where are the four liberties of the Atlantic Charter? Where is liberty and humanity for the sake of which your government has sent you into this war? All this is nothing as long as your government has the possibility of ruling the mob, of sabotaging Peace by means of intrigues, and of being fed with a constant supply from the increasingly despairing masses—America, who has fostered you upon a bereaved world only turns her masses of industry against that world, the muzzles of her howitzers of insanity and greed against a continent that she herself contaminates.

While you have been haranguing and speculating in Democracy, while you have branded and crucified continental Europe with your ideologies, Germany has risen. We proclaim that in the midst of the rubble left in your path there exists an honorable national spirit, a spirit conducive to the unification of the world and poisonous to the capitalistic states. The rise of the German people and their reconstruction is no longer questionable—the land, the Teutonic land, gives birth to the strongest of races, the Teutonic race.

People of Germany: We joyfully announce that tonight the Third Allied Commander, overseer

176

of Germany, was killed. The Allies are no longer in power, but you, the Teutons, are once more in control of your futures, your civilization will once more rise. The blood that is in your veins is inevitable and strong. The enemy is gone, and in this hour of extermination of our natural foe we give thanks to you, your national spirit that has flown, at long last, from Western slavery.

We pay tribute to the soul of Cromwell of the first war, who, realizing the power of the Goths and forsaking his weakened England, instigated the Germanic Technological Revolution. It is on his inspiration that the East looms gloriously ahead, and on his creed that the Teuton hills and forests will design their Native Son.

From the ruins of Athens rise the spires of Berlin.

I put down the tweezers. Without a word, but quivering with excitement, Fegelein locked the stick in place and the press murmured louder. Stumpfegle watched unmoved as the sheets, hardly legible, began to fall, like feathers, on the delivery table. Actually, I had never seen Berlin.

Madame Snow heard the animals rummaging in the shed, heard the foreign clatter disturbing the night.

"Ah, poor creature," she said, looking at the sleeping Kaiser's son, "they've come for you again." But Balamir did not understand.

Madame Snow's son eased himself laboriously back into bed, very much awake and excited with the effort of climbing, one leg, part of a leg, straight ahead, pulling as if it knew the way back up the stairs. The actress's face, just as bright as an usherette's, sniffed and startled, a smile on her lips, in the darkness. He pulled the covers up over his undershirt, leaned the canes against the bed. His wife did not breathe heavily enough to disturb him. He remembered with fixed pleasure, that night in the shed behind the boarding house and the girl from out of town with braids, who was pretty as a picture. She lost her pants in the shed and left them when the old Madame called and they had to run. In the late night he thought it was delightful, a skirt without the pants beneath.

"I haven't felt this way," he thought, with the Duke and child in the back of his mind, "since that ambulance ride four weeks after losing the leg. It was the bouncing of the car then, the driver said. Tonight it must have been jumping up and down the stairs."

Leg or no leg she'd lose them again. The boy certainly deserved the cane.

"Can't you wake and talk?" His voice was high and unnatural.

178

THREE

Balamir awoke with the sound of the engine in his ears and the arms of the Queen Mother holding him close. He wore his inevitable black trousers and black boots, the uniform that made the crowd in the streets bow down before their Kaiser's son, the black dress of the first man of Germany. For a moment he thought he was in the basement, in the sealed *bunker,* for the plaster of the walls was damp. But the Queen's hands, cooled with the mountain snow, touched his shoulder and the royal room, he laughed to himself, could not be mistaken for the cellar where he was sheltered in the first days. She had taken him from hiding, had evidently held his enemies at bay. Tonight the cabinet was re-formed, the royal house in state, and the crisis, for the nation, passed. The Queen Mother herself had sent the telegrams, the car would be waiting, and the Chancellor would arrive with reports of reconstruction.

Something kept Madame Snow awake and now the poor man himself, after his peaceful sleep, looked up at her with those spiritless eyes and the impossible happy smile. She felt that powerful forces were working in the night and despite the fact that his presence was an extra obligation, she was thankful for him now. Perhaps he was like a dog and would know if strangers were about, perhaps his condition would make him more susceptible than ordinary men to the odd noises of the night. Would he whine if a thief were at the window? Madame Snow hoped, covering his shoulders more with the robe, that he would make some sort of noise.

The Duke, standing alone on the hillside in the hour before dawn, drew his sword with a flourish. The bottoms of his trousers were wet and ripped with thorns. He had lost his hat. His legs ached with the weariness of the chase, the silk handkerchief was gone from his sleeve, he stumbled in the ruts as he went to work. It was a difficult task and for a moment he looked for the moon as he cut the brush from the fox and found he had cut it in half. Looking up, lips white and cold, he could barely see the top of the hill. Over the top and through the barbed-wire was the rough path home. He hacked and missed the joints, he made incisions and they were wrong as the point of the blade struck a button. The fox kicked back and he was horrified. He hated his clumsiness, detested himself for over-looking the bones. Men should be precise either in being humane and splinting the dog's leg or in being practical and cutting it off. He would have pre-ferred to have a light and a glass-topped table, to follow the whole thing out on a chart, knowing which muscles to cut and which to tie. Even in the field they had maps and colored pins, ways were marked and methods approved. The blade slipped and stuck in the mud, while his fingers, growing thin and old, fumbled for a grip, and his ruffled cuffs and slender wrists became soiled and stained. He should have had a rubber apron like a photographer or chemist, he should have had short sharp blades instead of the impractical old sword cane. The whole business bothered him, now after three or four hours of running about the town in the darkness. For the Duke was an orderly man, not given to passion and since there was a 'von' in his name, he expected things to go by plan. But the odds of nature were against him, he began to dislike the slippery carcass. It took all his ingenuity to find, in the mess, the ears to take as trophy, to decide which were the parts with dietician's names and which to throw away. At one moment, concentrating his energies, he thought he was at the top of it, then found he was at the bottom, thought he had the heart in his hand, and the thing burst, evaporating from his fingers. He should have preferred to have his glasses, but they were at home—another mistake. It was necessary to struggle, first holding the pieces on his lap, then crouching above the pile, he had to pull, to poke, and he resented the dullness of the blade. The very fact that it was not a deer or a possum made the thing hard to skin, the fact that it was not a rabbit made it hard to dissect; its infernal humanness carried over even into death and made the carcass just as difficult as the human being had itself been. Every time a bone broke his prize became mangled, every piece that was lost in the mud made the whole thing defective, more imperfect in death., It annoyed the Duke to think that because of his lack of neatness the beast was purposely losing its value, determined to become useless instead of falling into quarters and parts with a definite fore and hind. It lost all semblance to meat or fowl, the paw seemed like the foot, the glove the same as the shoe, hock and wrist alike, bone or jelly, muscle or fat, cartilage or tongue, what could he do? He threw them all together, discarding what he thought to be bad, but never sure, angry with his lack of knowledge. He should have studied the thing out beforehand, he cursed himself for not having a phial for the blood, some sort of thermos or wine bottle perhaps. He set something aside in a clump of grass and went back to work. But before he could lift the blade, he dropped it in indecision and searched through the grass. The piece he found was larger, more ragged. Perhaps the other was valuable and sweet, this was not. Tufts of the red fur stuck to his palm, a part of the shirtsleeve caught on his fingers. He wished for a light, a violent white globe in a polished steel shade, but this was the darkest part of the night. The task was interminable and not for a layman, and the English, he realized, never bothered to cut their foxes up. They at least didn't know as much as he. He sliced, for the last time, at a slender stripped tendon. It gave and slapped back, like elastic, against his hand. It would be pleasant, he thought, to pack these tidbits, be done with them, on ice. Someday, he told himself, he'd have to go through a manual and see exactly how the thing should have been done. The Duke put the blade back in its sheath and making a cane, he hooked the handle over his arm. The organs and mutilated pieces gathered up in the small black fox's jacket, he tied the ends together, used his cane as a staff, and trudged up the hill, his long Hapsburg legs working with excitement. Behind him he left a puddle of waste as if a cat had trapped a lost foraging crow. But the bones were not picked clean and a swarm of small cream-colored bugs trooped out from the ferns to settle over the kill.

182

I left Stumpfegle and Fegelein to distribute the leaflets. The sound of the press died out as I walked from the shed across the littered yard to the boarding house, the murmur of the canal grew louder with the rain from the hills that flowed, no crops to water, down into its contaminated channel. Somewhere near the end of the canal the body of Miller, caught under the axle of a submerged scout car, began to thaw and bloat.

Once more I climbed the dark stairs, deciding as I went, that in the weeks to come I'd turn the place into the National Headquarters. I'd use Stintz's rooms as the stenographic bureau, the secretaries would have to be young and blonde. I reached the third floor and a gust of cold wind, that only a few hours before had swept over the morning already broken in the conquered north, made me shiver and cough. My boots thumped on the wooden floor, my sharp face was determined, strained. It was a good idea, I thought, to make this old house the Headquarters, for I could keep Jutta right on the premises. Of course, the children would have to go. I'd fill the place with light and cut in a few new windows. That aristocrat on the second floor, the Duke, would perhaps make a good Chancellor, and of course, the Census-Taker could be Secretary of State. This town was due prosperity, perhaps I could build an open-air pavilion on the hill for the children. Of course I'd put the old horse statue back on its feet. Young couples would make love beneath it on summer nights. It might be better to mount it on blocks of stone, so that visitors drawing near the city could say, "Look, there's the statue of Germany, given by the new Leader to his country."

I pushed open the Census-Taker's door and by rough unfriendly shaking, roused my comrade out of a dead stupor.

"All the plans have been carried out. But there's something you must do."

I rubbed the man's cheeks, pushed the blue cap on more tightly and buttoned the grey shirt. I smiled with warmth on the unseeing half-shut eyes.

"Hurry, wake up now, the country's almost free."

After more pushing and cajoling, the old official was dragged to his feet, "What's the matter?"

"Nothing. Come with me."

"I'm too tired to sleep with that woman any more tonight."

I looked at him sharply. "We're not going to. Come along." I could not allow myself to be offended.

"I don't go on duty until eight o'clock."

I held my temper, for the old man was drunk and couldn't know what he was saying.

Together we climbed one more flight of stairs to Stintz's room, and pushing the tuba, with its little patch of dried blood, out of the way, we picked up the crouching body and started off with it.

"Nothing but water," said the Census-Taker struggling with the feet, "nothing but tuba and water and hot air out of his fat horn. Another pea in the fire of hell."

"Don't drop him."

"Don't drop him? I'd just as soon push him out of a window and let him get to the street by himself."

"We'll carry him, and you be careful."

The old man mumbled and pulled at the feet. "I won't even bother to take him off the roster."

184

Out in the street we propped the body against the stoop where the moon shone down on the upturned eyes and a hard hand lay against the cold stone.

"Go back to the paper, you know what to do. I'll meet you in front of the house." The Census-Taker, vice-ruler of the State, shuffled into the darkness and I went back to the shed to find the cart.

The Chancellery was still as cold as it was in its unresurrected days, and even at this hour the Chancellor, boarder of the second floor, was out. Madame Snow drew the curtains and found that it was still night, the smashed wall across the street was vague and covered with mist. Her loose hair hung in uneven lengths, where she had cut it, down her back, her face was white and old, pressed to the window. "If old Stintz wants to sit out there like a fool, well, let him. I'll make my imbecile some broth," she thought, and tried to stir up the stove but found it impossible. "You'll have to go without," she said to Balamir, and he started and grinned at the Queen Mother's words. Balamir knew that the village was like an abandoned honeycomb because somebody in airplanes had blown many of the roofs from the houses. But the Queen Mother should not look at the bleak night, it was his job and his alone to rebuild the town and make his subjects happy. He tried to attract her attention, but she was looking at the stove. Madame Snow herself wanted some broth, but collecting stove fuel from the basement was simply too great a task and she knew the fool, poor man, could never learn to do it. "Stintz is as bad as you," she said and crawled about the honeycomb chuckling to herself, tiara fallen to one side, grown loose.

Four flights up in my new rooms, the child got out of bed and once more stood by the window, beginning her vigil over the ageless, sexless night. The little girl, Selvaggia, was careful to keep her face in the shadow of the curtain, lest the undressed man in the sky look down and see. As much as she disliked Herr Stintz, she thought that someone should go and tell him to come back into the house. But she knew enough not to disturb her mother.

Jutta pulled the covers back over her shoulder. Now that I was gone, there was no need to expose herself to the cold, and even the Census-Taker was no longer interested in seeing. But she couldn't sleep. The peculiar thump of drunken feet, the droning of an engine, the footsteps of dead men echoed through the room, the branches scraped and whispered outside the window. She remembered the day that Stella went to be married and left her alone. Now Stella, the Madame, was old, only an old sterile tramp, and couldn't even keep the house quiet at night. Jutta drew her knee up, smoothed the sheets, and lay wide awake. She wished that I would hurry home. Men were so stupid about their affairs, running around with pistols, little short rods and worried brows. "Come to bed," she thought, "or one of these days I'll throw you out, Leader or not."

It was no use, there was no more sleep. She got out of bed and went to the three drawers under the washbowl stand and searched through her clothes. She found the letter under her week-day dress and it was covered with official seals and the censor's stamp. The letter from her husband before he was lost in Russia, imprisoned among Mongolians, was the only personal possession she had left. She held the paper up to the moonlight.

". . . I'm now at the front in a big field and the familiar world of men is gone. Yesterday a group went by and I shot the leader off his horse with a bullet right through his head. The rain sings and the streamlets reproduce every hour. I thought about him all last night and his horse ran off across the field. Now, Jutta, if it is true that I get what he used to own, I will send you the necessary papers so you can go and take possession of his farm. There may be a great deal of work to do on it so you had better start. I kept wondering last night if his wife was automatically mine or not. I suppose she is, and frankly, that worries me and I'm sorry I shot the fellow for that. I think she probably has red hair and the officials will dismiss the whole thing—but I will send you money as soon as it comes and you simply will have to make the best of it and fight it out with her and the children. His farm might be several acres, who knows? I'll send you maps, etc. plus the fellow's name and I don't think you'll have trouble crossing the field. I cannot make out what his wife will think of me now that she is mine along with the land. It's too bad for her that it had to be this way but perhaps there's a horse in the barn to replace the one that got away. I couldn't sleep at all because this field is in the open, which is most astounding, and I couldn't decide how much money he actually had that I could send you. I don't know how you feel about all this, perhaps you'll think I did wrong, but I struck the best bargain I could, and the Corporal in the dugout made it very difficult. Maybe I'll be able to end this slave rule and will certainly mend the roof on his farmhouse for you if you'll just do your share. There may be a few dogs on his farm who will keep the poachers off—I hope so. It's a terrible problem as you can see but if the Corporal comes on my side I think things will change. I hope the whole plan works out for you and the papers arrive safely through the rain, for at the same time I am doing nothing in the trenches and this excitement, over the wire and saddles, is disturbing my conscience . . ."

Jutta dropped the letter back into the washstand. She wished that it were a chest of drawers, a chest as tall as she and carved, with layer after layer of gowns and silk, something precious for every moment of the night, with a golden key and a gilded mirror on the top.

Stintz sat straight up in the cart, knocking heavily against the wood to the rhythm of the stones and fractures in the street. His face was set and he slipped, then righted, like a child in a carriage that is too large. He looked like a legless man hauled through the streets in the days of trouble, he was a passenger tensed for the trip with only his head rolling above the sides of the cart.

There was no straw in the bottom, his hands were locked rigidly apart, and he jiggled heavily when the wheels rolled over the gravel. If anyone else had been riding with him, he would not have spoken. He was surly, he was helpless, and his whole body had the defiant, unpleasant appearance that the helpless have. The shafts were too wide for me, and I had a difficult time pulling the cart, for sometimes it seemed to gather a momentum of its own and pushed me along while the heels behind me kicked up and down on the floorboards in a frightening step.

We met on the appointed corner and the Census-Taker put the tins, cold and unwieldly, into the cart. They quickly slid back into Stintz's lap, crowding him, pinning him down. He no longer slid with the movement of travel, he was no longer a passenger. The tins made the difference, they cut away his soul, filled the cart with the sloshing sound of liquid. His head was no longer a head, but a funnel in the top of a drum.

We stopped before the Mayor's door and struggled to get the martyr and the fuel out of the wagon. We dropped him and caught our breath.

"Are you sure he won't hear us?"

"He won't hear. And if he does, he won't do anything. I guarantee you he won't make a sound. He knows no one would help him."

With a great deal of effort, we dragged Stintz into the Mayor's hall and propped him against a table. We emptied the tins of petrol, ten *Pfennige* a cup, throughout the downstairs of the house.

It took a long time for the fire to reach the roof since the tins were diluted with water and the house was damp to begin with. The Census-Taker was forced to make several trips back to the newspaper office for more fuel and his arms and shoulders were sore with the work.

The Mayor thought that the nurse was preparing cups of hot broth and the kettle boiled as she stirred it with a wooden spoon. Little white pieces of chicken, whose head she flung in the corner, floated midway in the water. The warm fumes filled the room.

"Here, Miller," he said, "let's sit down to the soup together. That woman's an excellent cook and the bird's from my own flock. I have hundreds, you know. Miller, let me give you this broth." Tears were in the old man's eyes, he reached for the cup. But Miller wouldn't drink. The Mayor's nose and mouth were bound in the red bandanna, it choked about his throat, and at the last minute, Miller knocked over the tureen.

"I think we can go," I said. The fire was filling the street with a hot, small amount of ash.

The Mayor did not cry out, but died, I was very glad, without recompense or absolution.

The little girl had seen no fires since the Allied bombings, and in those days, she saw them only after they were well under way, after the walls had fallen and the houses did not look like houses at all. And the people crowding the streets after raids, running to and fro, giving orders, often made it hard to see.

Now, since the town had no fire apparatus, no whistles or trucks, and since there was no one in the streets, she could watch the fire as long as she wished; see it from her window undisturbed, alert. Firemen would certainly have destroyed the fire, their black ladders climbing all over the walls would have changed it, black slickers shining with water would have cried danger, covered with water they would have put it out.

The fire went well for a while, and then, because there was no wind to help it, no clothes or curtains to feed upon, it began to fade like an incendiary on the bare road, until only a few sparks and gusts of smoke trickled from the cracks of an upstairs shuttered window. The child soon tired of the flames that couldn't even singe a cat, but was still glad the fire-bell had not rung. She crept back under the covers to keep warm while waiting.

The Duke, his arms loaded with the shopping bag, wearily climbed the stairs and unlocked the door.

Madame Snow, hearing the noises overhead, knew that the second floor boarder was back.

The Signalman dozed in his chair and forgot the boy and the man with the upraised cane.

Madame Snow did not see the dying embers.

With his free hand the Duke put a few copies of the *Crooked Zeitung,* old unreadable issues, on a chair before resting his bundle; the white legs that dangled over the seat were too short to reach the rungs. A stain spread over the newspapers. He moved quickly about the majestic apartment, fit only for the eyes of a Duke, and now in his vest with his sleeves rolled up, he put two lumps of coal in the stove, rinsed his hands, and finally put the pieces in the bucket to soak. He put a few bones that he had been able to carry away, uninspected and unstamped, before the shop closed, on a closet shelf. After throwing the small fox's black jacket into a pile of salvaged clothes, he collected his pans and set to work. More newspapers over his knees, he gathered the pots about his feet and one by one he scoured, scoured until the papers were covered with a thick red dust, and the vessels gleamed, steel for the hearth. He scoured until his hands and arms were red.

The stove was crowded, for every pan and roaster that he owned was set to boil, lidded pots and baking tins, large and small, heavy and light, were all crammed together over the coals. The broth would last for weeks and months, his shelves would hold the bones for years. Through the shades a dull light began to fill the kitchen and at last, proudly, he was ready to go downstairs.

Madame Snow heard the footsteps, slow and even, stop before her door. She knew that something waited, that some slow-moving creature, large or thin, alive or dead, was just beyond, waiting to call. She heard the breathing, the interminable low sounds, the sounds so necessary to a nightmare, the rustling of cloth, perhaps a soft word mumbled to itself. If she turned on the light, he might disappear or *she might not recognize him,* she might never have seen that face, those eyes and hands, those rubber boots, and slicker drawn tightly up to the chin. It may swing an axe limply to and fro, large, ponderous, unknown. And if he did not speak but simply stood, hair wet over the eyes, face scarred, bandanna about the throat, and worse, if he did not move, never a step once inside the door with the white handkerchief, with the Christ by his head, with gauntlets and whistle that were never clutched, that never blew, on his belt, what would she do? She would not be able to speak, she would not recognize nor remember nor recall that peculiar way he stood, as if he held a gun, as if he had just climbed up from the canal with his slicker made of rubber rafts. She could hear him leaning closer against the door.

At last the knock came and cautiously and formally he entered.

"Ah, Herr Duke," she said, "good evening. You're visiting late, but it's a pleasure to see you."

He bowed, still in his vest, with arms red, and straightened stiffly.

"Madame Snow, I realize the hour, but," he

smiled slightly, "I have come on a most important mission."

She clutched the robe, the Queen Mother's before her, close to her chest.

"I would be most happy," continued the tall man, "if you would give me the pleasure of dining with me, full courses and wine, at ten o'clock this morning that is to come. I have been most fortunate, and the meal is now being prepared."

"It is an honor, Herr Duke."

With one more bow, sleeves still rolled, the Chancellor climbed the stairs. He was the bearer of good tidings.

Balamir was startled to see, only a few moments after the Chancellor took his leave, Madame Snow stoop to seize a piece of paper that had been thrust beneath the door. They heard the messenger, Fegelein, cantering off down the greying street, heard the slamming of several doors. Madame Snow squinted by the window, her long hair shaking with excitement. She read and disbelieved, then read again. This joy was too much to bear, too great, too proud. Tears of joy and long waiting ran down her cheeks, the pamphlet fluttered from her hands, she clutched at the sill. Suddenly, with the energy of her youth, she flung open the window and screamed towards the upper stories of the boarding house.

"Sister, Sister, the news has come, the liberation has arrived. Sister, thank your countrymen, the land is free, free of want, free to re-build, Sister, the news, it's truly here." She wept as she had never wept when a girl.

Only silence greeted her cries. Then the child called fearfully down, "Mother is asleep." A bright excited day was beginning to dawn and a few harassed and jubilant cries, no more, echoed up and down the drying streets.

Even though the print was smeared quite badly, and some of the pamphlets were unreadable, the decree spread quickly and most people, except the Station-Master who didn't see the white paper, heard the news and whispered about it in the early morning light, trying to understand this new salvation, readjusting themselves to the strange day. The decree was carried, faithfully, by Stumpfegle and Fegelein who walked in ever widening circles about the countryside. They walked farther and farther, growing tired, until even the spire, struck with sunlight, was no longer visible.

In Winter Death steals through the doorway searching for both young and old and plays for them in his court of law. But when Spring's men are beating their fingers on the cold earth and bringing the news, Death travels away and becomes only a passer-by. The two criers passed him on his way and were lost in an unbounded field.

The Census-Taker slept by the bottles in the newspaper office, his hands and face still grey with soot.

Madame Snow hummed while she tied up her hair.

Her son finally slept.

The hatches on the tank were closed.

The decree worked, was carried remarkably well, and before the day had begun the Nation was restored, its great operations and institutions were once more in order, the sun was frozen and clear. At precisely ten o'clock, when the Queen Mother went to dine, the dark man with the papers walked down the street and stopped at the boarding house. As Balamir left the castle with the shabby man, he heard the faraway scraping of knives and forks. At the top of the hill he saw the long lines that were already filing back into the institution, revived already with the public spirit. They started down the slope and passed, without noticing, the pool of trodden thistles where the carrion lay.

I was surprised to hear all the laughter on the second floor, but was too tired to stop and receive their gratitude. Beside the bed in Jutta's room I stripped off my shirt and trousers and with an effort eased myself under the sheets. I lay still for a moment and then touched her gently, until she opened her eyes. The lips that had waited all evening for a second kiss touched my own, and from the open window the sharp sun cut across the bed, shining on the whiteness of her face who was waking and on the whiteness of my face who had returned to doze. We shut our eyes against the sun.

Selvaggia opened the door and crept into the room. She looked more thin than ever in the light of day, wild-eyed from watching the night and the birth of the Nation.

"What's the matter, Mother? Has anything happened?"

I answered instead of Jutta, without looking up, and my voice was vague and harsh; "Nothing. Draw those blinds and go back to sleep . . ."

She did as she was told.

New Directions Paperbooks—A Partial Listing

For complete listing request complete catalog from
New Directions, 80 Eighth Avenue, New York 10011   † Bilingual

The Ethics of Jonathan Edwards

THE ETHICS
OF
JONATHAN EDWARDS

Morality and Aesthetics

Clyde A. Holbrook

Ann Arbor
THE UNIVERSITY OF MICHIGAN PRESS

Preface

Some thinkers possess the genius to set perennial religious and philosophical problems in such a profound and stimulating perspective that they affect not only their own times but also those to come. They so construe issues that their successors must either walk in their footsteps as commentators, or break decisively with the formulations they have inherited. In either case the crucial insights of the originators of these legacies prove to be the focal figures in man's wrestle with his nature and destiny.

In American theology and philosophy Jonathan Edwards stands preeminent among those who have thus decisively set in motion fresh currents of thought. He was not, as some have assumed, merely a belated defender of Calvinism or a crabbed exponent of a now outmoded evangelism. He was in some respects a conserver of what he took to be orthodox Christianity, but he was also an adventurous thinker who was willing to move beyond the strictures of Calvinism when he felt that to do justice to the great God he envisioned called for more expansive categories. As his pupil, Samuel

Hopkins, put it in his *Memorial* on Edwards, found in *Works of President Edwards* (1817) 1:44, "Though his principles were Calvinistic yet he called no man Father. He thought and judged for himself, and was truly very much of an original." Edwards placed under discriminating tribute the thought of Locke, Shaftesbury, Hume, Hutcheson, and the Neoplatonic tradition as well as many lesser known Biblical exegetes, theologians, and philosophers.

However, Edwards should be seen in an even larger framework than that suggested by these names. In the history of man's engagement with a Supreme Being, there has always been a large number, regardless of their religious and cultural traditions, who have conceived the deity as attendant upon man's desires and values. Paramount to these believers has been the more or less explicit conviction that God serves as an explanatory principle of the world, or as a Being whose sole purpose and interest is in man's salvation. Such views have ranged from the crassest forms of religious devotion, bordering upon superstition, to views that made of the deity a guarantor of the highest ideals of human conduct. But there has also been a smaller group of those who gloried in God for his own sake and felt deep rejoicing in the consciousness of his presence. These are the theological objectivists, who have found in their experiences of the great Being the whole aim and goal of life. Edwards concurred with both of these views, as may be seen in his various writings at different times in his life. However, it is the theme of this book on his ethics that the burden of his thought resides with the theological objectivists. In terms of this view, both his Calvinism and his Neoplatonism become part of one consistent and developing pattern of his thought. The vessels in which he placed this objectivistic conviction were Calvinistic and Neoplatonic, but it was as though he wanted to press these instruments to their uttermost to express what had fascinated him from his earliest religious experiences to his most mature writings. I find that this well-nigh overwhelming conviction of God's centrality, power, and beauty penetrated Edwards's use of language in both his imprecatory sermons and his more placid treatises on virtue and God's last end in creation. The connecting link is his aesthetic rhetoric, which was the proper style in which to express the depths to which man the sinner could descend as well as the heights to which God summoned men.

The complexities of interpreting Edwards present considerable difficulty, and I have certainly not intended to force him at each point into the objectivistic framework. To illustrate the complexities of my endeavor I have, I am afraid, introduced the reader to Edwards in a rather uninviting way by referring in Chapter I to a series of recent works which have in their respective ways also attempted to penetrate the corpus of Edwards's writings. The authors of these books or articles have in some cases reached conclusions different from my own, but none of them, except Roland A. Delattre in his fine study of *Beauty and Sensibility in the Thought of Jonathan Edwards,* has dealt systematically with the ethical import of Edwards's thought. One may detect in my footnotes a running debate with Delattre on precise points of interpretation, but this does not detract from my appreciation of his insightful book. However, I am inclined to hold with Douglas J. Elwood's contention that Edwards's primary emphasis was deposited upon the doctrine of God. I hope I have made clear to the reader that I have not scanted Edwards's attention to the human response to divine action. Important as it was to Edwards's case that the "affections be raised," that a "divine and supernatural taste" and religion of the heart be exercised, these were all to the purpose that man might enjoy and participate in the effulgent beauty of God himself. As Sereno Dwight commented on Edwards's preaching (in *Works of President Edwards* [Converse, often called the Dwight edition] 1829, 1:194), "He regarded it (the revival) as caused—not by Appeals to the feelings or the passions, but—by the Truth of God brought home to the mind, in a subordinate sense by the preaching of the Gospel, but in a far higher sense by the immediate agency of the Holy Spirit." I believe that Edwards did not swerve from this position even in his treatise on the *Religious Affections,* in which he defended the proper place of the affections in religion. But this tension between the finer subjective elements and theological objectivism is treated in its appropriate context in the body of the book.

Over the period of time during which this volume took shape, I have been forced to use several collections of Edwards's writings. In part this has been due to the availability of certain editions at the time of writing. But it has also been made necessary because different editions vary as to which works of Edwards are included. For evidence of this variation one should consult Thomas H. Johnson's *The Printed Writings of Jonathan Edwards* (Princeton: Princeton University Press, 1940). In several cases the editing itself of the treatise in question has determined my choice of edition. Such has been the case in my use of the volumes so far produced in the Yale Edition of Edwards's works. Professors Paul Ramsey and John E. Smith, referred to occasionally in the text, are the editors respectively of volume 1 (*Freedom of the Will*) and volume 2 (*Religious Affections*). All editions of collected works em-

ployed are cited in the bibliography. I have also provided references to H. K. Frankena's transcription of
the *Treatise on the Nature of True Virtue,* in order to
permit convenient access to a modern version, although
in some passages the flavor of Edwards's style has been
changed and the edition from which the transcription
has been made is not noted. To assist the reader of my
text to identify the work referred to, the title appears
either in the notes or in the text itself, lest my references
to different editions of the collected works be completely and infuriatingly mystifying. For most references
to Edwards's *Miscellanies,* a voluminous collection of
thoughts with which he worked, I have depended upon
H. G. Townsend's selections from this corpus. I have
also employed some citations from the *Miscellanies* in
the Yale collection. Some of the lengthy or variant titles
attributed to Edwards's sermons and major treatises
have been identified by short titles which I hope will
be clear to the reader.

This book originated in my doctoral dissertation,
supervised and encouraged by the late H. Richard
Niebuhr of Yale University. It has been thoroughly
revised from its earlier form, and is now offered as one
more contribution to the ever expanding body of theological and philosophical scholarship which Edwards
continues to inspire. Thanks are due to Raymond
Morris and Philip A. Muntzel of Yale Divinity School,
the Oberlin College library staff, and my secretary, Bar-
bara Turek. My deepest appreciation for assistance
must go to my wife, Dorothy, to whom this volume is
dedicated. I am of course also indebted to the many
authors before me who have wrestled with the sinewy
thoughts of one whom Fichte called "this lonely North
American thinker."

CLYDE A. HOLBROOK

Contents

I

The Major Patterns

MODERN INTERPRETERS of Edwards seldom agree completely on what Perry Miller called the secret of Edwards. Yet each interpreter seems to complement the other. Miller himself pointed to Edwards's *Original Sin* as the clue to Edwards's "glorified naturalism," by which he indicted utilitarian liberalism and the profit motive.[1] James Carse abandoned the possibility of knowing the "real Edwards" and settled for a portrait of a hero whose aim was to make God "visible" in this world.[2] Conrad Cherry's thorough reexamination of Edwards's theology finds its focus in the Calvinist's concern with faith.[3] Roland A. Delattre finds from beginning to end that one's appreciation of beauty unlocks one's understanding of Edwards.[4] Douglas J. Elwood treats Edwards as a metaphysician who, by means of his doctrine of religious immediacy, united his Calvinism with a Neoplatonic ontology of a panentheistic type.[5] William S. Morris finds the genius of Edwards to reside in his reinterpretation and combination of the rational and the empirical.[6] So the list runs, always with the danger present that the interpretive motif will distort or eliminate some aspect of Edwards's total perspective which for him was of importance.

No interpreter of Edwards's ethics is likely to escape from similar dangers, although at the same time the richness of Edwards's thought cannot be explored without the aid of some interpretive tool. In the first instance, the search for this tool must begin in the texts themselves, and not be imperiously imposed upon them from the standpoint of the twentieth century. For this reason, numerous citations have been unavoidable in the text. Yet something more than a recital of texts is called for. There is need for an interpretive instrument which will be sufficiently pliant to follow without distortion the contours of what was the living thought of Edwards. Nor need it be assumed that Edwards woodenly and consistently followed only one pattern at all times. Logician though he was, Edwards, like all systematic thinkers, could at times entertain and express views which were not completely compatible with the major thrust of his thought. There are recalcitrant fragments of his outlook which, even with the best of intentions on the part of his interpreters, cannot be made consistent with the main stream. Yet a total perspective must nevertheless be sought. Although it may not provide coherence for every phase of Edwards's thought, it must illuminate the main direction of his thought. Perspective must be attained through the use of an interpretive principle which, although rooted in Edwards's writings, is broader in scope than the system it purports to understand. The illumination, in short, must be provided by a pattern which has its basis in a range of thought more extensive than the system it aims to interpret.

Elwood has well said that Edwards was "a man of one idea, and that one idea was God." [7] This clue must be explored in depth as it relates to ethics; it cannot serve our purpose if it merely invites an analysis of the way in which Edwards moved from a Calvinistic to an essentially Neoplatonic form of theological ontology. But what we do find running throughout the Edwardsean corpus is a pattern of thought which may be called theological objectivism.[8] This pattern stands in tension with another which may be identified as theological subjectivism, wherein the human subject assumes the primary position in the religious consciousness. It is the usual fate of theological subjectivism that sooner or later it falls away into theological utilitarianism. Each pattern is intended at a minimum to indicate the primary direction which the religious process takes. Theological objectivism points the religious life to its source and goal in God or Being that does not lie at the disposal of man. Theological subjectivism primarily concentrates its attention upon the human being, his nature and possibilities, and the products of his social imagination. It finds its goal in the fulfillment of the human dimension, if not in this world, then in the next. Neither pattern is a stranger to the history of religious experience and thought.

Theological objectivism is at root a profound conviction, rather than a dogma, or the conclusion of argument. It affirms the absolute primacy of deity, metaphysically, morally, and spiritually.[9] It has had a variety of expressions in the history of western man's religions, wherever God-intoxicated figures appear. The Old Testament prophets, Plotinus, Spinoza, Calvin, and we believe Edwards, all represent this tendency. In whatever form the theme appears, there is expressed a sense of a dominant power with which man must come to terms, but which he cannot control. Mankind, it is maintained, is confronted not only by its own kind, nature, or simply with the projection of its own ideas reflected back to itself from a void, but with an in-

3

scrutable being who constitutes humanity and nature without complete identification with either. In contrast to those hearty souls who seldom if ever give thought to the presence of this reality or who, once having given thought, return to the comforting, provincial warmth of their own kind, the theological objectivist is likely to feel a deep and even agonizing disquietude in the presence of this reality. In this respect the subjective impact of theological objectivism may produce both profound humility and exaltation. The objectivist is haunted by the need to offer some interpretation of the Other upon which all depends and to develop a manner of life consistent with what he feels is his precarious position before the Other. Since power is the basic category from which theological objectivism arises, it also becomes essential that there be detected within that power some sign of beneficence, lest the human being be condemned to live continually in abject fear or at least in awe. He must be convinced that his experience of the divine object reveals not only awesome power, but also justice and some measure of graciousness. These attributes enter the picture not as secondary additions to the nature of supreme reality, nor are they to be interpreted as determinants of that reality which men find congenial to themselves. They are intrinsic to power. Value, moral and often aesthetic, inheres in the Being itself and cannot be divorced from it.

This pattern of thought and conviction will serve as the principal key to understanding Edwards's ethics. Thus, in its Calvinistic form, this motif was expressed by Edwards in the claim that God's right to rule his creation is bound up with the indubitable fact that he does indeed rule.[10] His credentials of kingship lie in his sovereignty and power to do what he wills. In one

4

way or another, inescapably, every man must come to terms with this Reality on its own grounds. God is the first, last, and ultimate fact about the universe. The wishes, hopes, and ethical norms which men entertain concerning their own nature and destiny must bend to the will of this Supreme Being, mysterious though it may be. Consequently, man does not begin his thinking about his appropriate conduct on the basis of moral values which he himself invents or intuits in separation from deity. God is not simply the exemplification of whatever values occur to men as desirable in their particular cultures. Their thinking on moral matters must rather begin with Him who is the determiner of all moral and spiritual imperatives.[11] Men do not sit in moral judgment upon deity.[12] They must instead think away from themselves toward God, who in his supreme authority and excellence is the source of all value. The vision of deity then is not first of all an insight into what men ought to do or what they themselves think they ought to do, but is rather an insight into the reality that is.

In his Calvinistic formulation of theological objectivism Edwards not only retained the notion of distance between man and God but he made it clear that the human subject was in a parlous state in the presence of a power which is untamable by human devices. The God who judges and redeems as he pleases is the God of initiative as to which of these possibilities lies before men. God is the principal actor in salvation and damnation. Therefore, there can be no scaling of the spiritual heights by mystical practices invented by finite man. Until he is brought to see his precarious condition before the dread and aweful majesty of God, he is not in a position to see himself as he actually is—a human subject with nothing in his hands by which to put God under obligation to save him. As Edwards rehearsed the theme of divine sovereignty, therefore, the human subject was correspondingly depreciated as to his moral and spiritual nature, a condition to be identified as sinfulness. It does not follow, however, that all forms of theological objectivism have the sinfulness of man as a correlate. However, given Edwards's Calvinistic and Augustinian cast of mind, this conclusion was inevitable. The more glorious the metaphysical and moral attributes of the deity became, the lower in Edwards's estimation man sank.[13] Correspondingly the deeper in sinfulness he considered man, the more impressive the harsher attributes of God became. By the same movement of thought, the greater God became as the savior of man from the abysmal depths, so the more gracious, sublime, and beauteous aspects of the deity shone for the regenerate. So Edwards was able to combine the absolute priority of the divine object both in its most austere, judgmental aspects and in its most beneficent attributes.

The theme of theological objectivism was finally to be released from its Calvinistic form, especially in Edwards's posthumous works, the *Treatise on True Virtue* and the *Dissertation concerning the End for which God Created the World*. In these works, as they pick up some of his earliest musings upon the notion of Being, theological objectivism is lifted to a position close to an all-inclusive monism or panentheism from which he escaped only by his continued differentiation between the subject and the Object, even in the ultimate salvation of regenerate men. The absolute priority of deity, the complete dependence of men upon God, God's own glory as the aim of all creation and of man's highest end all remained as indications that the princi-

6

ple of theological objectivism had not been finally surrendered.

It must be remembered, however, that the theme of theological subjectivism is a pattern of thought and conviction which, without denying the reality of God, puts to the foreground as the focus of human concern the human subject, his inner feelings, his needs, hopes, and values. Like theological objectivism, this pattern has left its indelible mark both on religion and upon interpreters of religion. From the religions of preliterates to the most sophisticated forms of religious consciousness it may be found. Indeed, its presence has been so impressively evident that some would interpret religion and God without remainder as completely functional. The characteristic form which theological subjectivism takes in its individualistic phase is one which reduces religion to an instrument by which men procure a private, emotional security. Its concern is with the inner workings of the human ego, especially its feelings. In its social and ethical forms theological subjectivism regards religion as a means to social cohesion and the sanctioner of moral values which have been independently arrived at without essential recourse to religious insight. All cases, however, share in regarding both religion and God in varying degrees in a utilitarian manner. Both are means to human fulfillment. They assuage human grief, guarantee immortality, the protection of society against divisiveness, and even procure material and professional advancement.[14] In a general sense theological utilitarianism shares with philosophical utilitarianism the goal of human happiness and the prevention of unhappiness, as distinguished from the goal of the glorification of God, as in the case of theological objectivism. So William Paley could define virtue as "doing good to mankind in obedience to the will of God and for the sake of everlasting happiness." [15] The goal of happiness, it is understood, stands as a value to which God serves as a means. It must follow then that there is a moral continuity between man and God, since by definition they share the same aims and values. By this means men may hold the divine being to account and may tame his sovereignty. Justice, moral goodness, and virtue, as these are recognized in the human domain, become criteria of what God should be if he is to be worthy to be worshipped. Newman Smyth therefore could take it for granted in any reading of Christian ethics "that the divine nature is moral, and that the moral is in essence the same in God and man." [16] The theological subjectivist, armed with this plausible view, finds it all but inevitable that the moral attributes, especially those of a beneficent character, should outweigh those metaphysical attributes of deity which are highly and equally regarded by the theological objectivist.[17] And the human moral sense becomes the vehicle by which the value of God and religion is determined. The worthiness of God to be worshipped is determined by the subjective end of the God-man polarity, and religion becomes a useful instrument for the satisfaction of human needs and a means of being persuaded that the universe or God is on the side of the moral values which occur to man or which God has implanted in humanity.

As we shall see, Edwards was not above the temptation to resort to some aspects of theological subjectivism when it suited his purposes. He was greatly concerned over the operations of God within the soul, as well as the happiness to which they led. His deeper conviction, however, was oriented toward theological objectivism. He was truest to that conviction when he wrote, "What makes men partial in religion is, that they seek themselves, and not God, in their religion, and close with religion, not for its own excellent nature, but only to serve a turn." [18] Few there may be who can live on the breathless heights to which theological objectivism points. The return to theological subjectivism and utilitarianism with its appeal to rewards and punishments and self-interest repeatedly occurs in the history of religions. The living to God for his own sake seems to some too barren a concept to attract the faith of men. Yet if there be a God, and if this is his world, what alternative remains? So thinks the theological objectivist.

It remains to be seen, in the context of Edwards's thought, how these two interpretive principles operate in respect to the question of morality. Can there be a perspective developed on the ground of theological objectivism that is recognizably ethical? Or must a theological ethic at last pay tribute to theological subjectivism and its inevitable utilitarian consequences?

The Patterns in Tension

EDWARDS did not come easily to his characteristic form of theological objectivism. Although reared in the Calvinistic tradition, he was far from convinced originally of the justice of a deity who used his power arbitrarily to determine men's destinies. In some way, of which he could offer no clear account, he did suddenly at an early age apprehend the justice and reasonableness of what he formerly called this "horrible doctrine" of divine sovereignty. Although he was later to reinterpret this conviction, he came to rest his life in it and to interpret the Christian life in terms of it. From the outset divine sovereignty was vastly more than an abstract doctrine impressed upon his mind. He wrote, "I have often, since that first conviction, had quite another sense of God's sovereignty than I had then. I have often since had not only a conviction, but a delightful conviction," one that "often appeared exceeding pleasant, bright and sweet." [1] In its light his soul was moved to an ardent longing for God and for a holy life in comparison to which "everything else was like mire and defilement." So overpowering was the sense of the divine presence that all nature sprang to new life and beauty. "God's excellency, his wisdom, his purity and love, seem to appear in everything; in the sun, moon and stars; in the clouds, and blue skies; in the grass, flowers, trees; in the water, and all nature." [2] Clearly, Edwards was here not merely indulging in a nature romanticism, but giving voice to a symbolic sense of an ordered nature through which God revealed himself in beauty, but with which God was not to be identified. God retained his objective status as the source of a beauty and holiness which deeply affected Edwards. Thus the conviction of the sovereignty of God can be seen as the ground of the most intense subjective effects. But these effects were not to be the goal of the religious experience. Rather they pointed beyond themselves to their source in God's own glory, and to a delight in that glory for its own sake.

When we find Edwards engaged in the revivalistic work of the Great Awakening, the theme of the theological objectivism takes a less attractive turn. In his *Personal Narrative* he remarked that no sermons had been more remarkably blessed "than those in which the doctrine of God's absolute sovereignty" had been insisted on.[3] However, the hues with which he painted the destiny of unrepentant sinners in hell showed a treatment of the doctrine that was to make it offensive to the more humane among his critics. Yet to Edwards the results were "surprising" and unexpected, since he had not aimed to do more than describe the precarious state in which the sinner stood before an awesome divine being.[4] Even his style of preaching, as Samuel Hopkins recalled, was dispassionate and calm, lacking the ostentatious flourishes which others emphasized to incite the emotions.[5] The results of preaching the sovereignty of God, without conscious attempts to manipulate the emotions of his listeners, convinced Edwards that the revival was nothing less than a work of God, not man. So, in the words of C. H. Faust, "He defended the outburst of emotionalism known as the Great Awakening because it seemed to him to be an expression of the kind of religion toward which a recognition of the sovereignty of God would lead." [6] And he was to make plain this contention when he wrote the *Religious Affections*. In that work he made clear that although raised affections were at the heart of vital religion, they were in danger of evaporating into "enthusiasm" or of being fruitless unless they were stimulated by an apprehension of the divine being and were fulfilled in their attachment to God. Whereas "False affections rest satisfied in themselves," that is in subjectivism, true affections or holy love "has a holy object." [7]

The objectivistic theme, which was to echo throughout much of his preaching, was heralded in his first published sermon, "God Glorified in Man's Dependence." Nothing could be clearer to Edwards than that God "be the cause and original whence" all of man's good comes. He is the medium by which it is obtained, and he is the good itself.[8] He is completely sovereign, possessing as he does an infinite number of perfections, and these in infinite degree. As he created out of nothing, and upholds and governs all things great and small "at one view," his power and understanding must be of infinite magnitude. Thus, being perfect and absolutely holy, it is impossible that he should do anything amiss.[9] Consequently his is the absolute and independent right to dispose of his creations according to his will. Without prejudice to his honor and righteousness he may save or damn whom he pleases.[10] In both cases God glorifies himself.[11]

But what manner of righteousness is this which operates arbitrarily? The moral sentiment of men finds offensive to their estimate of themselves the possibility

that there is a power in the universe which has determining power over their eventual destiny. Even to raise
this question is to move quickly into what Edwards
conceived as the spiritual correlate of his objectivism,
the sinfulness of man. The question above assumes what
cannot be assumed in the Edwards's scheme, namely,
the moral capacity and right to pass judgment upon
divine righteousness. As he put it, "What poor creature
are you that you should set up yourselves for judges over
the Most High: that you should take it upon you to call
God into account; that you should say to the great Je-
hovah, what dost thou?" [12] The question arises from
the abhorrent vice of pride, which masks itself in the
trappings of earnest intellectual and ethical inquiry. It
implies that God is not God, that although there may
be some superior being, he cannot act like God except
as he pays homage to the moral criteria men have established. But God to be God by definition not only possesses moral perfection, but also establishes the norms of
righteousness. If in the sight of this perfect being, man
falls short of what God requires, he is a sinner and from
that posture no valid challenge to God's moral demand
can be mounted. If there be a God, he must be the deci-
sive factor in respect not only to man's creation but also
to his destiny and the way to that destiny. To start to
think about morality, one must start from the fact that
the moral governance of the world is in other hands
than one's own, and that before the demands of that
moral governance man is in no position on ethical
grounds to raise his voice. It must be, argued Edwards,
"that God does take care, that a good moral government, should be maintained over men" lest all things
"remedilessly" be in "the utmost deformity, confusion
and ruin." [13]

Edwards's revivalistic sermons were to rehearse this
theme of man's sinfulness, and one of his major treatises

was to explore it thoroughly. He was persuaded that the Bible taught the doctrine of original sin, but he was also convinced that an examination of human behavior verified it beyond question. What the Bible taught, and what theologians had pondered was no abstractly conceived dogma. It was a doctrine which sprang from a candid look through the eyes of both Christians and pagans at the history of mankind, in which sottish stupidity in matters of morals and religion stood out unmistakably. There was no need to believe that misanthropic theologians and preachers had imposed the doctrine upon the innocent minds of men. Rather the doctrine explained why men constantly deceived themselves by self-assurances that they were fundamentally decent, upright creatures, whereas all the evidence pointed in the other direction. As Perry Miller put it, "The doctrines of original sin, of the depravity of man, and of irresistible grace were not embraced for their logic, but out of the hunger of the human spirit and an anxiety of the soul." [14]

Convinced as he was of the truth of this doctrine, Edwards in many of his sermons proceeded to set man before the majestic holiness of God in unrelieved tension and danger. By his rhetoric and logic he drove home the lesson with a vivacity which cut the ground from under all human pretensions to virtue. The familiar and comforting entrances to the divine favor by means of what appeared to be the sincere efforts of man were effectively blocked off. He assured his listeners that "you cannot bring him under the obligation by your works; do what you will he will not look upon himself as obliged." [15] Their strivings he regarded as "not so much an earnest seeking to God, as a striving to do themselves that which is the work of God." [16] Their frantic efforts to run from punishment in hell were merely prompted by negative motives. "There is a great deal of difference," as Edwards perceptively pointed out, "between a willingness not to be damned and a being willing to receive Christ for your Saviour." [17] Considering the torments which awaited the damned, it is understandable that fear would drive men to conversion. But Edwards was too keen an analyst of human emotions to suppose that fear of hell would automatically bring about salvation. The sight of hell, as he recognized "would doubtless be effectual to terrify and affright men, and probably to death." [18] It would as soon drive them away from God and make them hate God the more as it would bring them to a new estate. Nevertheless he drove home his lesson with picturesque imagery. There will be raging flames and dolorous shrieks of the damned when "their heads, their eyes, their tongues, their hands, their feet, their loins, and their vitals shall forever be full of glowing, melting fire." [19] As rebels against God who would even encompass God's death if that were possible, the damned deserve this horror.[20] But God is not only concerned for the punishment of sinners; he is jealous of his own honor which has been impugned and trodden on by men. In hell, "God will get himself honor upon you; then he will magnify himself in your ruin, in the presence of the holy angels, and in the presence of the Lamb; and will be praised upon that account by the saints, at the day of judgement: and by all the host of heaven throughout everlasting ages." [21] Here the objectivistic theme is set forth in a most imprecatory sense.

The saints, witnessing this scene of horror, are not to be considered lacking in moral sensitivity. True, "they will have the greater sense of their own happiness, by seeing the contrary misery," but this happiness arises not from an "ill disposition," but is the "fruit of an amiable and excellent disposition." Unlike the Devil's joy which springs from a delight in cruelty and malice, the saints' disposition arises from a conformity to Christ and a recognition of the majesty and justice of God now vindicated before their eyes.[22] So filled are they with a sense of God's justice that their moral criteria are entirely consonant with his. It is not the suffering of the damned as such that they enjoy; it is the objectivistic glory and majesty of God which claims their hearts.

The question arises as to how a being so great and sovereign in his sway could possibly be offended by a finite sinful subject. Again the objectivistic pattern sets the stage for Edwards's answer. The argument proposed to justify this seemingly asymmetrical relation was not uncommon in Christian theology, and Edwards was to return again to it in his treatise on Original Sin. The argument begins with an appeal to man's innate sense of right and wrong—in some ways an anomalous starting point, since man is supposedly entirely corrupt in his moral perceptions. This sense tells man that "every crime or fault deserves a greater or less punishment, in proportion as the crime itself is greater or less." Justice thus means proportionality between the fault and the consequent punishment. If it be accepted that a crime is more or less heinous depending upon the degree of obligation one has to the contrary, and if it also be allowed that man has an infinite obligation to love and obey God, by the same principle of proportionality, it must then be that man in his disobedience is infinitely at fault, since he is in a position contrary to an acknowledged infinite obligation. The degree of infinity in the obligation rests not in the ontological status of the human subject, but in the nature of God, who himself is infinitely excellent, beauteous, lovely, and is therefore infinitely worthy to be honored and obeyed. On these grounds sin is to be construed as nothing less than a

heinous condition of infinite degree, when judged
against the infinitely great object, and it follows that sin
deserves an infinite punishment. The "fault must be
infinite by reason of the infinite object," so there must
be punishment in the same degree.[23]

This dispassionate justification for eternal punishment establishes once more the objectivistic flavor of
Edwards's preaching and thought, but he was not willing to let the argument stand as merely a logical demonstration. A moral argument was also to buttress the doctrine of divine punishment. The entire sermon on "The
Justice of God in the Damnation of Sinners" is given
over to proving that God acts with complete justice in
carrying out his judgment. In this act "God glorifies his
justice," and since God's glory is the chief end of creation, his attribute of justice must also be glorified. The
glory of God would be lessened unless his moral attribute be given full play, and this, as Edwards elsewhere
put it, was one of the "several good and important ends"
served by eternal punishment of the wicked.[24] But there
is another side to the coin. The infinite greatness of God
is as much seen in the depths to which he stoops in saving men as in damning them. God's righteousness in the
form of justice as well as grace is exhibited in Christ's
work. Since Christ has fully satisfied justice, so now an
appeal to God's justice claims salvation for the believer.
"So it is contrived, that that justice that seemed to re-
quire man's destruction, now requires his salvation." [25]
The attributes of God which justify on moral grounds
the punishment of sinners are now even more glorious
in man's salvation. The majesty of God appears more in
the suffering of Christ than in the eternal sufferings of
mankind. The more heinous the condition of man, so
much greater, by infinite proportion, is God glorified in
redemption.[26] In both damnation and salvation, God's
glorious moral attributes are enhanced by their exercise

and exposure to the eyes of both the condemned and the saved.

Of course it is not accurate to suppose that the doctrine of divine sovereignty could be preached and taught without consideration of the subjective response to it. Even in the most vigorous of the imprecatory sermons Edwards held out hope to his hearers. The doctrine of divine punishment served as a threat, but it could be joined with encouragement and hope. Even in the notorious "Sinners in the Hands of an Angry God," by no means the most severe among his imprecatory homilies, the emphasis at last falls upon the phrase, "If God should withdraw his hand." The restraint of God's mercy is deposited in the word "if," without, however, completely relaxing the precariousness of the sinner's position. In one of his most reassuring sermons of the period, "Pressing Into the Kingdom of God," men are urged to seek the kingdom without allowing themselves to be entangled in needless worries over abstruse doctrines like the secret decrees of God, election, the unpardonable sin or original sin. By such fruitless distress of mind and spirit comes "the distemper of melancholy; whence the adversary of souls is wont to take great advantage." [27] To enter the kingdom one is not necessarily to become a theologian; neither is he to spend his time upon continual inspection of his soul's estate. God is to be trusted, since he has provided the means of which the soul is to take full advantage. "You must not think much of your pains . . . you must press towards the kingdom of God, and do your utmost, and hold out to the end, and learn to make no account of it when you have done" for "when you have done all, God will not hold himself obliged to show mercy at last." [28] The final result still is in God's hands, but one does not achieve salvation by resting. Although there is no place for a works righteousness, the subject also has his part to play. This conjoining of theological objectivism with his call to human effort is one of the most baffling of Edwards's concepts. It has been called the Edwardsean paradox, although its origin is rooted in Paul's advice to the Philippians to work out their own salvation with fear and trembling, "for God is at work in you, both to will and to work for his good pleasure." (2:13) For Edwards the paradox posits a natural power in all men that enables them to strive for the kingdom, but the kingdom is a gift, a prize granted only by the deity. One way out of the apparent difficulty, as Edwards saw, was to argue that "the work of obedience" was not necessary to merit salvation, but necessary to preparation for salvation.[29] But this move scarcely resolves the impasse. How can a preparation that has no inherent connection with salvation be considered a preparation? In fact, as Edwards elsewhere wrote, the convictions of conscience do not inevitably produce "saving faith or repentance" which seem to be the only valid preparations conceivable.[30] Thus the natural operations of spiritual and moral efforts guided by conscience at best have a restraining or negative effect on sinful promptings and acts, but are powerless in respect to the positive fruit of repentance. The objectivistic theme can be seen even more fully overriding the subjectivistic when Edwards affirms that God can bypass any preparatory work of man by shedding his grace on whomever he pleases.[31] For the moment the best that can be done to untangle this paradox is to say that God deals individually with men according to his pleasure. In some cases preparation is necessary, and God takes it as such; in other cases, although no moves have been made toward the kingdom, God simply takes hold of the sinner's life. If these alternatives are accepted, morality is virtually cast adrift from religious faith, a conclusion which, in the last analysis, was to prove totally unacceptable to Edwards. If good deeds, interpreted as acts of justice and mercy, have no weight with God, or if the evil men do is no hindrance to the divine act of salvation, the very nerve of moral effort is severed. Indeed, evil may be done so that God's glory will be the greater in rescuing the sinner, whereas the "good" man's salvation argues for a less majestic and sovereign act of the deity, if such a person be saved at all!

The remarkable situation, as seen from the standpoint of a spectator of the revival, was that men did strive to enter in at the straight gate in spite of the apparent contradiction between Edwards's urging men to strive for salvation and his austere denial of the efficacy of effort on the grounds that all depended upon divine grace. Logically, such efforts were doomed in advance, but psychologically, the very box into which the Edwardsean paradox drew them prompted many to frenzied attempts to win salvation in any way they could. The tighter the limitations placed upon them, the more frantic they became. No wonder that Edwards could note with satisfaction that no sermons were more blessed with results than those in which the sovereignty of God was preached.[32] The very desperation which theological objectivism produced appears to have hastened many toward the goal, even when no assurance could be confidently given that their strivings would be blessed. In retrospect, as the *Religious Affections* shows, Edwards reassessed the value of the tumultuous behavior of those who attempted the tour de force of entering the kingdom when they had been pronounced incapable of doing so. Not all had won through to the goal and so they had been lost in subjective feelings and bodily ex-

a testimony of his love of order," since "things should be together or asunder according to their nature." [38] It is not the moral and spiritual fitness of man which at last saves. The human act of "uniting," which Edwards does concede that man accomplishes, is sharply distinguished from the validity of Christ's excellence that graciously covers the individual's shortcomings. Salvation is by Christ's doing, not man's, but the whole drama is of God's will.

Although Edwards strongly emphasized the sovereign rule of God in all things, he nevertheless found it difficult to pass off the human act of "uniting" as a mere exercise without some measure of value. A natural fitness, as he was later to argue in the *True Virtue,* does enjoy a kind of good. There is, he admits, "something in man that is really and spiritually good, that is prior to justification." But lest his reader mistake his central point, he hastened to add, "Yet there is nothing that is accepted as any godliness or excellency of the person till after justification." [39] Here opens the distinction between a natural morality or spirituality and a true virtue consisting in love to God for his own sake. In spite of Edwards's contention that there is some kind of virtue in man prior to the operation of divine grace, he can go on to call persons who have that virtue "altogether hateful" in God's eyes.[40] This surprising evaluation of the human condition rests upon his conviction that the supernatural glory of the divine produces a whole new dimension in human consciousness. There is an incommensurability between the two levels which, although there may be an analogical relation between them, leaves man incapable by his own efforts to scale the extraordinary heights of holiness which Edwards believed he himself had tasted, and which was reserved for those chosen by God. At the last Edwards maintained that there is a natural morality, but denied that it fulfills the goal of true virtue which God alone brings about.

Theological objectivism is a recurrent theme of the majority of Edwards's sermons, but side by side with this motif runs the companion theme of theological utilitarianism. Nowhere is the latter more apparent than in the imprecatory sermons, where the appeal is made to the crassest instincts of self-interest and self-preservation in this world and the next. In sermons of this type especially, the pleasure-pain principle is unashamedly employed. Religion, Christ, and even God sometimes take on the character of devices by which to escape the torments of hell, to win earthly comfort, and to secure celestial happiness. The human being's aspirations and fears are freely played upon to bring him through to salvation. Pages could be filled with examples of Edwards's cudgeling of sinners by alternately spreading out the joys of heaven and the fearsome punishments of hell. It was totally in keeping with his objectivism and his conviction of the moral order of the universe that there should be a general judgment at which time rewards and punishments would be meted out. This truth is taught to men by natural conscience.[41] Vivid descriptions of this ultimate reckoning seemed appropriate means to bring sinners to a lively sense of what lay in store for them.[42] As previously suggested, if sinners will not take advantage of the opportunities for salvation so lavishly offered in this life, then in another world God will teach them "by severe means." "Their eyes in many respects shall be thoroughly opened in hell" and then there will be no chance for reconciliation with God.[43] In his mercy within this world God does not disdain to work upon "men's fears and self-love to restrain their corruptions" lest hell swallow them up.[44] But if these means fail, as they often do, men will find themselves in the hands of the one who made them and knows how to punish both in body and soul. By then it will be too late to offer objections to God's acting out his will.[45] It is all beside the point to comfort oneself with the notion that God is so merciful that "he cannot bear that penal justice should be executed." This line of thought, Edwards argued, "is to conceive of the mercy of God as a passion to which his nature is so subject that God is liable to be moved, and affected, and overcome by seeing a creature in misery, so that he cannot bear to see justice executed: which is a most unworthy and absurd notion of the mercy of God, and would, if true, argue great weakness." [46]

On the other hand, the beatitude of the saved is held out as a great reward. Happiness lies in the world ahead. No small part of that heavenly happiness lies in the prospect which the saved will have of the torments of the damned, since "the two worlds of happiness and misery will be in view of each other." As Edwards saw the connection between the two realms: "It is the nature of pleasure and pain, of happiness and misery, greatly to heighten the sense of each other." [47] Nor was the righteous life to be one of selfless devotion to the Lord. The "everlasting rewards" and "unspeakable infinite benefits" which were to come to men had as their ulterior purpose the advancement of "your own interest." [48] Neither was it to be necessary to await life after death to reap the promised benefits. Summons to conversion were buttressed by the promise that life in this world would prosper. "You will not only gain eternal life by it, but you will be richly rewarded while here, though that be little to your future reward. You cannot take a more direct course to make life pleasant." [49] Again Edwards reminds his hearers that "in seeking the glory of God and the good of your fellow-creatures, you take the surest way to have God seek your interests, and promote your welfare." [50]

The tension between the objectivistic, subjectivistic, and utilitarian strains in Edwards's thought also appeared in his treatises in defense of the Great Awakening. His defense was to incorporate objectivistic as well as subjectivistic considerations, but he also had to show that the means employed to bring about evangelical awakenings, including appeals to the emotions and even to terror and threats of pain, were justified. His objectivism led him to assert that certain criteria derived from the deity, and that others were dependent upon what happened in the souls of men, and thus were of subjectivistic origin. His utilitarianism, on the other hand, exposed him to the charge, never overlooked by opponents of the revival, that men had been threatened and lured into frantic emotionalism on an unethical and emotional basis.

At the outset an embarrassing problem met Edwards. The claim that all true "awakenings" had been from God could scarcely be defended when repeated references were also made to the sovereign pleasure and will of a deity who was bound by no rules as to his actions.[51] In a strict sense one had no business attempting to mount either a defense for or an attack upon such a remarkable outburst of spiritual power, because judgment as to what God could or could not do was in effect a denial of Edwards's central theme of objectivity. Too many times he had informed his listeners that they had no business questioning God's mercy and justice. The way around this difficulty was to revert to Scripture, the instrument backed by the authority of God himself for just such an eventuality. In its light such false grounds for judgment as were provided by "philoso-

phy," criteria not mentioned in the Bible, history or
"former observation," or present lack of experience
simply were to be put out of court.[52] Of course, the
same Scriptures had been pored over to establish the
principle of divine freedom, and this Edwards clearly
stated. "The great God has wrought like himself . . .
so as very much to show his own glory, and exalt his
own sovereignty, power and all-sufficing, and pour contempt on all that human strength, wisdom, prudence,
and sufficiency that men have been wont to trust, and
glory in." [53] But if men were not to trust their reason
and experience, or as Edwards called all such attempts,
their a priori approaches, then it was necessary to repair
to the high ground of criteria, the sacred scriptures
themselves. Unlike the querulous and inadequate attempts of the enemies of the revival to judge by pre-
conceived criteria arising from the unregenerate minds
of men, the Bible was possessed of divine authority itself. Here God had laid down the principles by which
to judge his operations in the hearts of men. The divine
could only stand in judgment upon its own work.

Edwards, however, was not content to base his defense on mere quotation of Scripture. In his treatise on
the *Religious Affections,* he set forth his most sophisticated answer to the critics of God's amazing work by
interweaving objectivistic and subjectivistic criteria,
those which centered upon the deity on the one hand,
and those which dealt with the subjective nature of all
true religion, the affections.

To counter the common charge that the revival
was merely a frantic emotional outburst rife with physical tantrums and social disorder, Edwards had found it
necessary to clear the ground by indicating the proper
role of the affections. The operative fallacy of his opponents lay in their assumption that "the affections of

the soul are something diverse from the will, and not appertaining to the noblest part of the soul, but the meanest principles that it has." [54] One does not have to accept all forms of emotional behavior to recognize that these principles are absolutely central to the dynamics of a person. And if they are crucial elements of the self, it follows that in the most important business which man has, that of religion, his affections will be called into play in a vivid and forceful way. "The very life and soul of all true religion" resides in the affections as the whole man responds to the divine initiative. The will, which is the exercise of "the soul's appetition or aversion" when at its highest pitch, is nothing other than the affections in full play, and as such involves the total person in religious activity.[55] But if the affections are equated with the workings of the will, it does not follow that Edwards's defense was to be one that opened the way to the exercise of raw, unbridled passion. As John E. Smith has carefully pointed out, "The point almost invariably missed is that in Edwards' view the inclination . . . involves both the will and the mind." The affections are "the expression of inclination *through the mind.*" Thus reason is not to be left to its own devices as would be the case with passion, in which instance "the mind is overpowered" and clear understanding suppressed.[56]

Once having cleared the nature of the affections, and having staked out his major thesis that "true religion in great part, consists in holy affections," Edwards was prepared to show what criteria were relevant to determining the validity of the affections.[57] He accomplished this task by skillfully blending criteria of an objectivistic type with those of a subjectivistic type, which gave evidence of the impact that the divine influence had on the self. Considered by themselves, the affections, which are the springs of action in man, are not holy. They become so when they arise from influences "which are spiritual, supernatural and divine," [58] when their "objective ground . . . is the transcendently excellent and amiable nature of divine things, as they are in themselves," [59] when the mind is enlightened in such a manner as "to understand or apprehend divine things," [60] and when there is a "beautiful symmetry and proportion" among the affections.[61] These signs may rightly be understood as objective, since they show clearly that holy affections arise from a source beyond the self, aim at a goal beyond the self, and are modeled on the ordered proportionality of divine reality itself. Or as Edwards succinctly summarized this aspect of the signs, "A holy love has a holy object: the holiness of love consists especially in this that it is the love of that which is holy, as holy . . . so that 'tis the holiness of the object, which is the quality whereon it fixes and terminates." [62] In these cases we have the grounds upon which true affections are brought into play. These signs point away from the human subject and any preoccupation with his own feelings toward the reality of God himself. It is not first of all certain states of consciousness which the self enjoys which determine the validity of the affections, but rather the source, the structure, and the goal which prompt their enactment.

Subjective criteria of valid affections are those in which a "reasonable and spiritual conviction of the reality and certainty of divine things" appears; [63] when there is "evangelical humiliation"; [64] when the whole nature of man is transformed,[65] when the temper of love, meekness, and tenderness in Christ is found,[66] and when "appetite and longing of soul after spiritual attainments" are increased.[67] These criteria or signs possess the immediacy of consciousness which is the appro-

priate response to a divine operation in the soul. But
they must at last be counted as sure signs of holy affections if they arise from and fasten upon the dimension
of the objective holiness of God or Christ.

By the time he put the *Religious Affections* in final
form, Edwards had left behind him the as yet unanswered charge of the opponents of the Great Awakening, that he and others had engaged in sheer terroristic
preaching to bring about conversions. Was it in any way
justifiable for a preacher to use such doctrines as heaven
and hell, or even God's sovereignty as lashes to drive
men toward salvation? What moral justification can
be offered for the employment of fear of punishment
and hope of reward, of appeals to pain and pleasure?

The first basis of Edwards's defense was Scripture,
wherein he could find abundant evidence that warnings
and promises had been given to mankind, but he went
on to develop his reply on two other grounds: the psychological nature of man, who is possessed of affections
including the fear of pain and the desire for happiness,
and the sinful nature of man. As to the first of these,
Edwards argued, if man is largely a creature of loves and
hates, then these affections are to be moved by suitable
means. Or as he put the matter in the *Religious Affections,* "such means are to be desired as have much of a
tendency to move the affections." [68] Therefore preaching which stimulates these affections is entirely appropriate to the task. In the second instance, the terribly
dangerous condition in which the naturally sinful man
finds himself calls for a mode of preaching which will
clearly set forth the dire plight in which he stands. Consequently in *Some Thoughts on the Revival,* Edwards
had boldly confronted the charge by asking, "Why
should we be afraid to let persons, that are in an infinitely miserable condition, know the truth or bring

them into the light, for fear it should terrify them?" [69] Men do not first of all need comfort, but as in the case of a patient suffering from a grievous sore, the doctor must thrust in his lance to the core, in spite of the anguish caused. It would be a dereliction of duty merely to apply a plaster and a patent immorality to allow the patient's shrieks to divert the doctor from his professional responsibility.[70] True, Edwards hedged to the degree that the condition of the sinner should not be painted in worse colors than was the truth. Nor should a melancholy person be pressed too hard. Nevertheless he maintained defiantly, "I am not afraid to tell sinners that are most sensible of their misery, that their case is indeed as miserable as they think it to be, and a thousand times more so; for this is the truth." [71] But the other side of the coin is no less important. Persons under conviction of sin, "whose consciences are awakened" must have the gospel preached to them. They must know of a Savior, who is sufficient to save them and who stands ready to receive them, for this is also the truth, as well as that they now are in an infinitely dreadful condition: this is the word of God.[72] Yet Edwards was reluctant to claim that men could be herded into the kingdom by forcible means. Mere fear of hell may serve as a negative impulse, causing consciences to be aroused, but it will not bring men home to Christ. "This forced compliance is not what Christ seeks; he seeks a free and willing acceptance." [73]

In view of Edwards's strictures upon the sinful nature of man, it would appear that saints in this world should have nothing to do with sinners. But this conclusion he did not draw. In the midst of his savage, denunciatory sermon on the *End of the Wicked Contemplated by the Righteous,* we find him arguing for a love to all men, regardless of their spiritual and moral estate.

"We ought now to love all, and even wicked men; we know not but that God loves them." [74] It may be, unknown to his contemporaries, that one of the wicked upon whom God has set his love will be a "companion in eternity." However, he went on to say, in the life after death what is "a virtue now . . . will be no virtue then." [75] The natural affections which men display in this world, the absence of which in this world is a "very vicious disposition," are "no virtue in the saints in glory." [76] From this premise Edwards went on to state his case for the enjoyment of the saints for the everlasting punishment of sinners that redounds to the glory of God. Thus in spite of Edwards's kind words for a benign spirit among all men in this world, sinners are still to be threatened with torment in the life after death and promised the highest rewards of happiness if they convert. The passage from this world to the next thus introduces a discontinuity in the meaning of virtue. What is virtuous in this world turns out to be no virtue in the next. The virtue of the saints will exercise itself in a higher manner, quite distinct from that found in the common life of mankind. Thus his utilitarianism seems to have won out over his conviction of the divine sovereignty when the means used to promote conversion are less those which promote the divine glory than they are tools by which to press people into the new order.

There remained another line of Edwards's defense of the great revival, that which was explicitly concerned with its ethical results. In his *Thoughts on the Revival,* Edwards had argued against his opponents that the results of the Awakening should be judged by the work of God, not by a priori criteria. If the results were found to be consonant with Scripture, "we are bound, without more ado, to rest in it as God's work." [77] He could point to transports of the soul which had been enjoyed, all in agreement with the Bible, but he did not rest his case at that point. He also insisted that there had sprung forth a rich harvest of moral results. While he freely admitted that there were unfortunate by-products of the revival, he tenaciously maintained that certain external expressions of genuine affections should be reckoned to its credit. He found "self-denial, righteousness, meekness and Christian love" flourishing among men.[78] Young people had been reformed in respect to "drinking, tavern haunting, profane speaking and extravagance" in apparel. The vanity of the wealthy and those of a "fashionable gay education" had been subdued, quarrels had been patched up and restitutions made. Indians, "those wretched people and dregs of mankind" as well as "many of the poor negroes" had been reformed. And there abounded a "love and compassion to all mankind" among the converted.[79]

The same theme was vigorously pursued by Edwards in the *Religious Affections* when he maintained that the chief sign of gracious affections lay in moral results. Both Scripture and reason testify that properly raised affections will exhibit themselves in a heightened morality.[80] The works of grace go "to the very bottom of the heart, and take hold of the very inmost springs of life and activity." Truly converted men are new creatures in whom the soul and body make up one entity of which good works are the end product. It is this total union which God at last judges, not merely the affections or the external acts themselves. "All Christian experience is not properly called practice: but all Christian practice is properly experience," Edwards claims.[81] Nothing is more active than true grace, so it follows as a matter of course that the heart truly moved will express itself spontaneously in beneficent acts. Although the presumptive saint may fail at certain points to bring forth the requisite moral deeds, the very perseverance and return to the ground of good works are indications that the persistent power of grace will reassert itself.[82]

It may be a sign of genuine faith that beneficial moral deeds inevitably proceed from it. But, in turn, it may be asked by what norms are the works themselves then to be judged. What makes a work good? One answer for Edwards was to repeat all the valid distinguishing signs which make up a major portion of the *Religious Affections;* however, he also placed emphasis upon two criteria. On the one hand there were what he called "Christian rules," [83] and on the other, the firm conviction and sense of God's honor, majesty, and glory. The first of these criteria guarded against the all too familiar danger of falling off into antinomianism, criteria that drew upon his objectivism. As he stated the latter, "Whenever a person finds within him an heart to treat God as God . . . and finds his disposition effectual in the experiment, that is the most proper, and most distinguishing experience." [84] The Christian rules to which he referred his readers were such as meekness and forgiveness, doing good to men's souls and bodies, temperance, mortification, and humble conversation, "walking as Christians in all places, in families, among neighbors, friends and enemies, superiors, inferiors and equals." [85] But these are rules, Edwards carefully pointed out, that were not to be used in judging the deeds of non-Christians: they apply only to professing Christians.[86]

Edwards's statement that practice was the best evidence of sincerity of conviction is not the straightforward, common-sense contention it appears to be when taken in connection with other "signs." Can practice be elevated to a primary position among the evidences of a transformed heart in contrast to that supreme, spiritual conviction "of the reality and certainty of divine things?" [87] What need for good works is there if, as Professor John E. Smith claims, "A man sees that it is really so" that he does have gracious affections.[88] It would seem that seeing that it is "really so" decides the question at the outset. Edwards himself is finally forced by his own logic and the pressure from the "liberal" critics of the revival to qualify his presentation of the significance of good works. His was a monumental dilemma. He had to show to Chauncy and his fellow critics that affections end in no narcissistic self-enjoyment; hence works do follow properly aroused affections, as Edwards's whole psychology and theology demanded. But he also had to remind the frenetic enthusiasts of revivalism that raised affections without reformed behavior were void of significance. In the context of this delicately poised dilemma he had both to affirm the significance of good works and yet to deny that they justify the moral agent. However, he could not keep the balances held even between the two sides of the problem without whittling away his bold affirmation that good works were the chief sign of conversion. He had at last to confess "that no external manifestations and outward appearances whatsoever . . . are infallible evidences of grace." Consequently, none can beget an absolute certitude as to the condition of one's soul. In fact, evidences of good work may even be imitated without suitable transformations of one's spiritual condition. It is "impossible certainly to determine, how far a man may go in many external appearances and imitations of grace, from other principles." The somewhat lame conclusion at which he finally arrived was that these manifestations were simply "the best mankind can have." [89] If conduct, or moral and spiritual consequences, under these limitations are the best men must settle for, much doubt is thereby introduced in Edwards's original purpose of distinguishing true from false affections.

The whole problem is directly connected with the larger, traditional theological question as to whether works can ever justify true piety or insure its existence. Justification by faith, which is the doctrine in question, is strongly linked with divine objectivity in the Calvinistic scheme where it becomes increasingly difficult to detect what role any human activity has in indicating which are truly gracious affections. God as the initiator and goal of the affections leaves little room for identifying precisely what obligations fall to man. As Professor Smith makes clear: "The point is that the more one stresses . . . the doctrine that God not only bestows grace on justification and sanctification but further provides all the conditions for grasping and receiving this grace, the more difficult it becomes to understand what can be meant by saying that a man has a duty to do this or that in connection with believing in God." [90] But Edwards argued that the union of the believer with Christ is not to be counted a spiritual or moral achievement of the believer, but a "natural fitness" between the two by means of which the repentant believer was to be treated as covered by Christ's righteousness. This being the case, there is no room for supposing that any human work, even faith itself, should be counted as a justifying operation. Confusion arises only from imagining that works are the price of divine favor, rather than being the sign of divine favor.[91] The sign, in short, is neither to be taken as a justifying fact nor as the sole purpose of the divine action. It is a result without which faith and true affections would stop short of their intended outcome, but the effect cannot be used to lay claim to salvation. By the same reasoning, however,

Edwards could not coherently argue that moral effects in any way provide a defense for the revival. They remain indications of gracious affections, which if treated in turn as "proof" of the value of the Awakening, lose their status and fall off into the doctrine of justification by works. They may be used as tests of sincerity within limits, but they may not establish the righteousness of the converted sinner without endangering the objectivistic bent of Edwards's thought at this point.[92]

The Great Awakening found Edwards employing all three distinctive motifs. He preached the doctrine of divine sovereignty, and his sermons were remarkably blessed with conversions. He spoke to and about the new and supernatural sense of the heart for divine matters, and thereby touched the deepest subjective tonalities of men's souls. But he also lured and menaced with promises of happiness and threats of eternal damnation, thus stooping to the crassest forms of utilitarianism. A reading of the form of morality which these devices were to bring forth was on the one hand that of an ethic which found its ground and goal in the supreme glory of the deity, and on the other an ethic of prudential self-interest which contradicted the thrust of his objectivism.

Morality without Grace: Foundations

IN THE *Religious Affections* Edwards had not only indicated the nature and manner in which genuine religious affections expressed themselves, he had also laid
down the framework for an understanding of the human
constitution apart from which it would be impossible
to understand the religious and moral life. He had
aimed at describing the self as a unity made up of the
affections, the will, perception, and understanding. Instead of a faculty psychology in which diverse elements
of the self operated in a quasi-mechanistic fashion, he
offered the notion of a self whose various modalities of
action were all centered in the concrete being of the
human personality. Thus "affections of the soul are not
properly distinguished from the will, as though they
were two faculties of the soul," he had written in
Thoughts on the Revival and echoed in the *Religious
Affections.*[1] To understand this structure of the self
then becomes the foundation of any system of ethics,
and to that task two of his most formidable works were
dedicated, the treatise on the *Freedom of the Will* and
that on *Original Sin.*

The treatise on the *Freedom of the Will* is by no means to be understood as an exercise in tortured dialectics designed to prove that several hapless Arminians did not know what they were talking about. Nor is it to be approached only as an ingenious exposure of the foundational dynamics of the self. Its first and abiding contribution, theologically and ethically, was to serve as an unshakable buttress to theological objectivism. True, the major part of the work was given over to a careful clarification of terms and a thorough analysis of the views of the proponents of the doctrine of free choice, but all of this was to show that without moral necessity mankind would make a shambles of the divine order and reduce God to the task of patching up his well-nigh ruined creation. If, with no moral cause, human wills spontaneously allow choices and events quite unforeseen by God, all manner of confusion would ensue. If choices are generated from nothing, as the Arminians seemed to argue, then "millions of millions" of other events might do the same, thus jeopardizing and denying God's sovereign reign. Under these conditions God would become a celestial utility ever in pursuit of correctives for the random and destructive pluralism to which man had reduced the divine creation.[2] To meet this obnoxious possibility Edwards bent his efforts to the demolition of what he counted to be the spurious and mischievous notion of the freedom of self-determination.

Much of the dynamite with which he destroyed his opponents was deposited in his careful assessment of the terms to be used in the argument. It was crucial, for example, to make clear that the will was not some self-determining faculty operating in independence of the mind or soul. Rather the term "will" is only a way of speaking of the mind as it acts in choosing: it is "that by which the mind chooses anything." Consequently it would be absurd to regard the will as having a will to choose! "For the will itself is not an agent that has a will . . . that which has the power of volition or choice is the man or the soul and not the power of volition itself." To be able to choose is "the property of an agent" and "not the property of properties." [3] Choices are made by men, not by the will operating autonomously, regardless of the motive set before the mind. Nor does the will act first in respect to such motives as may be placed before the self. To act, to choose is already to have been brought under the influence of a motive; otherwise, oddly enough, a choice would have already been made before any motive came into play.[4]

How then does the willing occur? Swerving aside from Locke's distinction between desire and will, Edwards brought the two together. "A man never, in any instance, wills anything contrary to his desires, or desires anything contrary to his will," [5] a conclusion anticipated in the *Religious Affections*.[6] What one likes, one wills positively; what he is disinclined toward, he wills against. But there are various degrees of disliking, liking, electing, and rejecting. How then could one ascertain which motive prompted the mind in the act of willing? The answer which Edwards gave cut the knot of speculation. It is the strongest motive as it appears to the understanding, a term which in Edwards's mind includes the whole faculty of perception or apprehension—not merely reason or judgment.[7] This is but to say that the strongest motive which moves the "will" is that which promises "good" or "agreeableness." It is that which in the purview of the whole personality, character, or mind appeals or disgusts so overwhelmingly that it is elected or repudiated. Edwards's use of terms in explaining what constitutes an act of willing is most precise. The motive comes to the mind in no other way than that "it is perceived or thought of." And, in the case of the strongest motive, this "determines" the mind in its willing.[8] The word "determines," however, carries the wrong meaning, for it implies a measure of discontinuity between the motive and the willing, a pressure exerted from the "outside" upon the mind, or apprehension without regard to the receptive posture of the mind. To be sure, the motive does play upon the perception externally, but only in accordance with the nature of the self at that moment, and it thereby becomes part of a total act of the mind. Edwards's account states the matter most carefully. "I have chosen to express myself thus, that the will *is* as the greatest apparent good, or as what appears most agreeable, is, than to say that the will is *determined* by the greatest apparent good . . . because an appearing most agreeable or pleasing to the mind, and the mind's preferring and choosing, seem hardly to be properly and perfectly distinct . . . The act of volition itself is always determined by that in or about the mind's view of the object, which causes it to appear most agreeable. I say, in or about the mind's view of the object, because what has influence to render an object agreeable, is not only what appears in the object viewed, but also the manner of the view, and the state and circumstances of the mind that views." [9] Thus the will does not act separately and freely, but is integrated with the mind by following after the strongest motive.[10]

Having gone so far in describing the act of volition, Edwards found it essential to cast this process in the framework of cause and effect. What he wished to argue was that nothing comes to pass in this finite world without a cause, and he was to use this formula repeatedly to the acute discomfiture of his opponents. But what is a cause? In a rough and ready way, cause has been understood as that factor which makes something occur or without which something could not be, that is, an effect. Occasionally Edwards lapses into this usage, but his more sophisticated notion of cause and effect is more congenial to the position of Hume or even more particularly that of Leibniz's principle of sufficient reason.[11] Philosophical necessity he defines as "the full and fixed connection between the things signified by the subject and predicate of a proposition, which affirms something to be true." [12] This definition repudiates the notion of efficient causation, and provides the basis for the highly important distinction between "moral determinism" and "compulsion." [13]

Every event is caused, and in this sense it may be said to be totally determined. The fixed connection between subject and predicate is a logical rendering of this fact. Nevertheless, it does not follow that every event is compelled by an extraneous force. Or as Paul Ramsey succinctly puts it, "Free acts are uncompelled acts, not uncaused or undetermined acts." [14] F. J. E. Woodbridge also caught the crucial significance of Edwards's use of "cause" and "necessity" when he noted that "necessity is not some exterior fate, compelling events, but the actual linkage which the events disclose in their existence," both in mind and nature. "The causes of volition, whatever they may be, do not affect its voluntary aspect or destroy the function of the will, any more than the causes of life destroy the functions of life." [15] Cause, then, is "any antecedent with which a consequent event is so connected that it truly belongs to the reason why the proposition which affirms that event, is true." [16] Moral necessity is that fixity of connection between inclination and motives which gives structure to the moral life, but as Edwards was to make clear in distinguishing moral necessity from natural necessity, the difference between these two forms does not lie in the nature of the connection between events —each is as fixed as the other—but in the nature of the terms connected in each case. Moral necessity involves dispositions, motives, or volitional acts; natural necessity involves such things as pain, sight, or the experience of gravity.[17]

Now unless there be "cause" in the sense of moral necessity in respect to human willing, and unless in a larger sense it be operative in the created, finite world, the universe would be a madhouse of random events, and "all arguing from effects to causes ceaseth, and so all knowledge of any existence, besides what we have by the most direct and immediate intention." [18] And with this "grand principle of common sense" Edwards set about to dispatch those who acknowledged effects without adequate causes or sufficient reasons, of choices made while the will is indifferent.[19] Relentlessly he pursued them into infinite regresses, where, if there be such a thing as cause, they were brought to a standstill when confronted by an act of will which was not freely chosen. If the first act of will is not freely chosen, neither are any successive acts of the will. It must be then that at the root of any so-called free act of will there lies an antecedent cause, that is, an apprehension or motive to which the mind as willing inclines, and this conviction is moral necessity.

What then is freedom, for Edwards does not deny that men are free? Edwards's answer rings clear. "Let the person come by his volition or choice how he will, yet, if he is able, and there is nothing in the way to hinder his pursuing and executing his will, the man is freely and perfectly free." [20] To be prevented from carrying out an act of will because of some natural impediment and defect exterior to the will robs man of freedom and excuses him of guilt, but moral inability signifies lack of inclination to act and does not excuse.[21] In the last analysis it is the nature of what is willed that is subject to judgment, not the manner by which it has come to be. It is the intrinsic character of the volitional act, not the cause, which must come under the criterion of "inherent deformity" or conformity to virtue.[22]

If his Arminian foes did not grasp the significance of his argument and continued to appeal to the feeling of free choice, Edwards was willing to meet them on the grounds of concrete experience as well as logic. If one will pay careful attention to what actually passes in man's mind, he will find, thinks Edwards, no evidence of a will determining itself or acting contingently. There is not the slightest evidence for the Arminian conclusions. Ignorance of the cause of a particular decision "may make some imagine, that volition has no cause, or that it produces itself. But I have no more reason from hence to determine any such thing, than I have to determine that I gave myself my own being, or that I come into being accidentally without a cause, because I first found myself possessed of being, before I had knowledge of a cause of my being." [23] There would seem to be as much evidence from experience for Edwards's form of determinism as there is for that freedom of choice to which repeatedly the Arminians repaired when hard pressed. Nowhere is this more evident than in those cases where virtue operating by moral necessity shows itself to be praiseworthy. After all, God is necessarily virtuous, as is also Jesus Christ— this all parties would allow—yet no one could properly deny to them the high praise due to their goodness.[24] So also in the case of a virtuous man. "Men don't think a good act to be the less praiseworthy, for the agent's being much determined in it by a good inclination or a good motive; but the more." In the same way a man determined by evil motives is the more blameworthy.[25] Since the whole man is involved in the act of willing, which is not some faculty distinguishable from the totality, the man is either praiseworthy or blameworthy, depending on the character of the motives to which he is responding.

If man be thus bound by moral necessity, how then can it be said that "means" can legitimately be employed to turn a person from an immoral course? But the question already reveals its impropriety. If man is operating in the context of moral necessity, then clearly means are necessary to achieve the end sought. There must be a full connection between means and ends, else the ends would not be achieved. The Arminians on the other hand, with their doctrine of the unfixedness between means and ends, and talk of contingency, would themselves find it impossible to account for the need of means. In the process of the development of character, these means are absolutely necessary, since an end without means to it, as in fatalism, would make no sense in the Edwardsean scheme. The fixity of the result is dependent upon the equal fixity of the means to that end. Thus the way is left clear for means to be employed. After all, man, as Edwards made explicit, is not a machine. His reason, understanding, capacity of choice and control of his actions make him "entirely, perfectly and unspeakably different from a mere machine." [26] Instead of being blown about by the winds of "blind contingence," he has built into him a structure which affords a purposeful integrity. Once having made secure moral necessity, Edwards had little trouble in showing that means and therefore commands and obligations were necessary, even when the will to obey was lacking. Else "inability will excuse disobedience" and wickedness would always carry with it that which excuses it.[27]

Ethical thought has for so long found plausible the notion that freedom of choice is the sine qua non of moral responsibility, that Edwards's views seem to provide meager grounds upon which to rear an ethical system. However, for him ethics not rooted in a "determinism" encompassing the total character in the moral act would be impossible. Human responsibility was not to be purchased by exacting from God the price of freedom of choice.[28] If men are to be counted as morally accountable, then the sure connection between motive and will must be established, and the self can then be understood as the total moral entity which stands behind and in the act itself.[29] This is the way in which God has ordered the structure of moral behavior, and it is fruitless to complain that matters might have stood otherwise.[30] And at this point, once more, his theological objectivism reveals itself as the undergirding thesis of the treatise on *The Freedom of the Will*. Not only is the moral structure of man ordained by God, but as the Arminians complained, God himself, rather than the freedom of the agent, accounts for virtue in man by acting as the "extrinsic cause" of virtue.[31] So also in the case of vicious or sinful volitions which God allows by the same structure of moral necessity which is operative in the case of virtue. But in all this, Edwards had no mind to deprecate man. Quite the opposite. Men might claim freedom of choice as "some dignity or privilege," but, he went on to ask, "what dignity or privilege is there, in being given up to such a wild contingence as this, to be perfectly and constantly liable to act unintelligently and unreasonably, and as much without the guidance of understanding, as if we had none, or were as destitute of perception as the smoke that is driven by the wind." [32] Where is the dignity of a man if he must continuously decide whether or not to tell the truth, must continuously behave honorably or generously to others as though every moral act were discrete from every other act? Such a creature would consist of atomistic moral or immoral jumps from which nothing sensible could be predicated.

If the treatise on *The Freedom of the Will* can be counted as a final demonstration of the folly of the Arminians and a successful defense of moral necessity as the ground of virtue and vice, an even more telling blow was to be launched against those of a Pelagian temper who not only claimed freedom of choice, but also claimed the generally benevolent nature of man. The unkindest cut Edwards offered was not to deny freedom of choice, but to assert that in the context of moral necessity man was caught irrevocably in the toils of original sin. The tones of the imprecatory sermons were to be heard again, this time in a systematic treatise.

The arguments adduced for this grim situation of the natural man do not, for the most part, sparkle with dialectical skill as did those on the will, but they were no less effective in crunching over the opponents' positions. From history and Scripture Edwards demonstrated that all men did in fact fall into all manner of evil, that this evil constituted an infinitely heinous affront to divine dignity for which men could offer no repayment, that this deplorable state of affairs could be accounted for only by reference to an underlying active steady cause, namely a corrupted nature brought about by Adam's fall, in which man participated by the principle of identity, and that God could not be held responsible as the active author of sin.

What is essential to an understanding of Edwards's

position is the point that sin does not consist solely of immoral deeds, although these are the symptoms of the deeper cancer inherent in the self, but rather that sin is a persistent failure to enjoy and cleave to the glory of God for his own sake. In that light it was folly to talk of man's doing at least as many good deeds as bad, thereby avoiding the dire consequences which Edwards saw lowering over mankind. Moralistic book-keeping of good and bad deeds showed that those who held such naïve ideas had no valid conception of either sin or virtue. They assumed, contrary to Edwards's conclusions in the *Will,* that man as an essence was a neutral being on whose strand of personality could be strung immoral and moral acts in at least approximately equal numbers. But of course all this concession to human virtues was beside the point. Edwards ridiculed this whole notion by likening it to a ship crossing the Atlantic, which might go much of the distance before sinking and which then might be justified as seaworthy because it sailed "above waters more hours than it will be in sinking." [33] In an even more pointed but less attractive analogy he noted that those who depended on their good works were like a wife who "though she committed adultery, and that with the slaves and scoundrels some times, yet she did not do this so often as she did the duties of a wife." [34] What John Taylor, his principal opponent in the *Original Sin,* failed completely to see was that the very character of sin itself infinitely outweighed the paltry quantity of supposedly virtuous deeds a person could muster. Quality not quantity at this point was at stake, and the quality of sin was such that it left men with an infinite debt before an infinite deity. No amount of pulling or hauling on the part of the natural man could ever make good that debt. Here Edwards employed, as he had in his sermons, the feudalistic argument formulated by Anselm.[35] The degree of hatefulness or demerit in sin is to be measured by the being against which it is committed. It is against God, who is an infinite being; therefore although it is a finite being who sins, the sin is to be counted as infinite.[36] Since it is infinite, man cannot hope to cast anything into the scale which would either make good the demerit or avert the punishment to follow.[37]

If men do without fail fall into the abyss of infinite demerit, there must be an adequate cause, since "a steady effect argues a steady cause." [38] But Taylor had argued that each man, being possessed of free choice, simply had misused his freedom and thereby had brought on himself the guilt which alone was properly his. No sin could be rooted in the moral necessity which Edwards had indicated in the *Will*, but only in that freedom of the will by virtue of which responsibility was vested in the single moral agent. Edwards in turn asked how it came to pass that if the "cause is indifferent, why is not the effect in some measure indifferent?" [39] Obviously with sin universally strewn across the pages of history and recorded in Scripture, free choice could not be offered as a sufficient cause. Only the deep stain of a perverted heart which ran throughout mankind answered the purpose.

Nothing outraged the Pelagian mind more than to be informed that Adam's sin had infected the whole human family. Sin and guilt are nontransferable properties, they argued. Each man stands for himself alone. Simple justice and good sense dictate no other conclusion, thought Taylor. However, Edwards was not to be put off by this atomistic conception of human nature. He forged an ingenious argument for personal identity. Whereas Locke had held that identity resided in memory,[40] Edwards cut deeper by arguing that identity de-

pended upon God's sovereign constitution, which upheld from moment to moment all existence, including
the function of memory. "In point of time," he argued,
"what is past entirely ceases when present existence begins; otherwise it would not be past." Therefore, since
one being in the created mind does not explain the
appearance of the next being in time, the agency of
God must be operative in each successive moment to
guarantee the existence of created substances. What appear in certain respects to be diverse, are nevertheless
identical by God's constitution, for it is his will that
"makes truth in the affairs of this nature." Humanity,
all there was of it, was in Adam, and he was so treated
by God, and so also man centuries later is identified
with Adam. Adam's sin is not imputed to man as Adam's
sin. It is properly humanity's sin and therefore is identified with humanity. When Adam fell, man fell, and
man's present vile estate is nothing more than a re-
capitulation or extension of the fall.[41]

The theological objectivism which repeatedly
sounds through his *Original Sin,* when he argues for
the infinite heinousness of sin and the principle of
identity which "makes truth" in these matters," led
straight to the most difficult problem of all, the origin
of sin in a world under God's supreme control. At the
outset Edwards swept aside the false notion that God
had implanted any wrong principle in man, and went
on to explain how the human venture went astray. Man
at creation was endowed with two sets of principles, the
inferior or natural ones such as self-love, and the superior or supernatural ones such as capacity for love
of God. But when man fell, the "superior principles
left his heart, . . . that communion with God, on
which these principles depended, entirely ceased." With
the departure or withdrawal of the supernatural prin-

ciples, the inferior principles took over human life, with catastrophic results. Ever seeking himself and "the objects of his private affections and appetites," man becomes an accursed rebel and one who has richly merited the awful punishment of outraged sovereignty. Nevertheless God cannot be held directly responsible for the human plight. His withdrawal of the supernatural principles was only fitting, considering the affront to his honor offered by Adam's disobedience. Furthermore, God's was a privative act, by which the natural principles were left to themselves. When once released from the domination of the superior principles, corruption followed. For his own mysterious reasons God allows these corrupted beings not only to live but even to flourish in sin until his own time comes to triumph, either by pure grace or dreadful punishment, over the evil spawned in individual hearts in this world and the next.[42]

Whichever way Edwards turns, his insistence upon the divine sovereignty leads to God's authorship of sin. It matters little whether God allowed sin to occur by withdrawal of the superior principles, or whether he directly caused at least the possibility of sin in Adam's heart by so ordering the natural principles that, left to themselves, would bring on the horrid consequences attributed to them by Edwards.[43] In the *Will* Edwards had canvassed this ground more thoroughly than he did in the *Original Sin,* and he was at last reduced to the concession that God was the author of sin. "If by 'the author of sin' is meant the permitter or not a hinderer of sin; and at the same time, a disposer of the state of events, in such a manner, for wise, holy and most excellent ends and purposes, that sin . . . will most certainly and infallibly follow: I say . . . I don't deny that God is the author of sin (though I dislike

and reject the phrase . . .)." [44] But, he added with a
flourish, the Arminians were in no better fix with their
doctrine of freedom, which explained sin as the result
of a free choice, but were also forced to accept the fact
that God permitted sin to exist and even to increase.[45]
Of course, Edwards was careful to defend God's honor
by insisting that his permission of sin was not an evil
act executed so that good might come from it. It did
not arise from being "unfit and insuitable in its own
nature," since God's purpose, not chance, disposes of
good and evil, and he knows how all events should
be arranged in respect to each other; nor is this permission due to any "bad tendency," in deity since he
has arranged matters to be in the best final state; nor
is it due to any "evil disposition" on his part, for what
he aims at is good "in the final result of things." [46] But
in spite of all his tortured moves, Edwards had not
satisfactorily answered how it was possible for an innocent being first of all to fall into disobedience. By
his own account, the withdrawal of the supernatural
principles came as an act of God subsequent to Adam's
fall, not before or during it. If there must be an adequate cause for every event, if there is an inclination
preceding every act of will, then how can natural principles, created by God as the identifying characteristics
of a human nature which had not been effaced by sin,
be credited as the source of sin? At last, Edwards has
to rest in the mystery of the whole transaction. "The
first arising or existing of that evil disposition in the
heart of Adam, was by God's permission; who could
have prevented it, if he had pleased, by giving such
influences of his spirit, as would have been absolutely
effectual to hinder it: which, it is plain in fact, he did
withhold: and whatever mystery may be supposed in
the affair, yet no Christian will presume to say, it was

not in perfect consistence with God's holiness and righteousness, notwithstanding Adam had been guilty of no offense before." [47] Thus when certain forms of theological objectivism are carried through to the end, there is no escape from making God in some sense the author of all, including sin.

Who then is the "natural man," who in spite of his sinfulness nevertheless has ethical duties to perform? Edwards had insisted in his *Original Sin* that the proper way to understand man as man was to analyze his condition apart from what divine grace could do. The natural man is he who is bereft of supernatural principles, not he who has lost all human capacities. He is one who still chooses, loves, rejects, hopes, acts, but all within the orbit of that self-interest to which his rebellion in Adam has condemned him. What is denied to him is not his humanity, but his capacity to love and cherish the excellence of God for his own sake, but this in no way excuses him from either having some rough notion of what true virtue is or being bound to certain moral responsibilities by virtue of which human society, ever marked by sin, carries on its business. What follows will be morality, but a morality in a lower key, one that has not broken through to that "relish" for divine love which is the capstone of the Christian's experience. Although it has been argued that "The doctrine of the sinfulness of even our best efforts cuts the nerve of morality," [48] Edwards thought otherwise. The moral life is not a closed issue, even with sin all about, and with the presence of God lowering over all. Man still has serious business with God, even in his estranged condition. In a context of theological objectivism, man, no matter how sinful, is not outside the range of the deity's action, nor stripped of obligations to him and his fellow creatures.

Morality without Grace: Its Nature

THE GRIM CONSEQUENCES described in the *Original Sin* and the imprecatory sermons appear to leave mankind in so deplorable a state as to foreclose all possibility of a moral or religious life. Edwards could claim that after the fall men are in a condition of "extreme and brutish blindness in the things of religion," but he had also hastened to add that no fault was to be found with their natural faculties. "God has given men faculties truly noble and excellent." [1] In a similar vein he had hotly replied to Taylor's charge that the doctrine of original sin poured contempt on human nature by asserting that "No contempt is by this doctrine cast upon the noble faculties and capacities of man's nature, or the exalted business, and divine and immortal happiness he is made capable of." [2]

The contrast between the dark picture Edwards had drawn of man's plight and his defense of the "noble faculties" man enjoyed is traceable to a distinction he had drawn concerning the image of God in man. In conformity with the nature of God man originally possessed two images. As it is that in God there are moral attributes which compose his holiness, so it is that in Adam there was once a spiritual image, now forfeited. As it is that in God there are natural attributes of strength and knowledge which compose his greatness, so it is that in man God's natural image remains "in men's reason and understanding, his natural ability and dominion over creatures." [3] Through these natural capacities, man is able to recognize that there is such a thing as the grace of God, which he understands only as "a profitable good to me." Because of the lack of the supernatural principles originally granted by God, natural man turns in upon himself rejoicing in religious feelings. Such persons "are wont to keep their eye upon themselves" and are taken up, not with the glory of God or the beauty of Christ, but "the beauty of their experiences." [4] However, this inversion toward the subjective and the utilitarian is not without its benefit in God's world. At least men by natural ability have some intimation of the natural attributes of God, and so are made aware of God's presence and control over human life. Thus a sense of God's greatness and natural attributes is "exceeding useful and necessary." [5] On this foundation something like a natural ethic can be reared.

The ethical motivation of the natural man is self-love, and to this concept Edwards gave special attention in *Charity and its Fruits,* in *Miscellany* 530, and finally and most explicitly in the treatise on *True Virtue.* In the first of these works he turned to the familiar pattern elaborated in the *Original Sin,* namely that man, having lost his noblest and most benevolent principles, fell under "the power and government of self-love." Man's mind "shrank from its primitive greatness and expandedness to an exceeding smallness and contractedness." "Sin, like some powerful astringent, concentrated his soul to the very small dimensions of selfishness," and "man retired within himself." [6]

However, self-love is a complex phenomenon and easily misunderstood. If it can be conceived as a love of one's own happiness, it is not necessarily contrary to Christian faith. "That a man should love his own happiness is as necessary to his nature as the faculty of the will is; and it is impossible that such a love should be destroyed in any other way than by destroying his being." [7] In this respect self-love is essential to the existence of humanity and is not as such the result of the fall. It "belongs to the nature of all intelligent beings" and "God has made it alike in all." [8] Even when converted, man's love of happiness is not diminished, but is only modified according to the object to which it is directed. Salvation lies in the expansion of one's happiness under the direction of those supernatural principles which reach out to God for his own sake. In what appears almost as a reckless concession, Edwards affirms that "wicked men do not love themselves enough," because they do not love in a way beneficial to their own welfare and happiness.[9] But if once brought under the influence of divine grace, men discover that in loving God's happiness they must needs love their own happiness.[10] By the same token, however, this understanding of self-love shows up the weakness, frailty, and limited character of the natural man's love. He may love his children and wife, do good to society, show kindness to others, and feel gratitude for good deeds done to him, but since "most of the love that there is in the world arises from this principle [of self-love] . . . it does not go beyond nature." [11]

Self-love fails as an adequate moral principle by being excessive and exorbitant, as well as limited.[12] Compared to the love of God and of one's fellow man, such love is disproportionate: the proportion of love is not commensurate with the greatness of the object to which it properly owes allegiance. A holy love, on the other hand, "does not spring out of self, so neither does it tend to self. It delights in the honor and glory of God, for his own sake, and not merely for the sake of self; and it seeks and delights in the good of men, for their sake, and for God's sake." [13]

Edwards had pursued in depth the notion of self-love in *Miscellany* 530. There he argued that self-love must be considered in two forms. In "the most extensive sense" self-love cannot be compared with a love to God, not because of the distance between them, but because they are intimately intertwined; "one enters into the nature of the other." In terms that suggest that Edwards was yielding too much to subjectivism, he claimed, "'T'is improper that our love to God is superior to our general capacity of delighting in anything." This, he argued, is true because a delight in God is a love of God and at the same time it is a love of delight, which is self-love. Thus, since the particular happiness in which one rejoices and loves participates in the general enjoyment of the one who delights, the two aspects are so intermixed as to defy all efforts to contrast them. Thus, when one loves another, he desires good for the other and delights in it if it is obtained, and is uneasy if it is not obtained. At the same time the well affectioned person rejoices in his own happiness at the sight of the good achieved and dislikes the uneasiness which results from the failure of the other to receive the good envisaged. And what is this, concludes Edwards, "but love to our own delight or hatred of our own uneasiness" in the form of self-love. Hence, "no love to another can be superior to self-love as most extensively taken." [14] In this respect self-love is not identified with sin. It is rather a basic component of human nature which comes into play in any delight which properly is one's own.

In this general or extensive sense, Edwards considered self-love to be "compounded" rather than "simple." Self-love arises not only from the nature of a perceiving and willing being, but also from another principle, namely, that principle by virtue of which the good of one person becomes the good of another. It is self-love, so understood, which permits one to love God, and yet to love the good which God brings to one as God's good. Then there follows an important corollary: " 'Tis impossible for any person to be willing to be perfectly and finally miserable for God's sake." To think otherwise would be to suppose that man does not desire his own true happiness, for "the more a man loves God, the more unwilling will he be to be deprived of this happiness." [15] To be truly happy one must rejoice in a good or happiness which is another's, i.e. God's, which in turn constitutes the love of one's own happiness. Self-love in this complex or "compounded" sense is therefore not to be condemned.

The ordinary or "simple" sense of self-love, however, is a quite different matter in Edwards's thought. It amounts to selfishness in a quite ordinary meaning. This kind of self-love constitutes a person's good by being a separate good, as something to which he clings as his alone, and in which he delights "directly and immediately." As such it arises from no other principle than that of the "nature of a perceiving and willing being" and is therefore completely distinct from the compounded self-love which may participate in a love to God.[16] With this kind of self-love natural men continually live, and from it they cannot free themselves by their own efforts. Of these persons Edwards concluded, "No matter what they may do or suffer, it does not change their character." [17] In this most intensive form of subjectivistic utilitarianism, natural men are enfolded in themselves, and even such intimations of God's existence or favor as they receive simply fall into the category of "a profitable good to me."

Although much of what Edwards offered in his posthumous *True Virtue* recalls his careful analysis in *Miscellany* 530, the major essay on virtue moves beyond his preliminary work. By indirection, at least, he is answering those like Mandeville and Hobbes, who would claim that all supposed virtue arises from self-interest, while at the same time he argues that true virtue goes far beyond that natural benevolence which Shaftesbury and Hutcheson held originated in man's uncorrupted nature.[18] In the light of his doctrine of original sin, Edwards appears closely linked to Mandeville and Hobbes, but his analysis of self-love showed that their views of the subject failed to encompass the subtleties of self-love, even as Shaftesbury and Hutcheson were over-optimistic in their estimates of the power of the moral sense in natural man. Against dark estimates of man's morality Edwards was willing to employ Hutcheson's theory of moral sense up to a point; against Hutcheson he was to use his own theory of self-love.

If self-love simply means a man's love of his own happiness, then in accordance with Edwards's views as worked out in *Miscellany* 530, it may be taken either as signifying "all the happiness or pleasure of which the mind is in any regard the subject" or as "the pleasure a man takes in his own proper, private and separate good." [19] But what does the first of these alternatives amount to? It is simply a way of saying that a man loves what he loves, or more fully, that man possesses a general capacity to be pleased or displeased "which is the same thing as a man's having a faculty of will." [20] In this sense, all that is signified by self-love is that it distinguishes man from trees and stones, but "it can never be a reason why man's love is placed on such and such objects." [21] Even if the proponents of this shallow view persist in arguing that self-love means love of "our own happiness," the notion is still absurd. Here the cause and effect have been confused with each other. "Our happiness, consisting in the happiness of the person beloved, is made the cause of our love to that person" but in fact the case is just the opposite. "Our love to the person is the cause of our delighting, or being happy in his happiness . . . the being of inclinations and appetites is prior to any pleasure in gratifying these appetites." [22] Therefore it is fruitless to claim that all morality arises out of self-love in this general sense, since it has not been shown why one's self-love has been stimulated in the direction which it has.

However, when Edwards turns to his second or simple sense of self-love, he mounts his opposition to those who would find in man a natural bent to virtue. Self-love, construed as those pains and pleasures which are private and personal, is what man has by certain principles implanted in his nature, and which sustain no direct "participation in the happiness or sorrow of others, through benevolence." [23] Men may love others in a certain sense, but they do so out of this natural aversion to suffering or out of a liking for one's own happiness. Consequently, "there is no more true virtue in a man thus loving his friends merely from self-love, than there is a self-love itself, the principle from whence it proceeds." [24] Even the pronouncements of the moral sense, which Hutcheson maintained to be a faculty uncorrupted by self-interest, Edwards found to be in part dictated by self-regard.[25] He could reduce the optimistic Hutchesonian estimate to a relatively simple formula: since we love ourselves, it is natural to extend that love to the same kinds of beings as ourselves—who express the same kind of self-interested love toward ourselves.[26] The vaunted disinterested moral sense is tainted with a tit-for-tat quality which amounts to no more than a sense of desert—important as that sense was to be in Edwards's full rendering of the notion of natural morality.[27] The examples offered of a benevolence springing forth spontaneously from a natural source in humanity were systematically reduced to instances of private self-interest. "If a man may from self-love disapprove the evils of malice, envy and others of that sort, which naturally tend to the hurt of mankind, why may he not from the same principle approve the contrary virtues of meekness, peaceableness, benevolence, charity, generosity, justice and the social virtues in general; which, he as easily and clearly knows, naturally tend to the good of mankind?" [28] What appears to be sheer spontaneous disapproval or approval of moral evils and goods amounts to no more than an association of ideas, inbred by custom and education and the play of natural psychological mechanisms.[29]

In spite of its obvious deficiencies when compared to Edwards's exalted conception of true virtue, self-love, like all natural principles, is nevertheless not without its benefits.[30] It is far from being useless in the world, since it is "necessary to society," while at the same time "everybody sees that if it be not subordinate to, and regulated by, another more extensive principle, it may make a man a common enemy to the general system." [31] There is, after all "something of the general nature of virtue in those natural affections and principles," Edwards allowed, or else it would seem there could be

61

no place for the natural morality, a conclusion which experience and reason denied to Edwards. There is a similarity between a natural morality based on self-love and a true virtue. Pity, compassion, gratitude, party loyalty, patriotism, the capacity to approve and disapprove which arises from a sense of natural agreement with benefits and disapprobation of vice and evil—all are possible. A certain restraint of moral evil, which Edwards counted as "negative moral goodness," may even put men in the way of seeking true virtue itself, although in the final analysis all these natural principles of morality rooted in self-love suffer from being "not subordinate to a regard to being in general." Self-love remains "the source of all the wickedness that is in the world." [32] It possesses all the limitations attendant upon a view of reality which has been confined to private systems, even that of society or humanity at large.[33]

Self-love is therefore the height of theological subjectivism, and expresses itself in a utilitarian search for happiness, regardless of the extent to which it is a social virtue. The social virtues come from a perspective which is askew, since they are stimulated by an interest in self or in private advantage. There is no way for men to convert their commendable virtues into the true virtue to which Edwards aspired and which he hoped to unveil to human understanding.

If self-love, necessary as it is to man's existence in certain respects, fails as virtue, is it not possible that there remain in men certain natural principles which by divine constitution lead to a natural benevolence? These principles which determine the mind to certain affections and actions "established chiefly for the preservation of mankind" are what Edwards calls instinct. It was largely on this basis that Shaftesbury and Hutcheson had relied in making their case for a natural virtue in mankind.[34] Nevertheless, Edwards veers off from this enticing view to show that the instinctive basis of virtue fails, as does self-love, to live up to his account of the definition of true virtue. The similarities to true virtue are once more recounted, but they fail because of their partiality. Love of one's children, or between the sexes, or the pity one feels in witnessing the distress of others has nothing of that disinterested benevolence to being in general which constitutes true virtue. Instincts, like self-love, to which they are closely allied, are beneficial, and men take pleasure or experience pain in their exercise, but they are bound to a graceless state. Pity, for example, is embedded in man as "an instance of his [God's] love to the world of mankind, and an evidence, that though the world be so sinful, it is not God's design to make it a world of punishment." So men feel pity over the calamities of others, even those at a distance from them, because they too stand in need of assistance in similar circumstances. However, unlike the case of extreme calamities which tend to human destruction, there is no instinct which rejoices in the prosperity and pleasure of others, since in the latter case men "do not stand in equal necessity of such an instinct as that in order to their preservation." [35] Natural instincts are therefore given by God even to graceless mankind by a divine favor, but they serve the purpose only of sustaining the human family, not that of raising it to a truly virtuous condition.

Natural morality may be motivated by self-love or by instincts, but it must call upon other principles for its guidance and prudential control. These principles, all closely interrelated, are natural reason, or the light of nature, conscience, and the moral sense. The light of reason has not been extinguished by the fall, hampered though it be by the consequences of that event.[36]

Although it by no means raises men to the level of gracious affections, it remains in man as a restraining grace of God. It is capable of teaching that there is a God who governs the world and will reward the good and punish the evil, and by it he works upon "men's fear and self-love to restrain their corruptions." [37] It is "the principal faculty by which God has distinguished this noble creature from the rest," but lacking the support of revelation it has failed to produce those fruits of knowledge and conduct which God demands. "If human reason is really sufficient," asks Edwards, "and there be no need of any thing else, why has it never proved so?" [38] Never by the improvement of mere human faculties, including reason, have men brought themselves out of superstition and darkness. Never have endless disputes and controversies been resolved in religion or morality by the use of unaided reason. "The increase of human learning does not bring these controversies to an issue, but does really increase and multiply them." [39] Yet with these strictures on the human reason, Edwards was not content to allow reason no part to play in morality. Thus in *Charity and its Fruits* he boldly asserts that "All things in the soul of man should be under the government of reason, which is the highest faculty of our being." [40] An even more vigorous defense of reason is offered when he claims that "Christian charity is not a thing founded on the ruins of reason." [41] In fact, Edwards pointed out in the *Original Sin* "the propensity to act contrary to reason, is a depraved disposition." [42] However, reason as a function of speculative knowledge does not yield "practical knowledge," which is the attendant of grace in the human heart.[43] But it does instruct mankind in his rightful duty, "for the light of nature teaches us as much that we ought to obey God as that we ought not to do the greatest injury to our fellow creatures from revenge and malice." This Edwards considers to be a duty of "eternal reason" itself.[44] Reason, while it bespeaks moral responsibilities, no less points men to their rational duty towards deity as well. In this respect the natural reason of man may lay the groundwork for salvation. Through reason men may recognize the danger in which they stand before a righteous God, and feel the need for an escape from punishment. This, thought Edwards, was God's "ordinary way" of preparing men for conversion. But he drew a line among men on the basis of their natural capacities. "The more unthinking people, such as husbandmen and the common sort of people" are not accustomed to the exercise of reason so God usually employs with them the notion of punishment. In the more knowing and thinking men, the Holy Spirit makes more use of rational deductions to convince them that 'tis worth their while to seek earnestly for salvation. He makes use of a "good nature, a good understanding, a rational brain, moral prudence, etc. as far as they hold." [45] In so doing the light of nature reveals the "law of God," states that particular duties must be completed because they are right and just, and because the law is God's law, it ought to be obeyed.[46]

A further distinction concerning reason must also be made. Edwards notes that men often confuse the process of reasoning with the norm of reason itself. In the former sense reason functions as an agency of choice; in the latter it serves as a ruling principle or authority for what is chosen. But in fact, for Edwards, in the latter sense reason must give way to the authority of that in which reason comes to rest, namely, the nature or law of God himself. However, reason does not then stand in judgment upon that power which constituted it. It yields itself by its own rational conclusion into the hands of God, or in the case of the natural man, at least it is subservient to the law of God or the law of nature, as Edwards called it.[47] An additional qualification of reason is seen in its relation to the will and understanding. The understanding, as Edwards claimed in the treatise on *The Freedom of the Will,* is a more capacious faculty than is reason, "as including the whole faculty of perception or apprehension, and not merely what is called reason or judgment." Therefore in the movement of the will, the motive factor of the human self, the entire context in which the reason operates must be taken into account. A dictate of the understanding is therefore a compound product which involves man himself rather than a strictly rational deduction. The whole affective and cognitive faculty is operative. What moves men to will and act is not "what reason declares to be best or most for the person's happiness, taken in the whole of his duration," but the whole complex view of happiness which is elected by the human subject.[48] Thus, however high the estimate which Edwards placed on reason—and it was considerable, as we have seen—it continues to be associated with God on the one hand and with the total composition of the human subject on the other.[49] It is limited also by the sinfulness of man, which places obstacles in its way by bending it to self-interest and by introducing prejudices which mar its complete autonomy. That reason emerges from a sinful being does not cancel out its limited effectiveness in following arguments or in recognizing moral duties within the circumscribed range to which sin has assigned it. Its capacities within that range are sizeable, but never do they overstep the boundaries set by the nature of the graceless man to enter the realm of true virtue. As Edwards viewed it,

"The light of nature teaches that religion which is necessary to continue in the favour of the God that made us; but it cannot teach us that religion which is necessary to our being restored to the favour of God, after we have forfeited it." [50]

It is all but impossible to draw any sharp or consistent line of distinction between natural reason, on the one hand, and conscience and the moral sense, on the other. As a rule of thumb, it may be suggested that the light of nature is capable of recognizing and guiding the mind to the proportionality and harmony not only of ethical relations, but also of such excellence as can be discovered in nature and by metaphysical speculation. Conscience, on the other hand, is more generally used by Edwards in the sense of a capacity to offer ethical judgments of right and wrong only.[51] In any case, Edwards made a place for the natural man's conscience as one of the principles which had survived the disaster of the fall and which could be depended upon to guide moral conduct in the absence of the rarer forms of divine grace.[52] Edwards esteemed conscience so highly that in his sermon on "True Grace Distinguished from the Experience of Devils" he stated that "God sits enthroned in the conscience." [53]

The operation of conscience, however, was most clearly expressed in the *Nature of True Virtue,* where Edwards seems to have equated it with the moral sense.[54] Natural conscience consists in that "disposition in man to be uneasy in a consciousness of being inconsistent with himself" and as such it is bound to the principle of self-love in the narrower sense already described. When men approve actions they recognize such actions as in agreement with themselves in the same way that in actions they disapprove they find something which disagrees with themselves. In neither case are they judging in the light of a general benevolence in regard to Being in general.[55] The operations of conscience unless "greatly stupified" habitually, spontaneously, and even insensibly, go into action in the presence of moral acts as the agent puts himself in the place of the actor of the moral deeds.[56] Thus natural conscience consists first of all in a consciousness of self-consistency or lack thereof.

In addition, this judgment is coupled with what Edwards calls a "sense of desert," that is, the realization of "natural agreement, proportion and harmony, between malevolence or injury and resentment and punishment; or between loving and being loved, between showing kindness and being rewarded etc." [57] When the conscience functions properly, that is, takes a broad view of human actions and attitudes and does not fall into "speculative error," it sees and relishes those just and equal relationships which obtain between doing evil and being punished, or doing good and being rewarded. It is this symmetry or proportion as applied to all virtue and vice which constitutes the essence of the natural beauty of a genuine morality.

Since all men are possessed of conscience by which they know right from wrong and recognize desert or justice in moral acts, Edwards feels that they may even recognize from afar the beauty and harmony of true virtue. True, natural conscience does not lift one to a true "taste" of the sweetness resident in benevolence to Being in general, yet the natural conscience "may approve of it from that uniformity, equality and justice which there is in it." Men can see that it is just to yield to God, though they are incapable of it; they can see the obligation men have to love God above all, yet not realize it, and they can see the fitness there is in a punishment exacted of them for failing to come to

that intimate union with Being in general wherein true
virtue consists. If their consciences were fully enlightened, however, men would approve nothing but true
virtue, but the door is barred against this possibility
so long as their view is limited to the private sphere
and obstructed by sensual objects and appetites.[58]
Merely having conscience, then, does not guarantee
virtue in its highest sense; if such were the case men
would repent upon approving the beauty of true virtue.
But men will continue to sin against the convictions
of conscience, since their hearts are not fully engaged
in the matter. The higher realms of virtue are closed
to them, and no amount of instruction will bring them
over into it. God alone accomplishes that final act of
reinstituting the supernatural principles. Shaftesbury
and Hutcheson had argued from the basis of the moral
sense or conscience to a natural inclination to virtue.
Edwards, however, while allowing their contention of
the presence of a moral sense in man, has accepted only
a natural or secondary virtue bound to a self-interest
which falls short of an inclination to Being in general,
although it extends to all humanity or society in general.[59]

A remarkable oversight of Edwards is his contention that natural conscience could approve of true virtue, while at the same time he insisted that the essence
of true virtue remained a closed book to the natural
man. No matter how well informed the conscience may
be, so long as it remained spiritually unenlightened, it
could never know virtue as it is in itself, and not knowing it in the fullest sense would seem to make impossible even the act of approval which Edwards posits.[60]
The way around this problem lay in Edwards's Platonic
inclination, nurtured by a Puritanical tendency to see
analogies between natural and supernatural entities.

"He has constituted the external world in analogy to the spiritual world in numberless instances." [61] What he called "some image of the true, spiritual, original beauty" was accordingly to be found in "secondary beauty" in a metaphysical or natural sense, and in respect to the appreciation or judgment of moral acts, some image of genuine virtue could be discovered. By correctly reading the nature of the natural agreement or harmony among moral acts at the natural level, some intimation of that supernatural beauty resident in true virtue might be spied. The difference between the two levels of ethical judgment, however, lay in the grounds upon which each is approved. The moral sense of the natural man approves the same things as does a spiritual and divine sense, but does so upon the basis of self-love, whereas the perception of true virtue derives from a cordial consent to Being in general, set in motion by divinely granted supernatural principles. In this way Edwards thought that he had surmounted the problem of the natural man's implicit testimony to a true virtue of which he possessed no first-hand acquaintance. [62]

Granted that all men were possessed of the instrument for a moral life, there remained a vexing question as to why men fell out among themselves in their judgments as to what was right or good. If all natural morality roots in self-love or private affections, one might expect more unanimity in these matters—and at times Edwards seems to suppose in a broad sense that this is the case. Yet men do variously estimate moral acts in contradiction to each other. If all natural morality is to be directed by the light of nature, the conscience and moral sense, why then do their judgments not more often coincide with the natural law? In general, of course, Edwards could fall back upon the power of original sin, which sent men off on different courses of action and moved them to contradictory judgments of what was right or good. However, this was not a sufficiently precise answer to the question of ethical relativism.

Edwards attempted an answer to this perennial question in the context of his discussion of sentiment as the basis of the moral good. What he wished to fend off was the notion that moral sentiments were entirely detached from the nature of things, so that morality became a completely subjective, individualistic and arbitrary affair. Of course he would not contradict the idea that virtue was founded on sentiment or affection rather than reason, if all the proponents of this view intended to say was that true virtue impinges directly upon the mind of man and receives approbation without recourse to a long and involved process of reasoning. What he would not accept, however, was the idea that such a sentiment was given arbitrarily by God without any connection between its pronouncements and the inherent structure of reality which God had created. Edwards rehearsed the arguments for his primary conviction that all reality and hence virtue consisted in harmonious relations among the parts, not only in sensed reality, but in God himself. That which was contrary to this harmonious interaction was irrational, and in fact, if Edwards's argument be worked out to its finest detail, was unthinkable! Thus, when men are moral they are consistent or in harmony with themselves, even in self-love, as he had demonstrated in his treatment of conscience and natural reason. When men see or intuit this principle of harmonious relationship in its highest form, they have knowledge of true virtue, which is founded on the same harmonious relationship. There is a correspondence between their ideas and what is objectively given, otherwise this would not be knowledge in any proper sense, but only a recognition of what is in their own minds and "no representation of any thing without." [63] Thus the spiritual sense in the case of true virtue is not arbitrary in the anarchistic sense which Edwards opposed, any more than it is in its limited sense in the case of natural morality, wherein some idea of harmony is present. In both instances there is "a disposition of the mind to consent to, or like, the agreement of the nature of things . . . and certainly," he concludes, "such a temper of mind is more agreeable to the nature of things than an opposite temper," as the contrary view maintained.[64]

He moved next to a slightly different line of defense, in which he strove to show that linguistic conventions of ethical terms indicated their relation to a firm basis in the nature of things. His line of thought was excessively compacted, but its direction and terminology have an astonishing resemblance to modern linguistic philosophizing. He posits that language has as its purpose the expression of "sentiments" or ideas. So the terms which signify moral acts or relations express moral sentiments, which for Edwards means that the moral sense governs the use of language and provides the mind's rule for the usage of ethical language. By appeal to a common usage of such terms as right and wrong, good and evil, he defines them as meaning deserving of praise or blame, respect or resentment. Then comes the nub of the difficulty he wished to crack. If sentiment is the rule of language, and yet "that sentiment, at least as to many particulars, is different, in different persons, especially in different nations . . . how therefore can virtue and vice be any other than arbitrary," i.e. determined only by the individual sentiments of men? [65]

In answering his own question, he first argued that

men's sentiments are not "casual or accidental" in the distinctive sense implied in the question. All men, he insisted, possess a sense of desert of love or resentment, "a natural uniformity and agreement between the affections and acts of the agent." Yet they may at the same time, depending upon their apprehension of various occasions and objects and their unique way of viewing the same, come to differing conclusions about these insights. Sociological and psychological factors, such as custom, education, and association of ideas also contribute to this apparent disparity of judgments concerning moral acts and affections. This disparity exists only in particulars, not in the general moral sense which remains when one looks sharply enough at the apparent diversity of ethical judgments. Thus, Edwards goes on to insist, the language in which ethics is couched is not "unfixed and arbitrary." The terms right and wrong or good and evil find their proper meaning in their general or common usage, and men in that usage are obliged to aim at consistency. Otherwise, language cannot be used as "a common medium of manifesting ideas and sentiment." Hence if men are to employ terms with meaning, they must call things right when they are deserving of praise, and wrong when they are deserving of blame, else men will be inconsistent with themselves, which is another way of saying that they flaunt the order of things as constituted by God. The need for consistent usage then points to the fixity of conviction between language and sentiment, on the one hand, and the order of being on the other. It is to this general principle that mankind returns in matters of ethical dispute, and there is no other way by which men can come to any agreement in moral matters except by this "general standard or foundation in nature." In fact, such an appeal is presupposed in all disputes about right and wrong, whether or not it is immediately recognized.[66] Diversity of moral views may exist, but this fact does not in the least endanger the reality of that moral sense of conscience, in terms of which adjudication is possible when consistency of usage of ethical terms comes into play as it must in any rational discourse.

When cast in the framework of Edwards's Neoplatonic outlook, natural morality becomes secondary or inferior beauty. As with self-love, conscience, and the moral sense, this formulation of natural morality fails to achieve the heights of true virtue, but like them has its role to play in the divine economy. Here the heavy dependence upon Hutcheson's views of beauty comes fully into focus, as Edwards borrows his aesthetic terminology to describe that beauty found in inanimate objects which has its counterpart in spiritual and moral relations as well.[67] The mutual consent or agreement of divine entities in harmonious symmetrical patterns, the uniformity in variety found in nature and the works of man have their parallels in the ethical realm where there is spiritual or mental harmony between motives and acts and among forms of behavior themselves.[68] The analogical motif which illuminates the relation between nature and supernature forms the basis upon which one can perceive, if not relish in a heartfelt manner, the divine operation which has created inferior beings and relations similar to their superior models. This is the law of nature, thinks Edwards, whereby the beauty of a plant becomes "some image of the consent of mind, of the different members of a society or system of intelligent beings, sweetly united in a benevolent agreement of heart." [69]

The misfortune of the natural man in respect to genuine virtue lies in the fact that although he may have an immediate apprehension of beauty in such things as geometrical forms, nature generally, the harmonies of music, or the physical features of an attractive face, he is totally ignorant of the principle of agreement and proportion which is the underlying basis of this apprehension. He does not perceive the "union itself" which makes such beauty attractive.[70] He goes no further than the law of nature or instinct takes him, by giving him the immediate sensation of pleasure when confronted with pleasing objects. The same principle operates in respect to material objects, and even more so in respect to immaterial objects which are more important. It is to be found in the appropriate ordering of society, in wisdom, "consisting in the united tendency of thoughts, ideas, and particular volitions, to one purpose." Again it appears in the ethical value of justice, where mutual relations are discernible in respect to good and evil, and when equal and proportionate duties are undertaken among men.[71] But in all these apprehensions, which Edwards insists bear some analogy to spiritual and virtuous beauty, "men do not approve" them "because of any such analogy perceived." If they did so, then the recognition of natural beauties would heighten as men became more virtuous, but reason and experience, Edwards holds, show that men may have such apprehensions of beauty in material and immaterial things, and still fail of virtue. In fact, "vicious and lewd" men would have no sense of these beauties if there were a close correlation between recognition of them and a sense of genuine benevolence to Being in general, but in fact persons of this type do have some appreciation of proportion and uniformity in things about them.[72]

Without the supernatural sense or divine relish two conditions for true virtue are lacking, knowledge of the basis of that agreement by which moral beauty exists, and a cordial consent to this foundation as it exists in Being itself. These two factors are in fact mutually implicative of each other. The clear perception of Being in general involves the affections, whereby the heart of man and his mind or reason themselves act in concert in the appreciation of the beauty inherent in the way being agrees with itself, even in God himself, the superlative example of beings' consent to Being.[73] Secondary beauty, of course, retains the characteristics of beauty, but suffers from taking into account only the private spheres, moved as it is by self-love. But these private spheres, says Edwards, counteracting Hutcheson, Shaftesbury, and Wollaston, contain but an infinitely small part of universal being. Furthermore, men of this stripe are content with their views of the social good, because they "leave the divine Being out of their view . . . as though he did not properly belong to the system of real existence, but was a kind of shadowy, imaginary being." [74] Thus when private affections are extended to many particular things, men remain closed in to the created order without regard to the creator, supposing mistakenly that because there is something of the universal in their perspective, they are aware of true virtue.[75]

Secondary beauty in respect to moral virtue falls into the category of theological subjectivism or utilitarianism. The divine object may even be referred to as it was by Hutcheson, but the conscience, moral sense, and natural reason are all held under the sway of a self-considering perspective, and the affections commensurate with this perspective. The virtues attendant upon this truncated outlook retain their beauty and serve in many ways to keep society together and operative. The natural man is not necessarily a totally immoral being, although his sinful character is not eradicated.[76] His narrowness of view, which he cannot overcome or from which no amount of ethical instruction can free him, condemns him to the lower level of morality, but it is still a moral theory which Edwards offers, in which the distinctions between good and bad, right and wrong must play their part, and for which his metaphysical speculations provide guidelines. Agreement, proportionality, and symmetry may not at first acquaintance seem terms appropriate to ethical discourse, but as he has shown in respect to pity, gratitude, charitable acts, and justice, there is a principle of order by which the natural man may correctly evaluate his actions.

V

Edwards on Practical Morality

It has long been recognized that Edwards was not especially concerned with "social ethics," in the sense in which that term is used today. He centered his attention upon the immediate and close relation of the human soul with God—a relationship which was so dynamic and vital that it necessarily operated in all areas of life. He did not have a full grasp of social problems which, as we know them, are constituted and made complex by impersonal factors and by a variety of individual responses of those who are under specific group pressures. His approach to such problems was, in the modern sense, a naive one, which assumed that a simple, personal approach to problems which existed in relationships of the self to others could be adequately handled by direct face-to-face contact. This did not mean that he was oblivious to the social responsibilities of men, but it is true that he followed, in the main, the formula that if men are changed in their hearts by God, all else will follow. Furthermore, he seldom played the part of a casuist. He did not outline the specific problems resident in the social character of men, nor point out appropriate moral attitudes for them. He firmly believed that if all men fastened their eyes upon God and committed their lives into his hands, society itself could be lifted up into the white light of God's glory. However, it has not been adequately recognized that Edwards did have something to say upon certain problems which in their modern form we call social problems.

Society and Government

Men are created in society and for society. They are essentially social creatures, dependent upon each other for all manner of sustenance, economic and otherwise, for mutual comfort and for the realization of the various values which arise out of the interplay of personalities.[1] This social nature is not sufficient, however, to provide the cement for all human society. There is a need for a moral government in all human societies, which will prevent men from rending each other to pieces as wild beasts; this moral government is the decree of God, backed by his threats and his promises.[2] There is, then, a coercive foundation to all human society, which operates jointly with the given social nature of man. As Edwards put the matter, "Public societies cannot be maintained without trials and witnesses: And if witnesses are not firmly persuaded, that he who holds the supreme power over them, is omniscient, just and powerful, and will revenge falsehood; there will be no dependence on their oaths, or most solemn declarations —God therefore, must be the Supreme Magistrate; society depends absolutely on him." [3]

It may be seen then that human society does not depend upon a social contract, but upon a legalistic basis, with its implied law, guilt, trials, witnesses, and judges, and depends as well upon an element of fear which deters men from falsehoods and other immoralities. Edwards had too low an opinion of men's natural tendencies to suppose that they could live together amiably without the dread coercion of an altogether righteous God to sanction their social and political commitments to each other. All human societies are upheld by "his restraining grace," which prevents the evil that men naturally do from running into totally destructive extremes.[4]

Even as God is the ultimate governor of all society, without whom no society would exist, so government, as it is known and developed by man, is modeled upon divine government, as Edwards understood it.[5] It is simply a fact that God has decreed or ordained that there shall be "human moral government." [6] "Here God hath set those to be moral rulers, who are the wiser and stronger, and has appointed those to be in subjection, who are less knowing, and weaker, and have received being from their rulers, and are dependent, preserved and maintained." [7] Such governments include not only those of the state or civil government, but that of the family as well. Even as God rules by telling what his rules and laws are—and of this there was little doubt in Edwards's mind—so human rulers make "visible" their laws and enforce them as does God, by just punishments and wise rewards.[8] As the deity carries on conversation—revelation—with his creatures, so between temporal rulers and their subjects there must be conversation so that the superiors may enlighten the ruled. Without such "conversation,"—which incidentally is somewhat one-sided, inasmuch as it implies that the ruler commands, and the subjects do not advise—no morality is possible, since "affairs of morality are affairs of society," [9] and without some conversation society itself would be impossible. All present governments and societies are temporal, not eternal. Their affairs are subordinate and purposefully related to those of the heavenly kingdom. They are not the chief ends of life, and should therefore be treated as necessities only for this life, and as possibly preparatory to the absolute government of God in heaven. "Civil, ecclesiastical and family affairs, and all our personal concerns, are designed and ordered in subordination to a future world, by the Maker and Disposer of all things." [10] Therefore, we may conclude that no temporal kingdom or government is to be equated with the kingdom of God itself.[11] In the "last days," however, all present societies and governments will be replaced by a great new society. It will be a "time wherein the whole earth shall be united as one holy city, one heavenly family, men of all nations shall as it were dwell together and sweetly correspond one with another, as brethren and children of the same father." [12] However, this "social end" of men is a society that all men will not enjoy, since it is reserved only for the saved.

What are the specific qualities desirable in a ruler of the people in temporal society? Edwards gave some general answers to this political question in a funeral sermon preached upon the death of the civic leader, John Stoddard, on June 26, 1748. A civic ruler, he contends, must have "great ability for the management of public affairs." He must possess "insight into the mysteries of government" and ability "for discerning those things wherein the public welfare or calamity consists." A civic leader will naturally have by experience great knowledge of human nature in general, and of his own people in particular, as well as knowledge of the peoples and laws of other countries. The civil magistrate will combine great understanding of mind with nobility of disposition and largeness of heart. He will not stoop to taking advantage of his high position for private gain. He is strong in the face of opposition, and resolute in his course of action. He is a religious man, of great integrity and piety. "He is not only a man of great ability to bear down on vice and immorality, but has a disposition agreeable to such ability; is one that has a strong aversion to wickedness, and is disposed to use the power God has put into his hands to suppress it; . . . He is one of inflexible fidelity, who will be faithful to God, whose minister he is, to his people for good, and who is unmovable in his regard to his supreme authority, his commands, and his glory; and will be faithful to his kind and country." [13] It is clear that the administration, as well as the foundation of civil society, is a theological one, since the civil ruler is the representative of God to a people, whose authority is sanctioned by the power and righteousness of the deity. The patriotism of the magistrate is rooted in the divine character of the government which he has been called to control. There is no thought of a political leader who operates upon a purely secular basis; political leadership always implies the moral and religious fitness of the ruler.

Edwards thought of government as predominantly monarchical. "Almost all of the prosperity of a public society and civic community does, under God, depend on their rulers. They are like the mainsprings or wheels in a machine, that keep every part in its due motion, and are in the body politic, as the vitals in the body natural, and as the pillars and foundations in a building. Civil rulers are called 'the foundations of the earth.' " [14] It would appear that the real vitality in government exists not in the dynamic relation between the governed and the governor, but solely in the power of the governor himself.[15] Political rights and obligations descend, as it were, from above, not from the consent of the governed, a conception which became less and less palatable to a New England which had begun to feel the ground swell of democratic influences from abroad, and which had begun to express itself vigorously in the direction of free institutions whose sanction derived from the governed. It is doubtful whether Edwards did anything more in his conception of civil government than to reflect a conservative attitude toward the status quo. It is certain that he did not spend much time directly thinking upon the problem of political sovereignty and the notion of civil government. His remarks upon the subject were more in the nature of implications derived from his ideas of God's moral government.

Family and Sex

The matter of family government was apparently an important one for Edwards. In his revival sermons, in his "Faithful Narrative" and "Some Thoughts," he often referred to the lamentable breakdown of the family institution or government as being productive of impiety and looseness in morals.[16] He maintained that "every Christian family ought to be as it were a little church consecrated to Christ, and wholly influenced and governed by his rule. And family education and order are some of the chief means of grace. If these fail, all other means are likely to prove ineffectual. If these are duly maintained, all the means of grace will be likely to prosper and be successful." [17] The family, then, is the basic moral and religious institution in human society. Where it fails, society fails. It must therefore be conducted as a government in which parents reprove, admonish, and restrain their children, bringing them up in the fear and love of God. "There must be government as well as instruction, which must be maintained with an even hand, and steady resolution, as a guard to the religion and morals of the family." [18]

The proper administration of the family is important, not only because it is the fundamental unit of society, but because the greater part of one's life is spent in the home or family, and consequently "a great proportion of the wickedness of which men are guilty . . . will be the sin which they shall have committed in the families to which they belong." [19] Edwards apparently recognized that the closer the physical and spiritual bonds in this particular institution, the greater the possibility of evil. The common bond of family life is not coercion, though Edwards sometimes expresses himself as if it were, but love.[20] The love which is found in the family has a particularly intense quality, which is based upon the idea that "the nearer the relation, the greater is the obligation to love." [21] Husbands and wives, having become one flesh, are truly one, not by mutual promise alone, but by virtue of God's witness to their marriage vows, which makes of them a "covenant of God." [22] In the sacredness of this bond, husbands and wives are to regard each other with the highest respect. Husbands are not to be of "an unkind, imperious behavior" towards their wives, treating them as servants and allowing them no freedom of action simply because they themselves are heads of the family. Wives are to be in subordination to the head of the household because God has thus ordained. The particular tasks of the parents are those of instructing and governing their families, servants, and children, all of whom are to be subservient to family authority. There is no indication in Edwards that chastity is a state superior to that of marriage, nor is marriage, so far as can be observed, simply a device to prevent men from falling into sexual sin. It is rather the proper condition of all mankind, as decreed by God. In other words, the foundation of the family, as that of society in general, is laid in the will or constitution of God. It is a holy institution, of supreme importance in temporal society, though in the world to come we may be separated from those whom we love upon earth. The authority of the family head and the subordination of the members of the family to him are accepted by Edwards upon scriptural basis as being the proper state in which God has destined men to live their temporal lives.

Edwards's theological view of the family and the high place which he accorded the institution of the family, as well as his general Calvinistic background, made him particularly sensitive to questions of sexual morality. At numerous times he preached against the "frolickings" of his young people, implying that such occasions went beyond the bounds of decency and led to moral turpitude. In at least one specific case he took a direct hand in criticizing and judging his young people for reading a dubious book on sexual matters. This event, which contributed to his downfall at Northampton, came to be called the "bad book affair." [23] Edwards took seriously his pastoral relation with his young people. In one of his strongest sermons, he preached against temptation in general, and sexual temptation in particular, warning his congregation that temptation usually overpowers those who consider themselves most impervious to its wiles.[24] Like all sins, he pointed out, sexual impropriety constitutes an infinite sin against God, and directly tends to kill the very soul of man. If one is to remain spotless from moral evil of this kind, he does well, counsels Edwards, to avoid evil imaginations, tavern-haunting, gaming, drunkenness, profanity, and association with vicious persons, since all these, as experience shows, are directly related to the grossest immoralities.[25] Nor was he squeamish about attacking particular sexual vices, especially the custom of bundling, which had become a more or less accepted method of courting.[26] "It has been one main thing that has led to the growth of uncleanness in the land . . . And there are other customs and liberties customarily used among young people in company, which they who use them know that they lead to sin. They know that they stir up their lusts; and this is the very end for which they do it, to gratify their lusts in some measure." [27] Another custom, as has already been suggested, Edwards severely censured, is "that of young people of both sexes getting together in companies for mirth and spending the time together till late at night, in their jollity." [28] This custom is not the innocent thing which it appears to be, said Edwards, since it leads directly to fornication and the doing away with all serious thought and vital religion.[29] Edwards made no distinction in matters of this kind between the morality which should be practiced by the saved and that of the unregenerate. Natural reason itself and the moral law that it recognizes condemn such things, he believed.

The Morality of the Economic Life

Edwards gave no general conception of the economic life of man, which is simply a part of the whole social life, within which God has placed man. It encompasses the necessary way men make their living, sustain their homes, and practise charity. He did make some moral observations upon this part of life, particularly in regard to trading and to the use of one's time.

It is dishonest, he said, to withhold what belongs to our neighbor by either stealing from him or by failing to fulfill the obligations which we have assumed. For example, if one contracts to do a certain piece of work, it must be done; "If they be hired to a day's labour, and be not careful to improve the day, as they have reason to think that he who hires justly expects it of them," [30] men commit the sin of stealing, for they have taken from another without his knowledge that which is by rights his own. A neighbor is wronged by another when he withholds the payment of a just debt. Edwards did not state that going into debt was an immorality in itself, but strongly suggested that it was by saying that one runs into debt usually through "pride and affectation of living above circumstances," or through a grasping, covetous disposition. Debts which run to too great an amount are customarily the result of some "corrupt principle." [31] The creditor is often put to great inconvenience by debtors who spend their funds upon "gay clothing for their children" or the advancement of their estates, instead of paying what they owe. The sin of withholding the payment of a debt consists in stealing what rightly belongs to the creditor. Whether the creditor be rich or poor, the principle holds that the debt should be paid as speedily as possible: "if the creditor be ever so rich, that gives no right to the debtor to withhold from him that which belongs to him. If it be due, it ought to be paid: for that is the very notion of its being due." [32]

One steals from the neighbor not only by withholding what rightly belongs to him, but by actually taking his property, and into this matter Edwards goes in some detail. Men steal by negligence, as when, for example, one's cattle destroy the produce of a neighbor's field through the failure of the former to provide a suitable enclosure for his beasts.[33] Another manner of taking what is our neighbor's is by fraud. "This is the case when men in their dealings take advantage of their neighbor's oversight, or mistake, to get something from him: or when they make their gains, by concealing the defects of what they sell, putting off bad for good, though this be not done by speaking falsely, but only by keeping silent; or when they take a higher price than what they sell is really worth, and more than they could get for it if the concealed defects were known." [34] These things Edwards flatly stated, "however common they may be in men's dealings one with another, are nothing short of iniquity." Obviously, Edwards was no Yankee trader! He believed in a scrupulous honesty as being paramount in all the business dealings of men.[35]

Men steal from each other by violence in its various degrees, as for example, by open force, by threatening, or by taking advantage of another's poverty.[36] Under this heading comes the sin of raising the price of provisions above the market price to take advantage of need when people are presently unable to pay. Edwards warned such extortioners that God may at any moment cast them down, and they may themselves soon be in a poverty-stricken condition. It is only the goodness of God which keeps those who have means from being poor, and from being in the same position as those of whom they take advantage. Nor is it right to seize by any method the wealth of the rich man, simply because he has more of this world's goods. It is wrong also to take advantage of the vagaries of the law to seize what is rightfully another's. "The best laws may be abused and perverted to purposes contrary to the general design of laws, which is to maintain the rights and serve the properties of mankind. Human laws have a regard due to them, but always in subordination to the higher laws of God and nature." [37] It is therefore a sin before God to avail oneself of any loophole in the human law for the purpose of contravening the law of God, who will judge us "by his own laws, not by the laws of the commonwealth."

In the last place, there is outright stealing, which Edwards defined as "a designed taking of our neighbor's goods from him without his consent or knowledge." [38] This act of stealing differs from "withholding," since it is a deprivation or a taking away from another; it differs from extortion, since the person sinned against does not know what is taken from him; and in the same way, it differs from fraudulent dealing. In stealing, the sinner does not intend the victim to know that he has taken from him, nor is there any consent given by the victim in such an act, as there may be in fraudulent dealing, even though, in the latter case, the consent be secured by deceit. No rationalization or excuse can wipe out the fact of stealing as defined above. Even if what one takes is owed to him by another, a theft has been committed. "That his neighbour is in debt to him, doth not give him a right to take it upon himself to be his own judge, so that he may judge for himself, which of his neighbor's goods shall be taken from him to discharge the debt." [39] If men did appropriate to themselves the right to judge and to take that which they desired from another without his knowledge, even if it be an honest debt, human society would fall into confusion.

Again, Edwards warned that it was dishonest to take, without the knowledge of another, something equal in value to a favor done previously. The very fact that one does such a thing secretly shows that the conscience is not clear. Stealing cannot be condoned, even when it involves taking things of slight importance. "If the thing be of little value, yet if it be worth a purposed concealing from the owner, the value is great enough to render the taking of it proper theft." [40]

If stealing has taken place by any one or a combination of the methods touched upon above, there is only one act of moral reparation, and that is complete restitution of the things stolen, or at least their equivalent value. Restitution operates on the principle that so long as one retains that which is not his own, he continually wrongs his neighbor.[41] Restitution not only reestablishes the relation between the culprit and his neighbor, but conditions the forgiveness of God to the guilty party. God cannot forgive one so long as he continues in his sin of stealing by failing to make proper restitution.

The matter of the use of one's time is also a moral and religious question, which has relation to the economic life. On this subject Edwards followed the Calvinistic idea of redeeming every possible moment of time by pursuing the precious business of religion, which is the main end of life.[42] The daily tasks of routine living are to be performed to the glory of God. As Edwards answered a critic of the Great Awakening, who charged that the daily business life of New England was suffering from too great attention upon religion, "worldly business has been attended with great alacrity, as part of the service of God: the person [referring to the testimony of a sympathizer with the revival] declaring that it being done thus, 'tis found to be as good as prayer." [43] Edwards himself was a hard worker, and he believed that all men should engage in their various means of making a living just as vigorously as he pursued his own tasks.

The proper use of leisure time, which can always be improved upon, was also important. "When we are most free from cares for the body, and business of an outward nature, a happy opportunity for the soul is afforded. Therefore spend not such opportunities unprofitably, nor in such a manner that you will not be able to give a good account thereof to God. Waste them not away wholly in unprofitable visits, or useless amusements. Diversions should be used only in subserviency to business. So much, and no more should be used, as doth most fit the mind and body for the work of our general and particular calling." [44] There is no place left for recreation simply for its own sake; all things, even the use of leisure time, must contribute in some way to the religious end of life. The proper improvement of leisure time is suggested in one place to be that of improving the mind, particularly upon religious subjects. Edwards naturally reflects his own scholarly attitude with this suggestion, apparently believing that for the man who works with his hands and muscles, the training of the mind would be a most welcome relief. Perusal of the Scriptures for learning Christian knowledge is especially recommended, which, if it has no other end, at least, if diligently followed, will result in no want of employment during leisure from common secular business.[45] In this manner time will be redeemed, since when one is not occupied with the business of making a living, he can be storing up knowledge of life itself. Almost grudgingly, Edwards admits that some diversion is lawful, but he conditions this somewhat dangerous idea by warning that evenings spent only in useless and amusing conversation are spent sinfully, and "tend to poverty of soul at least, if not to outward poverty." [46] There were to be no blank spaces in man's life; all was to be filled with meaningful work of some kind, more or less directly contributory to the chief end of man, namely, his salvation, or the glory of God. One misses in Edwards any feeling for the trifles or the amusing aspects of life, which ease the tension of human existence. There is no "animal joy" in his thought of the proper life for men, but a stern and serious never-ending business of seeking salvation, whether or not the individual has a sense of his own election.

Personal and Social Charity

Of the specific social virtues which Edwards mentioned, none is more concrete nor stands higher than the giving of alms or charity.[47] The alleviation of poverty and need was not to be realized by any change in society itself, but by the direct personal outpouring of generous gifts to the needy. Charity is a duty of the Christian, commanded by God, but a duty which is to be carried out cheerfully and willingly. Its sanction rests not only upon the word of God, the Bible, but upon its inherent reasonableness in the light of the general condition of mankind. Men are made in the image of God, and they are linked to each other by a common nature, which makes them worthy of loving and charitable deeds. "God hath made us with such a nature, that we cannot subsist without the help of one another." [48] A selfish spirit is therefore completely out of place in human society, and one who possesses such an attitude "deserves to be cut off from the benefit of human society, and to be turned out among wild beasts." To love our neighbors as ourselves, Edwards reckoned, is the sum of the moral law respecting our fellow creatures, and to contribute to their relief is the most natural expression of this love. Men should be prompted to practice charity, furthermore, because God has so richly blessed them and has acted upon their behalf, unworthy though they be. "How unsuitable is it for us, who live only by kindness, to be unkind." [49] By Christ's redemption of us, we are made as of one body, and should therefore bear each other's burdens in poverty and in wealth.

The giving of charity is particularly conditioned by the important fact that all that a man possesses is his only by subordinate right. "Your goods are only lent to you of God, to be improved by you in such ways as he directs." [50] The clear implication of this stewardship is that one should use God's goods only for God's purposes, the most obvious of which is to refrain from hoarding and to express one's love of God by freely giving to the needy. If this is not done, Edwards argued, God is robbed of what is his right, since giving to the poor is regarded by the deity as a gift to himself. There is a utilitarian element which also enters into the motivation, for if one gives charity, or alms, it is to be expected that God will repay these gifts, not only in eternal things, but in temporal goods as well. By the giving of charity, one provides against a future calamity, when the donor himself may be in need; giving to the needy is like laying up against winter, or against a time of disaster. It is the best way of laying up for yourselves and for your children.

No Christian is exempt from the absolute obligation placed upon him by God to perform charitable acts. Simply upon the basis of natural moral virtue, men are commanded to provide for the needy. Whatever objections to charity can be mustered, Edwards bears down by his logic. If a man argued that he has given, and has never been better off for it, Edwards replied "you have probably given in a niggardly spirit, not with liberality," and reminds him that "the promises are made to mercy and liberality, not to the giving of the gift itself." [51] Or if perhaps a person has given cheerfully for the welfare of others, and has not received reward, he has been protected, unknown to himself, from far greater calamities which might have been visited upon him. Or again, how can anyone know but that God is holding in reserve some great blessing which he will award in a moment of particularly great need?

It makes no difference, reasoned Edwards, whether the person toward whom the charity is directed is in only moderately poor circumstances, completely destitute, or even an "ill sort of man." The duty to charity still obtains.[52] The love of the neighbor does not take into consideration the moral condition of the particular neighbor; it acts directly toward such a person's needs without cavil or question. However, if a person be reduced to want by his own fault, there are several conditions which should be brought into consideration. If he be in want because of the lack of some inner natural faculty to manage his affairs to advantage, he is to be pitied and helped; God has simply not conferred upon him the same gift for handling this world's goods which he has bestowed upon the prospective donor, and the latter may be thankful for God's goodness to him. If a man's want derives from an oversight or carelessness upon his part, the obligation to charity is in no way abated, since to refrain from giving under such circumstances would amount to making the sin of oversight an unpardonable one, and we would be guilty of a lack of forgiveness. Even if the needy person be reduced to want by vicious idleness or prodigality, men are to succor him, but only if he breaks off from his former vices. If he continues in his evil course, yet his family is to be cared for, even though this charity finds its way at least indirectly to the sinful person. "We had better lose something of our estate, than suffer those who are really proper objects of charity to remain without relief." [53]

The fact that each town was by law required to care for its poor, Edwards felt, should provide no excuse for lack of Christian charity. Such a law is eminently necessary, for "it is not fit that persons who are reduced to that extremity should be left to so precarious a source of supply as voluntary charity"; [54] but there is yet a place left for charity, since there are always those who, although not in extreme want, nevertheless need Christian help. Even those who are helped by the law stand in need of something beyond what the town can provide.

Edwards saw the problem of poverty from the standpoint of his time. He regards it as due to personal shortcoming, either from some natural ineptitude in handling one's own affairs, or from ignorance or sheer prodigality. It is not a problem affected by industrialization and technological unemployment which creates poverty regardless of personal abilities. The social problem of poverty, for Edwards, was simply concerned with particular poor people in a community, the solution of whose economic problems lay in personal charity. The fact that by law the town provided for its poor was not discussed as to its social efficacy; Edwards accepted it as a beneficial regulation, but gave it no particularly vigorous support. In fact, he was not so much interested in social change by the enactment of law as in the reaction of individuals to the needs of others. So in his fight for the protection of the Indians at the Stockbridge mission, he was not involved in a crusade for social justice as we understand the term today, but simply with a remedy for certain poor people, mistreated in a specific situation.[55] He was not a social reformer by direct intent, but his theological ethics of universal benevolence had a social outthrust which was later given expression in the antislavery crusade and "humanitarianism" of Samuel Hopkins.[56]

As in the individual life, so for society the ground of all is God. Without any systematic exploration of various social, economic, political responsibilities, Edwards accepted the general framework of social life as the work and designed purpose of God. Behind the laws of human society stood the awesome majestic power and justice of the divine magistrate and ruler. If society's laws were inadequate and subject to the perversion of sinful men, yet there was always a reckoning to be made with the deity. Although Edwards did not overtly challenge the status quo, it is nevertheless true that he assisted in setting in motion a religious movement which substantially altered the social and political order of the time.[57] If his attitude made for acquiescence in the face of social injustice and wrong, as some may think, it is even truer that his exalted conception of divine sovereignty contained a social dynamic, inasmuch as God's judgment was conceived as standing over against all human institutions in a righteousness which could never be ultimately flouted.

True Virtue: From Ethics to Aesthetics

WHEN Edwards turned his attention from natural morality or "secondary virtue" to "true virtue," he was not inclined to repeat his earlier studies which dealt with the question of how men were to achieve this precious quality. His task now was to analyze the structure and foundations of a moral life in which the religious affections, the "divine and supernatural light," and justification by faith were all already operative. He was to lay bare "the principle of morality which is eternally at the foundation of reality," regardless of the fact that on the basis of human calculation few could look forward to achieving it.[1] This treatise on true virtue was to be nonpolemical and normative, rather than prescriptive in tone.

His initial definition of true virtue as a kind of beauty or excellence catches up his own earlier aesthetic experiences. The "delightful conviction" of divine sovereignty which made that hitherto repulsive doctrine "exceedingly pleasant, bright and sweet" was now to receive fresh expression in something akin to a Neoplatonic vision.[2] In that calm cast of mind to which such insights brought him, he could discover a nature so replete with analogies of things spiritual that he concluded that men, in spite of their miseries, would cling to life "because they cannot bear to lose sight of such a beautiful and lovely world." [3] "When we are delighted with flowery meadows and gentle breezes of wind, we may consider that we see only the emanations of the sweet benevolence of Jesus Christ. When we behold the fragrant rose and lily, we see his love and purity . . . The crystal rivers and murmuring streams are the footsteps of his favor, grace and beauty." [4] This aesthetic sense, now given fresh impetus by his study of Shaftesbury and Hutcheson, was to be transferred to the ethical domain, where he found once more indications of that intrinsic amiability with which God had been pleased to constitute a nature in conformity with the supernatural realm and one to which a divinely given sense alone gives access.

The moral beauty which Edwards assigned to true virtue was constituted of three factors, all of which coalesced in the final analysis, each supporting and shedding light on the other. After distinguishing among various types of beauty, he came to the first of his determinants of moral beauty. The beauty of which he wished to speak was associated with those qualities and acts of mind where praise and blame are relevant. This is as much as to affirm that this kind of beauty has to do with the affections or the will, Edwards's favorite word here being "the heart" as distinguished from the speculative reason.[5]

This aspect of true virtue may be designated the emotional or affective factor. To this must be immediately added a second aspect of true virtue, for the affections left to themselves without direction, as the treatise on the *Religious Affections* made clear, may be seized with intensity without due respect as to their range and object. Therefore there must be a cognitive factor involved, which makes good the incipient possibility of disarranged and misdirected affections.[6] As he put the matter in the *Original Sin*, "Tho it is not easy, precisely to fix the limits of man's capacity as to love to God; yet in general we may determine that his capacity of love is coextended with his capacity of knowledge. The exercise of the understanding opens the way for the exercise of the other faculty." [7]

The implication of this is made clear when Edwards offers a preliminary definition of true virtue as a beauty belonging to the heart of an intelligent being, which is beautiful when seen "in a comprehensive view, as it is in itself, and, as related to every thing with which it stands connected." [8] The cognitive aspect of true virtue thereby contributes breadth and disinterestedness, since it breaks through the limitations by which lesser, more confined and private affections might otherwise be bound. It also connects the affections to the principle of being itself, thereby providing an object to which religious affections may, in proportion, fasten. True virtue, it then appears, is an affection of consent or benevolence on the part of an agent, directed to Being in general. The subjective element, that is, the will or affections, is thereby harnessed to the objective element, and in that consonance of agent and object moral virtue consists.

It is crucial to note that although true virtue is a matter of the heart, the defining feature of the authenticity of the affections lies in the nature of the object, rather than in the intensity of the affections. "No act of the mind or exercise of love" as Edwards put it, "is of the nature of true virtue, but what has being in general, or the great system of universal existence, for its direct and immediate object." [9] He had echoed the same conviction in the *Miscellanies* when he wrote, " 'Tis from the nature of the object loved rather than from the degree of the principle in the lover" which determines the value of the love the agent may have.[10] Secondary virtue on the other hand falls short of genuine benevolence, because its affection rests in itself or turns back upon the self in self-centered enjoyment.[11]

If true virtue is a kind of beauty, a third feature of it must be brought into play. This is the structural factor which operates with the affective and cognitive. The roots of this structural notion are to be discussed in Edwards's *Notes on the Mind,* where he had wrestled with the concepts of being and excellence. They explicitly appear in the *Religious Affections,* where he identifies gracious affections as those which possess a "beautiful symmetry and proportion." [12] Beginning with the data which sense and pure reason offer, Edwards had approached the notion of excellence by inquiring why one thing is excellent and another evil, "one beautiful and another deformed." Here the aesthetic connection between good and proportion, as well as that between evil and deformity, were established. But granted that proportion is more excellent or pleasing than disproportion, he pressed on to ask why this is so. The answer lies, he thought, in understanding the concept of proportion as an equality or likeness of ratios, a fact he proceeded to demonstrate in relation to inanimate nature by geometric diagrams.

Following the same principle, he moved on to consider "spiritual harmonies" that he designated as being of "vastly larger extent" which called for "a larger view to comprehend them." In this category, as in nature, he found that "equality thus pleases the mind and inequality is unpleasing . . . because disproportion or inconsistency is contrary to being. For being, if we examine narrowly, is nothing else but proportion." [13] The clear implication of this unexpected conclusion is that excellence lies in harmony or proportion as inherent in being as such. Perception of this agreement of being with itself is immediately pleasing, as is also the perception of those beings which in turn have similarly perceived the harmony or consent of being with itself.

His next step carries Edwards to the position from which he derived his principle of symmetry or proportion in respect to man's relation to God. "The greater a being is, and the more it has of entity the more will consent to being in general please it." But this is to say that God is the proper entity in which greatness and consent to being cohere. "So far as a thing consents to Being in general, so far it consents to Him." [14]

To this point Edwards's analysis has been couched in abstract and impersonal terms. But to come to moral excellence, this terminology was translated into the language of personal entities. Consent of being to being thus recast is an act of the mind toward other minds, which he now identifies as love, distinct from a consent directed toward things, which is designated as choice.

The crucial outcome of this understanding of consent as love to other minds is that such love must be a proportional love, that is, "to greater spirits, more and to less, less." "The want of this proportion is a deformity because it is a manifestation of a defect of such a love. It shows that it is not being in general, but something else that is loved, when love is not in proportion to the extensiveness and excellence of being." [15] But God, as Edwards was to state in the *True Virtue*, "is in effect being in general," in which there is perfect unity and love of himself.[16] He is therefore most to be loved or consented to, and any lack thereof produces a deformity or jarring in the total system of being, which is abhorrent to any perceiving being who has risen to the heights of viewing reality in its most comprehensive extent.

In writing his *True Virtue,* Edwards did not swerve from his conclusions reached in *The Mind.* The beauty which resides in true virtue is the structure of a benevolence which takes being as its first or primary object, simply considered, and "that object who has most of being, or the greatest share of existence, other things being equal . . . will have the greatest share of the propensity and benevolent affection of the heart." [17] Then it follows, according to Edwards, that other beings will be loved proportionately to the degree of being and benevolence, i.e., the degree of the love to Being in general. The latter is the second object of a truly virtuous person, and was designated as complacence, in distinction, but not in separation, from benevolence.[18] It follows that if one loves Being in general, he will "value good will to Being in general, wherever he sees it," and the more beings in which he finds this consent to Being in general, the greater will be the value he finds, since then there will be more being in agreement with Being in general than before. Thus on the human level a kind of "chain reaction" occurs, as more persons discover in each other a similar agreement to Being. Thereby they not only consent to each other, but also bind themselves closer in harmonious relation to God.[19]

There is then a hierarchy of being and excellence extending from God down through his creatures, which by the principle of proportion gives direction and structure to true virtue, and prevents it from becoming merely an indiscriminate merging of beings with one another and with God.[20] The beauty of virtue resides.

in the cordial consent of beings to Being in general, which flows out freely "to particular beings, in a greater or lesser degree, according to the measure of existence and beauty which they are possessed of." By the same principle it is affirmed that God's love of his creatures "is derived from and subordinate to his love to himself." [21] Since God loves himself infinitely, all subordinate intelligent beings have as their end nothing less than the same end, that for which they have been created. The objective element reigns supreme, since nothing can be counted as true virtue or the supreme good "in which God is not the first and last." [22]

The absolute primacy of God or Being in general in Edwards's moral theology moves the emphasis in morality from the human subject and his capacities to a plane where the nature and purpose of deity are determinative of virtue. True, in man there must be holy affections, divine sensibility and a sense of proportion when true virtue occurs, but in each case the deity is the originative power as he is also the supreme end. The moral good or right is not then determined by an analysis of the inherent ethical powers, insights, or valuations of man. Shaftesbury, Butler, Hutcheson, Hume, and Kant, in their various ways, had gone down that path.[23] Hutcheson, for example, had pointed out that human laws might be called good "because of their conformity to the Divine," but he concluded that calling the laws of God holy, just, or good was nothing but "an insignificant tautology, amounting to no more than this, 'that God wills what he wills.' " [24]

For Edwards to take humanity, in its graceless condition, as the source of norms of genuine morality, would be to select only one aspect of total reality to the exclusion of the entire context within which the human subject plays its part. Such a move would, at the outset, destroy the harmony of the whole structure of being. It would permit the human aspect, important though it be, to be considered as capable of laying down rules and principles for Being in general without reference to the ground of all existence and value. Only when the heartfelt recognition of the principle of Being itself was operative was it proper to speak of true virtue. And to say as much as this, for Edwards, was to span the alleged gap between value and being and thus to orient ethical thought to the ontological domain. Consequently, when he speaks of the beauty of true virtue, making that beauty consist in cordial consent with Being in general proportionate to its own degree of being and cordial consent to itself, he has established an ontological framework for the highest morality.

In the *End for which God Created the World,* Edwards deposited explicit evidence of this ontological interest. It is here that the clearest indications of his departure from the theological objectivism in a Calvinistic vein show, as he embraces the parallel stream of Neoplatonic thought which ran through Augustine, the Reformers, and the Cambridge Platonists.[25] But to cast the moral life in this Neoplatonic perspective is tantamount to transcending ethics, understood in its more familiar guise as concerned with laws, principles, precepts, and "oughts." Or, in agreement with *True Virtue,* it construes rules and principles in aesthetic terms, rather than in terms of specific moral categories.[26] Indeed, as ethics comes to be subsumed under aesthetics, it has seemed that Edwards has left behind him all ethical discourse. The aesthetic vision of reality has so swallowed up ethical insight and discrimination that it appears that nothing is left but the poetic or mystical outpourings of a mind which has lost all contact with the hard business of ethical decision wrought out in daily life.

Before this conclusion can be accepted, however, Edwards must be permitted to buttress his theory of true virtue by offering his exposition of theological objectivism cast in largely Neoplatonic terms. According to the dictates of reason, he thinks, God is not only infinite and perfect in every respect conceivable by man —a doctrine well attested in Scripture—but also is perfect in the expression of his supreme excellency in his attributes.[27] If the expression of his perfect attributes, which would otherwise lie fallow, is excellent, so also must be the knowledge thereof. "It is a thing infinitely good in itself that God's glory should be known by a glorious society of created beings." [28] This follows from Edwards's conviction that existence is more worthy than defect or nonentity, and the existence of a being's knowing the divine perfections is then more valuable than the absence of such beings. So the perfection of God, expressed and known, is to be valued and esteemed, loved, and delighted in for its own sake. In a passage which breathes the very essence of Neoplatonism, Edwards sums up the relation of God to his world. As there is "infinite fulness of all possible good in God," it overflows as an "infinite fountain of good." It emanates or communicates its being and value, and this multiplies good. As the fountain or the sun, each of which pours forth spontaneously its streams or beams, so God in his goodness and power as Supreme Being streams out to his creation his joy and happiness, moral excellence and beauty. And this is the end or purpose of his creation or emanation of the world, "to communicate himself or diffuse his own fulness." Emanation, the overflowingness of being and value, was what was aimed at. Lest he be misunderstood as suggesting that the existence of the creature in any way limited or exercised control over the original intention and act of deity, Edwards hastened to add that the very existence of intelligent beings as well as the divine communications to them once they exist, all arise from the same general diffusive character of God.[29]

It would be easy to conclude that once intelligent beings came into existence, the divine purpose would be exhausted in providing for them. But this conclusion would subvert the entire Edwardsean scheme by establishing man as the center and ultimate goal of God's actions in creation. "The doctrine that makes God's creatures and not himself, to be his last end, is a doctrine the farthest from having a favorable aspect in God's absolute self-sufficience and independence." [30] The same logic and conviction of proportionality which had driven Edwards to insist that greater respect and love was owed to that Being possessed of the greatest degree of being and excellence, now also brought him to the conclusion that God owes greatest respect to himself in all he does. Because he is "infinitely the greatest and best of beings" in comparison to which, "all things else, with regard to worthiness, importance and excellence are perfectly as nothing," no other alternative exists as to his purpose in creation.[31] What flows forth from the divine source is nothing other than God's love of himself and his delight or happiness in that same love or agreement with himself.[32] This intention to display his beauty, power, love, and excellence precedes the existence of his creatures.

Thus in what Edwards called the larger sense God's love is the foundation of the existence of his creatures and is exercised without respect to "any particular present or future created existence for its object." But in the stricter sense, because love presupposes "the existence of the object loved, at least in idea and expectation" there were in God's mind particular created objects of his love, of which it is proper to conceive that God was moved by a benevolence to them. But this is not to say that God has anything less than himself and his glory in view when he acts for the sake of these potential or created beings. The two aims are not to be set in disjunction. "They are rather to be considered as coinciding one with the other, and implied one in the other." The creature is "the object of God's regard consequentially and by implication as it were comprehended in God." [33] At no point therefore does the human subject become the chief aim of God's creation; he is completely subordinated to God's glory and contributes to it. Theological subjectivism has no place in this view of reality, nor do all notions of man's virtue as a private possession or an end in itself. Such virtue as is brought about in man can but be a reflection of the divine graciousness wherewith he is created and maintained in existence.

It is not only existence which God in his diffusive nature brings about. He communicates three aspects of himself to the creature as he delights in himself. The first of these is knowledge of himself, which is to be understood as "conformity to God." It is the image of God's own knowledge of himself. It is "a participation of the same." [34] Secondly, he communicates virtue or holiness whereby the creature "partakes of God's own moral excellency," which is his beauty.[35] Again, since God delights in his own moral excellence, he also delights in its multiplication in his creatures. And thirdly, God communicates his happiness. Just as he enjoys himself, so now he rejoices in the happiness of those who participate in his happiness.[36] In all these acts of communication, which in a sense are all one, it is not the welfare and the benefit of his creatures at which the deity first aims. He remains his own end. But as they grow and are enriched in these three respects they come ever closer "to an identity with that which is in God." The creatures' aim is then to approach ever nearer to God through eternity until they are "as it were swallowed up in him." [37] Or as Edwards put it in a summary fashion, "In the creature's knowing, esteeming, loving, rejoicing in and praising God, the glory of God is both exhibited and acknowledged; his fulness is received and returned. Here is both emanation and remanation. The refulgence shines upon and into the creature and is reflected back to the luminary. The beams of glory come from God, and are something of God, and are refunded back again to their original." [38]

If then virtue merges into beauty and beauty is resolved into aesthetic harmony with the deity, to whose glory all else exists, the question of virtue cannot be raised or answered without reference to the "virtue" of the deity himself. Because he is infinite, he is most worthy to be worshipped; his attributes, both metaphysical and ethical, are of the highest excellence, and he emanates his nature for his own glory so that all will participate in the cordial agreement, knowledge, and happiness of which he partakes in himself. But this is to conclude that he needs nothing but himself to be happy, and by which he would enjoy his own excellence. As an infinite Being possessed of all appropriate attributes he is seemingly self-contained, and nothing could be added to him, in respect to either being or value.[39]

The questions which must be raised are twofold: why does God create, since he already has all being in infinite degree, and no being can be added to that which is already infinite? And more significantly for ethical theory, how can a being, already self-sufficient in respect to excellence and happiness, in any way profit by the virtue of his creatures? Indeed, what conceivable role has the morality of mere man in relation to this self-contained absolute being? If man can be of no value to the deity, he has lost all dignity, and whatever measure of virtue exists in him counts for nothing in the cosmic scheme. Either the self-sufficiency of God or the value of man must be surrendered, so the two questions imply.

These are questions which Edwards himself raised and to which he felt he had an adequate answer. The Neoplatonic strain which runs through these late works served to maintain the infinite self-sufficiency of God while it made place for the multiplication of being and value. Although it is true that God's glory and happiness are "infinite and cannot be added to," and are also unchangeable, nevertheless God, being infinitely good, pours out himself in respect to both existence and value, and delights in so doing. His happiness consists not in the objects so emanated from the fulness of his being, but in their happiness, which is nothing other than the exercise of his own goodness in their happiness and existence. So the "delight which God has in his creatures," happiness, cannot properly be said to be received from the creature.[40] It is but his own work, reflected back to himself. His joy is "dependent on nothing besides his own act, which he exerts with an absolute and independent power." He is "absolutely independent of us," and there is nothing the creature has which in the last analysis is not from him.[41] To be sure, his creatures, their virtue, happiness, and existence are in time, but he has enjoyed all this as present to his mind from all eternity, and therefore undergoes no mutability.[42] To speak of man's value or his virtue in this context is but

to speak of God's operations, and man has no independent status from which to judge of the righteousness of
God's work, since his existence and virtue are all from
the deity. Man's dignity lies simply in being a creation of God, through whom God glorifies himself. It
does not depend upon his achievement of moral virtue.
It is a dignity conferred ontologically, not morally.

Again, men may persist in asking about the morality of a God who does all, is curiously enough independent of all existence and value humanly considered,
and yet is recognizable in and through all creation. If
a human being were to claim that all he does is for his
own sake, such a person would be adjudged as a selfish
individual, yet in the case of God, Edwards feels that
this aspersion as to moral character is completely out
of place. It is not to be counted selfishness in its most
sordid connotation when God, being omniscient and
infallible, knows that "he is infinitely the most valuable
being" and pursues ends in agreement with this truth.
His interest is not set in opposition to the good of all,
as is the case in human self-interest, but instead it seeks
the good of his creatures as a way of expressing his own
innate goodness.[43] The good or happiness of the creature, Edwards repeats, is not to be thought of as separate from or independent of God's glory or happiness.
The two go together as one. In seeking his own glory,
he seeks the glory and happiness of the creature as
well.[44] Man's true virtue is the playing back to the
supreme original of that harmonious beauty, the source
and end of which is God. It is the continuing dynamic
process of drawing ever closer to that Being in whom
the supreme agreement or harmony already exists in
infinite degree, and to whom both reason and revelation
attest.[45]

At first appearance, Edwards's conclusion would

seem to be that the virtuous person would be "swallowed up" in God.[46] However, if this is the end of the matter, ontological problems of the first order would exist. A form of pantheism known as panentheism would seem to eliminate totally the foundation upon which Edwards had built his concept of true virtue understood as cordial consent of intelligent beings to Being in general.[47] The minimal condition of polarity between the human subject and the divine object necessary to true virtue would be lost by engulfing the subject in the nature of the object. That Edwards came perilously close to this conclusion cannot be denied. He had dared to write in the *Miscellanies* that "if we should suppose the faculties of a created spirit to be enlarged infinitely, there would be the deity to all intents and purposes," and he had affirmed that God "is present everywhere, as the soul is in the body." [48] Yet to say this much is not to claim identity between God and man. He seems rather to hold that the divine, infinite essence of God does not become identical with the creation. Distinctions still remain, as God and man differ in manner and degree, while at the same time no ontological independence can be posited for man. In this sense God is everywhere as the ground of the being of all, without loss of the differentiation between the created and the creator, the emanated and the emanator.[49] Edwards undoubtedly is moving into the area of pantheism, though not pure pantheism in which all creation would itself be divine. The mystical absorption of the creature into the very essence of the creator, which pantheism demands, is forestalled by Edwards's dynamic view of the relation of the creature to God. He held that the identity between man and deity would never be complete. In the case of truly virtuous mankind, the relation was to be one going on throughout eternity, in which asymptotically the creature would be ever approaching perfect union with God, but never reaching it. "It is no solid objection against God's aiming at an infinitely perfect union of the creature with himself, that the particular time will never come when it can be said, the union is now infinitely perfect." Although the saints will be glorified in heaven with "eternal felicity," the moment will never arrive when "this infinitely valuable good has been actually bestowed." [50] In this respect the polarity necessary to theological objectivism had the last word, and pantheism faltered, close as Edwards's mystical tendencies came to winning the day.[51] Individuality was preserved in the total relation as contributing to the aesthetic harmony at which God aimed. And Edwards's ethical system was saved from the dead end of static mysticism by his insistence upon a dynamic interaction between God and mankind.

"True Virtue" and Its Early Critics

THE TREATISE on *The Nature of True Virtue* appeared posthumously in 1765, probably brought to press by the good offices of Samuel Hopkins. The work was placid and serene in tone, lacking either the pyrotechnics of the *Will* or the incessant citations of Scripture in the *Original Sin*. With the exception of a few brief, respectful references to Hutcheson, Wollaston, and Hume, Edwards's exposition and argument is devoid of support from extraneous sources. As to both content and style it lacked the polemical touch, and seemed rather to be a piece of amiable, disinterested metaphysical speculation. It was not, apparently, the kind of writing which sparks controversy, as did Edwards's other major works.

Six years after the publication of the *True Virtue,* the Reverend William Hart of Saybrook, Connecticut, believing he had detected certain pernicious errors in the work, published a slim volume in answer to it. Hart's book, *Remarks on President Edwards's Dissertations concerning the Nature of True Virtue,* proved to be the first of a series of criticisms launched against

Edwards's treatise.[1] The controversy was to run well on into the nineteenth century, when it exhausted itself in the dry sands of dispute between the advocates of the New England theology and the orthodox Calvinists of Princeton Seminary.

What annoyed Hart at the outset was Edwards's insistence that benevolence fastened upon Being as such, a notion which at most might be regarded as referring to a Being possessed of perception and will, but one which lacked all moral attributes. Being, abstractly considered, Hart argued, "is neither wise nor foolish, neither morally good nor evil, neither self-existent nor created and dependent upon neither God nor a creature. It has no relation," he concluded, "to the benevolent mind." [2] It is evident that no clear moral directions for man can be derived from such an entity as Edwards offers. Furthermore, Edwards has substituted this virtually featureless metaphysical being for the living God of the Bible. God is therefore "not the primary object of virtuous regard, nor is love to him the root of virtuous affections," since God and being simply considered are "exceeding divers from each other." [3] In fact, as Edwards had maintained that true virtue did not identify itself with any particular being, it followed that a benevolence directed to God was only a second best virtue, since God, as Hart understood matters, was in fact a particular being. Or to press the matter further, loving consent to being simply considered produces a form of idolatry in which Being itself and benevolence to it take the place of God. Love to God, under these conditions, becomes the consequence of our own love to simple being, "virtue's idol," as Hart calls it, rather than the result of God's love to sinful man. If Edwards is correct, these virtuous affections toward the deity comprise merely secondary, not primary, virtue.

Edwards's insistence upon the notion of Being in general further irritated Hart, because he found Edwards to be arguing that God loves himself because he has the greatest amount of being. But this is ridiculous. God's holiness, thinks Hart, does not depend upon his first viewing himself as possessed of infinite degrees of being and therefore exercising pure benevolence to himself. If this were the case, God would be "reflecting on himself as thus virtuously benevolent" and thereby he would make himself the secondary object or "greater benevolence and the first object of his own complacence." [4] The upshot of this strange internal operation in the Godhead would be that all the divine perfections such as "justice, equity, moral proportion, faithfulness" turn into secondary or subservient qualities in respect to benevolence to being as such, whereas all virtues in God are "equally original and primary." [5]

Hart was further outraged to learn that good, or common morality, was in Edwards's view only an inferior form of virtue. After all, in ages past prophets, apostles, and other men had praised and exercised such virtue, whereas Edwards had demeaned all such efforts. In fact, Edwards was so far lost in his high metaphysics of virtue that he had interpreted virtue in terms of geometric figures and physical bodies. "The truth," sneered Hart, "is this marvellous scheme has changed the natural, moral beauty and glory of true virtue, into an image made like to the beauty of an equilateral triangle or a chess-board." [6] This charge, of course, missed entirely Edwards's nuances of meaning in respect to secondary beauty. He had in fact turned aside such a charge by his rhetorical query: "Who will affirm, that a disposition to approve of the harmony of good musick or the beauty of a square or equilateral triangle is the same with true holiness or truly virtuous disposition of mind!" Appreciation of forms of natural beauty, he added, does not increase with achievement of true virtue or decrease with viciousness. " 'Tis evident in fact, that a relish of these things does not depend on general benevolence, or any benevolence at all to any Being whatsoever." It is precisely the confusion of man's natural sense of beauty with the transcendent beauty of true virtue by which some moralists—probably referring to Shaftesbury and Hutcheson—have been misled.[7]

Hart's criticisms came nearer a sensitive point when he fastened upon what he regarded as Edwards's inconsistent use of the notion of natural conscience. How can natural conscience approve of true virtue, he asked, when in fact the natural conscience can't appreciate the beauty of true virtue? And how can it be that natural conscience approves nothing, as he understood Edwards to say, that falls short of true virtue and yet approves secondary moral beauty? And if in the last judgment sinners will finally see what true virtue is, does this not mean that men, hitherto sinners, are mysteriously transformed into saints because they at last apprehend true virtue?[8] Even in this workaday world, moral matters are confused enough, especially since the natural conscience gives no inkling of how men are related to Being as such. There is no need therefore to project into eternity the conundrum as to how sinners become saints because they finally know what true virtue is. Hart admits that there may be a distinction between a natural moral sense and a divine relish, but the former is the firm basis of the latter, and is an ingredient in man's moral constitution. Common moral sense shows man to be destined for the virtue with which his happiness is connected, although it is not guaranteed.[9]

True virtue, Hart affirms, appears only when the

heart relishes and when practice follows what the moral sense dictates. Being as such has nothing to do with this determinant of moral virtue. Edwards, on the other hand, has insisted that under the spell of a "divine and supernatural sense" men should pursue moral virtue in a higher dimension. But, jibes Hart, "You might as reasonably preach to your horse, as St. Francis did to the fishes, and exhort him to see and admire the secondary beauty of moral things, as, on these principles, exhort natural men to see and relish their primary beauty." [10] All the horse lacks is a moral sense, and all natural men lack is a spiritual sense; one is as unattainable in the one as in the other, except by sheer miracle. So Edwards has simply ruined the idea of true virtue and religion with his high-flown distinctions which have made virtue "unnatural" and impossible to attain. By his demeaning ordinary virtuous actions to the status of secondary moral beauty, he has set morality in such a light as to "disgust enlightened and virtuous men and perplex the simple . . . and involve practical religion (the plainest thing in the world, adapted to the capacities of the vulgar) in a cloud." The consequence will be that men will suspect "there is nothing real in it," or if there is, it is so far removed from view as to make it fruitless to trouble themselves about religion.[11]

The moralistic tendency in Hart is obvious. It vitiates the aesthetic component to which Edwards aspired, as the distinction between true virtue and its inferior forms was thoroughly confounded in a semantic wrangle over the idea of a supernatural sense and the word "virtue" itself. Hart was incapable of making anything of Edwards's metaphysical grounding of morality, in which being as such provided an order of reality to which the categories of aesthetic valuation apply. Ethics for Hart may glorify God, but its true aim is a good life, not a holy life, an honorable life, not one of disinterested affection for Being in general, a happy life rather than one subordinated to the harmonious good and beauty of all being. God's purpose, in fact, aims at "as great a measure of happiness as can be communicated by the exercise of a paternal government upon rational creatures. In keeping with his own attributes God cannot communicate more than happiness without defeating his own designs, and thereby destroying the happiness of his children." [12] Cordial consent to Being thus becomes a notion quite distinct from human "happiness" as ethics in a moralistic vein part company with aesthetics. The subjectivistic and utilitarian phase of American Protestant ethics had come to expression as God's purposes were reduced from his own glory to the congenial confines of humanity's benefit.

In spite of Hart's fragile grasp of Edwards's thought, he had fallen upon certain deficiencies in it which would continue to haunt discussions on Christian ethics. He had seen the difficulty in Edwards's idea that a natural moral taste or conscience could approve true virtue while at the same time failing to come to a full appreciation of its radiant beauty. He had raised the question as to how ethical injunctions, responsibility, or moral claims could derive from Being as such. He had skirted the formidable issue as to how God could possess true virtue, since Being as such would seem to be a simple entity from which all cordial consent would be absent. Some of these problems were to surface again in the discussions of the later eighteenth and nineteenth centuries, as the Edwardseans attempted to defend their master against Robert Hall, Archibald Alexander, and the Princeton critics.

First in the field against Hart was Samuel Hopkins,

who rose promptly to his mentor's defense. In the Appendix to his own "Inquiry into the Nature of True Holiness," Hopkins attempted to answer systematically Hart's objections. Hart's criticism of Edwards's notion of Being in general had amounted to treating that entity as a "tertium quid," distinct from God and lacking in all definite ethical features. Hopkins did not fully come to grips with this contention, but outflanked the objection by insisting that the troublesome term included God and his sentient creatures. Consequently when men are called to consent cordially to Being in general, they are summoned to love God and their neighbors. "He who loves being in general loves God and his fellow creatures and, therefore, obeys the two great commandments." [13] Once having identified Being in general with God and his creatures, there was no longer any need to suppose that God, to be virtuous, must first love Being before loving himself, as Hart had contended. God's holiness does not consist in some action prior to love or distinct from it.[14] The ethical ingredient that Hart had held to be lacking in the notion of Being in general had been accounted for when Hopkins smoothly coalesced God and Being in general. God could issue moral demands and at the same time be a proper object of benevolence. However, Hopkins had shifted Edwards's emphasis from Being in general as the principle of ultimate reality to the view of Being in general as a collection of beings, composed of God and his creation. As a result, the door was opened to the charge that to love Being in general, one would have to love each specific being, of which there may be an infinite number. The result would be that true virtue would be a logical and actual impossibility, since to love each concrete being would be an endless task.

In fact, to love any particular being all beings would have to be loved at the same time, which brings the whole matter to absurdity.[15]

Hart had touched the quick when he raised the issue as to whether, on grounds of the natural moral sense, one could heartily approve of true virtue without possessing it. Unless one could do so, it seemed that the nerve of moral obligation had been cut, and mankind set loose to seek whatever good it pleased. Hopkins would not have it so. He argued, following Edwards's thought quite closely, that a wholly selfish person might be pleased with some things which accompany true virtue, but fail completely to take in the genuine beauty of benevolence. Just as a mathematician may recognize the proportion and symmetry of the lines within a picture without grasping the beauty of the whole, so one lacking in true virtue may prize something of the structure of true virtue but fail to relish its full beauty. So also one who lacks the capacity or inclination to enjoy the harmony of a tune may nevertheless be pleased by the "exact proportion and harmony in the vibrations of the chords" in a piece of music.[16] A heart disaffected from true virtue simply cannot relish its intrinsic value and beauty. Without holiness in the heart, there is no hope of a genuine appreciation of true virtue. "It is even a self-evident proposition," thought Hopkins, "that the love of holiness is holiness, and therefore has passed for an incontestable truth, till Mr. H. has risen and contradicted it." [17] Actually Hopkins's answer to Hart had not met the objection squarely. Whereas for Edwards proportion and symmetry were not mere accompaniments of true virtue, but ingredients of it, Hopkins had treated them as though they were secondary features of true virtue. Furthermore, since they are essentials in true virtue, to approve of them with the natural moral sense is to see something, if not all, of that upon which the beauty of true virtue depends. Although one's heart may not relish the full beauty of virtue, one is nevertheless able to perceive that without which beauty could not exist. To this extent Hart was correct in his judgment of the adequacy of the natural moral sense.

But if Hopkins be right, as Hart's inquiry implied, what is the value of the natural moral capabilities of men? Does not the moral sense mislead men if it does not lead to or fails to appreciate true virtue? It seems that the moral conscience, in fact, does not tell men the right direction as to where moral responsibility lies. Not so, argued Hopkins. The natural moral sense of men does tell him the truth. It provides judgments that are valid concerning benevolence "independent of the exercises of the heart and in direct opposition to them," for it "judges of what it sees, and not of that which it does not see." As a result, "the reason and judgment may be fully convinced that true virtue consists in benevolence, while the heart is wholly opposed to it." Men may possess a true "speculative" idea of virtue without possessing it.[18] But to relish, taste, or possess true virtue as a reality rather than a speculative possibility depends upon whether the person wills it. And this, according to Hopkins, means that "he is furnished with every thing needful in order to see and exercise virtue, except it be virtue itself." [19] This conclusion scarcely answers Hart's original questions, since Hopkins has already offered the idea that seeing holiness and being holy are identical.

Hart then returns to his principal point. What obligation does man have to pursue true virtue if all that his moral capacities can do is to bring him to a speculative idea of virtue, but cannot enable him to achieve a disinterested benevolence? If men do not actually see, that is, relish and enjoy true virtue, then they are like blind men, suffering under a natural inability for which they are not responsible. Again Hopkins, enlarging upon Edwards, attempts to set Hart straight. When blind men do not see, it is a natural inability for which they cannot be blamed; but the blindness of the heart "lies wholly in the indisposition and perverseness of the will or heart." Consequently it is men's fault, for which they are to be held responsible, that they do not fully see and relish true virtue.[20] Of course, according to Hopkins's reading of the problem, men are able to reason correctly and come to valid judgments about true virtue. They may approve the conclusion that disinterested benevolence constitutes true virtue, but they close their eyes to the beauty of holiness because of the lusts of their hearts. The result is an inexcusable ignorance, a deficiency or a misdirection of affections, for which men themselves are responsible. And the natural conscience assents to the justice of this condemnation of their own inexcusable waywardness, thus showing that the moral faculties God has implanted in mankind are serviceable within the limits that the self's comprehension has afforded. If Hart's claim be allowed that men are freed of obligation by virtue of the fact that they are lacking a spiritual sense which lies beyond their powers to achieve, then one's responsibility to true virtue, disinterested benevolence, or Being is completely slackened. Moral obligation stops at the limits of moral ability. But, argued Hopkins with some cogency, "Shall the blinding lusts of men's hearts take off all obligations to love what they disrelish and hate, though conscience tell them that it is excellent and lovely, when this same blindness of heart, if it binds the conscience too, and bribes that to agree with it, would be altogether blamable."[21]

Early in the nineteenth century the scene for criticism of Edwards's *True Virtue* moved across the sea to England, where a clergyman named Robert Hall professed to have discovered that certain "fashionable infidels" had embraced a definition of virtue which coincided with that of Edwards.[22] To his famous sermon, "Modern Infidelity Considered," he added a footnote in which he discussed his major objections to Edwards's work. These remarks served as a goad to the adherents of the New England theology, as they soon entered the controversy. Hall traveled a familiar path in arguing that infidelity spawned immorality and licentiousness, and offered marriage as a bulwark against the intemperance which infidelity had let loose. It followed, to his way of thinking, that men should be made benevolent and unselfish first in their private affections before attempting the exercise of broader affections. This program of moral development was especially to be developed in the culture of those affections which sprang out of close, intimate family relations. "As in the operations of intellect," he argued, "we proceed from the contemplation of individuals to the formation of general abstractions, so in the development of the passions, in like manner, we advance from private to public affections." This principle is one embedded in nature itself, the order of nature being "evermore from particular to generals." [23] It is this eternally fixed order that has been inverted by the infidels—and by implication by Edwards. Instead of inculcating private affections as a preparation for broader moral affections, they want "to make us love the whole species more by loving every particular part less . . . [when] virtue is limited to a passionate attachment to the general good." [24] But such advice leads to indifference to one's family, estrangement from friends, insults to benefactors, absence of gratitude and pity, and generally leads men to divest themselves of their humanity. Selfishness, not generosity would ensue, and the "perpetration of every crime" would have its source in the callousness of the heart which attends the infidel's view. Moreover, the notion of pursuing the good of the whole in its abstractness "is a motive so loose and indeterminate, and embraces such an infinity of relations, that before we could be certain what action it prescribed, the season of action would be past." On the other hand, the affections implanted in the self, developed according to certain rules, are definite, and "the boundaries of virtue are easily ascertained." In developing these affections as parts of the whole, the good of the whole will be secured.[25]

With this line of thought before him, Hall proceeded to show how Edwards's thought led to precisely the same fallacies as were to be found in the infidels. On Edwards's grounds virtue is an impossibility. Since the system of being—including God—is infinite, it is impossible to maintain the proper proportion in one's affections between infinite Being and particular attachments, the latter being "infinitely less than the passion for the general good." But the human mind is simply incapable of assessing or achieving this difference in degree. Furthermore, men's views of the universe can be perpetually enlarged, even if the sum of existence remains the same, so at each step of the enlargement of one's views of existence, one must also reduce the strength of particular affections lest they become disproportionate and ultimately vicious. The result is a constant fluctuation in the nature of virtue. And, at last, if love to Being in general be the exclusive property of virtue, private or particular affections become useless or "even pernicious." Nevertheless Hall concluded, erroneously as it turned out, by affirming that "we have no dispute respecting what is the ultimate end of virtue, which is allowed on both sides to be the greatest sum of happiness in the universe." The question remaining is what is virtue itself, or as Hall put it, changing the whole meaning of this question, "what are the means appointed for the attainment of that end?" The difficulty with such a view as Edwards's is that it sought simplicity by placing virtue in one disposition of the mind without regard for the "infinite variety of moral phenomena and mental combination." [26]

Hall's views were not far distant from those taken up by the Princeton critics of Edwards and his followers. Archibald Alexander, professor at Princeton Seminary, left behind him at his death a slender and unimpressive volume entitled, *Outlines of Moral Science*. The editors of *The Biblical Repertory and Princeton Review* produced a laudatory review of the book, which was enlarged by a general attack upon The New Haven Divinity and the New England Theology. Along the way several slighting remarks were made to Edwards's treatment of virtue, "which is supposed to have given the first start to the peculiar speculations of some New England divines on this subject." The treatise itself was referred to as "a sort of tentative effort, made late in life," which was out of joint with some of Edwards's basic principles and "had very little influence on his views of practical and theoretical theology." It noted that even Edwards's closest follower and student, Joseph Bellamy, had not followed his master "in this single exceptional case." [27] The implication left was that Edwards had slackened off as an older man from his former Calvinistic zeal, and had lost his intellectual powers, whereas Alexander's posthumous volume was the ripe vintage of his full powers, for which that author could be held responsible "not only at the bar of human criticism, but at the tribunal of God." [28]

There was much in the review that coincided with the theological objectivism of Edwards. The Princeton reviewers inveighed against what they regarded as the prevailing utilitarian spirit of the time in a vein reminiscent of Edwards's insistence upon the intrinsic beauty of true virtue. "The idea that truth, beauty, goodness, have an inherent worth in themselves seems to be lost," they lamented, and charged "spurious ethical systems" with responsibility for interpreting moral goodness only as a means to happiness.[29] While agreeing with Hall and Alexander, they differed sharply from Edwards's placement of all sin in selfishness and all true virtue in benevolence. They argued that when men give up their own welfare as "a sacrifice to the overbearing demands of others," they sin not from selfishness, but from a lack of justice, since benevolence without justice is no longer virtue. By the same token, if benevolence be taken as the sum of all virtue in God, without regard to his justice, the question arises as to why he does not make all men happy by making them holy. On the other hand, if it be understood, as it should be, that God's justice operates to punish some by withholding salvation, then the righteousness of the deity is upheld, and the question as to the lack of complete happiness among his creatures here and in the hereafter becomes tractable.[30]

The Princeton reviewers were also deeply disturbed by their understanding of the views of the New England theologians concerning the will of God as the only foundation of moral obligation. If the New England divines, following Edwards, insisted that God's will determined by fiat the good to be good, then it is conceivable that all manner of evil could be counted as virtuous simply because God willed it. But the moral sense of man is revolted by this conclusion, and may, if further light is not shed on the problem, lean to the view that a standard of right exists independent of the divine will to which God conforms. The notion of such an independent criterion was not acceptable to the Princetonians, for they saw that this state of affairs would rob God of his "supremacy, independence and exclusive divinity." The true answer lay in affirming that the eternal rule of right exists in the Divine Being, in the "eternal, inimitable, immaculate sanctity and goodness of his own nature." To this norm his will infallibly conforms, "for he cannot deny himself." His creatures in turn have been empowered to perceive this right or moral good by means of conscience or the moral faculty.[31] On these several grounds the Edwardsean position seemed highly vulnerable to the Princetonians.

The New Divinity men could not allow the assaults of Hall, Alexander, and "The Princeton Review" to pass without challenge.[32] They too produced a review of Alexander's book on moral science. They found that Alexander had confused Cumberland's theory of virtue with that of Edwards, had falsely ranged Bishop Butler against Edwards, and generally had deprecated Edwards's "illustrious treatise." They correctly pointed out that Edwards's views were not simply a "tentative effort" of his declining years, but were offered in the "full vigor of his manhood" when he was younger than the venerable Alexander. Furthermore, the ideas for true virtue were to be found in Edwards's youthful notes, which they proceeded to cite to establish the fact that Edwards's dissertation was but the maturing of ideas long held. Its depths had not been plumbed by its critics; they had failed both to understand it and, fairly, to answer it. "Nothing have we ever seen which appears to us more superficial, than the arguments which have been arrayed against it." [33]

The answers to Hall and the Princeton divines were made in a point-by-point refutation. The charge that Edwards had simplified moral phenomena by reducing them to benevolence was turned aside by noting that all science seeks simplicity. Hence, "The simplicity of a thing . . . is no proof that the thing is false," but rather may recommend its validity.[34] Or again, to narrow virtue to benevolence was not an error, since virtue so conceived includes benevolence to one's self as part of Being in general.[35] But the more serious objection to Edwards which had to be met was that his conception of virtue had made virtue impossible. If, as Hall had argued, one had to hold an infinite number of infinite ideas of an infinite being, the whole notion of virtue fell to the ground of its own weight. But, argued the New England authors, no one need suppose that there must be infinite ideas of an infinite being. All that Edwards had intended was that men should cleave to "the universal system so far forth as they comprehended it" with proportionate allowance of affection for the "different parts of it." Nor would such finite views of "the universal system" hamper the expression of concern for private individuals closely related to the moral agent. To be sure, instinctive attachments may have more force than general preferences, but there may also be a governing affection, which is "less impetuous." "The ruling sensibility is not always the most highly excited." Thus, in a figure of speech which was bound to outrage natural moral sentiments, the authors went on to suggest that a mother might choose to offer up her first born sooner than "renounce her supreme love to God." Deliberate esteem, as distinct from the sheer force of affection for her child, would thereby control the "pathematic affections." "There may be a governing power in calmness," blandly concluded the Andover theologians—although it would be difficult to see how calmness could be enjoyed in the situation described. This line of thought, in fact, came dangerously close to agreement with Hall's charge that as views of the universe expanded, the strength of particular affections would dwindle in significance. But the Edwardseans put a different interpretation on this possibility. Their theory of virtue, they claimed, "does not diminish our interest, absolutely, in our friends, but it does so, relatively to God." Therefore, since all particular beings are part of the universal system, men are under obligation to love friends, relatives, and countrymen. "If we have the right feeling toward that part of the universe of which we are more immediately cognizant. . . . Virtue must be proportioned to our ideas of sentient being." [36] In fact, in loving those who are close and dear to us, we are loving God's glory, concluded the New England divines. "The great object which we have in view, when we cherish our love of parents, children, brethren and neighbors, is the glory of God." [37]

The critics of Edwards had hammered home the notion that his view of true virtue was too indiscriminate, lacking in precise weighing of advantages and disadvantages, as in the case of justice. In fact, if Alexander was correct, benevolence would so soften the moral agent's heart and so blind him to moral distinctions that he would free criminals and malefactors. Thus benevolence, instead of being an all-encompassing term for virtue, turns out to be a vice! The Edwardseans tugged hard to pull themselves out of the difficulty, and in the process gave away the whole game. They began to make distinctions among various forms of benevolence, thereby showing in fact that the term "benevolence" was too broad a characterization of virtue unless another norm such as justice be introduced. The benevolence which was genuinely virtuous, they held, was indeed a discriminating act, because it was "a free choice of the general above the private good." It was an act of moral judgment whereby the most valuable as well as the beings with the most existence are chosen to be loved. The conclusion must then be that God is to be chosen above all as "the most valuable of all existences." [38] But in so arguing, the Andover apologists let loose a problem which, boldly put, bade fair to being unanswerable on their own grounds or upon Edwards's as they interpreted him. Why is the "largest amount of existence" more worthy of benevolence than a smaller amount? This troublesome inquiry was smoothly glossed over by assimilating the term "amount" to the notion of "relative value in the great scale." So each individual, to return to Hall's pertinent criticism, was in the last analysis to be loved "on account of, as well as in proportion to, his relative value"—a proportion determined on the basis of the amount of existence in question.[39] And this conclusion signified that the weakest and most needy, those least in possession of existence, were the least to be cherished, whereas it would appear in Christian thought that these would be the ones most in need of a benevolent concern. So long as Edwards's defenders insisted on treating this question as one of "amounts" of empirical existence rather than as one regarding Being in general as the principle of being itself in all existents, the system they proposed would be distasteful to man's moral sense.

The most egregious fallacy with which the Princeton group charged the Edwardsean view was that his

position led straight to utilitarianism. In their replies
the New Englanders were back on more solid ground.
Of course happiness was to be a result of cordial consent,
but where, they asked, did Edwards ever assert that
virtue itself was not a real good and only a means to
happiness? In his *Religious Affections,* and *Dissertation
concerning the End for Which God Created the World,*
as well as the *True Virtue,* Edwards had repeatedly held
to the objectivistic theme. God's glory for its own sake,
holy affection fastening upon the holiness of God, and
moral virtue for its own sake, all oppose the utilitarian
notion that happiness is the sole good or that happiness
of God's creatures is what is sought as the chief or supreme end. Several passages from the *Dissertation concerning the End for Which God Created the World*
proved embarrassingly close to utilitarianism, they admitted, but these "unguarded suppositions," although
regrettable, did not lead to utilitarianism in any form.
In any event, it might be argued, God's seeking his own
happiness in the outpouring of his being was a very
different case than that of men's seeking virtue as a
means to their own happiness rather than God's.[40] Or
to say that God wills man's happiness is not to claim
that this is the same as men's seeking first of all their
own happiness. Flatly put, "the love of being in general
is a good in its own nature." [41] The issue was not to be
so easily settled. After all, happiness does have a part
to play in morality. The Christian life does have the
aim of a joyous fulfillment. Edwards himself had repeatedly spoken of virtue as a beauty which was "immediately pleasant to the mind." [42] What place then
does happiness have? That which is ultimate as to temporal sequence must be distinguished from what is ultimate in respect to dignity and worth, argued the New
England divines. The mind may therefore by its se-

quence of choices fasten upon happiness as a goal, but that fact does not prove that general happiness is a greater good than love of holiness. Holiness is lovable, as the "highest bliss of the universe," and even the wicked are to be loved not for their holiness, which obviously they lack, but because they are "capable of happiness and misery unending." [43] Happiness, it was allowed, might be the motive for which men seek true virtue, but it is not the essence of virtue itself.[44] In this sense then, love of general happiness turns out to be the foundation of virtue, but then the Edwardseans added that it was also the fruition of virtue as well. Since holiness is the highest bliss, it must be the highest happiness. So in loving others we love them as capable of happiness, and do so as an act of "choosing the bliss of the universe." [45] But by this time the argument against utilitarianism flounders into confusion as the authors of the *Bibliotheca Sacra* claim that "mere bliss is not the highest good, yet it must be the object to which holiness, which is the highest good, finally directs itself." [46] This line of thought seems to make holiness a means to bliss or happiness, a view totally inconsistent with the views previously stated. What was being attempted apparently was a way of maintaining that happiness accompanied true virtue, but that it was not a self-interested concern for happiness. In any case, it was a distinction not clearly enough wrought out to pacify or adequately answer the Princeton critics.

The controversy over Edwards's *True Virtue* died, to all intents and purposes, by the mid-nineteenth century, but A. V. G. Allen as late as 1889 was echoing the complaints of Hart and Hall, as he lamented that Edwards had not become a great ethical theorist because of his narrow theological principles and his insistence upon grounding virtue in the nonethical foundation of

Being as such.[47] The proponents and opponents of Edwards on virtue passed from the picture and left the field to an emergent liberalism, a liberalism which held to the notions of a beneficent deity who ruled the world to man's fulfillment rather than his own glory. The pragmatic, utilitarian spirit which Edwards, the New England theology, and the Princeton critics had fought was coming to the foreground, and was to hold the field well into the twentieth century. The early controversy had proved to be something of a dead end in which there were no victors or vanquished, although pertinent issues had been raised on all sides.[48] Edwards himself, however, was to rise again from the limbo of antiquarian interest in the twentieth century, as Perry Miller, Joseph Haroutunian, and many others began the difficult task of interpreting him in the light of his own thought, rather than with the presuppositions of liberal Protestant theology.

Being and True Virtue

To EDWARDS'S CRITICS, nothing seemed so outrageously out of keeping with ethical discourse as his disposition to refer benevolence to Being as such. In their eyes he had surrendered his Calvinistic emphasis on the personal character of God. Where once he had spoken of a God who commanded, punished and rewarded, threatened and promised, now in his later works God is spoken of as pouring forth his being and goodness as a fountain might or as the sun emanates beams. Where once God could be said to will, now he spontaneously erupted in a flood of beneficence and power which permeated the whole cosmos. The whole tone of Edwards's position had been transformed, to the confusion of his opponents. The modes of his expression had become more impersonal than were his earlier works. Yet he had always employed the terminology of being, perfection, excellency, proportion, and the like, as his "Notes on the Mind" showed. The question was how to mix the metaphors of the personal character of God with those of Being as such. Could divine love and effulgence of Being ever be identified with each other? [1] In fact, these two modes of expression were never to be completely and satisfactorily correlated, but Edwards found comfort and support in his attempt to do so in the moral philosophy of Shaftesbury and Hutcheson. These thinkers could employ the terminology of personal affections and moral sense, and at the same time speak of the harmony of not only moral sentiments but also of nature's laws. As Vereker has pointed out, "Hutcheson equated the whole collection of moral rules with the law of nature and particular actions which promote happiness with special laws of nature." [2] All reality must then be permeated by some principle of unity which explained the interconnections between morality and nature, and provided the ground for the harmony of the whole. As Edwards saw the matter, moral principles ran parallel to the natural order by divine fiat, and therefore a language suited to ethical reflection would find its counterpart in a terminology which referred to the nature of that principle by which the subtlest harmonies existed between the natural and moral spheres. God's "regard to harmony and fitness and beauty in what He does as the governor of the natural world, may strongly argue that He will maintain the most strict and perfect justice in proportion and fitness in what He does as the governor of the moral world." [3] What remained to be done then to provide a clearer understanding of the nature of that principle of harmony between the two orders was to explore the very nature of being itself. And this task had been left undone by Shaftesbury and Hutcheson. They had left the problem hanging as to what the ground of unity, harmony, and beauty was, just at the point Edwards found the question interesting and of supreme importance. The language he would employ in that task was that of an impersonal character, but it would be shot through with references to God as a personal being as well. He would speak of God as Being itself, but the personal reference was ever on the horizon.

Being, as he had long held, was excellence itself, thereby depositing at the outset both value and power in Being itself.[4] Value did not have to be imported from elsewhere into the realm of power, since both were inherent in Being. God does not create value, law, or ethical essences which he then obeys. They are constitutive of Being itself.[5] Being as power is dynamic, and therefore since Being is infinite as well, there would be a constant outgo of both value and sustaining power in the creation and sustenance of creatures. If Being is so understood, it would be easy to pass to the conclusion that there would be a diminution of existence and value the further creatures were from the source of Being. It cannot be denied that Edwards sometimes fell into this way of expressing himself as he did in the notorious note where he claimed that an archangel might be supposed to have more existence than a worm or flea.[6] However, the main thrust of Edwards's thought lay in another direction. Being in general was not merely the sum of particular beings at a given time, but an ontological concept referring to the power of being in whatsoever may be said to exist. "All things are in Him, and He in all." To think otherwise is finally to try to think of "an absolute nothing" at the root of all which is impossible.[7] As a modern commentator points out, what Edwards intended in spite of his quantitative expressions was to affirm God as Being in general, not God as a particular form of being like all other beings.[8] As such Being has the capacity and efficacy of promoting power in the form of goodness and excellence, which when converted into personal terms, is love. Since all value, as we have seen, is in Being as such, the ancient argument over whether the good is what God disposes because it is good, or the good becomes good by his disposal of it, is put out of court by the assimilation from the beginning of both factors equally in Being as such. The crowning feature therefore of Being itself is beauty, because in infinite degree both power and good inhere in it. Being then is attractive and evocative of man's attention, loyalty, and in Edwards's terms, "cordial consent." [9]

With beauty as the crowning feature of Being itself, the familiar landmarks of ethical reflection seem to disappear when regarded from the standpoint of man. The ethical norms and universal moral laws important to traditional theological ethics had vanished in the realm of beauty, the intrinsically valuable.[10] Nowhere in the *True Virtue* is there any mention of the Decalogue.[11] Neither is the concept of the moral "ought" prominent in that work—a word Hutcheson had called "another unlucky Word in Morals." [12] "Duty," a term which does appear, is entirely limited to the inferior form of ethical beauty. It is clear then that true virtue is not something men "ought" to pursue or can be summoned to achieve because in the last analysis it is a gift of God. No course of instruction can be offered which leads to it. It is not a teachable attribute. As Edwards noted in criticism of "our new philosophers," discipline and gradual culture along with the notion of the will's freedom "tends exceedingly to cherish presumption while in health and vigor, and tends to their [men's] utter despair, in sensible approaches of death by sickness or old age." [13]

The issue of moral obligation in the context of the idea of Being in general had been effectively skirted. The question of the derivation of a moral ought from Being as such had been handled in advance by his theory of the divine and supernatural taste for divine reality. Moral obligation was thereby converted into a new state of the agent to which the sheer power of Being itself proved attractive. The persuasive power of Being as such drew from the moral agent the truly cordial consent to itself which was the nature of true virtue. In place of duty or obligation there stood consent, benevolence, or love, which had its origin and ground in that which was supremely and intrinsically beautiful and worthy.[14]

Lofty as this conception is, it nevertheless called up the problem of the ontological status of the natural man who by definition had no hopes of achieving true virtue in his unregenerate state. What had been left hanging was the question of what in Calvinistic terms was the "fall." How in an essentially monistic system could one account for the declension in being or metaphysical status of the natural man? In the Neoplatonic form which colors Edwards's late works, it would be possible to argue only that lower forms of being, those that did not as fully participate in being as those above them in the scale, were in some metaphysical sense "fallen away" from the true source of their being. But this means, in turn, that their place in the scale has somehow been ordained by Being itself, thereby making deity responsible for their declension from the original. In terms of Edwards's theological objectivism this conclusion, unpalatable as it may seem to moralists, nevertheless guards the supremacy of God and retains the sense of ordered proportionality necessary to the existence of an intelligible universe. At the same time the peculiar weakness of theological objectivism carried to its extreme is exhibited. The outward thrust of God's goodness is jeopardized by the fact that as it disseminates itself, so the farthest reaches of its creative power are diluted. As such what begins in perfect spontaneity of goodness, beauty, and power, now proliferates into levels of beings, necessary to the divine expression, but still less than fully good in the sense in which the original outpouring occurred. To this degree then it can be said that Edwards's monism accounts for the fallen status of man when that concept is cast in Neoplatonic terms.

However, there is another ontological puzzle that is associated with Edwards's concept of overflowing Being. Such a system is haunted by the metaphysical and logical need for another principle than that of Being itself if it is to be said that Being emanates its fullness. Since in Edwards's figures of speech the nature of God is not static, but ever dynamic and active, there must be that by which or into which this process distributes itself proportionately. There must be that which at least reflects, to use Edwards's own phraseology, the glory of God. Polarity or duality is then presupposed even if it is only envisaged as a possibility anterior to the existence of created or emanated creatures. Otherwise monisms such as Edwards's tend to be as sterile ontologically as they may be ethically.

How close Edwards came to wrecking his system upon the problem of duality or polarity may be seen in his ruminations on the infinity of God. His argument ran that God was unitary and therefore infinite; an infinite being "must be an all-comprehending being. He must comprehend in himself all being." If there were an "independent and underived" entity, God's infinitude would be cancelled, as there now would be another entity whose being would not be dependent on God. But, on the contrary, since God is infinite, all other entities are but communications of the great Original and add no being to the infinite sum of Being in

God.[15] If taken in a totally empirical fashion, these reflections lead straight to an all-inclusive monism in which all that is, is God. But if taken in the sense that whatever there is, is finite and therefore dependent on the power of being itself, the problem is relieved somewhat by allowing "distance" between God and his creation. There may be many beings created, but no increase in Being as such, so the necessary polarity is maintained. Without this supposition, Edwards's favorite notion that God continues by his "diffusive disposition" to communicate himself to his creation would be jeopardized, as would also the possibility of the intelligent creation reflecting back to God in beauty and benevolence the rays of light, power, and love which he sheds upon them.[16] Without some element of polarity, there would be no sense in concluding that God had effected anything by his communication of his fullness. As there is both unity and trinity in God, as we shall see, so there must be a diffused plurality to account for the actual differentiation in the world which the mind contemplates.

We see then that a measure of polarity is necessary to the total metaphysical scene, but it is one to be understood as created by God, by virtue of Edwards's insistence upon degrees of being and value or proportionality. Some measure of the original excellence of Being as such is to be recognized in all beings, even those, like fallen mankind, who retain the capacities of reason, moral sense, and natural affections. Even when men act against Being as such, they do so by virtue of Being itself, and do so in a structured manner. In short, although Being pours itself out spontaneously in power and love, order and structure are also created, lest the ultimate range of the divine dissemination end in sheer chaos or absolute nothing, an idea which Edwards argued was not "supposable." [17] Creation or emanation is a continuous activity without which "the whole universe would in a moment vanish into nothing; so that not only the well-being of the world depends on it, but the very being." [18] And to say so much was to affirm that the universe is totally dependent upon God, and that its existence was in some sense necessary to the fullest manifestation of his glory. "So God looks on the communication of himself and the emanation of the infinite glory and good that are in himself to belong to the fullness and completeness of himself; as though he were not in his most complete and glorious state without it." [19] This is the reason, at last, why true virtue must be cordial consent to Being as such, not simply a love or benevolent regard to the creation itself, even the totality of mankind. It also provides the metaphysical grounds on which one may properly speak of "consent" in any form, since the notion of "distance" or polarity between being as such and particular beings is maintained. Without it, consent would be meaningless. However, although polarity is maintained, it is important to see that God's purpose in glorifying himself is not to be set in opposition to his acting for the sake of his creatures. His action in pursuit of his last end coincides with the purpose of the benefit of his creatures. They are still "creatures," and therefore subordinate to deity, so their welfare is "consequentially and by implication as it were comprehended in God," the original object of his own creative act.[20] Creatures are distinct from God, but not separate from him, and therefore are not assimilated without remainder into deity. They remain finite beings, and as such are in polar relation to Being as such.[21]

The beauty which Edwards ascribed to true virtue was "consent, propensity and union of heart to Being in general, that is immediately exercised in a general good will." [22] In what sense then is it possible to describe Being as such or God as virtuous? Answers to this question are not taken up in either the *True Virtue* or the *End for which God Created the World*. In the *True Virtue,* indeed, he speaks of "the mutual love and friendship which subsists eternally and necessarily between the several persons in the Godhead" as the basis of divine virtue.[23] But in the *End for which God Created the World,* God appears as a single, unitary Being in whom no persons or beings exist that might be said to consent cordially to each other. In the early *Notes on the Mind* and the *Miscellanies,* however, we find Edwards spelling out more fully the grounds upon which God may be called virtuous. Just as there must be a duality between creature and creator in order to substantiate the possibility of consent, so also must there be at least a duality in God if virtue is to be posited of him. The typical expression for this duality can be found in Edwards's statement that "His infinite beauty is His infinite natural love of Himself." [24] More explicitly put, "But He exerts Himself toward Himself, in the mutual love of the Father and the Son. This makes the third—the personal Holy Spirit, or the holiness of God—which is His infinite beauty. And this is God's infinite consent to Being in general." [25] It must then be that God was primordially at least dual in character, else there would have been no object toward which he could "exert" himself, or which could return his love. "There must have been an object from all eternity which God infinitely loves," as Edwards put it.[26] But to love or consent even in God must mean that there is a significant distinction between two entities which are therefore able to consent to each other. Edwards leaves the nature of this distinction unclear as he put his emphasis on what these entities have in common.

" 'Tis necessary," he states, "that that object which God infinitely loves must be infinitely and perfectly consenting and agreeable to Him. But that which infinitely and perfectly agrees is the very same essence: for if it be different, it don't infinitely consent." [27] On the other hand, if there are no distinctions among the consenting partners, neither is there consent. There is no point in speaking of consent of being to being unless one being differs from another in some specifiable sense. Edwards saw this point clearly when he went on to state "that one alone cannot be excellent" because then there would be no consent. "Therefore," he concluded, "if God is excellent, there must be a plurality in God." [28] This plurality, of course, is the Trinity. Edwards's treatment of the Trinity salvages the notion of the cordial consent of being to being, but his equal insistence upon the unity of deity tends to reduce in importance the trinitarian distinctions.

As we have seen in dealing with the concept of the fall in the context of Edwards's Neoplatonism, the problem of evil in a world in which the effulgence of God's beauty, power, and love reign becomes a difficult issue. We have seen that the "fall" presupposes a negativity in the world, a privation which logically in Edwards's scheme would be accounted for not first by an act of will, but by an act of emanation in which certain beings are further removed from the divine source than are other beings. Emanation flows out of the fullness of God, toward a nonentity which, as we have already seen, never can be, since there is no polar principle of nonbeing or pure nonentity for Edwards. Yet in one sense, moral evil is always a privation or a loss. It is lack of the supernatural principles with which primordial man was created, but which were lost to him in the fall. The principles of self-love and natural appetite, without the infusion of any positive evil principle, when left to themselves with no "superior principles to regulate or control them" became "absolute masters of the heart." [29] Negatively, moral evil is lack of love for God for his own sake; but positively it is self-love, which has been left detached from the superior love of God. In the former sense, moral evil is due to deprivation; in the second sense, it is a radical and positive affirmation of the human subject against God. What Edwards could never answer, however, was the question as to why God should deprive man of his supernatural principles or taste for divine beauty and love, just at the moment man most needed the divine assistance.[30] Edwards's assertion that it was unfit for a holy God to company with a fallen creature accentuates his theological objectivism, but denies at this point the divine compassion Edwards elsewhere attributes to the deity.

Moral evil, when once on the scene, could be regarded as ignorance—a very disastrous type of ignorance.[31] This ignorance or limitation of view led men to mistake "private systems" or "a particular circle of Beings" for the true object of their love.[32] The consequence of this ignorance or self-love was to set up that jarring inconsistency in being as it was experienced in this world, which ran counter to the proportionality necessary to genuine benevolence. An otherwise harmonious structure of being would then fall into disorder. Relationality would be broken. A perversion of being would have occurred.[33] But how could this occur in the world picture Edwards described in his later works? Would not God be ever set at naught by created beings whose wills are set in opposition to him? If God's overflowing power and love emanates and remanates from the creature, there must be in the remanation a loss in the total process, as unending as is God's outpouring.[34] Only a relatively small "amount" of the emanation of God returns to the original so long as sin continues, and it does continue in this world as it is constituted. The only answer possible, and that a dubiously valid one, is that the quality of that love returned to God is of such a high degree as to compensate for the quantitative loss! But this is to suggest in turn that the creature does in fact add something to the Divine Being, a position Edwards stoutly denied. The self-sufficiency and independence of God was to Edwards an unassailable doctrine.[35]

What role does moral evil play in the total scheme when construed as a perversion of being, a jarring inconsistency with Being in general? One answer, a familiar one in similar ontologies, is that discordance or deformity enhances by contrast the beauty of the totality. Or, as a variation of the same theme, when being is spread out as a whole, as seen by God, the more inclusive harmony of being overcomes the disproportionality among the parts.[36] The aesthetic vision thereby makes place for the incongruities apparent only to the eye of finite man, whose own limited perspective sees, as it also occasions, the discordant component of the whole. For God, however the argument runs, may hate a particular act "as it is simply," but "may incline to it with reference to the universality of things." Thus he permits sin or ugliness for the sake of "promoting of the harmony that there is in the universality, and making it shine the brighter." [37] Furthermore, without default in the finite reality, God would not be able to display the full range of his attributes. Without evil, he could not fully communicate himself. Therefore, not only is the sense of good heightened by the sense of evil, but also the "display of the glory of God" is heightened and made expressible. Or to put it as flatly as did

Edwards, "evil is necessary, in order to the highest happiness of the creature" since the creature's happiness depends upon the full, not partial, communication of God and his love.[38] God, therefore, since he wills all, is ultimately responsible for evil in the sense that he permits it to happen, but not that he enacts it. But he is also the one who brings it to heel by incorporating its disharmonious nature into the universal order and beauty of the whole.[39] Better this conclusion, with its degree of unpalatability, than the notion that all happened by chance, which is the only alternative Edwards could conceive.[40] Thus when seen from the divine perspective, the evils of the world fall into place in a harmonious whole. The human subject cannot ultimately defy or question this view because he is part of the picture and does not have the infinite view which God alone possesses.[41] The evil is finite, as it comes from a finite being, but in the infinite view the finite is skillfully woven into the texture of being to produce that harmony to which God ever advances. The narrowness of vision which self-love brings is expanded in the infinite and for those who, by grace and love, are opened to the aesthetic vision in true virtue. Thus out of the conditional pessimism to which natural man is logically driven, there arises for Edwards a cosmic optimism at a higher level than that envisioned by the more secular moralists of the moral-sense school.

What is the impact of this total view on morality? It has been argued that views which subscribe to the essentially Neoplatonic view may be optimistic as to the cosmos, but at the lower levels they lean toward moral pessimism. Because all is as it should be, men should keep their position in what A. O. Lovejoy identified as "The Great Chain of Being." [42] There is no place for man radically to reform his life or his social,

political, or economic portion, since he has been placed
as a link in the "chain" to exhibit the fecundity and
rich variety of being which descends from God to whatever limit he assesses. In this sense the inferior parts of
the universe are essential, even in their incapacities, to
the beauty and self-sufficiency of the whole. The beauty
of the whole cosmic scheme might therefore be interpreted in optimistic terms, but also as "an apologia for
the status quo" at the level of the mundane. In any case
it is an oppressive conclusion.[43] Superficially, much of
this view might be attributed to Edwards, were it not
for the activism with which Edwards endowed Being.
His is no static world order, but one that is filled with
movement from God to man, from man to God. If one
appeals to God's moral governance, it is clear that God
has an end in mind, an eschatology toward which his
activities move, and the image of the "great chain of
being" proves to be too static a term by which to describe this divine activity. As Edwards remarked of nature's revolutions, "These revolutions are not for nothing . . . Does God make the world restless, to move
and revolve in all its parts, to make no progress? . . .
The wheels of God's chariot, after they have gone round
a thousand times, do not remain just in the same place
that they were in at first, without having carried the
chariot nearer to a journey's end." [44] What is true for
nature is true for man, thought Edwards, namely, that
some great end of God's is what is being achieved on
earth, which ends with dissolution, although man sur-
vives, he being of eternal duration. But the end toward
which man moves is God's purpose, an infinite good of
infinite duration, which alone is worthy of an infinite
Being.[45] Thus, instead of a static order presided over
by a static Being, Edwards's complex view was one of
activity moving ever closer to some great denouement

in which the ever-increasing perfection of God would at last be increasingly realized beyond history and time. Nor is man bound to a ceaseless, meaningless process in which no moral improvement is possible. At least a sector of humanity, by divine grace, will increasingly move into the nearer orbit of the divine love. The contemplative aspect of true virtue is not set aside, but it is the contemplation of an active subject, even as God's contemplation and joy in himself is conceived as an active eternal process.

However, a contemplative interpretation of ethics is strangely out of place in the thought of a man as strongly Calvinistic as Edwards. Calvinism seemed set on turning the kingdoms of this world into Christ's kingdom, whereas in Edwards we find a delicacy of feeling, sensibility over the beauty of moral relations, and the persuasive, attractive power of deity. The revolutionary power of Calvinism spends itself in aesthetic satisfaction. The concept of beauty provides at last the context in which to understand the moral good; harmony is the sign of the moral right and love, and consent or benevolence overcomes the austerity of the ought or duty. It remains then to explore more fully that end to which morality in the Edwardsean framework aspires to—the state wherein virtue and happiness are conjoined.

Happiness and True Virtue

THE TENSION between theological objectivism and theological utilitarianism comes prominently to the foreground when the question is asked as to the role of happiness in respect to true virtue. Theological utilitarianism normally exalts the utility of God and religion as a means to the realization of human happiness. Theological objectivism exalts the deity above all, as the beginning and end of all creativity and as the object whose glory is to be sought at all costs. In the case of Edwards, the happiness of the creature—if such be an adequate goal of the moral life—must be in some way closely connected to the happiness of the deity—if happiness also be an end for which deity acts. Since we have found both theological utilitarianism and theological objectivism in Edwards's works, the questions arise as to whether happiness and its cognates are to be associated only with Edwards's earlier explicitly utilitarian writings, and how happiness can be incorporated into the objectivistic phases of his thought.

If one reads Edwards, as did Hall and the Princeton critics, with the idea of happiness to the foreground, it is not difficult to make a case for theological utilitarianism.[1] In his *Miscellanies* Edwards states that eternal happiness should be bestowed on man as a reward for obedience.[2] Or again, he refers to "even the making the creature happy by redemption" as "the end of all God's other works," as though God's primary purpose were aimed at the creature's satisfaction.[3] Strong support for the notion that happiness is the goal of virtue can also be found in Edwards's denunciation of the idea that a man could properly will to be "perfectly & finally miserable for God's sake . . . Love to God will make a man forever unwilling utterly & finally to be deprived of this part of his happiness which he has in God's being blessed & glorified & the more he loves him the more unwilling he will be."[4] A different emphasis, however, can also be found in Edwards's comment that "unless men would love God from some real respect to God or sense of duty . . . and not merely from an aversion to pain and desire of pleasure, it is no wise from any good principle."[5] Again, he wrote, "The happiness of the greater part of mankind, in their worldly enjoyments, is not great enough or durable enough to prove such a supposition, as that the end of all things in the whole visible universe is only that happiness."[6] In the light of these last citations, it would appear that pleasure or happiness cannot be the reason why persons would seek to be united with God.

To make clear the apparent contradiction between these two perspectives on happiness, it is necessary to turn back to the treatise on the *Freedom of the Will*. In that work Edwards made clear that the human will always is as the greatest good, the latter term meaning "agreeable" or "pleasing to the mind."[7] What appeals to the mind is by definition that which in pleasing is to be considered as either contributing to happiness or bringing it directly. A more certain or more readily accessible pleasure or happiness will be a stronger determinant than a less probable or more distant one.[8] This means that the unregenerate person will seize upon those pleasing objects which accord with his present temper of mind, and he will consequently find his happiness at a lower level than will the person who, enlightened by divine grace, finds his happiness at the level of a genuine affection for God or Being as such. In both cases, however, men seek happiness by means of the same psychological mechanism, although for the truly virtuous the divine and supernatural sense has been added. The degree of happiness is determined by two factors. One focus is the level of appreciation available to the human subject, which is the degree to which the understanding "as the whole faculty of perception or apprehension" allows him to be aware of the desirable object. The other is the drawing power of the object in which happiness is to be sought. In the case of the truly virtuous individual, the apprehension has been opened to the attractiveness of the divine object as such; in the case of the natural man, he seeks what is immediately desirable in his environment. The structure of the search for happiness remains the same in both instances, as we have seen, but true virtue and the happiness it brings is contingent upon "the holiness of the object which is the quality whereon it fixes and terminates." [9]

In turning to the *Treatise on True Virtue,* one is struck by the lack of extended treatment of happiness. Once more the natural man is depicted as one pleased with the beauty of natural objects and moral virtues such as justice, but this appreciation is due simply to an instinctual basis.[10] The kind of agreeableness which solicits man's attention and with which he is pleased is but an extension of self-love. However, Edwards makes an important distinction concerning happiness among persons. The happiness one appreciates in another person is not founded upon happiness as such, but rather upon the measure of love one feels for the other, for the "inclinations and appetites" are "prior to any pleasure in gratifying these appetites." The love in question, of course, remains that of self-love.[11] Edwards does not deny that man seeks and loves happiness, since "every being who has a faculty of will must of necessity have an inclination to happiness."[12] What he wants to affirm is that the love of a being must logically precede happiness, although in practice when true religious affections are operative, happiness will inescapably follow the consent to Being.

There is then in benevolence to Being in general a delight and joy in the beauty of that object upon which the mind fixes. And the goal of a person so situated is to seek "to promote the happiness of the Being" and to rejoice in its happiness. When true benevolence reigns in the heart, it rejoices "in the prosperity and pleasure of the object of it. . . ."[13] This is a lost possibility for the unregenerate, since they do not possess the perception of the intrinsic amiability and agreeableness of virtuous beauty. Such a view cannot be realized even "by argumentation or its connexions and consequences, but by the frame of their own minds, or a certain spiritual sense given them of God, whereby they immediately perceive pleasure in that presence of the idea of true virtue in their minds or are directly gratified in the view or contemplation of this object. . . ."[14] Happiness then comes by a direct intuition into Being itself and a recognition of the power and beauty of Being as exhibited in one's fellow creatures. It is not a reward for virtue, for virtue is the basis of happiness, not the result of happiness. At the same time, virtue is no joy-less affair, for it incorporates the joy which one feels in cordially consenting to Being as such in its full beauty.

What then constitutes happiness? The answer in one form is given in *The Mind,* where Edwards explained the notion of "pleasedness." Here he found that pleasedness arises "from a perception of Consent to Being in general, or of consent to that Being that perceives." It followed that "agreeableness of the object" perceived must please the perceiving being if it perceives being as an object. But then intrudes a thought strange in the light of much else Edwards was to write. "Pleasedness does not always arise from a perception of Excellency but the greater a Being is, and the more it has of Entity, the more will consent to Being in general please it." [15] It would seem highly inappropriate to deny that excellency always stimulates "pleasedness," but this is what Edwards apparently meant to deny. What he seems to be arguing, however, is that "pleasedness" is a natural operation of the self, since it is clear that men in fact are pleased by many things that do not pertain to excellence in the sense in which he used that word. Men are pleased with being, even if it be at a lower level or only as a faint pattern of the truly excellent. In an exasperatingly compressed statement Edwards went on to state more concisely what happiness was. It is the perception of three things: "the consent of being to its own being: of its own consent to being; and of being's consent to being." [16] It is not easy to decipher Edwards's meaning from this cryptic comment. It may be suggested that happiness conceived on the model of consent to being in some sense may be understood as follows. Since Edwards means by "be-ing," intelligent being, the passage signifies that an intelligent being is happy when he is in fact at one with or consents to himself as having existence. Secondly, he may be said to be happy when he is aware that in consenting to his own being, he has enlarged the range of consent by becoming aware of his consent. And lastly, he is happy when he perceives the truth that underlies the whole transaction, namely that metaphysical principle which Edwards rehearsed in *True Virtue,* when he referred to virtue as the cordial consent of intelligent being to the principle of being itself. Happiness, in this reading, inheres in the coalescence of all three perceptions, none of which can independently be rightfully considered as an adequate definition of happiness. If only the first perception be allowed, man's happiness would be virtually self-love, a satisfaction of oneself with oneself. The second perception allows for the awakening realization that more than self-satisfaction is involved. And the third perception not only crowns the whole, but turns out to be the basic principle underlying the whole by identifying happiness with the principle of the operation of being as consenting being. The upshot of this analysis of happiness is the realization that there is a structural basis of happiness laid in the ontological realm and that the happiness concurrent with true virtue is not just any kind of passing amiability, liking, or feeling, but a consent which is grounded in the nature of Being as such, or God.

To speak of happiness in these terms seems to direct attention to human happiness, but the role of happiness in the Edwardsean scheme is not fully depicted until the testimony of the *End for which God Created the World* is heard. God's happiness in its relation to human happiness must be explored. In this work Edwards made clear that the happiness of his creatures is not what he called the "original ultimate end" of God's work.[17] In fact, quite deprecatory comments are made as to the value and nature of the human creature in this respect.[18] "No part of his [God's] happiness originates from man." [19] However, in emanating his own fullness God gives vent to that which is in himself, inclusive of his own happiness, and that happiness consists in his love of himself in which he delights.[20] In so doing, instead of receiving happiness from his creatures, he communicates his infinite happiness and so makes the creature happy.[21] This rich outpouring of his own beauty, goodness, and happiness thus blesses the creature. But in this emanation he acts for himself as his own chief end, and consequently for the good of his creatures.

Three attributes of deity are thus poured out, and in the creature's reception of them they participate in the glory which is in God's own last end in creation. The knowledge of himself which God gives is in the creature a "conformity to God" in which, in turn, God delights. Secondly, God communicates virtue and holiness so that the creature "partakes of God's own moral excellency" to the delight of God. And thirdly, the happiness which God has within himself is emanated to the creature with God and his glory as "the objective ground of it." So joy, and rejoicings in deity on the part of the creature, redound to God's own happiness.[22] But one must be careful not to suppose by these rhapsodic expressions that the creature in any way contributes independently to God's glory or enjoyment.[23] It is God's own happiness, expressed and returned to him, just as it is God's power, knowledge, and virtue which constitutes the foundation of the existence and fulfillment of the human subject. Hence the subject's good is not to be considered in separation from his.[24]

If happiness at this high level is to be properly

understood in the Edwardsean context, it must be seen
first of all not as a particular human emotion of fulfillment conditioned upon the satisfaction of man's natural desires or appetites. To accept this view as definitive
is only to affirm that man is possessed of choice or will
and that he is happy or finds pleasure by the exercise
of willing. He is then happy with whatever he wills.
True happiness, on the other hand, as one major ingredient in true virtue, cannot be conceived apart from
the divine joy in which the self participates. Happiness,
even for the creature, is "objectively" grounded in the
sense that it is totally contingent on the cordial consent
to Being. It is not to be understood as deriving from
the parochial emotional drives of individual men. It
is "objective" in the additional sense that God alone is
the source of happiness, since it is his happiness, not
man's, in which the human subject delights. It is therefore difficult to make out a case for any of the traditional
forms of utilitarianism in respect to human happiness.
Joy and happiness are an essential part of the Christian
life, rather than grim duty or obedience to rules and
demands of the deity. The persuasive power of God
relieves the elect from the grosser legalisms and authoritarianism to which late Calvinism tended to bind
mankind. True religion or virtue has the verve, delight,
and joyous enthusiasm which only a believer who has
consented totally to Being can possess. A religion of this
character is one which glorifies the Creator for his own
sake, and moves away from ethical structures in the
direction of aesthetic satisfaction as one participates in
harmonious concert with the deepest reality. Nor is this
a happiness which exists solely in the individual's fulfillment. Edwards made clear that this was a happiness
to be shared socially. No being can be happy without
communicating his happiness, so the happiness of so-

ciety consists "in the mutual communications of each other's happiness." Each communicates to the other.[25] Thereby God wills a harmony of mankind wherein there is joy and happiness for all. Nothing less than a society of happy beings is contemplated.

Now it can be said, in a special guarded sense, that "Happiness is the end of creation." This insight Edwards carefully spelled out in *Miscellany* 3.[26] Certainly God created out of his goodness, but, Edwards went on to ask, "how can we conceive of another end proposed by goodness than that He might delight in seeing the creatures He made rejoice in that being that He has given them? . . . What is glorifying God but a rejoicing at that Glory He has displayed?" A man may understand the perfection of God, but if that is all, "he had as good not understand it as see it" if he is not moved to joy at the sight of these perfections. So also it is good for nothing if the human being simply declares the glory of God to his neighbor, unless he also raises joy in himself and others in doing so. "Wherefore such happiness is the highest end of the creation of the creator of the universe." And intelligent beings are the immediate subjects of this happiness.[27] The height of objectivistic religion then is a happiness and joy which transcends all earthly joys. God's aim is to glorify himself in making his creatures happy. The two are inseparable.

A God whose main concern was his own delight would seem to be a curiously introverted being. Moreover, by human standards of benevolence, he could be counted as a "selfish" being. As such God would be as unworthy of man's devotion and love as a human being who sought only gratification of his own impulses. Edwards was not unaware of this line of thought, and he felt that he had met the objection of God's

seeking his own happiness. His answer lay in the structure of true virtue itself. Even as true virtue rests upon
proportional consent to Being, so the highest virtue
must consist in the fullest consent of being to greatest
Being. This can be the case only in God himself. He,
being the fullness of Being, proportionally and most
lovingly consents to himself in the persons of the Trinity. And this is also to say that his happiness is not
then to be reckoned as a self-interested affection, in the
manner which it would be in a finite man. The infinity
of God's being, by definition, makes that happiness
which inheres in the relations of the Godhead a transcendent joy unmarred by the finitude to which even
the best of man's virtue is subject. But Edwards had
gone further in his answer to the charge of a selfish
deity. God's joy rests not only in the communion he
has with his own perfections, but in the overpowering
expression of that same beatitude toward his creation.
His joy is not limited; it is infinite, and as such ever
seeks to fulfill itself in outward expression. As God
comprehends all in the sense that he is the ground of
all being as well as its goal, he takes into consideration
his whole creation, into which he is constantly and
inexhaustively pouring his power, beauty, goodness, and
happiness. Consequently, as the creature reflects back
to him its joy and love, he enjoys this remanation of
his happiness, all of which redounds to his glory.[28] "If
God's holiness consists in love to himself, then it will
imply approbation of and pleasedness with the esteem
and love of him in others; for a being that loves himself, necessarily loves love to himself." [29]

God rightfully makes his own glory the end of his
creative powers. Into this concept of glory, Edwards
poured all the attributes he had found to apply to God
in Scripture. Glory therefore signified inherent excel-

lence, dignity, and worth, a great height of happiness and an exhibited worthiness which culminates in a knowledge of divine excellence, praise, and joy in God by the creatures.[30] Thus, in short, we come again to sheer joy in God's perfections for their own sake on the part of human beings, even as he also rejoices in the amplitude and exercise of those same attributes. As men achieve a closer union with deity, so does the saint's joy mount higher, even as God's joy also increases as his creative powers exercised in creation return to him. Happiness is indeed the crown of life for the human being, as it is for God, but it must always be seen as dependent upon the ontological fitness of God as infinite Being to be glorified as his own end. Virtue is not to be reduced to happiness in either God or his creation, but without happiness virtue or genuine religious affections would lack that glorious joy which is properly theirs. Happiness is thus objectively grounded in Being itself, not merely in subjective feelings unattached to the source and end of all creation.

In any intelligible sense of the term "utilitarian," as used in moral philosophy, Edwards cannot be classified as a theological utilitarian in spite of the high place he accorded to happiness in his scheme. As has been pointed out, utilitarian considerations are to be found in certain of his sermons, but he is consistent even there with his later writings, when he argues that mere fear of hell and God's wrath are inadequate and even pernicious grounds for seeking salvation. Only genuine faith, a true love to God or Christ engendered by grace, will bring the redeemed person through to the joyous fulfillment of salvation. Men are happy in the highest sense when they are worthy to be happy, and their worthiness depends upon their loving consent and harmonious relation to Being as such. In the

same manner God is happy because he is worthy by
his infinitude of excellent attributes, and their exercise,
and by the loving consent among the persons of the
Godhead.

X

Aesthetics and Ethics in Retrospect

THE EFFORT to interpret ethics in aesthetic terms has proved to be a hardy motif in western thought. The Neoplatonic strand has usually borne its impress.[1] The moral sense philosophers of the eighteenth century found it appealing.[2] The late British Hegelians were drawn to it.[3] In the twentieth century Whitehead explicitly embraced it. Working with a cosmology in many ways quite different from that of Edwards, he insisted that the universe "is directed to the production of Beauty," the one aim "which by its very nature is self-justifying." The moral order, he held, was merely an aspect of this purposive trend to which it was virtually assimilated. "The real world is good when it is beautiful." However, he did see that some tension existed between ethics and aesthetic categories when he wrote, "The charge of immorality is not refuted by pointing to the perfection of art." [4]

At first appearance, it seems remarkable that Edwards, usually counted both as a product and a creative mind of late Puritanism, should have fallen in with this aesthetic temper of mind, since popular opinion has

often regarded Puritanism as rigorously ascetic and opposed to beauty in any form. The moralistic strain of
late Puritanism especially has been seen to be in bitter
conflict with forms of beauty which endanger the soul's
duty to God and hence its salvation. What this reading
of the Puritan mind sometimes forgets is the deep yearning for an ultimate beauty beyond all earthly beauties,
which would crown the saints' never-ending discourse
with the Creator. The Neoplatonic philosophy which
informed the Cambridge Platonists and lured them toward the beautiful had also fed the springs of early
Puritanism. And this tradition found its heir in Edwards.[5] Its intuitive, penetrating grasp of realities beyond the deliverances of the senses found its counterpart in Edwards's "divine and supernatural sense." The
possibility of beauty's seduction of the soul was tamed
and brought within the bounds of the divine perspective when the true good of man was seen to lie in a
transcendent beauty beyond that which the sensory
world offered. But the rhetoric and play of images
which portrayed the glorious and transcendent beauty
of the saints' joyful reconciliation with God had its
counterpart in the dolorous, vividly described scenes of
the sinners' ultimate punishment. Here, for Edwards,
was an aesthetic terminology which in embracing both
the beauties of heaven and the horrors of hell was congenial to the Puritan temperament. It was not one
which was satisfied to revel in nature for its own sake
or in the workmanship of human hands. Rather it was
a sense which pierced through a nature ever alive with
signs and images of God's purposes. And the beauties
wrought by man, although not without their attractive
power, could only be of secondary importance at best,
or at most a seduction to idolatry.

Edwards's picture, in terrifyingly vivid detail, of

the fate of the sinners in the grasp of divine punishment is therefore no abrupt break with this tradition. His thought-world was one of drama to which an essentially aesthetic reading was appropriate.[6] Neither is there a discontinuity in Edwards's thought when, in his posthumous works, he caught up in aesthetic terms his early meditations on excellence and beauty. In Edwards the Puritan aesthetic was expressed not only in terms of beauty compatible with the thought of moral sense philosophers of his century, but also as the proper medium in which to depict the entire scope of the soul's adventure as it either mounted to virtue or descended into eternal punishment. The highly imaginative language of damnation in the imprecatory sermons thus stands at the opposite pole from the placidly metaphysical language of *True Virtue* or the almost rhapsodic expressions of the *Dissertation concerning the End for which God Created the World*. The former casts theological objectivism in a starkly Calvinistic mode; the latter is suffused with a Neoplatonic perspective, but both employ a rhetoric and imagery consonant with an aesthetic consciousness. Beauty, consent, fullness of Being are balanced in the total aesthetic continuum by the images of horror, fear, and ugliness which drench the most severe of the imprecatory homilies. The concept of beauty then is not the only sign-manual indicating the aesthetic consciousness. The vision of the glorious beauty of divine Being and the beauty inherent in true virtue does not preempt the aesthetic field so long as Edwards's clinically unyielding gaze into the depths of hell remains in the field.

The horrendous scenes of divine punishment, to be sure, occupy relatively little space in Edwards's literary output. It also seems probable that the calmer cast of mind represented in his *Notes on the Mind* and

Personal Narrative has been swept aside temporarily by the emotional excesses of the Great Awakening, although there can be no doubt but that he was sincerely in earnest when he wrote and delivered his awakening sermons. Among his major works the *Religious Affections* shows his return to a position of "distance" from the dangers of an enthusiasm which by his own testimony he had not planned as an appeal to emotionalism. The dramatic imagery appropriate to sermonic presentation yields to the need to work out an ontology or metaphysic which does justice to the affections by setting them in a context where the beauty of the structure of being is made explicit. In this return to the insights of *The Mind* a rhetoric and model for the expression of the aesthetic different from that employed in the sermons came to the foreground. As his major posthumous works reveal, the form which his aesthetic consciousness assumed was that of an essentially Neoplatonic ontology. However, this ontology is not developed as an exercise in aesthetics for its own sake, a rendering of beauty for the sake of beauty. Rather, the aesthetic tendency which informs the ontology is put in the service of spelling out the deepest and highest structures of religious and ethical experience, for which only the category of beauty could be conceived, as the crowning virtue for both God and man.

Beyond the Kantian attempts to limit religion within the bounds of rational moral obligation, there have been thinkers who would not confine the religious life to bare moral essentials.[7] Morality, it has been felt, must itself stand in a broader context than afforded by the moral rationalism of the Enlightenment. There has also been a yearning in such minds for a context of morality which breaks with the supposition that morality should be construed only as a feature of inter-human relations. It seems imperative to thinkers of this disposition that there be some agency or being that accounts for the fact of morality, even when it is conceived in purely interhuman terms; but even more that both directive or guidance as well as provision for sanction are rooted in some dimension of being more extensive than that provided by the interplay of human beings in society.

The Calvinistic formulation tended toward a legalistic reading of this situation, but for Edwards finally this was found wanting. It lacked what he had sensed even in his early awakening to be the powerful presence of divine sovereignty, namely beauty. Although clearly Edwards's sensitivity to beauty can be traced in his earliest experiences and writings, he had not formulated in a systematic way a world view which could do justice both to the power and to the beauty of deity. He did render his ethical concerns within the structures of an essentially Calvinistic framework, but as he began to show in the *Religious Affections,* he was intent on providing fuller treatment of being which would encompass both the ethical and theological dimensions of human experience. To accomplish this feat, he found it necessary to adopt or readapt that type of ontology in which harmony was a ruling conception. Organic interrelatedness, rather than radical discontinuity, was to mark any outlook by which to account not only for morality but also for the relations of God, nature, and man, and even natural and moral evil.[8] This was to be accomplished without contradicting the principle of the divine priority, that is, theological objectivism.

God therefore cannot be simply the sum total of beings in their infinite variety, as a consistent pantheism would hold. Rather he must be conceived as the ground or principle of harmony and interrelatedness among otherwise discrete beings and events. If he is to be understood as beauty or as that which beautifies, his must be a type of beauty which far excels all forms of beauty apparent in his creatures. As Edwards put it, "God is God, and distinguished from all other beings, and exalted above 'em, chiefly by his divine beauty, which is infinitely diverse from all other beauty." [9] In respect to the moral qualities of creatures, however, there is also a beauty. The "good" and "right" take criteria, sanction, and ground in intelligibility from this structure of being which Edwards immediately intuited as both power and value. Where there is consent in personal beings to Being in general, there the good or right appears as beauty; where there is dissent, incompatibility, or lack of harmony with Being in general, then wrong and evil appear as ugliness and deformity.

Important as the category of beauty is for a full understanding of Edwards's position, it is also important to understand that the notion of beauty was not consistently maintained as the criterion of morality. Granted the difference in style and mode of expression between the *True Virtue* with its normative but non-prescriptive nature, and many of the sermons with their definitely practical purpose, there remains the fact that beauty is seldom alluded to as central in the latter, whereas it continually and centrally appears in the former writings. This contention is supported in such works as *Charity and Its Fruits,* the sermons on social problems, some of the Awakening sermons, and the *History of Redemption,* where beauty is more often treated as culminating and eschatological fulfillment than it is a this-worldly possibility.

Charity and Its Fruits, one of Edwards's most practical expositions of the meaning of Christian love, serves as a test case in his use of the category of beauty. However, surprisingly enough, in the course of the sermons which make up this work, while benevolence is often mentioned, beauty, the surrogate of true virtue, is scarcely referred to. Scattered references to the love of God for his beauty and the beauty of holiness do appear, but not until Edwards speaks of the high reward of Christian love in heaven does the rhetoric of beauty appear full-blown. Beauty then comes into its own as an eschatological sanction and fulfillment of Christian love. In heaven all is to be "lovely" and "harmonious." It is a beauteous, loving place where no "unlovely persons" appear, where every saint is a "flower" in the garden of God and every soul "is as a note in some concert of delightful music, that sweetly harmonizes with every other note." [10] Nowhere, however, is the austere language of symmetry and proportion employed as a guide to the proper expression or defining characteristic of love, as *True Virtue* maintains. The primary ethical message is couched in terms of the love of God and the neighbor, with warnings of punishment to those who fail to practice such love. The sermons which deal with civil government, the economic life, family order, and alleviation of poverty fail also to support the view that beauty is the ruling concept of all morality. God's constituted order, the principle of super- and subordination, justice, and honesty provide the moral substructure in these areas, although love is not forgotten in respect to family and as the motive for providing charity for the indigent. Edwards obviously leaned heavily upon the notion of order in these sermons, but it was an order which was not explicitly associated with beauty.[11]

Beauty, however, is not totally missing from other representative sermons which move in the orbit of God's legalistic judgment and promise. Thus, for example, in his sermon entitled "Ruth's Resolution," Edwards held forth on the theme of the glorious excellence of God, picturing him in the terms familiar to "God's Elect" as an "infinite fountain and ocean" of love.[12] The theme of beauty appears again in "The Peace which Christ Gives His True Followers," where it is associated with peace and dignity as the position of the saints.[13] Sinners, on the other hand, fail to pursue the Christian life because they see in Christ "no beauty nor comeliness" which would draw their hearts to him.[14] One of Edwards's most explicit appeals to the incentive which beauty provides is found in "The Excellency of Christ" where he repeatedly stresses the harmony or "wonderful meeting of divine excellencies in Christ" as an inducement to salvation.[15] Ordinarily, however, Edwards's sermons indicate that the hardened sinfulness of man is too strong a power in daily life to yield easily to appeals for moral and spiritual beauty. In this respect he differs sharply from the assumptions of the British benevolence and moral sense philosophers who assumed a natural benevolent spirit in man.[16]

The *History of Redemption* views the history of mankind and the church in the familiar Biblical pattern of judgment, punishment, reward, and renewal. Not until the climax of God's work in redemption is brought into full view does beauty provide the fitting category. At last the triumph of the saved is realized in terms of light, knowledge, praise, joy, holiness, and glory. Then the church will be united in "one amiable society," and all parts of the world will be united in sweet harmony. In fact, the world will be as "one church, one orderly, regular, beautiful society," a body beautiful in which all parts are "in proportion to each other." Then Christ will come in his true beauty and glory, and punishment on Satan, devils, and sinners will be carried out.[17] It is noticeable that order, discipline, and proportion are essential ingredients in the beauty which will exist at the denouement of history. But it is also clear that although beauty and excellence are God's aim in redemption, beauty is not the means by which the whole process is to be carried out.[18] Beauty on earth and beyond history will be realized, since God cannot be frustrated in his purposes, but his means are still judgment and conversion, by which this high goal is to be realized. Thus moral beauty, as the glory of the redeemed society, was not at the same time the instrument by which the goal was to be reached. Rather, men, as the *Religious Affections* makes plain, may have only intimations of this beauty in holy affections which are distinguished by their symmetry and proportion.[19]

A review of the evidence indicates that beauty was not the sole organizing principle about which Edwards consistently interpreted the moral and religious life, either for the individual or society. But it also becomes clear that he maintained a sense of beauty in the natural world even while he retained a spiritual and moral beauty as the height toward which the life of the redeemed aimed. Edwards was always persuaded of the reality and necessity for order, to be sure, but this order in the private and social life, although concerned aesthetically, was not uniformly identified with beauty even of the secondary type. The sinfulness of man, as well as essential human nature, made it necessary to posit a level of morality appropriate to the natural man while reserving to the elect the full vision and achievement of true virtue as beauty. In spite of his desire to view reality in an unified aesthetic fashion, Edwards had found it necessary to introduce a measure of discontinuity in moral and spiritual reality to allow for the operation of the natural moral sense. Although the concept of beauty was retained to refer to this lower order of morality, it is clear that secondary beauty partook more of "equality and justice" than it did of the supernatural relish for Being in general for its own sake.[20] The distinction suggests that Edwards's appeal to beauty in both cases masked the fact that natural morality was the more basic, universally operative value in daily life, whereas true virtue or the beauty of benevolence in its comparative rarity was differentiated by valuational height rather than by comprehensive application in the common sense world.

Nowhere is this fact more obvious than when he attempted to show in the *Religious Affections* what religious and moral acts might be taken as evidence of a changed heart in the fruits of practice. There in summing up the signs of holy affections, he has great difficulty in mentioning any external acts that could not be imitated by graceless men. Repeatedly he attempted to set forth virtues such as justice, charity, mercy, meekness, gentleness, and devoutness as being the unique qualities of true Christians.[21] But he had also to admit that natural men both in this world and at the last judgment can appreciate the moral attributes of God, and even with joy respond to the great goodness of God and Christ. All that is lacking is the appreciation of the beauty of these moral attributes.[22]

Although he admits that common reason shows that deeds are more reliable interpreters of men's minds than are words, he wants to claim that the positive signs of holy affections apply only to Christians, "let the visible practice and virtues of others be what they will." [23] He finally confesses that there are "no infallible evidences of grace," that the manifestations of grace are simply "the best that mankind [not just Christians] can have" and "Tis impossible certainly to determine, how far a man may go in many external appearances and imitations of grace from other principles." [24] Thus no external acts, the supposed final evidence of true and holy affections can be taken as positive proof of grace, since the natural man can at worst counterfeit them or at best carry them out without reference to true virtue's beauty. Furthermore, moral beauty, as conceived in the *True Virtue,* obviously does not command or comprehend the entire field of ethics if "external appearances" are within the scope of unconverted men's powers. Men may carry out moral acts without a sense of beauty, although to Edwards there is still beauty in such acts.

Edwards was to make clear the role of beauty in *True Virtue.* Whereas complacence fastened upon the beauty discoverable among consenting beings, benevolence fastened upon Being as such. Thus Being, not beauty, was to be foundational to true virtue. As he put it, even as there may be benevolence "or a disposition to the welfare of those that are not considered beautiful," so in the divine nature benevolence is prior to the "beauty of many of its objects" as well as their existence.[25] Beauty is the crowning category of moral value, but as Edwards's *Notes on the Mind* made explicit, beauty or excellence depends upon a proportion or harmony in being itself. Beauty used without qualification as a single term is simply vacuous without structure, and cannot therefore be employed as a model of the highest moral life.[26] Nor is structure or proportionality simply reduced to a function of secondary virtue.[27] It is an ingredient in Being itself. The term "beauty" by itself explains nothing unless it is considered not only in terms of both proportion and symmetry, but also in terms of certain spiritual and moral attitudes.

Beauty is thus not simply beauty, but holiness, charity, loving kindness, glory, etc., as numerous passages of the *Religious Affections* show.[28]

Beauty is less the underlying basis of true virtue than it is the product of harmonious relations of beings with each other and ultimately with Being itself. As such it is the teleological justification of virtue itself, for Edwards had kept his priorities clear by insisting that whatever is pleasing in ethical relations is pleasurable because of the relations themselves. Moral relations are not beautiful because they are pleasing; they are pleasing because they are beautiful, and they are beautiful because the structure of proportionality and symmetry inheres in the cordial consent in the relation to Being as such. Cordiality of consent is not itself a sufficient ground of beauty unless the structure of beauty is also present. If anything is clear about Edwards's treatment of true virtue, it is his conviction that beauty is built into the nature of being as constituted by God. It is not a sentiment first of all, but a structure of relations harmoniously proportioned, of which one is sensitively aware and appreciative. Hence Edwards describes moral beauty as "that, belonging to the heart of an intelligent Being, that is beautiful by a general beauty, or beautiful in a comprehensive view as it is in itself, and as related to every thing that it stands in connexion with." [29] Interrelationships are thus crucial.

It has been argued to this point that Edwards's portrayal of the soul's adventure was cast in aesthetic terms, but that the category of beauty applied primarily to two areas of his thought, his ontological speculation and his late ethical views. This perspective was already implicit in his own early religious experiences and intuitive conceptions of reality. It has also been suggested that the beauty attributed to secondary virtue, although reflective of true virtue, nevertheless for life in this world was more basic to human existence than true virtue, whereas true virtue as moral beauty reached heights of value and appreciation which transcended ordinary standards of morality.[30] For this reason Edwards found it very difficult to frame words adequate to describe the heights of true virtue, which at the same time would treat this unique and transcendent experience without danger of confusion with ordinary ethical values. Whenever the meaning of beauty was analyzed, it appeared to be a form of moral virtue incumbent upon any moral agent. Therefore "holiness," "glory," "happiness" of a rare kind were employed to fill out the rich amplitude of meaning which Edwards strove to impart to his readers. It is little wonder that his early critics could make little of his references to Being as such as the ground of moral beauty, and that they failed to see how ethics derived in any significant way from what appeared to be a neutral omnibus term like Being in general.

The principal questions which remain then relate to the justification Edwards found in interpreting true virtue as beauty. Can moral right or good be logically or experientially assimilated to an aesthetic good? Are there not significant differences between beauty and moral good? In the light of Edwards's *God's End* dissertation, is it possible to avoid the conclusion that natural and moral evils are both necessary to the fulfillment of harmonious beauty, thereby destroying the notion that beauty provides a criterion by which to discriminate between good and evil? In respect to natural evils, Edwards appears to have had no final persuasive answer.[31] Although he was not so lost in his conviction that reality constituted a harmonious whole, he could not deny actual evils for which men were not responsible. In the light of his late works, this issue could conceivably be resolved by interpreting the presence of such evils as unmerited suffering according to the judgments of a finite human mind. And it is true that in the case of death he gave it a theological meaning by interpreting it as the consequence and punishment for sin, thus making it more than a natural evil.[32] But of these dolorous sentiments there is no hint in the *True Virtue* or the *God's End*.

However, as we have seen, moral evils in a world constituted by the outpouring of divine power, love, and beauty remained a perplexing problem.[33] They would seem to be contrary to harmony and as such infectious of the totality of being, although logically eventually contributing to the glory of God. Beauty, at the same time, would not then enable one to discriminate between them and moral good, because at last they would all be subsumed under the category of divine glory and beauty. This line of thought moves one to conclude that God may permit moral evil and sin to exist so that good may eventually come from them. At the same time and on the same grounds, men cannot perform or permit moral evil since they, unlike God, do not possess the infinite wisdom of deity.[34] Thus no justification for the presence of moral evil can be offered to the man not convinced of divine objectivism which will not at the same time challenge the authority and validity of his egocentricity. The request for an explanation of the occurrence of moral evil in God's world is but the sign of unconverted man's estrangement from the source of his being, whereas the saint has already moved beyond the querulous posture of the sinner. The question as to how in Edwards's ontology disharmony or "jarring" could occur may be thus damped by questioning in turn the spiritual and moral status of the questioner!

If there be no justification offered, convincing to the natural man, is he not then free of moral responsibility? Since he cannot free himself from his finitude, which he shares with the saint, and from his sinful blindness to the true end of creation and the beauty inherent in the totality, he seems free to go about his business as best he may. Not so, argued Edwards. The moral sense of man is not eradicated even in sinful man. Secondary virtue is still both a possibility and a demand, whether or not beauty be mentioned. The foundation for moral criteria has been implanted in man as a "disposition . . . to be uneasy in a consciousness of being inconsistent with himself, and as it were, against himself in his own actions." [35] This sense of disorder within himself is the indication that even in a state of self-interest some remaining intimation of conscience or moral sense assists in keeping the moral and social world in "a kind of disordered order." [36]

The tension between ethics and aesthetics is more pertinent when the question of moral obligation in relation to beauty comes to the foreground. This question cannot be dismissed immediately as one from an unconverted man, since even the man of secondary virtue may well inquire as to why he ought to seek the higher form of virtue. At least he has some intimation of the beauty of both natural and moral relations.[37] He may well inquire if the world, coming as it does from God's hand, is as it ought to be, whether there remains any further moral obligation for him if already he is placed as he ought to be in the system of being. Why ought one strive to be in loving consent to the great system of Being under these circumstances? In an aesthetic model of being it would appear that no place is left for moral or spiritual obligation unless beauty is firmly identified with the moral good and right. This alternative looks suspiciously like the "supernaturalistic fallacy" in which what is the case, the already extant, ordered structure of harmonious reality, determines what ought to be the case. The treatise on *True Virtue,* after all, reads like such a description of what true virtue would be like, if and when it exists. But from such a description, can any ethical responsibility be derived, even in the name of contributing to beauty? [38]

It must first of all be clear that Edwards did not deal with this question in *True Virtue,* largely because the treatise does not purport to answer the question as to why or how one enters into true virtue. But in keeping with his aesthetic formulation of being and true virtue, an answer to the problem may be found. Edwards's vision of the beauty of the divine nature moves in a different orbit from that observed in his polemical and homiletical productions. In the latter, as we have seen, the motives for man's obedience to the divine will rest in the sovereign right of God to rule his world and the threat of everlasting punishment for those who disobey or the promise of heavenly felicity to those who do obey. Men ought to obey God because he rules by right of his power, greatness, and justice, and he provides the familiar sanctions of reward and punishment.[39] However, in the case before us the situation is changed. It is the divine grace in Christ which transforms the fallen creature at the very center of his being so that what previously he did because he ought to, he does now from changed inclination and a renewed sense of divinity. His motivation is changed from a simple obedience to duty to a cordial consent to Being as such for its own intrinsic beauty. Cordial consent to Being not only is manifested in the symmetry and proportionality of holy affections, but marks the shift from the imperative to the indicative mood, from obligation to "relish" for the beauty which characterizes Being itself. Thus beauty draws the self to its goal in Being and reveals itself in the benevolence of the moral agent. God lures or persuades rather than commands. The rigor of moral obligation is thus converted into aspiration in response to the beauty of holiness. And "holiness comprehends all the true moral excellency of intelligent beings," as it does in God himself.[40]

Understood in these terms, the aim of man in his new estate would seem to be that of sheer contemplation of beauty, a relatively static goal. Not a little in Edwards's writings suggests that the mingling of religious and aesthetic sensibilities in his own life led to quiescent contemplation rather than to action. He had referred to his early experience of God as "a calm, sweet abstraction of soul from all the concerns of this world" in which "far from all mankind" he felt "wrapt and swallowed up in God." [41] And it is true that in describing the beauty of God and the beauty of those truly virtuous, Edwards maintained that such beauty was to be enjoyed.[42] In this sense, beauty was an end in itself. However, in the broader sense of Edwards's system, the beauty ascribed to deity and the nature of true moral beauty was something more than a static condition. The vision of beauty, opened to the heart of man by grace, was itself an active principle. In figures of speech echoed later in his *God's End,* Edwards set it down in the *Religious Affections* that godliness in the heart had a direct connection with practice, even "as a fountain has to a stream, or as the luminous nature of the sun has to beams sent forth, or as life has to breathing, or the beating of the pulse, or any other vital act." [43] Beauty is thus the nature of holy affections which provide the dynamics for moral practice, which in turn reveal the beauty inherent in the moral agent. Thus, contemplation may well have its place in the life of the "saint," but beauty does not rest in itself. It expresses or communicates itself even as the supreme instance of beauty, God, pours out his power and goodness.

Neither is it accurate to read Edwards as a perfectionist, if by that term we mean one who is immediately made holy. The advent of the "divine and supernatural taste" does not make sinful men into saints in the moment of the entry of grace into the soul. Too many disappointing experiences with those caught up in paroxysms of emotion during the Great Awakening of those who had imagined themselves made holy in an instant, had taught him to treat with care this murky area. As he once put it bluntly, "The reason why many good men behave no better in many instances, is not so much that they want grace, as they want knowledge." [44] Neither was he unaware of the incipient antinomianism which afflicted these emotional ravishments. Neither the lure of true virtue's beauty, of Christ's love, nor of raw subjective emotionalism could wipe out in a moment the accumulated weight of sinful, contrary affections. Grace implants a new nature, to be sure, but it is a dynamic principle which must grow in spite of opposing forces in the self.[45] The "evil, natural temper" is not rooted out at a blow. Men are still tempted. Grace is hindered by lack of "proper instructions," "errors of judgment," defects in education, thus reducing "the symmetry of virtues" to which the saint aspires. But, Edwards insisted, "the monstrous disproportion" of the affections found in false religion is eradicated. The true saint, however he backslides, will never so fall away from true righteousness as to fail "to observe all the rules of Christianity, and do all the duties required" of a Christian.[46]

Moral and religious obligations thus remain as a floor below which the saved could not sink, even in the face of strong, contrary influences. The ideal spontaneity of grace may not operate at full force, but the predominant direction of the soul is set. Even while the battle between sin and grace goes on, the moral ought remains, sometimes hidden within the embrace of cordial consent to Being, sometimes exposed when the remaining traces of sin rear up to deflect the soul's progress. In the latter case God's implacable "ought" continues to sound, even while he grants the power to overcome and fulfill, in some measure, the "ought." It is within the context of Edwards's concentration upon this result of God's outpoured grace that the aesthetic notion of beauty comes to the foreground in the *True Virtue.* This aesthetic impetus thus takes priority in describing the full-blown concept of virtue, although the road to this virtue may still be haunted by the inexorable presence of duty and moral obligation. The lure of beauty which invests benevolence rises above duty, but never falls beneath it.

Nowhere is this reading of the relation of beauty and obligation better seen than in Edwards's own life. As his *Farewell Sermon* made plain, he was not himself a saint, but if not, how could he describe true virtue unless he had himself experienced it? Could he, in fact, point to a single instance, in this world, of being's cordial consent to Being in general? And did he dare to claim so much for himself?

Part of the answer to these perplexing questions is to be found in the *Religious Affections,* where he claims, not for himself, but for anyone who sees the glory in divine things, that the "mind ascends to the truth of the gospel, but by one step, and that is its divine glory." [47] This intuitive grasp is enough, apart from arguments which could but lamely, if at all, reach to the heights of divine beauty. The force of *Miscellany* 260 leads in the same direction. "Seeing the perfect idea of a thing is, to all intents and purposes, the same as seeing the thing . . . Now, by seeing a perfect idea, so far as we see it, we have it." [48] Edwards's experiences, often designated as mystical or quasi-mystical, certainly would fit these comments. He had seen the beauty of God; he had therefore had holy affections, and he had, if even spasmodically, consented to Being as such. But it is also important to recognize that his sense of the overwhelming "otherness" or objectivity of God would not allow him confidently to assert that he had "arrived" once and for all. He was to preserve "distance" from deity, even after having been ravished by the beauty of the divine Being.

This insight into Edwards's experience returns us once more to this underlying theme of theological objectivism, as it is presented in the *True Virtue* and the *End for which God Created the World*. The distance between the human subject and the divine object is not difficult to recognize in Edwards's Calvinistic writings. But theological objectivism in these late writings seems jeopardized by monistic, Neoplatonist imagery. The aesthetic expression, which attributes virtually all existence and value to the divine Being, endangers the moral dimension by removing all essential duality and diversity in being. This metaphysical justification for degrees of being, which he insisted upon,[49] was never made clear, thus endangering the ethical distance between subject and object necessary for the working out of theological objectivism. Yet it was clear that he did not intend at any time to deny reality to subordinate beings or private systems of being, to which secondary virtue was attached. This ambiguity leaves ajar the door for the retention of the objectivity of deity. To this difference he clung. The divine emanation was not such as to collapse all particular beings into divine being, thus eliminating all possibility of distance between the creature and the creator, even in the case of the saved. Union of the soul with Being as such was not interpreted as the envelopment of the concrete individual into Being as such. True virtue continued to be a matter of relations between them, and relations indicated diversity or at least some ontological distinction.

The glorification of God for his own sake was the purpose of creation and the final goal of the soul, and so stated, souls had to remain to glorify God. Their end was not obliteration in deity. So as we have seen we find Edwards at the end of *God's End* writing that the nature and tendency of the creature is to the union of soul with God "though the time will never come when it can be said it is attained to, in the most absolutely perfect manner." True, the interest of the soul is one with God's interest, but it does not follow that the soul ever completely and finally unites with deity. "It is no solid objection against God's aiming at an infinitely perfect union of the creature with himself, that the particular time will never come when it can be said, the union is now infinitely perfect." So with the final happiness of the saints. There is also a never-ending process of asymptotically ever arriving at its end, but never resting in final completeness. "I suppose it will not be denied by any, that God, in glorifying the saints in heaven with eternal felicity, aims to satisfy his infinite grace or benevolence, by the bestowment of a good infinitely valuable, because eternal; and yet there never will come the moment, when it can be said, that now this infinitely valuable good has been actually bestowed." [50]

In this manner the fundamental pattern of theological objectivism with its denial of theological utilitarianism remains the key concept about which Edwards wove his metaphysic and late theological ethics. Moral beauty inheres in the interplay of intelligent beings with Being itself, even as within the Godhead, itself the Trinity, consists in the beauty of relationships among the three persons. [51]

XI

Conclusion

FOR MANY, Edwards's mode of ethical speculation is not in vogue today. For those who carry on their work without reference to theological issues, Edwards probably remains a distant, somewhat shadowy figure, at best only of passing historical interest. With the exception of H. Richard Niebuhr, the major theological moralists of this century have rarely taken Edwards as the point of departure for their speculations.

For both groups the premise of man's moral freedom has been so widely accepted that Edwards's logical demolition of the freedom of the will can find its modern counterpart only among psychological or genetic determinists. Original Sin is out of fashion, except occasionally as a dramatic theme among some authors and filmmakers, because human dignity is affronted when informed of man's deep-seated tendency to waywardness. The dignity of man supposedly depends upon his clutching some shred of virtue to himself, rather than upon his status as a child of God's creation, whereby he is made invulnerable to those forces which seek to demean him. Edwards's highly conservative occasional comments upon political, economic, and social problems are couched in a theological and cultural framework largely outdated except in the minds of a few people among the more conservative church members of the American public. His development of an ethic which reached its climatic expression in a Neoplatonic affirmation of the sublime nature of beauty seems sadly out of place in a tough world torn by wars, social tensions, poverty, and the despoliation of a planet.

In the light of such considerations as these, men are apt to turn their attention less to the cosmic proportions of an Edwardsean vision than they do to the purely intrahuman struggles that daily confront them. It seems unlikely today that they will easily surrender their utilitarian interest in ethics and religion to a contemplation of divine beauty for its own sake. So long as ethics continues to be conceived in this purely intrahuman framework, and religion is viewed as a prudential device for escape from the ills of human existence, Edwards would seem to offer little that is relevant to the present situation. Men will continue to embrace religion, to be sure, but, as Edwards put it, "not for its own excellent nature, but only to serve a turn."

Yet the twentieth century has seen a continuing interest in Edwards among scholars. Partly this has been due to the intrinsic interest he holds for those who find in him a profound thinker who shaped much of the religious and cultural life of America. But interest in Edwards also arises from a peculiar, if belated, relevance he has to the spiritual situation of contemporary man. More than one person has discovered that purpose and zest has gone out of life when it is treated solely in moralistic terms. Moral energy can flag when it is repeatedly frustrated by daily failure, and when nothing greater summons the soul to new effort. Then even the reason for minimal moral conduct is lost.

A religion which serves only to supply individual psychological satisfactions, or finds its sole goal in urging people to do right, or promotes servile conformity to existing cultural values soon exhausts the patience of its adherents and weakly succumbs to tedium. When there is no vision of something greater than the self and society to lure men beyond the confines of the solitary self or the amenities of society, the prophetic thrust of religion is lost. Even some aspects of the revolt of the youth in our society reveal that the soul of man yearns for an enlargement of vision which will break the boredom of a life weighed down by religious and cultural conventionalism. What Edwards offered in place of this malaise was a sense of the heart which had been seized by the coherence of all being. It was an affectionate concern for the implicit unity of existence. He was prophetic in respect to the present situation when he wrote, "He that sees the beauty of holiness, or true moral good, sees the greatest and most important thing in the world, which is the fulness of all things, without which all the world is empty, yea, worse than nothing." (*Works,* 1817, 4:170)

Perhaps ethics in company with Edwards, but not in slavish imitation of him, will see that morality, without escaping the mundane problems of human life, must be placed in the larger perspective of the reality to which Edwards pointed. Beauty may not become a cheap substitute for moral discrimination and action, but there is, as he showed, an ethic of responsibility which moves more by attraction of the final good in being than by the stern call of duty. Such an ethic finds its highest justification in a spontaneous virtue, which, lacking self-consciousness, takes the form of a beauty of personal character. Calvinists have been noted for their suspicion of the holiness of beauty, but never for their suspicion of the beauty of holiness. Their eyes, at their clearest, were set upon a transcendent beauty beyond those visible beauties which seduced men from their true goal as often as they ushered them into its presence. It is fitting therefore that Edwards the Calvinist should at last represent this aesthetic fulfillment in terms of a Neoplatonic configuration of a world which for him was replete with the beauteous evidences of God's presence.

Notes

CHAPTER I

1. Perry Miller, *Jonathan Edwards* (New York: William Sloane Associates, 1949), p. 276.
2. James Carse, *Jonathan Edwards and the Visibility of God* (New York: Charles Scribners Sons, 1967), pp. 11–12, 162.
3. Conrad Cherry, *The Theology of Jonathan Edwards, a Reappraisal* (New York: Doubleday Anchor, 1966), pp. 6 ff.
4. Roland A. Delattre, *Beauty and Sensibility in the Thought of Jonathan Edwards* (New Haven and London: Yale University Press, 1968), pp. 1–3.
5. Douglas J. Elwood, *The Philosophical Theology of Jonathan Edwards* (New York: Columbia University Press), 1960, p. 3.
6. William S. Morris, "The Genius of Jonathan Edwards," in *Reinterpretation in American Church History*, ed. Jerold C. Brauer, (Chicago: University of Chicago Press, 1968), p. 65.
7. Elwood, *Philosophical Theology*, p. 11.
8. The use of the term "object" in this context does not necessarily imply passivity, but in its broadest usage leaves open the question of whether that which confronts man ontologically has will and initiative. It is intended as an ontological distinction which pertains to human existence and is logically prior to epistemological duality. As such it signifies that which man cannot dispose of by assimilating whatever is present to his own consciousness. It carries the meaning of "over-againstness." Cf. C. A. Holbrook, *Faith and Community* (New York:

Harper and Brothers, 1959), pp. 65–66; cf. also J. Brown, *Subject and Object in Modern Theology* (London: SCM Ltd., 1953), chap. 1.

9. Cf. Andre Dumas, "De L'Objectivité de Dieu" in *Revue d'histoire et de philosophie religieuses*, no. 4 (1966), pp. 309–22. Edwards seldom mounted arguments for God's existence, but *Miscellany* 880 represents one of his attempts to do so. H. G. Townsend, *The Philosophy of Jonathan Edwards* (Eugene, Oregon: The University of Oregon Press), 1955, pp. 87 ff.

10. "The God that is the Creator of the world, is doubtless also the Governor of it: for he is able to govern it . . . He that gave being at first, can continue being, or put an end to it; and therefore nothing can stand in his way . . . so that it is evident God has the world in His hands, to dispose of as he pleases." *Works* (1843), 1:565, "Miscellaneous Observations on Important Doctrines."

11. "The moral imperative is not based on a possibility but on an order of reality." E. P. Dickie, *Revelation and Response* (New York: Charles Scribner's Sons, 1938), p. 64.

12. "If we would know how the Puritan felt we must resolutely divest our minds of all ideas relating to the divine Being, derived from the habit acquired by men in these last ages of sitting in judgment on the character of God . . . The Puritans had not risen or sunk to that tender French conception of the Almighty as 'le bon dieu'." Peter Bayne, *Documents Relating to the Settlement of the Church of England by the Act of Uniformity of 1662* (London, W. Kent, 1862), p. 16.

13. As R. Otto pointed out, the sense of a "numinous" object brings with it "a depreciation of the subject in his own eyes." *The Idea of the Holy* (London: Oxford University Press, 1925), p. 11, n. 1.

14. Cf. Abraham Heschel's criticism of theological utilitarianism: "Religion did not come into existence to console the desperate, to guarantee immortality, or to protect society. It is a reality in itself, not a function of man." "The Holy Dimension" in *The Journal of Religion*, XXIII, 2 (1943), p. 119.

15. William Paley, *The Principles of Moral and Political Philosophy* (New York: Harper and Brothers, 1849).

16. Newman Smyth, *Christian Ethics* (New York: Charles Scribner's Sons, 1923), p. 44.
17. In answering the Arminian criticisms of Calvinism, Edwards replied that the natural perfections as well as the moral perfections of God should be taken into account. "His moral perfections are proved no otherwise than by arguing from his natural perfections." Similarly Edwards answered by reference to Scripture the Arminian contention that only those doctrines concerning the moral nature of God which could be reconciled with human reason were acceptable. "The scripture itself supposes that there are some things in scripture that men may not be able to reconcile with God's moral perfections." *Works* (Worcester ed.), 5:375 ff.
18. "Religious Affections," *Works* (Yale ed.), 2:394.

CHAPTER II

1. "Personal Narrative," as quoted by Samuel Hopkins, *Works* (1817), 1:30.
2. Cf. ed. Perry Miller, *Images or Shadows of Divine Things* (New Haven: Yale University Press, 1948), pp. 1–41; also A. C. McGiffert, Jr., *Jonathan Edwards* (New York: Harper and Brothers Inc., 1932), p. 30; A. Heimert, *Religion and the American Mind* (Cambridge: Harvard University Press, 1966), pp. 103 ff.
3. *Works* (1817), 3:30–31.
4. Ibid., p. 15.
5. Ibid., 1:50. E. A. Gaustad refers to the revival sermons as "notable for their lack of stirring emotional appeals." *The Great Awakening in New England* (New York: Harper and Brothers, 1957), p. 22.
6. C. H. Faust and T. H. Johnson, *Jonathan Edwards, Representative Selections* (New York: American Book Co., 1935), p. xcvii.
7. Cf. "Religious Affections," *Works* (Yale ed.), 2:376, 260.
8. *Sermons on Various Important Subjects*, 1785, p. 320.
9. "The Sole Condition that God is God, Sufficient to Still all Objections to his Sovereignty," in *Practical Sermons*, 1788, pp. 41–42.
10. "God's Sovereignty," *Works* (1843 in Four Volumes), 4:550 ff. Henceforth, *Works* (1843).

11. *Practical Sermons,* 1788, p. 212.
12. Ibid., p. 48.
13. "Concerning God's Moral Government," *Works* (1843), 1:567.
14. *The New England Mind* (New York: The Macmillan Company, 1939), p. 22.
15. "The Justice of God in the Damnation of Sinners," *Works* (1843), 4:252.
16. "The Vain Self-Flatteries of the Sinner," *Works* (1817), 5:453.
17. "The Justice of God in the Damnation of Sinners," *Works* (1843), 4:241.
18. "The Warnings of Scripture . . . ," *Works* (1817), 7:462.
19. "A Fearfulness which shall Hereafter Surprise Sinners in Zion," *Works* (1843), 4:495.
20. "Man's Natural Blindness in Religion," *Works* (1817), 5:290–93.
21. "Wicked Men Useful in their Destruction Only," *Works* (1843), 4:312.
22. "The End of the Wicked Contemplated by the Righteous," ibid., 4:290–92.
23. "The Justice of God in the Damnation of Sinners," ibid., 4:228–29.
24. "The Eternity of Hell Torments," ibid., 4:276.
25. "The Wisdom of God Displayed in the Way of Salvation," ibid., 4:150.
26. Ibid., 4:151.
27. Ibid., 4:384.
28. Cf. ibid., 4:387, 391.
29. "A Farewell Sermon," *Works* (1817), 7:399.
30. "True Grace Distinguished from the Experience of Devils," *Works* (1843), 4:460–61.
31. "God Makes Men Sensible of their Miseries before He Reveals his Mercy and Love," *Works* (Dwight ed.), 8:59.
32. "Personal Narrative," *Works* (1817), 3:31.
33. *Sermons on Various Important Subjects,* 1785, p. 320.
34. "Justification by Faith Alone," *Works* (1843), 4:67.
35. Ibid., 4:67–68.
36. Ibid., 4:72–73. "The thing that the Scripture guards and militates against, is our imagining that it is our goodness, virtue or excellency, that instates us in God's acceptance and favor." Ibid., p. 102.
37. Ibid., 4:102.

38. Ibid., 4:73.
39. Ibid., 4:76. "Some natural men have had better natural tempers than others; and some are better educated than others; and some live a great deal more soberly than others: but one has no more love to God than another." "Men Naturally God's Enemies," ibid., 4:40.
40. Ibid., 4:76.
41. "Men Naturally God's Enemies," ibid., 4:55.
42. Edwards explicitly stated that the doctrines employed in his revival sermons were to be used as a means "to awaken and terrify the impenitent." "Natural Men in a Dreadful Condition," *Works* (Dwight ed.), 8:32.
43. "Man's Natural Blindness in Religion," *Works* (1843), 4:34–35; "Men Naturally God's Enemies," ibid., 4:58.
44. "Men Naturally God's Enemies," ibid., 4:55.
45. Ibid., 4:60; "Justice of God in the Damnation of Sinners," ibid., 4:245; "Future Punishment of the Wicked," ibid., 4:258–59.
46. "The Eternity of Hell Torments," ibid., 4:267.
47. "End of the Wicked . . . ," ibid., 4:289–90, 292.
48. *Practical Sermons* (1788), pp. 220–21.
49. "God Makes Men Sensible . . . ," *Works* (Dwight ed.), 8:38.
50. *Charity and its Fruits* (New York: A. D. F. Randolph and Co., 1851), p. 264.
51. E. A. Gaustad accurately touches on this point when he comments that Edwards, unlike Chauncy, claimed that the Great Awakening "was unique and that there were no rules for it." *The Great Awakening in New England* (New York: Harper and Brothers, 1957), p. 96.
52. "Some Thoughts on the Revival of Religion in New England," *Works* (Worcester ed.), 3:93, 97, 104, 109.
53. Ibid., 3:91. Also "It is a great fault in us to limit a sovereign, all wise God, whose judgments are a great deep, and his ways past finding out, where he has not limited himself, and in things, concerning which, he has not told us what his way shall be." 3:101–2; cf. also 104.
54. Ibid., 3:93.
55. Ibid., 3:94; cf. also "Religious Affections," *Works* (Yale ed.), 2:97.
56. *Works* (Yale ed.), 2:13–14.
57. Ibid., 2:95.

58. Ibid., 2:197.
59. Ibid., 2:240–53.
60. Ibid., 2:266.
61. Ibid., 2:365.
62. Ibid., 2:260; cf. also 394.
63. Ibid., 2:291.
64. Ibid., 2:311.
65. Ibid., 2:340.
66. Ibid., 2:344, 357.
67. Ibid., 2:376.
68. Ibid., 2:121; cf. also 9.
69. *Works* (Worcester ed.), 3:195.
70. Ibid., 3:196.
71. Ibid., 3:198.
72. Ibid., 3:196.
73. "Justice of God in the Damnation of Sinners," *Works* (1843), 4:242.
74. Ibid., 4:293.
75. Ibid., 4:294.
76. Ibid.
77. *Works* (Worcester ed.), 3:89, 90.
78. Ibid., 3:343.
79. Ibid., 3:124–28, 137.
80. *Works* (Yale ed.), 2:409–10.
81. Ibid., 2:450–51; cf. also 392, 391, 422–23, 424–25.
82. Cf. ibid., 2:390.
83. Cf. ibid., 2:383, 390.
84. Ibid., 2:452–53.
85. Cf. ibid., 2:419.
86. Cf. ibid., 2:412–13.
87. Ibid., 2:291 ff.
88. Ibid., 2:33–34.
89. Ibid., 2:420. "Our wisdom and discerning with regard to the hearts of men, is not much to be trusted. We can see but a little way into the nature of the soul, and the depths of man's heart . . . no philosophy or experience will ever be sufficient to guide us safely through this labyrinth and maze, without our closely following the clues which God has given us in his world." Ibid., 2:460.
90. Ibid., 2:469.
91. Ibid., 2:455 ff.
92. Cf. ibid., 2:436.

CHAPTER III

1. "Some Thoughts on the Revival of Religion in New England," *Works* (Worcester ed.), 3:94; cf. also "Religious Affections," *Works* (Yale ed.), 2:97.
2. "Freedom of the Will," *Works* (Yale ed.), 1:9–10, 239 ff., 257 ff.
3. Ibid., 1:137, 163–64.
4. Ibid., 1:227.
5. Ibid., 1:139. F. H. Foster considered this lack of distinction between desire and will one of the most serious defects of the treatise. "Thus he confounded the emotions, the action of which is necesary, with the will, the action of which is free, and attributed to the latter, as a matter of self evidence, all the necessity of the former." *A Genetic History of the New England Theology* (Chicago: University of Chicago Press, 1907), p. 64.
6. Cf. *Works* (Yale ed.), 2:97.
7. Cf. *Works* (Yale ed.), 1:148.
8. Cf. J. Haroutunian, *Piety Versus Moralism* (New York: Henry Holt and Co., 1932), p. 222. "An act of volition is a consequence which is inseparable from the mind's perception of the strongest motive."
9. *Works* (Yale ed.), 1:144, 146–47. The character of the self is not a totally passive ingredient in the process of willing for "The state of mind . . . contributes to the agreeableness or disagreeableness" of the object. The "particular temper" one has by nature, by education, example or custom plays into the degree of strength which the motive has.
10. Ibid., 1:217, 225. Cf. "The dispute about grace's being irresistible is perfect nonsense . . . it is nonsense, except it be proper to say that a man with his will can resist his own will . . . that is, except it be possible for a man to will a thing and not will it at the same time, and so far as he does will it." "Concerning Efficacious Grace," *Works* (Worcester ed.), 5:448. Also, p. 473: "In efficacious grace we are not merely passive, nor yet does God do some, and we do the rest. But God does all, and we do all. God produces all, and we act all."
11. Cf. *Works* (Yale ed.), 1:34–35.
12. Ibid., 1:152.
13. Edwards also pressed on to the equally important distinction

between "moral necessity" and "natural necessity." Cf. ibid., 1:38, 156 ff.

14. Ibid., 1:37.
15. F. J. E. Woodbridge, "The Philosophy of Edwards" in *Exercises commemorating the two-hundredth anniversary of the birth of Jonathan Edwards* (Andover: Andover Press, 1904), p. 55.
16. *Works* (Yale ed.), 1:181.
17. Cf. ibid., 1:156–58.
18. Ibid., 1:181.
19. Cf. ibid., 1:213 ff., 195 ff., 207.
20. Ibid., 1:164.
21. Cf. ibid., 1:159, 309, 359.
22. Cf. ibid., 1:337 ff.
23. Ibid., 1:426, n. 2.
24. Cf. ibid., 1:277 ff., 375 ff., 384 ff., 281 ff.
25. Cf. ibid., 1:361.
26. Ibid., 1:370.
27. Cf. ibid., 1:302 ff. on Edwards's defense of the view that obligation is consistent with moral inability; also p. 309.
28. Cf. the conclusion of W. T. Jones on Kant's theory of moral freedom. "Morally significant conduct, in a word, is that with which our self-feeling is associated; and to the fact that some acts are so felt it is completely irrelevant that their occurrence in this way is completely determined (if it is determined) by antecedent events in time." *Morality and Freedom in the Philosophy of Immanuel Kant* (London: Oxford University Press, 1940), p. vi.
29. "When a thing is *from* a man, in that sense, that it is from his will or choice he is to blame for it, because his will is *in* it: so far as the will is *in* it, blame is *in* it, and no further." *Works* (Yale ed.), 1:427. In the same vein, as John Hick points out, "It is difficult to see how such concepts as responsibility and obligation could have any application if human volitions occurred at random instead of flowing from the individual nature of the agent." *Evil and the God of Love* (London: The Macmillan Co., 1966), p. 312.
30. As Edwards put it in his Conclusion: "For, as the being of the world is from God, so the circumstances in which it had its being at first, both negative and positive, must be ordered by him . . . and all the necessary consequences of

these circumstances, must be ordered by him . . . all events whatsoever are necessarily connected with something foregoing, either positive or negative, which is the ground of its existence." And this "something which is connected with nothing preceding" is God's "own immediate conduct." *Works* (Yale ed.), 1:432.

31. Ibid., 1:433.
32. Ibid., 1:272–73.
33. "The Great Christian Doctrine of Original Sin Defended," *Works* (Yale ed.), 3:129.
34. Ibid., 3:133.
35. "Cur Deus Homo," I, 21, in *St. Anselm,* trans. Sidney N. Dean (La Salle, Ill.: Open Court, 1951).
36. One of the logical curiosities of this argument lies in the attempt to prove a conclusion about an infinite being from principles held by a finite being who is also a sinner by the very terms of the argument. Furthermore, it would seem to be equally impossible for a sinful man to argue to God's infinite righteousness, since by definition he has no insight or knowledge of this aspect of the divine nature. Edwards was not unaware of the difficulty presented by a finite being's incurring an infinite debt, and he attempted, not too successfully, to show in *Miscellany* 44 that only in God's mind was the sin and its punishment infinite, whereas in the human mind it was only finite. Since he was trying to persuade finite minds of the infinitude of sin, his proposed demonstration falls short of conviction. Cf. H. G. Townsend, *The Philosophy of Jonathan Edwards* (Eugene: The University of Oregon Press, 1955), pp. 241 ff.
37. *Works* (Yale ed.), 3:130 ff.; cf. also "Justification by Faith," *Works* (1843 ed.), 4:74–75.
38. *Works* (Yale ed.), 3:108 ff., 123–27, 158, 206–9.
39. Cf. C. A. Holbrook, "Original Sin and the Enlightenment," in *The Heritage of Christian Thought,* ed. E. Grislis and R. E. Cushman (New York: Harper and Row, 1965), pp. 155–56.
40. Cf. Terence Greenwood, "Personal Identity and Memory," *The Philosophical Quarterly,* 17:69, 334 ff.
41. Cf. *Heritage of Christian Thought,* pp. 158–60. Cf. also *Works* (Yale ed.), 3:403–12. Arthur B. Crabtree finds the argument on identity ingenious but unconvincing. "It tells

us absolutely nothing about the identity of Adam and his progeny." He "contents himself with the negative claim that 'no solid reason can be given why God may not establish' this union. The question whether God actually does is still unanswered." *Jonathan Edwards' View of Man* (Wallington, Surrey, England: The Religious Education Press, 1948), p. 35. Of course Edwards depended upon what he regarded as evidence that in fact God had treated mankind as one, just as in all and varying circumstances it had fallen into sin without exception. His metaphysical demonstration for identity was the undergirding structure of his "empirical" inquiry into the human condition. Even Taylor's admission that all men suffer from Adam's sin, but are not guilty because of it, indicates a unity of mankind which, Edwards felt, called for some metaphysical and theological justification.

42. Cf. *Works* (Yale ed.), 3:380–88.

43. "It matters not what the form in which the cause is stated, whether privative or positive; it at least is referred to God as its only cause." S. J. Baird, "Edwards and the Theology of New England," *The Southern Presbyterian Review*, 10:4, p. 584.

44. *Works* (Yale ed.), 1:399.

45. Ibid., 1:414. "On the premise that the creature in his unfallen state dwells consciously in the supremely glorious and joyous presence of God, his fall is not sufficiently accounted for merely by attributing to him a pure freedom of spontaneous creativity." Hick, *Evil and the God of Love*, p. 314.

46. Ibid., pp. 410 ff.

47. *Works* (Yale ed.), 3:394.

48. T. E. Hill, *Contemporary Ethical Theories* (New York: Macmillan Co., 1950), p. 112; cf. also A. V. G. Allen, *Jonathan Edwards* (Boston and New York: Houghton Mifflin and Co., 1889), p. 313.

CHAPTER IV

1. "Men's Natural Blindness to Religion," *Works* (1843), 4:17.

2. "The Great Christian Doctrine of Original Sin Defended," *Works* (Yale ed.), 3:423.

3. "Religious Affections," *Works* (Yale ed.), 2:256; cf. *Works* (Yale ed.), 3:370–71.

4. *Works* (Yale ed.), 2:251.

5. Cf. ibid., 2:266.
6. *Charity and its Fruits* (New York: A. D. F. Randolph and Co., 1851), pp. 226–28.
7. Ibid., p. 229.
8. Ibid., p. 232.
9. Ibid., p. 236.
10. Ibid., p. 238.
11. Ibid., pp. 249–50.
12. Ibid., p. 233.
13. Ibid., p. 252.
14. H. G. Townsend, *The Philosophy of Jonathan Edwards* (Eugene, Oregon: The University Press, 1955), *Miscellany* 530, pp. 202–3.
15. Ibid., pp. 203–5.
16. Ibid., p. 203.
17. *Charity and its Fruits*, p. 93.
18. Cf. C. H. Faust and T. H. Johnson, *Jonathan Edwards, Representative Selections* (New York, Cincinnati: American Book Co., 1935), p. lxxxviii.
19. "The Nature of True Virtue," *Works* (1817), 2:34; see also *The Nature of True Virtue by Jonathan Edwards*, with a foreword by William K. Frankena (Ann Arbor, The University of Michigan Press, 1960), p. 42.
20. *Works* (1817), 2:34; Frankena, *True Virtue*, p. 43.
21. Ibid.
22. *Works* (1817), 2:35–36; Frankena, *True Virtue*, p. 45. Edwards here appears to follow the line of thought which Hutcheson had employed to answer those critics who claimed that all virtue arises from a refined form of self-love which finds satisfaction in the beauties of a benevolent virtue. Cf. Faust and Johnson, *Jonathan Edwards*, pp. lxxxii–lxxxiii.
23. *Works* (1817), 2:36; Frankena, *True Virtue*, p. 46.
24. *Works* (1817), 2:38; Frankena, *True Virtue*, p. 48.
25. "This moral sense, either of our own Actions, or of those of others, has this in common with our other Senses, that however our Desire of Virtue may be counterbalanced by Interest, our Sentiment or Perception of its Beauty cannot; as it certainly might be, if the only Ground of an Approbation were Views of Advantage." F. Hutcheson, *An Inquiry Concerning Moral Good and Evil* (London: D. Midwinter, 1729), p. 119.

26. Cf. *Works* (1817), 2:39; Frankena, *True Virtue,* p. 50. "Self-love is sufficient, without Grace, to cause men to love those that love them, or that they imagine love them and make much of them." "True Grace Distinguished from the Experience of Devils," *Works* (1843), 4:467.

27. Cf. *Works* (1817), 2:40; Frankena, *True Virtue,* p. 51.

28. *Works* (1817), 2:43; Frankena, *True Virtue,* p. 57.

29. Cf. *Works* (1817), 2:44–45; Frankena, *True Virtue,* p. 58. Hutcheson had attempted to refute this reduction of moral discrimination by insisting that there was an intuitive approval or disapproval of behavior prior to the operation of these secondary influences. Cf. F. Hutcheson, *An Inquiry,* pp. 127, 214 ff.

30. "These natural principles, for the most part, tend to the good of mankind. . . . But this is no proof that these natural principles have the nature of true virtue." *Works* (1817), 2:65; Frankena, *True Virtue,* p. 94.

31. *Works* (1817), 2:62; Frankena, *True Virtue,* p. 89. Shaftesbury had also recognized the necessity of confining self-interest within bounds, but he regarded the relationship between self-interest and the public good as one of complete compatibility. "To be well affected towards the Publick Interest and one's own, is not only consistent, but inseparable." *Characteristicks of Men, Manners, Opinions, Times* (London: John Darby, 1737), 2:81; cf. also pp. 140 ff., 175. Hutcheson inclined to the same view. *An Inquiry,* pp. 174–77 ff.

32. Cf. *Works* (1817), 2:60–65; Frankena, *True Virtue,* pp. 90–94. Although Edwards asserts that self-love may lead to true virtue (p. 65) he makes clear elsewhere that private affections "have no tendency to true virtue." The contradiction may be more apparent than substantive. Self-love, since it does have some intimations of the beauty of true virtue, may produce a yearning for true virtue which it is impossible to achieve by oneself, since there is nothing of true virtue in the person which would move him to achieve it.

33. Cf. *Works* (1817), 2:56; Frankena, *True Virtue,* p. 88.

34. Cf. Faust and Johnson, *Jonathan Edwards,* p. lxxxix.

35. *Works* (1817), 2:58–59; Frankena, *True Virtue,* p. 83.

36. "True Grace Distinguished from the Experience of Devils," *Works* (1843), 4:454.

37. "Men Naturally God's Enemies," ibid., 4:54–55.

38. "Man's Natural Blindness in Religion," ibid., 4:30. In his "Dissertation Concerning the End for which God Created the World," Edwards made clear both the strengths and the limits of reason in deciding the main issue before him. Having paid tribute to the high attainments of human reason, which he was later to use, Edwards went on to say "it would be relying too much on reason, to determine the affair of God's last end in creation of the world, only by our own reason, or without being herein principally guided by divine revelation." *Works* (Worcester ed.), 6:21.

39. Cf. ibid., 6:22, 24, 25.

40. *Charity and its Fruits*, p. 280. Reason tells men that anger "cannot be for the glory of God." Thus reason allows one to see what is done.

41. Ibid., p. 304.

42. "Original Sin," *Works* (Yale ed.), 3:153.

43. Ibid., 3:387; cf. Townsend, *Philosophy*, pp. 119, 121, *Miscellany* 782.

44. Townsend, *Philosophy*, p. 208, *Miscellany* 4.

45. Ibid., p. 110, *Miscellany* 116.

46. Ibid., *Miscellany* 353.

47. Cf. C. A. Holbrook, "Edwards and the Ethical Question," *Harvard Theological Review*, 60:2, 172.

48. "Freedom of the Will," *Works* (Yale ed.), 1:148.

49. In his *Notes on the Mind* Edwards remarked on the influence which the general disposition of a person had on one's reasoning. "A person may have a strong reason, and yet not a good reason. He may have a strength of mind to drive an argument, and yet not have even balances. It is not so much from a defect of the reasoning powers, as from a fault of the disposition." Either a tendency to prejudice or a want of love of truth may interfere with reason's powers. *Works* (Dwight ed.), 1:680 (n. 68); cf. also "On Prejudice," ibid., p. 690 (n. 22).

50. "The Portion of the Righteous," *Works* (Dwight ed.), 8:236.

51. However, even this distinction between natural reason and conscience suffers in the light of Item 39 of the *Notes on the Mind*, where Edwards refers to conscience as an assent of the mind "arising from a sense of the general beauty and harmony of things." *Works* (Dwight ed.), 1:693. A similar view of the metaphysical competence of conscience was ex-

pressed in Item 14, where conscience is referred to as a "sense the mind has" of the consent of perceiving being to the general consent which all being has to Being in general, or the dissent of the mind from any dissent to Being in general. Ibid., 1:701.

52. "Conscience is a principle natural to men; and the work that it doth naturally, or of itself, is to give an apprehension of right and wrong, and to suggest to the mind the relation that there is between right and wrong, and a retribution." "A Divine and Supernatural Light," *Works* (1843), 4:440; cf. also Townsend, *Philosophy, Miscellany* 353:110 and 626: 111.

53. *Works* (1843), 4:459. The force of this quotation is lessened by Edwards's later formulation, when he referred to natural conscience "implanted in all mankind as it were in God's stead." *Works* (1817), 2:63; Frankena, *True Virtue,* p. 90.

54. He also refers to "that moral sense which is in natural conscience," ibid. "That moral sense which is natural to mankind, so far as it is disinterested, and not founded in association of ideas, is the same with this natural conscience." *Works* (1817), 2:51; Frankena, *True Virtue,* p. 70. A curious contradiction appears in Edwards's insistence that conscience arises in self-love, while at the same time admitting that "some of the arguments used by these writers (Shaftesbury and Hutcheson) indeed prove that there is a moral sense or taste universal among men, distinct from what arises from self-love." Ibid. He went on to point out, however, that there was some confusion in their discourses, since at least some of their examples were in fact instances of self-love.

55. Cf. *Works* (1817), 2:46–47; Frankena, *True Virtue,* p. 62.

56. Cf. *Works* (1817), 2:47–48; Frankena, *True Virtue,* p. 63. "Conscience is not infallible; it can be weakened by habitual wickedness and 'long acting from the selfish principle' or sensuality. *Works* (1817), 2:64; Frankena, *True Virtue,* p. 92.

57. *Works* (1817), 2:49; Frankena, *True Virtue,* p. 66.

58. Cf. *Works* (1817), 2:50–51; Frankena, *True Virtue,* p. 67.

59. Cf. Shaftesbury, *Characteristicks,* 42, 53–54, 120; Hutcheson, *An Inquiry,* pp. 114, 119, 125–28, 228; *Works* (1817), 2:56; Frankena, *True Virtue,* p. 72.

60. While arguing for the capacity which the natural man has to approve the nature of true virtue, Edwards seems to over-

look what he elsewhere claims to be the opposition which private affections have to Being in general. Not only do private affections "have no tendency to produce it," but since they are "unsubordinate" to Being in general, they imply "opposition" to it. If the mind of the natural man is in opposition to true virtue, it becomes difficult to see how he can approve it. *Works* (1817), 2:56; Frankena, *True Virtue,* p. 72. In the same vein, if man is naturally blind to spiritual matters, as Edwards had argued in his sermon in "Men's Natural Blindness in the Things of Religion" (*Works,* 1843, 4:16 ff.), it would seem to be impossible that he could have the slightest intimation of the beauty of true virtue. Cf. Arthur B. Crabtree, *Jonathan Edwards' View of Man* (Wallington, Surrey, England: The Religious Education Press, 1948), p. 38.

61. *Works* (1817), 2:27; Frankena, *True Virtue,* p. 30. Perry Miller worked over the Edwards manuscript which dealt with symbols, types, allegories, etc., and published the edited results in *Images or Shadows of Divine Things.* (New Haven: Yale University Press, 1948) Throughout these occasional and truncated writings of Edwards the dominant theme is that of the analogy and typology between divine and natural realities. See especially p. 44, no. 8; p. 54, no. 43. In view of the many instances of types and analogies which Edwards found in nature, it is difficult to understand Miller's judgment that "Edwards was too thorough an empiricist ever to become any sort of a 'Platonist'." (p. 151). For further consideration of Edwards's use of typology see Ursula Brumm, *Die Religiöse Typologie im Amerikanischen Denken* (Leiden: E. J. Brill, 1963), pp. 73 ff.

62. Cf. *Works* (1817), 2:75; Frankena, *True Virtue,* p. 99. "When conscience is well informed and thoroughly awakened, it agrees with him [God] fully and exactly, as to the object approved, though not as to the ground and reason of approving."

63. *Works* (1817), 2:75; Frankena, *True Virtue,* p. 99.

64. *Works* (1817), 2:76; Frankena, *True Virtue,* p. 100.

65. *Works* (1817), 2:80; Frankena, *True Virtue,* pp. 104–5.

66. Cf. *Works* (1817), 2:76–78; Frankena, *True Virtue,* pp. 100–104. The rationalistic tone of this line of argument is enhanced when it is observed that no appeal is made to Scrip-

ture as the supreme authority. In fact, unlike his practice elsewhere in his writing, Edwards does not quote Scripture to bolster his views in *The Nature of True Virtue*. There is a reference to Saul and David on p. 60 (1817) but no quote. This fact along with other evidence to the same intent should qualify V. Tomas's conclusion that Edwards was without remainder "a medieval philosopher," defined as one who "took orders" from Scripture. V. Tomas, "The Modernity of Jonathan Edwards," *The New England Quarterly* (1952), pp. 25, 60 ff.

67. Cf. Hutcheson, *An Inquiry into the Original of our Idea of Beauty and Virtue*, 3rd ed., 1729, pp. 16 ff.; also Shaftesbury, *Characteristicks* (London: John Darby, 1737), 2:28 ff.

68. Cf. *Works* (1817), 2:26–27; Frankena, *True Virtue*, p. 30.

69. *Works* (1817), 2:28; Frankena, *True Virtue*, p. 31. Although Edwards calls this a law of nature instituted by God, the source of this idea may be less that of a clear dictate of reason than it is a derivative of his fascination with the types and images he found in scripture. At the same time the Newtonian sense of order and pattern of the world of nature, coupled with the Platonic cast of these later views of Edwards, cannot be discounted.

70. *Works* (1817), 2:28–29; Frankena, *True Virtue*, p. 32.

71. Cf. *Works* (1817), 2:30–31; Frankena, *True Virtue*, p. 37.

72. Cf. *Works* (1817), 2:33–34; Frankena, *True Virtue*, p. 39.

73. Cf. Townsend, *Philosophy*, p. 258, *Miscellany* 117 on the trinity, and 262, *Miscellany* 697 on the unity of God. In the latter Edwards reaches toward a pantheism when he states, "An infinite being, therefore, must be an all-comprehending being," and also "to be infinite is to be all."

74. *Works* (1817), 2:61; Frankena, *True Virtue*, p. 87.

75. Cf. *Works* (1817), 2:61; Frankena, *True Virtue*, p. 88.

76. Edwards even allowed that natural principles may on occasion be mixed with truly benevolent affection, which "mixes its influence with the natural principles, and guides and regulates its operations. . . . Genuine virtue prevents that increase of the habits of pride and sensuality, which tend to diminish the exercises of the useful and necessary principles of nature." *Works* (1817), 2:66; Frankena, *True Virtue*, p. 96.

CHAPTER V

1. Cf. "The Great Christian Doctrine of Original Sin Defended," *Works* (Yale ed.), 3:411

2. Cf. "Miscellaneous Remarks on Important Doctrines," *Works* (1817), 8:306. ". . . without any divine government over the whole, the world of mankind could not subsist, but would destroy itself." Ibid. Cf. also "God's Awful Judgment . . . ," *Works* (1817), 8:87–88.

3. "Miscellaneous Observations on Important Theological Subjects . . . ," ibid., 8:184; cf. also "On the Medium of Moral Government," ibid., 8:215.

4. "Men Naturally God's Enemies," ibid., 5:308 ff.

5. Edwards's description of government and society in terms of a sovereign ruler and serflike creature or subject, as Haroutunian points out, was a thought-pattern whose original atmosphere belonged to a far different period than that of the eighteenth century. It reflects the medieval feudal culture. The revolutionary spirit abroad in the eighteenth century was destined to weaken the grip of this political figure of speech, not only in the sphere of the political, but also in that of the theological. Cf. J. Haroutunian, *Piety Versus Moralism* (New York: Henry Holt and Co., 1932), pp. 159–60.

6. Cf. "Miscellaneous Remarks . . . ," *Works* (1817), 8:307.

7. Ibid. The term "received being" reflects the family conception of civil government.

8. Cf. "Moral Government," *Works* (1817), 8:215.

9. Ibid. 8:218.

10. "A Strong Rod Broken and Withered . . . ," ibid., 5:531.

11. Ibid.

12. "Humble Attempt at Extraordinary Prayer," ibid., 2:453. The sermon is a result of the Great Awakening. Edwards never gave up the idea of the final end of man being a social one in the kingdom, whether in history or beyond history.

13. Cf. "God's Awful Judgment . . . ," *Works* (1817), 8:85.

14. Ibid., 8:86.

15. "Miscellaneous Remarks . . . ," *Works* (1817), 8:468. "The authority of a ruler does not consist in the power or influence he has on another by attractives, but coercives."

16. Edwards lamented in one sermon, "How is family government in a great measure vanished! This is one principal ground of

the corruptions which prevail in the land. This is the foundation of so much debauchery . . . family-government is in a great measure extinct." "Christian Cautions or the Necessity of Self-examination," *Works* (Dwight ed.), 6:359.

17. "Fifteen Sermons on Various Subjects," *Works* (1817), 7:378
18. Ibid.
19. "Christian Cautions . . ." *Works* (1817), 6:355.
20. Edwards, with Augustine, believed that all societies were based ideally upon love, although some of his ideas of civil government by no means make this evident. "Love is the uniting bond of all society." Ibid., 6:356.
21. Ibid.
22. Ibid., 6:357.
23. Cf. O. E. Winslow, *Jonathan Edwards* (New York: The Macmillan Co., 1941), pp. 220 ff.
24. "Men come into the world with many strange and violent lusts in their hearts, and are exceedingly prone of themselves to transgress; even in the safest circumstances in which they can be placed." Cf. "Joseph's Great Temptation and Gracious Deliverance," *Works* (1843), 4:592.
25. Ibid., 593–94.
26. Cf. A. C. McGiffert, Jr., *Jonathan Edwards* (New York and London: Harper and Brothers, 1932), pp. 115 ff.
27. *Works* (1843), 4:596.
28. Ibid.
29. Ibid., 4:593–96.
30. "Dishonesty or the Sin of Theft and Injustice," *Works* (Dwight ed.), 6:519.
31. Ibid. Cf. also a portion of a sermon which Edwards preached upon material excesses, debt, and gaiety, and costliness of apparel, in *Selections from the Unpublished Writings of Jonathan Edwards,* ed. A. B. Grosart, (Edinburgh: Ballantyne and Co., 1865), pp. 208–9.
32. *Works* (Dwight ed.), 6:520.
33. Ibid., 6:520–21.
34. Ibid., 6:521.
35. Cf. "Christian Cautions . . . ," ibid., 6:350.
36. Ibid., 6:522.
37. Ibid., 6:523.
38. Ibid., 6:524.
39. Ibid., 6:526.

40. Ibid., 6:527.
41. Ibid., 6:534.
42. "The Preciousness of Time . . . and the Importance of Redeeming it," ibid., 6:486–97.
43. *Some Thoughts on the Present Revival of Religion in New England* (Boston: S. Kneeland, 1742), p. 77.
44. "The Preciousness of Time . . . ," *Works* (Dwight ed.), 6:496–97.
45. Cf. "Christian Knowledge . . . of Divine Truth," *Works* (1817), 5:389.
46. Ibid., 5:390.
47. Cf. "Personal Narrative," quoted by Samuel Hopkins, ibid., 1:48–49, for an account of his personal practice of charity.
48. "Christian Charity," *Works* (Dwight ed.), 6:541.
49. Ibid., 6:542.
50. Ibid., 6:544.
51. Ibid., 6:556.
52. Ibid., 6:559–62.
53. Ibid., 6:566. In specifying the conditions of charity on this point, Edwards indulges in a casuistry which is not typical of him.
54. Ibid., 6:567.
55. Cf. O. E. Winslow, *Jonathan Edwards,* pp. 276–83; also A. C. McGiffert, Jr., *Jonathan Edwards,* pp. 143–46.
56. Cf. J. Haroutunian, *Piety,* pp. 86–87; cf. A. V. G. Allen, "The Place of Edwards in History" in *Jonathan Edwards, a Retrospect,* H. N. Gardner ed., (Boston & New York: Houghton Mifflin Co., 1901), pp. 10–11; David S. Lovejoy, "Samuel Hopkins: Religion, Slavery, and the Revolution" in *The New England Quarterly* (1967), pp. 40, 222 ff.; O. W. Elsbree, "Samuel Hopkins and his Doctrine of Benevolence" in *The New England Quarterly* (1935), pp. 8, 534 ff.
57. Cf. Frederic I. Carpenter, "The Radicalism of Jonathan Edwards" in *The New England Quarterly,* 4:644; J. C. Miller, "Religion, Finance, and Democracy in Massachusetts" in *The New England Quarterly,* 6:28 ff.

CHAPTER VI

1. Cf. Rufus Suter, "The Concept of Morality in the Philosophy of Jonathan Edwards," *Journal of Religion,* 14:268.

2. Cf. "Life of President Edwards," *Works* (Dwight ed.), 1:60–62.

3. *Images and Shadows of Divine Things*, ed. P. Miller, p. 137. In this respect Edwards is removed from the strictly Neoplatonic view.

4. Quoted by A. V. G. Allen, *Jonathan Edwards*, pp. 335–36.

5. Cf. "The Nature of True Virtue," *Works* (1817), 2:7; Frankena, *True Virtue*, p. 9.

6. "Holiness and the knowledge of God are the two aspects of the same experience . . . Where there is holiness, there is the knowledge of God: and where there is no holiness, there can be no vision of God." J. Haroutunian, "Jonathan Edwards: a Study in Godliness," *Journal of Religion*, 11:410.

7. "Original Sin," *Works* (Yale ed.), 3:147.

8. *Works* (1817), 2:8; Frankena, *True Virtue*, p. 3.

9. Ibid. "The first object of a virtuous benevolence is being, simply considered . . . being in general is its object." *Works* (1817), 2:12; Frankena, *True Virtue*, p. 5.

10. H. G. Townsend, *The Philosophy of Jonathan Edwards*, p. 205, *Miscellany* 739. The same conviction is found in the *Religious Affections*. Cf. *Works* (Yale ed.), 2:260, 240, 253.

11. *Works* (Yale ed.), 2:376.

12. Cf. ibid., pp. 365 ff. In view of this passage and others, it is difficult to see the basis upon which Roland A. Delattre identifies secondary beauty solely with harmony and proportion, and distinguishes this usage from primary beauty, which consists in cordial consent of being to being. Without proportion and symmetry, secondary beauty would lack that resemblance to true virtue which Edwards counted as essential to his total view. Cf. R. A. Delattre, "Beauty and Theology," *Soundings*, 51:1, 66. Cf. also his *Beauty and Sensibility in the Thought of Jonathan Edwards* (New Haven: Yale University Press, 1968), pp. 9, 18, 20; cf. also, "It is fit that the regard of the creator should be proportioned to the worthiness of objects, as well as the regard of creatures." "End for Which God Created the World," *Works* (Worcester ed.), 6:26, 28. Even as God loves in proportion and even as he is by definition perfect in virtue, so also must man judge proportionately which guarantees truth and justice in the case of true virtue.

13. Cf. Townsend, *Philosophy*, pp. 21–25.

14. Ibid., p. 26.

15. Ibid., p. 47.
16. *Works* (1817), 2:73; Frankena, *True Virtue*, p. 100.
17. *Works* (1817), 2:12; Frankena, *True Virtue*, p. 9. After Edwards's heavy emphasis upon proportionality as essential to moral excellence, it is odd that he should write, "No proportion is the cause or ground of the existence of such a thing as benevolence to Being. The tendency of objects to excite that degree of benevolence, which is proportional to the degree of Being, etc., is the consequence of the existence of benevolence; and not the ground of it." *Works* (Worcester ed.), 2:421. In agreement with this view, in the *Religious Affections* he had made loveliness or beauty of the "moral excellency of divine things . . . the first beginning and spring of all holy affections." *Works* (Yale ed.), 2:253–54. However, in *True Virtue* benevolence is not necessarily founded upon beauty: "There may be such a thing as benevolence, or a disposition to the welfare of those that are not considered as beautiful; unless mere existence be accounted a beauty." *Works* (Worcester ed.), 2:398. Proportion may not be the ground of benevolence or moral beauty, but it is a necessary ingredient and a controlling factor.
18. *Works* (1817), 2:12; Frankena, *True Virtue*, p. 9. Edwards worked out the idea of proportionality at radical lengths in his *End for which God Created the World,* when he decided that all created or emanated being was in comparison to God "as nothing and vanity." *Works* (Worcester ed.), 6:24–27.
19. *Works* (1817), 2:12; Frankena, *True Virtue*, p. 10.
20. The similarity of Edwards's views to that provided in A. O. Lovejoy's *The Great Chain of Being* (Cambridge: Harvard University Press, 1942), pp. 43–44, 59, 63, is too obvious to be overlooked, although Edwards cannot be totally assimilated to that motif. Cf. also D. J. Elwood, *The Philosophical Theology of Jonathan Edwards* (New York: Columbia University Press, 1960), p. 28.
21. *Works* (1817), 2:13, 23; Frankena, *True Virtue*, pp. 10, 23.
22. *Works* (1817), 2:24–25; Frankena, *True Virtue*, p. 26.
23. Cf. H. Sidgwick, *Outlines of the History of Ethics* (London and New York: Macmillan and Co. Ltd., 1931), pp. 184 ff., 193 ff., 201 ff., 207 ff.; C. S. Broad, *Four Types of Ethical Theory* (London: Routledge and Kegan Paul Ltd., 1950), p. 55; C. Vereker, *Eighteenth Century Optimism* (Liverpool: University of Liverpool Press, 1967), p. 59.

24. *Inquiry concerning Moral Good and Evil*, sec. 7. Hutcheson did allow that love and veneration of God was the purest of motives to the exercise of virtue, "since the admiration and love of moral perfection is a natural incitement to all good offices." Quoted in Thomas Fowler, *Shaftesbury and Hutcheson* (New York: G. P. Putnam's Sons, 1883), pp. 199–200.

25. "In this treatise we see the climax of Edwards's attempt to 'Neoplatonize' Calvinism." D. J. Elwood, *Philosophical Theology*, p. 91. It is equally important to note that in many crucial respects Edwards deviates from Plotinian thought. For example, the realm of becoming, for Edwards, was not a realm of unmitigated evil; the world of sense experience is not partially without order; the One, or for Edwards God, is not beyond Being; virtue, as it was not for Plotinus, is a category that does apply to God. Cf. Joseph Katz, *Plotinus' Search for the Good* (New York: King's Crown Press, 1950); Philippus V. Pistorius, *Plotinus and Neoplatonism* (Cambridge: Bowes and Bowes, 1952), chaps. 5, 6, 7.

26. "Logical monisms sooner or later take art as the analogue of the true nature of reality." H. G. Townsend, *Philosophical Ideas in the United States* (New York: American Book Co., 1934), p. 61.

27. *Works* (Worcester ed.), 6:30–31.

28. Ibid., 6:31.

29. Cf. ibid., 6:32–34.

30. Ibid., 6:47.

31. Ibid., 6:23.

32. Cf. ibid., 6:35. To speak of God's agreement with himself surreptitiously introduces the problem of the Trinity. For perfect love to exist in the Godhead, there must be a society of beings among whom there is perfect consent. This conclusion Edwards reached in *Miscellany* 117, where he stated, "That one alone cannot be excellent, inasmuch as, in such case, there can be no consent. Therefore, if God is excellent, there must be a plurality in God; otherwise there can be no consent in Him." *Miscellanies* 259, 308, 309 also bear on the subject of the role of the Trinity in God's nature. Cf. Townsend, *The Philosophy of Jonathan Edwards*, pp. 258, 259–61.

33. Cf. *Works* (Worcester ed.), 6:36–39.

34. Ibid., 6:39.

35. Ibid., 6:40. Exception must be taken to Delattre's insistence that divine beauty is a substantially independent attribute of deity. In the passage cited above Edwards explicitly identifies beauty with the moral excellence of God. The same position was taken in the "Religious Affections," *Works* (Yale ed.), 2:255–57, 394. Delattre places heavy emphasis upon Edwards's statement that "God is . . . distinguished from all other beings . . . chiefly by his divine beauty." *Works* (Yale ed.), 2:298. But this quotation does not necessarily presuppose that beauty is any kind of addition to the other attributes of God's nature. Rather, the passage emphasizes the familiar pattern of theological objectivism by which God is distinguished from the beauty of all other creatures. In omitting the remainder of the quotation Delattre loses the comparative emphasis Edwards intended. The passage concludes with the words, "which is infinitely diverse from all other beauty." Beauty is excellence, and excellence resides in the harmonious proportion of all divine attributes possessed in infinite degree. Cf. R. A. Delattre, "Beauty and Theology, a Reappraisal of Jonathan Edwards," *Soundings*, vol. 51, no. 1, pp. 66, 69–72.

36. Cf. "End for Which God Created the World," *Works* (Worcester ed.), 6:40, 117–23.

37. Cf. ibid., 6:41–42.

38. Ibid., 6:120.

39. "No notion of God's last end in the creation of the world is agreeable to reason, which would truly imply or infer any indigence, insufficiency and mutability in God: or any dependence of the Creator on the creature for any part of his perfection or happiness. . . . The notion of God's creating the world in order to receive any thing properly from the creature, is not only contrary to the nature of God, but inconsistent with the notion of creation; which "implies a being's receiving its existence, and all that belongs to its being, out of nothing." Ibid., 6:21–22. Cf. also *Miscellany* 679, "God stands in no need of creatures and is not profited by them . . . but yet God has a real and proper delight in the excellency and happiness of His creatures." Townsend, *The Philosophy of Jonathan Edwards*, p. 138.

40. *Works* (Worcester ed.), 6:43.

41. Ibid., 6:45. "If all things be of him, and to him, and he is the first and the last, this shows him to be all in all: He is all

to himself. He goes not out of himself in what he seeks, but his desires and pursuits as they originate from, so they terminate in himself." 6:48. In *Miscellany* 697 Edwards had flatly stated that since God is infinite he is all: "He must comprehend in himself all being." Creatures, therefore, do not add to his being. "Communications of being be'nt additions of being. The reflections of the sun's light don't add at all to the sum total of the light." H. G. Townsend, *Philosophy*, p. 262.

42. "End for Which God Created the World," *Works* (Worcester ed.), 6:46.

43. Cf. ibid., 6:48–50; also 6:58–59.

44. Cf. ibid., 6:55–56.

45. For Edwards's scriptural basis, cf. ibid., 6:60–115.

46. Cf. ibid., 6:41.

47. The term "panentheism" signifies that the ultimate encompasses the finite, but the nature of the ultimate is not exhausted in the finite. Even as some aspect of the divine transcends the finite, so some aspect of the finite, lacking as it does the attribute of infinity, is not totally identical with the ultimate. Elwood is undoubtedly correct in stating, "The idea of seeing all things in God and God in all things, is incompatible with the very different idea of seeing that God is all things." D. J. Elwood, *Philosophical Theology*, p. 100.

48. H. G. Townsend, *Philosophy*, pp. 183–84.

49. Cf. ibid., pp. 61, 63–64, 98–99.

50. *Works* (Worcester ed.), 6:124: "The nearer any thing comes to infinite, the nearer it comes to an identity with God," 6:57; cf. also 6:122–23. I. W. Riley held that Edwards's ecstatic desires properly led to a mysticism in which there would be a substitution of the divine for human nature, but that Edwards's Calvinistic beliefs resulted in dualism. Cf. *American Philosophy: The Early Schools* (New York: Dodd, Mead and Co., 1907), p. 186.

51. The debate over Edwards's alleged pantheism has had a long history. G. P. Fischer found Edwards's emphasis upon the complete independence of God the basis for concluding that "Every pantheistic hypothesis of this nature he repels." "The Philosophy of Jonathan Edwards," *The North American Review*, 128:297. A. V. G. Allen felt that the *Dissertation Concerning the End for Which God Created the World* was a form of pantheism which "while seeming to honor the divine

name, does so in appearance only." *Jonathan Edwards* (Boston and New York: Houghton Mifflin and Co., 1889), p. 336. J. Haroutunian opposed the idea of a pantheistic interpretation. "Jonathan Edwards, a Study in Godliness," *Journal of Religion,* 11:413. Erich Voegelin interpreted Edwards mainly in terms of mystical pantheism: *Ueber Die Form Des Amerikanischen Geistes* (Tübingen, 1928), p. 119. Perry Miller pointed out that the heirs of Augustine "always verge so close to pantheism that it takes all their ingenuity to restrain themselves from identifying God with the creation." *The New England Mind* (New York: The Macmillan Co., 1939), pp. 14–15. D. J. Elwood claims that Edwards struck a "delicate balance of traditional theistic and classical pantheistic elements, which can only be called a variety of panentheism or mystical realism." *Philosophical Theology,* p. 57.

CHAPTER VII

1. (New Haven, Connecticut: T. and S. Green, 1771). This tract was not the first brush Hart had had with the New Divinity men, Samuel Hopkins and John Smalley. He had quarreled with them over regeneration. Cf. J. Haroutunian, *Piety Versus Moralism* (New York: Henry Holt and Co., 1932), pp. 62–71.
2. Hart, ibid., p. 4.
3. Ibid., p. 5; "Being in general, or simply considered is not God; It has none of the peculiar, distinguishing characters of the Godhead," p. 10.
4. Ibid., pp. 18–19.
5. Ibid., p. 12.
6. Ibid., p. 21.
7. "The Nature of True Virtue," *Works* (Worcester ed.), 2:423; Frankena, *True Virtue,* p. 41.
8. Hart, *Remarks,* pp. 27–28.
9. Ibid., pp. 32–33.
10. Ibid., p. 36.
11. Ibid., pp. 45–46.
12. Ibid., pp. 42–43.
13. *Works,* ed. Samuel Hopkins, 3 vols. (Boston: Doctrinal Tract and Book Society of Boston, 1852), 3:69. Cf. Haroutunian, *Piety,* p. 83.
14. Hopkins, ibid., 3:76.

15. Haroutunian erroneously assumed that Hopkins had further debauched Edwards's idea of Being in general by limiting its extent to intelligent being. *Piety,* p. 83. However, Edwards himself explicitly stated that he had in mind "intelligent Being in general. Not inanimate things or Beings that have no perception or will, which are not properly capable objects of benevolence." *Works* (Worcester ed.), 2:398; Frankena, *True Virtue,* p. 5.

16. Hopkins, *Works,* 3:78. Hopkins virtually paraphrases Edwards in the *True Virtue. Works* (Worcester ed.), 2:417; Frankena, *True Virtue,* p. 32.

17. Hopkins, ibid., 3:81.

18. Ibid., 3:83–84.

19. Ibid., 3:85.

20. Ibid., 3:88.

21. Ibid., 3:94.

22. Robert Hall (1764–1831) was a Baptist pulpit orator of marked eloquence. He had once been a Calvinist, but had moved to Arminianism. The sermon on infidelity mentioned above is considered to have created a sensation in its day, and was repeated several times. Cf. *Dictionary of National Biography,* 8:969–71.

23. Robert Hall, *Works,* 4 vols. (New York: Harper and Brothers, 1849), 1:41.

24. Ibid., 1:41–42.

25. Ibid., 1:43.

26. Ibid., 1:43–44.

27. *The Biblical Repertory and Princeton Review,* 25 (1853), p. 21; cf. pp. 19–21.

28. Ibid., p. 1.

29. Cf. ibid., p. 11.

30. Cf. ibid., pp. 23–24.

31. Cf. ibid., pp. 24–25.

32. Sydney Ahlstrom refers to the New Divinity men, the successors to Edwards as "a self-conscious and brilliantly articulated movement. Probably no 'school' of American thought, in fact, has been graced by so many men of originality and intellectual power as the New England Theology founded or set in motion by Jonathan Edwards. . . . Yet none of these men, with the exception of Tyler, were docile Edwardseans." "The Shaping of American Religion," *Religion in American*

Life, vol. 1, eds., James Smith and Leland Jamison (Princeton: Princeton University Press, 1961), p. 255.

33. Cf. *Bibliotheca Sacra* 10:28, 403–13.
34. Ibid., p. 710.
35. Ibid., p. 715.
36. Ibid., p. 712.
37. Ibid., p. 714.
38. Cf. ibid., pp. 716–18.
39. Ibid., p. 717.
40. Cf. "Miscellaneous Observations concerning the Divine Decrees in General and Election in Particular," *Works* (Worcester ed.), 5:361.
41. Cf. *Bibliotheca Sacra,* pp. 718–23. In answer to Alexander's charge the Andover divines stated "The Edwardsean scheme is not utilitarian." Ibid., 409.
42. Cf. *Works* (Worcester ed.), 2:464; Frankena, *True Virtue,* p. 98.
43. *Bibliotheca Sacra,* p. 732.
44. Ibid., p. 735.
45. Ibid., p. 736.
46. Ibid., p. 737.
47. Cf. A. V. G. Allen, *Jonathan Edwards* (Boston: Houghton, Mifflin and Co., 1889), p. 317.
48. F. Foster, after citing the enormous influence of the New England theology on American religious life, comments "as it were, in a night, it perished from off the face of the earth." *A Genetic History of the New England Theology* (Chicago: University of Chicago Press, 1907), p. 543.

CHAPTER VIII

1. "Order is impersonal; and love, above all things is personal," A. N. Whitehead, *Adventure of Ideas* (New York: The Macmillan Co., 1933), p. 376.
2. Charles Vereker, *Eighteenth Century Optimism* (Liverpool: University of Liverpool Press, 1967), p. 60. Cf. also, "Empirical investigation and moral and political standards of conduct could be assumed to share a common theoretical foundation . . . ," p. 5.
3. H. G. Townsend, *The Philosophy of Jonathan Edwards* (Eugene: University of Oregon Press, 1955), p. 184; *Miscellany* 1196; cf. also *Miscellany* 651, 261.

4. Cf. "Notes on the Mind," *Works* (Dwight ed.), 1:695.
5. Cf. R. A. Delattre, *Beauty and Sensibility in the Thought of Jonathan Edwards* (New Haven and London: Yale University Press, 1968), chap. 3.
6. "True Virtue," *Works* (Worcester ed.), 2:401; Frankena, *True Virtue*, p. 9. Edwards tended to a quantitative explanation of virtue in several instances, e.g., "If he sees the same benevolence in two beings, he will value it more in two than in one only." *Works* (Worcester ed.), 2:403; Frankena, *True Virtue*, p. 12. "That being who has the most being or the greatest share of universal existence has proportionately the greatest share of virtuous benevolence." *Works* (Worcester ed.), 2:404; Frankena, *True Virtue*, p. 14.
7. Townsend, *Philosophy*, p. 87; *Miscellany* 880.
8. Cf. Douglas J. Elwood, *The Philosophical Theology of Jonathan Edwards* (New York: Columbia University Press, 1960), p. 29; cf. also J. Haroutunian, *Piety Versus Moralism* (New York: Henry Holt and Co., 1932), p. 78.
9. Cf. Ronald Hepburn, " 'Being' as a Concept of Aesthetics," *The British Journal of Aesthetics*, 8:2. Hepburn argues that "Being" language retains power because it has "aesthetic evocativeness," p. 139. Cf. also Vereker, *Optimism*, p. 56.
10. Vereker notes of the moral sense philosophies: "The renewed plea for virtue for its own sake was certainly in part a reaction against the morally inadequate legalism of traditional Christian ethics." *Optimism*, p. 41.
11. "The Religious Affections and True Virtue are complete antitheses of any authoritarianism and legalism. The Ten Commandments are strikingly neglected." Haroutunian, *Piety*, p. 90. In the *True Virtue* Edwards does refer to justice as a form of proportionality which includes "all duties that we owe to God." *Works* (Worcester ed.), 2:420; Frankena, *True Virtue*, p. 37. He also remarks in *Miscellany* 45, no. 10, that love is the sum of the Ten Commandments. Townsend, *Philosophy*, p. 49.
12. Quoted in Vereker, *Optimism*, p. 66.
13. "Concerning Efficacious Grace," *Works* (Worcester ed.), 5:418.
14. Edwards's solution of the derivation of moral obligation from Being as such leaves untouched the question of what particular acts we should undertake in expressing benevolence. This point concerning idealistic monisms was made by Wil-

mon H. Sheldon, when he pointed out that in such schemes even "the good gives no information about what we had better do." *Process and Polarity* (New York: Columbia University Press, 1944), p. 55.

15. Townsend, *Philosophy*, p. 262; *Miscellany* 697.
16. "End for Which God Created the World," *Works* (Worcester ed.), 6:33, 37, 39–40, 120.
17. Cf. Townsend, *Philosophy*, pp. 1, 9.
18. *Works* (Dwight ed.), 1:724. There is a correct use of the word "nothing" in respect to particular entities, even of the universe, but that there could be "nothing with respect to entity, 'being' absolutely considered" was sheer nonsense for Edwards. Cf. Townsend, ibid.
19. "End for Which God Created the World," *Works* (Worcester ed.), 6:37.
20. Ibid., 6:38–39.
21. Cf. Edwards's *Miscellany* 150; Townsend, *Philosophy*, p. 183, where he asserts that created spirits if "enlarged infinitely, there would be the deity to all intents and purposes." Finitude establishes the basis of polarity.
22. "True Virtue," *Works* (Worcester ed.), 2:397; Frankena, *True Virtue*, p. 3.
23. *Works* (Worcester ed.), 2:410; Frankena, *True Virtue*, p. 23. Here Edwards veers away from the viewpoint of Plotinus. For Plotinus the term "virtue" would have been a delimitation of the One, since the One is the norm of virtue, but not virtue itself. Cf. Phillipus V. Pistorius, *Plotinus and Neoplatonism* (Cambridge: Bowes and Bowes, 1952), p. 137.
24. Townsend, *Philosophy*, p. 47, *Miscellany* 45; cf. also 48, no. 7.
25. Ibid., 48, no. 9.
26. Ibid., 258, *Miscellany* 117.
27. Ibid.
28. Ibid.
29. "Original Sin," *Works* (Yale ed.), 3:382; also Townsend, *Philosophy*, p. 243, *Miscellany* 301.
30. *Works*, ibid.
31. In this respect Edwards is reminiscent of Hutcheson, who attributed lack of virtuous disposition to lower instincts gaining control over higher ones, leading to self-love. This state of affairs Hutcheson attributes finally to ignorance or "partial

views of the public Views of Good." Cf. Vereker, *Optimism,* p. 63.

32. Cf. "True Virtue," *Works* (Worcester ed.), 2:407–8, Frankena, *True Virtue,* p. 18.

33. Cf. Elwood, *Philosophical Theology,* p. 69.

34. Cf. "End for Which God Created the World," *Works* (Worcester ed.), 6:120.

35. Ibid., 6:43–59.

36. Cf. Elwood, *Philosophical Theology,* pp. 75, 83.

37. "Divine Decrees," *Works* (Worcester ed.), 5:356.

38. Ibid., p. 358.

39. "Freedom of the Will," *Works* (Yale ed.), 1:397 ff.

40. "Is it not better, that the good and evil which happens in God's world, should be ordered, regulated, bounded and determined by the good pleasure of an infinitely wise Being . . . than to leave these things to fall out by chance, and to be determined by those causes which have no understanding or aim?" Ibid., p. 405.

41. The question as to how any finite person could know what God's perspective would be is a perplexing question which stands unanswered unless by revelation.

42. A. O. Lovejoy, *The Great Chain of Being* (Cambridge: Harvard University Press, 1942), pp. 200 ff.

43. Basil Willey, *The Eighteenth Century Background* (London: Chatto and Windus, 1946), p. 48.

44. "Miscellaneous Observations on Important Doctrines," *Works* (1843 ed.), 1:573.

45. Ibid., 1:573–74.

CHAPTER IX

1. Cf. Robert Hall, *Works,* 4 vols. (New York: Harper and Brothers, 1849), 1:44; also *The Biblical Repertory and Princeton Review,* 25 (1854), p. 23.

2. *Miscellany* 664b, Yale Collection, par. 1.

3. *Miscellany* 710, Corollary, Yale Collection.

4. *Miscellany* 530, Yale Collection.

5. *Miscellany* 631, Yale Collection.

6. "Miscellaneous Observations on Important Doctrines," *Works* (1843 ed.), 1:571.

7. Cf. *Works* (Yale ed.), 1:142–43.

8. Cf. ibid., p .145.
9. "Religious Affections," *Works* (Yale ed.), 2:260.
10. Cf. *Works* (Worcester ed.), 2:417; Frankena, *True Virtue*, p. 32.
11. Cf. ibid., 2:407–8, 425–26, 437; Frankena, *True Virtue*, pp. 18, 43, 55.
12. Ibid., 467; Frankena, *True Virtue*, p. 101.
13. Ibid., 452; cf. Frankena, *True Virtue*, p. 88.
14. Ibid., 465; Frankena, *True Virtue*, p. 99.
15. *Works* (Dwight ed.), 1:696.
16. Ibid., 1:697.
17. *Works* (Worcester ed.), 6:54–55. See also his statement that if God made his creatures his chief and ultimate end in creation, this doctrine would be the "farthest from having a favorable aspect on God's self-sufficiency and independence." Ibid., 6:47.
18. Cf. ibid., 6:23, 25, 54.
19. Ibid., 6:45.
20. Ibid., 6:45.
21. *Miscellany* 1066, Yale Collection. Cf. R. A. Delattre, *Beauty and Sensibility*, pp. 154, 175.
22. *Works* (Worcester ed.), 6:39–40, 43, 117 ff.
23. Ibid., 6:44–45.
24. Ibid., 6:56.
25. Townsend, *The Philosophy of Jonathan Edwards*, p. 195; *Miscellany* 97.
26. Ibid., p. 193; *Miscellany* 3.
27. Ibid.
28. Cf. *Works* (Worcester ed.), 6:51 ff.
29. Ibid., p. 53.
30. Ibid., pp. 105 ff.

CHAPTER X

1. Cf. E. Cassirer, *The Platonic Renaissance in England* (Austin: University of Texas Press, 1953), p. 101.
2. "The language in which the moral sense school spoke of moral problems was predominantly aesthetic." C. Vereker, *Eighteenth Century Optimism* (Liverpool: University of Liverpool Press, 1967), p. 56.
3. Cf. F. H. Bradley, *Appearance and Reality* (New York: The

Macmillan Co., 1902), p. 177; cf. also D. J. Elwood, *The Philosophical Theology of Jonathan Edwards* (New York: Columbia University Press, 1960), pp. 83–84.

4. A. N. Whitehead, *Religion in the Making* (New York: The Macmillan Co., 1926), pp. 104–5; *The Adventure of Ideas* (New York: The Macmillan Co., 1933), pp. 341–42, 345.

5. Cf. R. A. Delattre, *Beauty and Sensibility in the Thought of Jonathan Edwards* (New Haven and London: Yale University Press, 1968), pp. 120–22.

6. It is interesting and important to note that Edwards employed the notion of proportionality in respect to the fear produced by hell-fire preaching as he did in describing true virtue. "Distinguishing Marks of a Work of the Spirit of God," *Works* (1843 ed.), 1:548.

7. However, as Delattre points out, there are also certain similarities between Kant and Edwards in their respective attempts to treat morality as a form of beauty. Delattre, *Beauty and Sensibility,* pp. 196–97.

8. "It is evident, by the manner in which God has formed and constituted other things, that he has respect to beauty, good order and regulation, proportion and harmony. . . . Surely, therefore, he will not leave the principal part of the creation . . . without making any proper provision for its being in any other than a state of deformity, discord, and the most hateful and dreadful confusion." "Miscellaneous Observations on Important Doctrines," *Works* (1843 ed.), 1:566.

9. "Religious Affections," *Works* (Yale ed.), 2:298.

10. The category of moral beauty appears as follows in *Charity and its Fruits* (New York: Anson D. F. Randolph and Co., 1851), pp. 7, 209–10, 357, 398, 470 ff., 473, 505 ff.

11. Cf. *Works* (1843 ed.), 1:568–69.

12. Ibid., 4:414.

13. Ibid., 4:435.

14. "Men Naturally God's Enemies," ibid., 4:57.

15. Ibid., 4:193.

16. "A general tendency towards benevolence, the possession of a virtuous disposition, come to be thought of as a natural determination, previous to choice." Vereker, *Optimism,* p. 42.

17. Cf. *Works* (1843 ed.), 1:490–98.

18. Cf. ibid., 1:304.

19. Cf. *Works* (Yale ed.), 2:365 ff.

20. Edwards pointed out that natural conscience could approve primary beauty as benevolence to Being in general "from that uniformity, equality and justice, which there is in it." "True Virtue," *Works* (Worcester ed.), 2:443, Frankena, *True Virtue*, p. 68.
21. Cf. *Works* (Yale ed.), 2:255, 387.
22. Cf. ibid., 2:264, 277.
23. Cf. ibid., 2:409–10, 412.
24. Ibid., 2:420.
25. Cf. *Works* (Worcester ed.), 2:398–99; Frankena, *True Virtue*, p. 3; cf. also Delattre, *Beauty and Sensibility*, pp. 83, 96.
26. Samuel Hopkins was correct in commenting, "Some have attempted to tell what holiness is, by saying, It is not properly a distinct attribute of God, but the beauty and glory of all God's moral perfections. But we get no idea by these words till we are told what is this beauty and glory." Preface to "An Inquiry into the Nature of True Holiness," *Works* (Boston: Doctrinal Tract and Book Society, 1852), 3:6.
27. I see no basis for R. A. Delattre's insistence that proportionality and harmony relate only to secondary or natural moral beauty. Cf. Delattre, *Beauty and Sensibility*, pp. 9, 11, 29, 45, 106, 211. Edwards explicitly identified holy affections by this "beautiful symmetry and proportion." *Works* (Yale ed.), 2:365. Delattre himself is forced to admit symmetry and proportion in distinguishing true virtue from the sublime. *Beauty and Sensibilty*, pp. 146–47.
28. Cf. *Works* (Yale ed.), 2:256–57, 273.
29. *Works* (Worcester ed.), 2:398; Frankena, *True Virtue*, p. 3.
30. "Indeed most of the duties incumbent on us, if well considered, will be found to partake of the nature of justice." *Works* (Worcester ed.), 2:420; Frankena, *True Virtue*, p. 37.
31. Cf. Elwood, *Philosophical Theology*, p. 67.
32. Cf. "Original Sin," *Works* (Yale ed.), 3, chap. 2.
33. Delattre finds a pattern in Edwards's thought which positions good and evil in the system without alleviating the problem of how moral evil, conceived as dissent, may occur. "The scales of good and evil, being and nothing, consent and dissent, beauty and deformity, all correspond to each other ontologically as well as morally in Edwards's grand system of being, which runs from the 'fullness of being' and beauty in God toward 'absolute' nothing, his boundary concept for that

which is 'the essence of all contradiction.'" Cf. *Miscellany* 21a, *Works* (Yale ed.), p. 78. The question of how ethics can be thus joined to an aesthetic ontology, however, remains, as does also the question of whether there is a central principle in reality which makes possible the degradation and disharmony of being.

34. Cf. "Miscellaneous Observations Concerning Decrees and Election," *Works* (1843 ed.), 2:545.
35. *Works* (Worcester ed.), 2:438; Frankena, *True Virtue*, p. 61.
36. Cf. W. Beach and H. R. Niebuhr, *Christian Ethics* (New York: Ronald Press, 1953), p. 388.
37. *Works* (Worcester ed.), 2:417 ff.; Frankena, *True Virtue*, p. 32.
38. Burton F. Porter has met this problem by arguing that since the concept of God "already embraces the notion of absolute goodness," when God wills X, X is good. "God is good is on this reading an analytic proposition." *Deity and Morality* (New York: Humanities Press, 1968), p. 125. This logical answer to the "supernaturalistic fallacy" does not occur in Edwards, who simply takes for granted that whatever God wills is good. He was willing to say that what is, is good; or more specifically that Being is intuited as both power and value.
39. Cf. "Observations on Important Doctrines," *Works* (1843 ed.), 1:568.
40. "Religious Affections," *Works* (Yale ed.), 2:255.
41. "The Life of President Edwards," *Works* (Dwight ed.), 1:61 ff.
42. Cf. Delattre, *Beauty and Sensibility*, p. 108; cf. preceding chapter.
43. *Works* (Yale ed.), 2:398.
44. "The Importance of Divine Truth," *Works* (1843 ed.), 4:13.
45. The work in a particular soul has its ups and downs . . . But in general, grace is growing: from its first infusion, till it is perfected in glory, the kingdom of Christ is building up in the soul. "A History of the Work of Redemption," *Works* (1843 ed.), 1:315.
46. Cf. *Works* (Yale ed.), 2:341, 365, 390.
47. Ibid., 2:299.
48. Yale Collection. Quoted in *Images or Shadows of Divine Things*, ed. Perry Miller (New Haven: Yale University Press, 1948), p. 22.

49. *Works* (Worcester ed.), 2:401. Note omitted in Frankena edition.
50. "End for Which God Created the World," *Works* (Worcester ed.), 6:123–24.
51. H. G. Townsend, *The Philosophy of Jonathan Edwards* (Eugene, Oregon: University of Oregon Press, 1955), pp. 258–59; *Miscellany* 117, 259.

Bibliography

PRIMARY SOURCES

Anselm of Canterbury. "Cur Deus Homo" in *St. Anselm*. Translated by Sidney H. Dean. LaSalle, Illinois: Open Court, 1951.

Beach, Waldo, and Niebuhr, H. Richard. *Christian Ethics.* New York: Ronald Press, 1953.

Edwards, Jonathan. *Charity and its Fruits.* New York: D. F. Randolph and Co., 1951.

————. *Practical Sermons.* Edinburgh: M. Gray, 1788.

————. *Sermons on Various Important Subjects.* Edinburgh: M. Gray, 1785.

————. *The Works of Jonathan Edwards.* New Haven and London: Yale University Press. Vol. 1, *A Careful and Strict Inquiry into . . . Freedom of Will,* edited by Paul Ramsey, 1957; vol. 2, *A Treatise Concerning Religious Affections,* edited by John E. Smith, 1959; vol. 3, *The Great Christian Doctrine of Original Sin . . . ,* edited by Clyde A. Holbrook, 1970.

————. *The Works of President Edwards.* 8 vols. First American ed. Worcester, Mass.: Isaiah Thomas, June 1808.

————. *The Works of President Edwards.* 8 vols. London: James Black and Son, 1817.

————. *The Works of President Edwards.* 10 vols. Dwight ed. New York: S. Converse, 1829.

————. *The Works of President Edwards.* 4 vols. Reprint of Worcester ed. New York: Leavitt and Allen, 1843.

Bibliography

Faust, Clarence H., and Johnson, Thomas H. *Jonathan Edwards, Representative Selections.* New York: American Book Co., 1935.

Hall, Robert. *Works.* 4 vols. New York: Harper and Brothers, 1849.

Hart, William. *Remarks on President Edwards's Dissertations concerning the Nature of True Virtue.* New Haven: T. and S. Green, 1771.

Hopkins, Samuel. *Works.* 3 vols. Boston: Doctrinal Tract and Book Society of Boston, 1852.

Hutcheson, Francis. *An Inquiry concerning Moral Good and Evil.* London: D. Midwinter, 1729.

———. *An Inquiry into the Original of our Idea of Beauty and Virtue.* 3d ed. London: D. Midwinter, 1729.

Miller, Perry, ed. *Images and Shadows of Divine Things.* New Haven: Yale University Press, 1948.

Shaftesbury, Anthony A. C., 3d Earl. *Characteristicks of Men, Manners, Opinions, Times.* London: John Darby, 1737.

Townsend, Harvey G. *The Philosophy of Jonathan Edwards.* Eugene: University of Oregon Press, 1955.

SECONDARY SOURCES
Books

Ahlstrom, Sydney. "The Shaping of American Religion." In *Religion in American Life,* edited by James Smith and Leland Jamison, vol. 1. Princeton: Princeton University Press, 1961.

Allen, Alexander V. G. *Jonathan Edwards.* Boston and New York: Houghton Mifflin and Co., 1889.

Bayne, Peter. *Documents Relating to the Settlement of the Church of England by the Act of Uniformity of 1662.* London: W. Kent and Co., 1862.

Bradley, Francis H. *Appearance and Reality.* New York: The Macmillan Co., 1902.

Broad, Charlie S. *Four Types of Ethical Theory.* London: Routledge and Kegan Paul, Ltd., 1950.

Brown, James. *Subject and Object in Modern Theology.* London: S.C.M. Ltd., 1953.

Brumm, Ursala. *Die Religiöse Typologie im Amerikanischen Denken.* Leiden: E. J. Brill, 1963.

Bibliography

Carse, James. *Jonathan Edwards and the Visibility of God*. New York: Charles Scribner's Sons, 1967.

Cassirer, Ernst. *The Platonic Renaissance in England*. Austin: The University of Texas Press, 1953.

Cherry, Conrad. *The Theology of Jonathan Edwards, a Reappraisal*. New York: Doubleday Anchor, 1966.

Crabtree, Arthur B. *Jonathan Edwards' View of Man*. Wallington, Surrey, England: The Religious Education Press, 1943.

Delattre, Roland A. *Beauty and Sensibility in the Thought of Jonathan Edwards*. New Haven and London: Yale University Press, 1968.

Dickie, Edgar P. *Revelation and Response*. New York: Charles Scribner's Sons, 1936.

Elwood, Douglas J. *The Philosophical Theology of Jonathan Edwards*. New York: Columbia University Press, 1960.

Foster, Frank H. *A Genetic History of the New England Theology*. Chicago: University of Chicago Press, 1907.

Fowler, Thomas. *Shaftesbury and Hutcheson*. New York: G. P. Putnam's Sons, 1883.

Gaustad, Edward A. *The Great Awakening in New England* New York: Harper and Brothers, 1957.

Haroutunian, Joseph. *Piety Versus Moralism*. New York: Henry Holt and Co., 1932.

Heimart, Alan. *Religion and the American Mind*. Cambridge: Harvard University Press, 1966.

Hick, John. *Evil and the God of Love*. London: The Macmillan Co., 1966.

Hill, Thomas E. *Contemporary Ethical Theories*. New York: Macmillan Co., 1950.

Holbrook, Clyde A. *Faith and Community*. New York: Harper and Brothers, 1959.

————. "Original Sin and the Enlightenment." In *The Heritage of Christian Thought,* edited by Egil Grislis and Robert E. Cushman. New York: Harper and Row, 1965.

Jones, William T. *Morality and Freedom in the Philosophy of Immanuel Kant*. London: Oxford University Press, 1940.

Katz, Joseph. *Plotinus' Search for the Good*. New York: King's Crown Press, 1950.

Lovejoy, Arthur O. *The Great Chain of Being*. Cambridge: Harvard University Press, 1942.

Bibliography

McGiffert, Arthur C., Jr. *Jonathan Edwards.* New York: Harper and Brothers, 1932.

Miller, Perry. *Jonathan Edwards.* New York: William Sloane Associates, 1949.

————. *The New England Mind.* New York: Macmillan Co., 1939.

Morris, William S. "The Genius of Jonathan Edwards." In *Reinterpretation in American Church History,* edited by Jerald C. Brauer. Chicago: University of Chicago Press, 1968.

Otto, Rudolph. *The Idea of the Holy.* London: Oxford University Press, 1925.

Paley, William. *The Principles of Moral and Political Philosophy.* New York: Harper and Brothers, 1849.

Pistorius, Philippus V. *Plotinus and Neoplatonism.* Cambridge: Bowes and Bowes, 1952.

Porter, Burton F. *Deity and Morality.* New York: Humanities Press, 1968.

Riley, I. Woodbridge. *American Philosophy, the Early Schools.* New York: Dodd, Mead and Co., 1907.

Sheldon, Wilman H. *Process and Polarity.* New York: Columbia University Press, 1944.

Sidgwick, Henry. *Outlines of the History of Ethics.* London and New York: Macmillan and Co. Ltd., 1931.

Smyth, Newman. *Christian Ethics.* New York: Charles Scribner's Sons, 1923.

Townsend, Harry G. *Philosophical Ideas in the United States.* New York: The American Book Co., 1934.

Vereker, Charles. *Eighteenth Century Optimism.* Liverpool: University of Liverpool Press, 1967.

Voegelin, Erich. *Ueber die Form des Amerikanischen Geistes.* Tübingen: J. C. B. Mohr, 1928.

Whitehead, Alfred N. *Adventure of Ideas.* New York: The Macmillan Co., 1933.

Willey, Basil. *The Eighteenth Century Background.* London: Chatto and Winders, 1946.

Winslow, Ola E. *Jonathan Edwards.* New York: The Macmillan Co., 1941.

Woodbridge, Frederick J. E. "The Philosophy of Edwards." In *Exercises Commemorating the Two-hundredth Anniversary*

Bibliography

of the Birth of Jonathan Edwards. Andover: Andover Press, 1904.

PERIODICALS AND PAMPHLETS

Alexander, Archibald. "Outlines of Moral Science." *The Princeton Review*, 25 (1853), 1–43. Later catalogued as *Biblical Repertory and Princeton Review*.

Allen, A. V. G. "The Place of Edwards in History." *Jonathan Edwards, a Retrospect*. Boston and New York: Houghton Mifflin and Co., 1901.

Baird, J. "Edwards and the Theology of New England." *The Southern Presbyterian Review* 10 (1858), 576–88.

Carpenter, Frederic I. "The Radicalism of Jonathan Edwards." *The New England Quarterly* 4 (1931), 629–44.

Delattre, Roland A. "Beauty and Theology, a Reappraisal of Jonathan Edwards." *Soundings* 51 (1968), 60–79.

Dumas, Andre. "De L'Objectivité de Dieu." *Revue d'Histoire et de Philosophie Religieuses* 4 (1966), 309–22.

Elsbree, Oliver W. "Samuel Hopkins and his Doctrine of Benevolence." *The New England Quarterly* 8 (1935), 534–50.

Fischer, George P. "The Philosophy of Jonathan Edwards." *The North American Review* 128 (1879), 284–304.

Hepburn, Ronald. " 'Being' as a Concept of Aesthetics." *The British Journal of Aesthetics* 8 (1968), 138–46.

Heschel, Abraham. "The Holy Dimension." *The Journal of Religion* 23 (1943), 117–24.

Holbrook, Clyde A. "Edwards and the Ethical Question." *Harvard Theological Review* 60 (1967), 163–76.

Lovejoy, David S. "Samuel Hopkins' Religion, Slavery, and the Revolution." *The New England Quarterly* 40 (1967), 227–43.

Miller, John C. "Religion, Finance and Democracy in Massachusetts." *The New England Quarterly* 6 (1933), 29–58.

"President Edwards's Dissertation on the Nature of True Virtue." *Bibliotheca Sacra*, 10 (1853), 705–38.

Suter, Rufus. "The Concept of Morality in the Philosophy of Jonathan Edwards." *The Journal of Religion* 14 (1934), 265–72.

Tomas, Vincent. "The Modernity of Jonathan Edwards." *The New England Quarterly* 25 (1952), 60–84.